MURDER
AT
RENARD'S

by Margaret Addison

A Rose Simpson Mystery

Rose Simpson Mysteries (in order)

Murder at Ashgrove House
Murder at Dareswick Hall
Murder at Sedgwick Court
Murder at Renard's

Chapter One

'But this is a disaster. No less than a catastrophe. My clientele will be devastated and my reputation will be in ruins. It will lie in tatters. They will say that I have gone back on my word, that I promised something I could not fulfil ...' Madame Renard, proprietor of Renard's dress shop, let her words falter and hang in the air before herself collapsing into a convenient chair. She was in the room she referred to grandly as her office but which, in actual fact, was little more than a glorified box room. She wrung her hands in front of her theatrically, her well made up face becoming unattractively distorted by her distress. This gesture was followed by the passing of a limp, but well-manicured, hand across her brow with the air of a doomed maiden in some Greek tragedy. Lips pursed, she regarded her employee, the bearer of such unwelcome tidings, with a mixture of sorrow and contempt as if it were all that young lady's fault that her very world was falling apart around her ears.

Rose Simpson, being accustomed to her employer's ways, had anticipated just such a reaction to the news she had to impart. She therefore merely sighed softly to herself and tried to smile reassuringly at the older woman despite feeling no less aggrieved and alarmed by the news than Madame Renard herself. She resolved however to keep her true feelings concealed from the proprietor, who she felt was demonstrative enough in showing her emotions for the both of them.

Renard's, as Madame Renard's ladies' outfitters was rather unimaginatively called, was an establishment with grandiose pretentions of being a dress shop of the superior type despite its singularly unprepossessing location in a London back street, squashed between a tobacconist that had seen better days on one side and an equally run down cleaners and dryers business on the other.

Notwithstanding these various locational disadvantages, Madame Renard had made considerable strides to turn her premises into what she most coveted. True, the sign above her shop did not declare House of Renard as she would have wished, and indeed envisaged, in her dreams. Sensibly she had reined herself in from making such a claim no matter how well she regarded her merchandise. A couture house in Paris her establishment was clearly not. But still 'Renard's' was written in impressive bold gold letters on a background of royal blue. The window displays were elaborate and boasted wax mannequins with glass eyes and fur eyelashes, moulded and painted eyebrows, dazzling eye make-up, and mouths that were inset with porcelain teeth and painted lips. Madame Renard had also invested in two or three of the full-length plaster mannequins which had newly become available and which had the twin advantages of looking more lifelike than their wax predecessors while also being more durable.

'Please, Madame, I don't think the situation is quite as bad as you might think,' Rose said, trying to sound more confident than she felt. 'Of course it is most unfortunate that Lavinia should choose this moment to become ill.' She paused a moment to consider Lady Lavinia Sedgwick in not the most favourable of lights. 'But it really couldn't be helped. I understand she is very poorly and has taken to her bed. But as I've already said, she hasn't left us in the lurch. She has made alternative arrangements.'

'Alternative arrangements?' Madame Renard removed her hand from her brow and looked at her shop assistant inquisitively and rather suspiciously, her manner still despondent. 'What precisely do you mean by alternative arrangements? The clothes display is tomorrow night. It will be a disaster without dear Lavinia there to model Marcel's gowns ... Oh, Marcel! How will he take the news?' Madame Renard's hand shot up to her mouth and her eyes bulged large and bright. 'We must not tell him yet. Promise me, Miss Simpson, you will not breathe a word of this to him or to anyone. Not until we have decided what to do.'

'But Madame, I told you – '

'*Oui, oui, oui,*' Madame Renard said irritably. 'But what do you mean? Explain yourself more clearly, come. Tell me quickly. And do speak up. *Très anglais.* You English, you always mumble. Can you not see how this news has affected me? I am quite done in as you say.'

'As I've said already,' Rose said slowly and with emphasis, 'Lavinia has arranged for someone else to model Marcel's gowns.'

'But whom?' Madame Renard sat up, looking interested despite herself. However, she was not yet ready to abandon her portrayal of malaise. 'If it is not another member of the aristocracy, it will not do. I promised my customers that the gowns would be modelled by the daughter of an earl.'

'And Lavinia does not want to disappoint. Does the name Lady Celia Goswell mean anything to you, Madame? She is the second daughter of the Marquis of Perriford.'

'Oh? I do not think I have heard of her. Let me see … *Non.* I have not seen photographs of her in the society pages. Tell me, the daughter of a marquis she is higher than the daughter of an earl, is she not?'

'Yes, she is.'

The proprietor brightened visibly. If she was aware that Rose still looked troubled then she gave no sign of it.

'No doubt she is a fine young lady like our Lady Lavinia, this Lady Celia *n'est-ce pas*?' purred Madame Renard. 'Tall and elegant with the same slender figure and delicate features that become clothes so magnificently. Her complexion will be the English rose, will it not?'

'Hmm … I'm afraid I don't know,' said Rose rather hesitantly. 'I daresay she carries herself well,' she added rallying a little, trying to forget the feeling of apprehension that she had experienced earlier that day following her telephone call to Sedgwick Court. 'We shall soon see for ourselves. Lavinia was so good as to ask Lady Celia to come to the shop tomorrow morning for a fitting.'

'A fitting?' Madame Renard looked alarmed. 'But we have not the time to make any changes to the outfits. The display, it is tomorrow evening.'

'But even so it will be necessary, I think,' said Rose firmly. 'But don't worry, Madame. I daresay only one or two very minor adjustments to Lavinia's outfits will prove necessary.'

'*Very* little adjustments, perhaps,' Madame Renard agreed grudgingly, giving Rose a sharp look. 'But remember this is couture. Marcel has designed these outfits to Lavinia's precise measurements. It has taken several fittings and a number of days to produce such garments. Couture cannot be rushed, Rose, as well you know. These dresses do not have generous seams that can be let out to accommodate the size and shape of any Tom, Dick or Harry. No, they fit Lavinia to perfection. But as to whether they will fit or suit someone else … who is to say? Marcel has chosen and designed these gowns to accentuate Lavinia's figure. On someone else the same outfits could look like the woman is wearing a sack of potatoes. Worse still, they could accentuate the very worst parts of her body. What you are saying, and this hesitating manner in which you are saying it, makes me anxious. You are keeping something from me I think? You – '

'I am sure we are worrying unnecessarily,' Rose said quickly, despite her misgivings. 'I am being silly, of course. There is no reason to suppose Monsieur Girard's gowns will not fit Lady Celia as well as they do Lavinia, no reason at all.'

'Is that so? But of course, you are right. Dear Lavinia would not be so unkind or so unthoughtful as to send us someone unsuitable.'

Personally, Rose was of the view that this might indeed be something her friend would do, not necessarily maliciously, but because she did not wish to be upstaged.

'Ah, dear Lavinia,' continued Madame Renard, rising majestically from her chair, suitably reassured and once more in control of her surroundings. She threw out her arms in a flamboyant gesture that encompassed not only the dress shop and the accompanying rooms, but also the girl who stood before her. 'I knew she would not let me down. She was always such a dear girl when she was working here, so diligent, so obliging.'

Rose nodded while all the time trying not to laugh. It was true that Lady Lavinia Sedgwick, only daughter of the then Earl of Belvedere, had worked for a short time in Madame Renard's dress shop. This had happened as the result of a bet that the lady in question had taken up with her brother, namely that she could earn her own living for six months. But Lavinia had been spared the most tedious aspects of the job of a shop assistant. She had not been expected to sweep the floor or wrap up garments in brown paper in preparation for their being sent out to customers on approval. Neither had she been required to deal with Madame Renard's more awkward or demanding customers. Unlike Rose, she had not suffered sharp words from customers or the indignity of being ignored or looked down upon. Madame Renard's treatment of her had been little short of deferential. For the proprietor had quickly ascertained that Lavinia's presence behind the counter was good for business and had not wished to lose the most attractive addition to her shop by giving her too tiring or mundane work, or subjecting her to the niggles or complaints of the shop's most tiresome customers.

4

'It's almost a year, is it not,' continued Madame Renard, 'since the dear girl worked here? It seems only yesterday that she was helping my customers with their ensembles. So very generous and unselfish. What Lady Lavinia does not know about fashion … But we will not speak of that now. We have not the time. Now, back to work we must go. Remember we are closing the shop early tomorrow to get ready for the show.' She beamed at Rose. 'We must therefore make the most of this afternoon, I think. Our customers are depending on us.'

'Where's Mama?' enquired Jacques Renard, strolling leisurely into Renard's, a wide grin on his handsome face.

He was a dark-haired, bespectacled young man of twenty-three and was dressed in a smart wool worsted suit with silk stripes which he thought became him rather well. It was true that while he did indeed require the spectacles for reading purposes, he wore them also out of vanity, being of the opinion as he was that they gave him a rather learned air. Indeed, he was aware that glasses made him look distinguished because one or two of the girls of his acquaintance at Harridges had told him so. Such endorsement also proved beneficial to his eyesight. He was no longer inclined to screw up his eyes and squint, the effect of which had been rather detrimental to his looks.

'I thought I'd find Mama out here in the shop cracking the whip and having you polish and clean every nook and cranny until the place shone. I'm surprised she's left you to your own devices. Why, there won't be a stroke of work done with her not here!'

'You're a cheeky one, so you are, Jack Renard,' retorted Sylvia. 'I'll have you know I'm the most hardworking one of the lot. Your mother's lucky to have me, and that's a fact. I'm not like Miss Simpson with all her airs and graces thinking that she's better than us just because she's friends with the gentry.'

'Rose isn't a bit like that, as well you know,' replied Jacques, pretending not to have heard Sylvia deliberately mispronounce his name. 'Now, don't be such a beast, my sweet.' He perched himself rather uncomfortably on the edge of a table on which there was a display of angora berets and hand painted and braided band hats. 'You're just jealous because she's done rather well for herself.'

5

'And who's to say she has?' demanded Sylvia. 'She's still working here, isn't she?'

'Oh, do leave off, Sylvia. What's Rose Simpson ever done to you? No,' Jacques Renard held up his hand and laughed before she could protest, 'I don't want to hear any more about it. I didn't come here to talk about Rose. Now, don't scowl, it's hardly flattering, you know. It will give you wrinkles which would be such a shame. It would spoil your fine looks and I came here just because I wanted to see your lovely face.'

'And see how your mother's faring with the preparations for this fashion show of hers, you said as much yourself,' said Sylvia, permitting herself a smile in light of the compliment. 'She's out back with Rose in that little room she calls her office.' She bent towards him conspiratorially. 'I think something's up with the show. Don't ask me what, because I don't know. But Rose telephoned Sedgwick Court a half hour or so ago and then came out of the office looking all worried and flustered although she tried not to show it. She asked your mother to go into the office and I've heard Madame's voice raised as if she's having hysterics.'

'Now that does sound like dear Mama,' Jacques said.

'Likely as not Lady Lavinia's changed her mind about coming. I wouldn't put anything past that madam. Have I told you how she hardly lifted a finger while she was working here? Although I wouldn't have called it working. Complained about the smallest thing, so she did, something rotten. Why, she – '

'Yes. Yes, you did,' said Jacques quickly. 'Hello, where's Mary? Don't tell me it's her day off?'

'Of course not. She's out in the storeroom wrapping up the garments to be sent out.'

'Well, I can't stop here chatting.' The young man rose from his makeshift seat on the table and hastily tidied the arrangement of hats that he had brushed so carelessly aside. 'I only popped out for a moment to undertake an errand and took the opportunity to come here. They'll be expecting me back in a few minutes otherwise they'll dock my wages.'

'As if they would! I don't know why you want to work at that fancy department store. I'm surprised your mother doesn't have you working here where she can keep an eye on you.'

'She wants me to learn the trade, don't you know. We receive specific training at Harridges, undertake proper training programmes and all that.'

'On how to wait in shops?' said Sylvia dismissively. 'I could tell them a thing or two about that.'

'I'm sure you could. But it's not just training in waiting on customers, no. We receive training on merchandise and selling techniques and we're also taught how to do accounts. It'll all come in jolly useful when I'm the proprietor here, you wait and see if it doesn't.'

'I doubt I'll be here then,' Sylvia said, giving him a knowing look. 'You mark my words, I'll be married and well provided for by the time you come into your inheritance. No working in shops for me then, I can tell you.'

'If anyone will have you, Sylvia. Now, don't look at me like that. You know I don't mean anything by it.'

'Don't you?' Sylvia asked sulkily.

'Of course not. I was only ribbing. You know you're my best girl.'

'No, I'm not. I daresay I used to be, but I'm not now. I've hardly seen anything of you lately. Not since you went to work at Harridges. I've heard about what you all get up to on a Saturday evening. Drinks and dancing, that's what. I suppose you've taken a shine to some girl at that fancy department store, one that's received all that shop training that you're so fond of.'

Jacques went red, but said nothing.

'I'm right then, am I?' Sylvia looked away for a moment. 'I thought as much. That'll explain why you're not on at me any more to go to the pictures with you.'

'It's not – '

'You needn't waste your breath making excuses, Jack Renard. I know your mother doesn't approve of me walking out with you. Not that it matters now,' Sylvia added haughtily. 'I've got myself a proper young man, so I have. One that's up in the world and has prospects.'

'Have you indeed?' said Jacques, not knowing quite what to think. He gave Sylvia a curious look. His first inclination was to think she was lying and just trying to make him jealous. But one could never tell with Sylvia. She was a girl who kept things close to her chest. And it did not escape his notice that her colour had risen. There was also something in the defiant way she had made her claim that made him wonder if she might not be having him on after all.

Sylvia was watching him closely, a smug look on her face. It was obvious that she found his confused reaction to her words amusing.

'Well just you wait and see,' she said beaming. 'You'll eat your words, see if you don't, Jack Renard. I can do better than the likes of you and no mistake!'

Chapter Two

Rose stood behind her glass counter feeling particularly restive, the afternoon seeming to drag horrendously as it always did when there were too few customers to while away the time, or she had a particular reason for wishing her working day to come to a close. In this instance her impatience was not due to her eagerness to embark on a visit to some ancestral home to attend a weekend house party as it had been on other occasions. Rather she had a desire that the day come to as hasty a close as possible so that tomorrow would dawn and bring with it the opportunity to see Lady Celia in the flesh.

Rose allowed her thoughts to drift back to the unsettling telephone call that she had had earlier that day with the various inhabitants of Sedgwick Court. Snatches of remembered conversation floated into her mind and she found that if she concentrated sufficiently, which was not difficult as there was little else to occupy her mind as the shop was at that very moment free of customers, she could play back the various conversations in her mind almost word for word. If she remembered correctly, the dialogues had gone something like this:

'Hello. I say, is that Manning? It's Miss Simpson here,' Rose had said as soon as she had been connected to Sedgwick Court. In her eagerness she had not allowed the other person to speak first.

'Hmm …' said rather a dignified voice. 'No, it isn't Miss Simpson. It's Torridge, the head-butler, miss.'

'Oh. Oh, I see.'

Rose raised her eyebrows. It was all she could do not to exclaim the man's name out loud in surprise. It was a few months since she had last seen the head-butler, and she had not expected him to still be employed in his position. Instead she had assumed that by now the old man would have given in to his old age and inevitable retirement, however reluctantly. A pension and a cottage on the Sedgwick estate awaited him, she knew.

'I'm so sorry. I assumed you were Manning. How are you, Torridge?'

'I can't complain, miss.'

'I was wondering if I might speak with Lady Lavinia? To tell you the truth,' Rose admitted rather confidentially, 'I'm rather surprised that she hasn't contacted Madame Renard already to make arrangements to come in for her final fitting. For the clothes, you know. The gowns she will wear tomorrow night for the presentation of haute couture to Madame Renard's private clientele.'

'I'm afraid Lady Lavinia is unavailable, miss. She is rather under the weather and has retired to bed.'

'Under the weather? Oh, no! How do you mean "under the weather"? Is she poorly, or has she been overdoing things a bit?' Visons of Lavinia sipping one too many cocktails immediately sprung to Rose's mind.

'Lady Lavinia is quite unwell,' retorted the old butler sounding shocked at any implied slur on his mistress's character.

'Yes. I'm sure she is,' Rose said hurriedly. 'What I meant to say ... well, what I'm getting at, Torridge, is, will she be well enough to participate in the fashion show tomorrow do you think? I daresay it isn't that important that she comes for a final fitting. Monsieur Girard has all her measurements and, from what I've seen, the gowns fit delightfully. But understandably Madame Renard is rather anxious. You see, it's the first time that she – '

'I very much doubt that Lady Lavinia will be well enough to attend tomorrow's event, miss,' Torridge said gravely.

'What? But that's impossible!' exclaimed Rose. 'Mayn't I speak to Lady Lavinia? Only for a few minutes? I won't keep her out of bed for long, I promise.'

'I am afraid that is quite out of the question, miss. Lady Lavinia was most particular that she not be disturbed on any account.'

'Oh.'

For a moment Rose was at a complete loss. With a dreadful sinking feeling forming in the pit of her stomach she began to wonder if Lavinia might be having second thoughts about coming to Madame Renard's grand event. Perhaps the prospect of returning to the shop where she had once worked, or playing the part of a mannequin, had been too much for Lavinia. It was possible that it had all suddenly made her feel nervous, although it seemed unlikely given that Lavinia had a fondness for being looked at and admired. Rose felt that if only she could speak to the girl herself instead of going through the formidable Torridge, then she might ascertain what precisely was wrong.

'Of course, her ladyship appreciates the predicament in which she has placed Madame Renard,' Torridge was saying. 'She has arranged for another young lady to model the gowns in her absence.'

'Oh, has she?' Rose said. 'And when exactly did she intend to let us know?' she added with feeling. 'On the day of the event itself?'

Her words were met with a frosty silence followed by a discreet cough by Torridge at such impertinence.

'Which young lady, Torridge?' Rose asked more sweetly in an attempt to appease the old man.

'Lady Celia Goswell, miss, second daughter of the Marquis of Perriford.'

'Oh, I see.' Rose pondered for a moment wondering how she might best go about enquiring whether Lady Celia resembled Lavinia in physique.

As if he could read her thoughts, the butler said: 'Her ladyship asked me to inform you that Lady Celia will be calling at Madame Renard's shop early tomorrow morning to ascertain what will be expected of her at the fashion occasion and for any alterations to be made to the outfits as required.'

'I see. Very good, Torridge,' said Rose, quite resolved to end the conversation, full in the belief that she had gleaned as much as she was going to obtain from the discreet old butler. How she wished that it was Manning, the young man being trained up to replace Torridge, who was on the other end of the telephone. She remembered that the under-butler had a tendency to be more forthcoming and certainly more approachable than his superior. She was just about to hang up the receiver when a sudden thought occurred to her.

'I say, Torridge, Lord Belvedere hasn't by any chance returned to Sedgwick, has he? I know he isn't expected back until tomorrow but – '

'His lordship returned an hour ago, miss.'

'Did he indeed?' exclaimed Rose. 'Oh, but that's delightful. Would you ask him to come to the telephone please, Torridge? I should like to speak with him.'

'But, Miss Simpson –'

'I'm afraid I must insist, Torridge' said Rose, feeling herself on surer ground. 'You know full well he will want to speak with me.'

'Very well, miss, if you say so ...'

Rose heard the old butler tottering off, tut-tutting as he went. She was under no illusions that he approved of her or her relationship with his master. She sighed. How awkward everything would be when finally ... No, she wouldn't think about that now. She had more immediate and pressing things to attend to at this moment. What was Lavinia playing at? And why did she have to be so awfully mysterious?

It seemed to Rose she had been kept waiting a very long time. She was certain that Torridge, however much he might personally disapprove of her, would carry out her instructions to the letter. But there was no escaping that the man was doddery and possibly forgetful. There was a chance that she may have been forgotten, hanging on the other end of the telephone as she was. She was in no doubt the butler had set off determined to summon one of the footman to deliver her message to the earl. But what if he had been waylaid by some unseen event in the servants' hall and she had slipped from his memory?

Rose was just about to hang up the receiver, with a view to telephoning Sedgwick Court again later that morning, when she heard the sound of approaching feet and fancied that she even felt rather than just heard the receiver being physically picked up the other end, such was the enthusiastic and earnest manner in which the person appeared to undertake the task.

'Rose, darling, is that you?'

'Yes, darling, of course it is. I've had to wait an awfully long time. I think that butler of yours deliberately kept me waiting. Oh, Cedric, I don't think he likes me very much. He's dreadfully formidable, isn't he?'

'Whom, Torridge? Is he? I can't say I've observed that he is. I can't believe that he doesn't like you, and as to being kept waiting on purpose, I was in the bath, don't you know.'

'Oh, were you? I'm awfully sorry to have summoned you from it –'

'Think nothing of it. I can't imagine anything better than –'

'Darling, I'm awfully sorry to interrupt you when you are in full flow. You know full well there is nothing more that I would like to do than to stand here talking to you for ages and ages. But I'm in Madame Renard's office at the moment, supposedly firming up arrangements with Lavinia for tomorrow's fashion show. Do you remember that I told you about it?' Rose paused a moment to turn and look guiltily behind her shoulder to make certain that her proprietor had not entered the room unobserved.

'Your sister had graciously agreed to be the main mannequin. But I understand she's ill and Torridge resolutely refuses to let me speak to her. He says she is very unwell and has taken to her bed and is not to be disturbed on any account. Do you know what's going on?'

'I say, is the fashion show tomorrow?' Cedric sounded distinctly despondent to Rose's ears, even from down the other end of the line. 'That's dashed bad luck. For some reason I had it in my head it was next week.'

'Are you saying Lavinia really is ill?' asked Rose concerned. 'It occurred to me, rather uncharitably I must admit, that she might simply have changed her mind. It is the sort of thing she might do, isn't it? I had hoped that if I had an opportunity to actually speak with her myself I might be able to persuade her to go through with it after all.'

'I'm afraid that's quite out of the question, Rose. She certainly won't be well enough to appear at your fashion show if it's tomorrow.' There was a distinct pause. 'I say, it isn't possible to delay it by a week or so, is it?'

'No, it isn't. The invitations have gone out and Madame Renard will be beside herself if it doesn't take place tomorrow. She'll feel that she'd let her customers down. And besides, one or two of them can be rather catty. They might take some satisfaction if she couldn't pull it off. It's rather a coup for Madame, you know. And then of course there's Marcel Girard.'

'Marcel Girard?'

'He's the designer of the couture that will be displayed at the show and which Madame will be selling in her shop. I believe he's an up and coming designer, or so I'm told. Madame Renard is awfully fortunate that he has agreed to supply her dress shop rather than a more fashionable boutique. I expect it's something to do with him being a friend of her son's.'

'And Lavinia was to model these gowns of Girard's?'

'Yes. Not only was Madame to have the prestige of having the daughter of an earl model her gowns, but Lavinia has the most perfect figure for the current fashions, tall and slender and willowy with pale delicate features and an English rose complexion that Madame will keep going on and on about.'

'If you say so.' said Cedric. 'But I say, Rose, I'm awfully sorry. I can say with absolute certainty that my sister won't be well enough by tomorrow to play at being a model.'

'Won't she? Really?' Rose was desperate. 'Won't you tell me what's wrong with her?'

'I'd love to, but unfortunately I have been sworn to secrecy on pain of death.'

'Oh, do be serious, Cedric.'

'I'm sorry, darling, I am. I've promised Lavinia that I won't breathe a word about what ails her, even to you.'

'Oh, very well,' said Rose, annoyed but fully aware that nothing would persuade Cedric to break his promise to his sister. 'I won't try and make you go against your word. But it's left us in the most awful lurch, I can tell you.'

'Can't someone else model the gowns in Lavinia's place?'

'Well, Lavinia has arranged for someone else to do so,' Rose admitted rather grudgingly.

'There you are then,' said Cedric, sounding relieved. 'The show will go on, what. As a matter of interest, who has she asked to do the deed?'

'Lady Celia Goswell.'

'Oh, I say. I wouldn't have thought … but one can never tell, can one?'

'You know her?'

'Oh, rather. At least I did. I haven't seen her for a few years. I wouldn't have said she and Lavinia were particular friends. I wonder what made my sister ask her.'

'Never mind that,' Rose said. 'I want to know what you meant when you said "I wouldn't have thought". You sounded awfully surprised that Lavinia had arranged for Lady Celia Goswell to take her place. Don't you think she'll be suitable?'

'I only meant by that that she and Lavinia aren't by way of being friends. That's not to say they dislike one another. They don't have an awful lot in common, I would say.'

'Are you certain that's all you meant?' Rose asked somewhat suspiciously.

'Well, if you must know, darling, I was rather surprised to hear that she'd want to be a mannequin. Didn't you say that the attributes that attracted Madame Renard to Lavinia were that she was tall and slender? Just the thing to carry off the current fashions?'

'That, and that she's an earl's daughter. Madame Renard is something of a snob, I'm afraid. But if I'm right in supposing that you are hinting that her figure doesn't resemble Lavinia's, then the gowns that your sister was to wear won't fit Lady Celia, let alone be particularly flattering to her form. Oh, dear, I don't know what's to be done. Monsieur Girard chose the dresses to be modelled with Lavinia in mind.'

'Well, as I say, I haven't seen Celia for a few years or so. She was at that difficult age, neither girl nor woman, if you know what I mean. I daresay she's changed a lot since then. No doubt she's the image of Lavinia now and all that. Really, darling, I don't think you need worry.'

'Needn't I?' said Rose, feeling none too sure.

'Of course not. My sister wouldn't have put her forward if she had any doubts as to her suitability.'

'Wouldn't she?' Rose was not so certain. As she similarly thought later when standing before Madame Renard, it seemed to her highly unlikely that Lavinia would suggest anyone who would outdo her in terms of figure and beauty.

'I'm afraid, darling, I must go, estate duties call and all that. Now, when may I speak to you next? I daresay tomorrow night is out of the question isn't it, because you'll be busy with your fashion show?'

'Yes, and Saturday we'll be busy clearing up and then opening the shop for an hour or two to hopefully take one or two more orders for the couture.'

'I tell you what, I'll motor down on Sunday and take you out for luncheon and you can tell me all about how it went. Honestly, darling, I'm sure you're worrying about nothing.'

When Rose at last hung up the receiver she felt a little more relieved although she still felt somewhat apprehensive as to what the morrow would bring. She was not to know then that Lady Celia's physique was to prove the least of her worries. Had she and Madame Renard but had an inkling of the tragic events that were to unfold, they would gladly and with little regret have cancelled all plans associated with the holding of the fashion show, even if it had resulted in a few spiteful and catty remarks made by some of their more objectionable clientele.

Chapter Three

Rose arrived at the shop before opening time to find Madame Renard already there and, from the amount of screwed up pieces of paper on the counter before her and in the overflowing wastepaper basket at her feet, apparently fully immersed in the task at hand. As Rose approached she saw that the proprietor was poring over a sheet of paper, on which she had made a number of crude sketches, many of which had subsequently been scribbled out or written on or drawn over.

'Ah. There you are, Rose. I cannot recall how we intended to stage this event, the exact positioning of the chairs and where we put the refreshments. Did we decide that we would serve the guests drinks at their seats or that they should be handed a glass before they sit down? I cannot remember. All these things, they have gone from my head. I am too anxious, you understand? Until I have laid eyes on Lady Celia, I can think of nothing else.'

'If you remember, Madame –'

'*Ma foi*, look at the time, it flies. We shall be opening in half an hour. I must clear away this mess at once.' Madame Renard put a hand to her forehead. 'I look around this shop and I think it is too small and cluttered to hold a fashion event. What was I thinking? We are not a grand department store like Harridges.'

Rose looked around the shop which indeed was full of merchandise. Every available surface was bedecked and festooned with every imaginable accessory to a woman's attire, arranged in artful displays designed to attract and tempt each shopper to stop and admire the goods on show or, better still, to pick them up and handle them. Madame Renard was very much of the view that once a customer had picked up a scarf and draped it around her shoulders to admire the effect in one of the many looking glasses located conveniently around the shop, a purchase would be forthcoming. The proprietor's philosophy, similar to that of the department and chain stores, was that goods should be out on display rather than hidden away. Handkerchiefs and scarves were not shut up in boxes or mahogany drawers to be produced only on request as happened in the provincial shops. The majority of Madame Renard's wares were both visible and touchable and most definitely formed part of her shop's décor and allure.

'Don't fret, Madame. There is room,' Rose said soothingly. 'Don't you remember that Monsieur Girard measured out the area and made suggestions as to the layout? The chairs are to be arranged in little clusters around the room and everyone will be seated. At the top of the steps Lady Celia will pause and twirl so that everyone can admire her outfit. She will then come down the steps, walk into the centre of the room like this.' Rose gave a quick demonstration, swirling this way and that as if she were wearing some magnificent gown rather than her usual rather drab shop assistant's attire of blouse and skirt. 'She will then go to each group of chairs like this,' Rose paused before an imaginary cluster of customers, 'and stop for a moment or so to enable the cut and fabric of her outfit to be admired.'

'I suppose one or two of the ladies might even rise to feel the fabric. You know what Mrs Milton is like. I do hope she will show some restraint and not try and pull Lady Celia this way and that.' Madame Renard shuddered at the thought. 'That would never do.'

'She will be hindered from doing so because she will be holding a glass,' Rose reassured her. 'And you know how she likes a tipple. The girls and I will ensure that her glass is kept topped up.'

'But all these tables, these counters, where are they to go if Lady Celia is to parade around the room? Surely she will knock into things or be obscured from sight?'

'We'll positon them around the very edges of the room and in between the clusters of chairs keeping the middle of the room clear. Don't you remember? Monsieur Girard showed you a sketch. And,' Rose went over to one of the many occasional tables, 'we will be changing the displays on the tables so that the only accessories on show will be ones that complement the outfits in the exhibition.'

'Yes … I think I see,' said Madame Renard, although she sounded rather hesitant.

'At the end of the event, or if there happens to be a lengthy break in the proceedings, Sylvia and Mary will also be encouraging customers to look at the accessories and will be making suggestions as to which will go best with which outfit.'

'*Bon,*' said Madame Renard, although she still looked worried.

Almost wearily the proprietor gathered up the pieces of spoiled paper and put them in the wastepaper basket. Picking up the basket in a somewhat distracted manner she went to the steps which, while being small in number made up for it in breadth, running almost the full width of the back of the shop as they did. That evening they were to form the makeshift stage from which Lady Celia would descend in all her finery. Their normal, everyday function was to lead up to a large arch, which opened out onto a narrow corridor which itself ran the full width of the back of the shop. Off the corridor were a few rooms huddled together, jostling for space, the most significant of which were Madame Renard's office and the storeroom. During the fashion event it was intended that the proprietor's office would take on the mantle of a dressing room where Lady Celia would change and emerge in her various outfits.

'Four stairs,' said Madame Renard despondently, turning back. 'Is it high enough, do you think, for a stage?' She did not wait for a reply but instead retreated to her office, visions of models descending grand staircases in her head, very much aware that four stairs looked rather meagre in comparison.

Rose was minded to follow the proprietor into her office to enquire when Monsieur Girard would be joining them. On reflection, she thought better of it. From the raised voices that she had heard coming from Madame Renard's office the previous day she was aware that the designer had not taken the news well when he had been informed that he would have a new mannequin to clothe. His mood had worsened when Madame Renard had admitted rather hesitatingly to being ignorant of Lady Celia's figure. Consequently the amount of alterations and adjustments that would be required to be made to the chosen gowns to ensure that they fitted Lady Celia as adequately as they had done Lavinia, remained unknown.

The sudden opening of the door to the street brought Rose to her senses, preventing her from following her employer into her sanctuary. Instead she turned around and found herself facing the very man who had been in her thoughts.

Monsieur Girard, a small shadow of a man, stood before her, his eyes large with dark shadows beneath them as if he had slept badly. One delicate hand toyed with the end of his moustache, the other was clasped to his chest as if he were preparing himself for some fearful ordeal. It seemed to Rose that he did not see her at first, so preoccupied was he in scouring the room for someone else as if he imagined them to be lurking behind the mahogany counters or plaster mannequins. Satisfying himself that they were indeed alone he said at last:

'Is she here yet, the mademoiselle?'

'Lady Celia? No, not yet.'

At the sound of the young man's voice Madame Renard rushed from her office and appeared at the top of the stairs, as agitated as the designer.

'Marcel,' she wailed, waving a sheet from the society pages. 'Marcel!'

'She's here now, Rose. In the office with Madame. Mr Girard's with them. There's been ever such a to-do.'

These were the words that greeted Rose when she returned to the shop an hour or so later that morning after undertaking an errand for Madame Renard. She looked at Mary, the meek little shop assistant who had delivered such news and noticed that the girl's usually rather expressionless and vacant face was now flushed with excitement, her eyes shining.

'Lavinia's friend is here?' It was on the tip of Rose's tongue to enquire as to the woman's appearance, but she thought better of it. She already feared the worst, believing as she did that the proprietor's earlier outburst had been the result of discovering an unflattering picture of Lady Celia in the society pages. Besides she thought it unlikely that Mary could contain herself from giving a vivid description whether or not she received any encouragement to do so.

'She's large and stout, not a patch on Lady Lavinia as regards looks.'

'Shush, Mary. She might hear you.'

'I'm only saying what's true, Rose,' protested Mary, but she lowered her voice a shade nevertheless before continuing. 'Mr Girard, he doesn't want her to wear any of his gowns. Says she hasn't the figure for it. Most particular he is about it. Not that what he's saying isn't right, because it is, but fancy saying as much to her face.'

'He never did!' Rose looked appalled. An unwelcome vision sprung up before her of Monsieur Girard giving forth as to the inadequacies of Lady Celia's figure and the lady in question, outraged by such insults, marching out of the shop and slamming the door behind her.

'He did as well,' exclaimed Mary, enjoying herself having now got into her stride. Her obvious enthusiasm, Rose noticed with dismay, had attracted the attention of the other shop assistant, Sylvia, who made her way over to them, a smug look on her face.

'He threatened to take all his dresses away, so he did,' continued Mary, in her element. 'Or at least cut them to shreds so they couldn't be worn. Madame Renard is beside herself, what with the fashion event being tonight. '

'I'm sure she is,' said Rose.

'I don't know what she was thinking, a fashion event indeed!' exclaimed Sylvia, smiling rather unpleasantly. 'We're not one of those posh department stores where famous Parisian fashion designers decide to show their London collections. Renard's is just a little backstreet dress shop selling factory made garments. Haute couture indeed! Mr Girard isn't a proper designer either, even if he is French. He's just a friend of Jack's who thought he'd have a bit of a dabble at designing clothes.'

'That's very unfair,' admonished Rose. 'Monsieur Girard has remarkable talent. That silver evening gown for instance, it's quite exquisite.'

'It is, I'll give you that,' admitted Sylvia rather grudgingly. 'But I don't think so much of some of his other outfits. They don't look much better than the factory made garments if you ask me. I can't see Madame's customers paying the fancy prices he'll be demanding for them, I can tell you that now.'

'That's why it is to be an exclusive event by invitation only. Madame has only invited a select few of her most affluent customers, as you well know.'

Sylvia sniffed and looked unimpressed.

'How has Lady Celia taken it?' Rose asked turning to Mary. 'Monsieur Girard's rudeness I mean about her wearing his gowns.'

'Lady Celia?' enquired Sylvia, looking curious. 'Who's she?'

'Lavinia's friend of course, the lady we've just been speaking of. It's Lady Celia Goswell, didn't you know?'

'No, we didn't know her name. Madame doesn't tell us anything, Rose, you know that,' said Mary. 'Lady Celia Goswell? I don't think I've heard of her, have you, Sylvia?'

'No, I don't think … Wait a bit. Isn't she one of the Marquis of Perriford's daughters?' said Sylvia. 'Now I come to think of it, I think she is. You don't see many photographs of her in the press and now I see why.'

'Don't be so unkind,' said Rose. 'And don't let Madame hear you say that. It's important that this fashion event is a success for all our sakes. For one thing we owe it to Madame and for another, who knows where it might lead?'

'To the House of Renard and a move to Oxford Street, I don't think!' retorted Sylvia, but Rose noticed that the girl looked less smug now and more thoughtful. Really, she didn't know why Madame Renard kept her on. Sylvia wasn't above being rude to customers although Rose admitted that, when she chose to be, Sylvia could be quite charming.

'Well, that's the funny thing. To answer your question, Rose,' said Mary. 'Lady Celia seems to think it's all a great hoot.'

'Gosh, does she? Well, I suppose that's something. Should I go in to see them, do you think?'

'Yes, Madame asked most particular that you go to her office as soon as you arrived back, and here we've been keeping you talking.' Mary touched Rose's arm. 'You will tell us what happens, won't you? It's better than being at the pictures!'

Rather reluctantly and with a growing feeling of trepidation, Rose made her way to Madame Renard's office and knocked on the door. It was immediately flung open by the proprietor herself, as if she had been awaiting her arrival.

'Rose. At last. I thought you had got lost. It was the smallest of errands that I sent you on, was it not?' Madame Renard ushered her into the room and quickly closed the door behind her as if she thought the girl might make a bid to escape. She moved aside. 'Lady Celia, may I introduce Miss Simpson? She is a particular friend of Lady Lavinia's. Miss Simpson, this is Lady Celia.'

'How do you do?' said Rose.

Now that the proprietor had moved away to the edge of the room Rose had a clear view of the other occupants. Monsieur Girard was seated behind Madame Renard's Edwardian satinwood desk. He looked so engrossed in his own thoughts with his head bent and his hands covering his face so completely that Rose wondered whether he was even aware of her presence. Lady Celia was seated in the chair opposite and had turned slightly away from the desk so that she might view the newcomer more easily. She beckoned with her hand for Rose to come forward. The gesture was made so exactly as if she were signalling to a servant to pour coffee or lay supper that Rose's initial inclination was to remain standing where she was. An imploring look from Madame Renard however resulted in her feeling compelled to comply with the command no matter how humiliating she felt it to be.

'Well, well, well. So you're the famous Miss Simpson, are you?' said Lady Celia in a voice that sounded surprisingly young and light given the woman's appearance. 'I have to admit I've been rather dying to meet you. I've heard so much about you. A shop girl who has made rather an impression on young Cedric and a bit of an amateur sleuth as well, so I've been told. Well, well, well.'

Lady Celia rose in order that she might scrutinise her more closely, which gave Rose the opportunity to do likewise. Lady Celia, she found, was rather older than she had anticipated. She would have put the woman closer to thirty than twenty, and while tall like Lavinia, her build was so completely opposite as to make the idea that she should take Lavinia's place and wear the clothes that had been made to her friend's measurements seem quite ludicrous. What had Lavinia been thinking? Had Lavinia even given the matter any thought, she wondered?

Tall and heavy as she was, Lady Celia still cut an impressive figure, although some of this was surely due to the good cut of her jacket and skirt which emphasised her height rather than her girth. Her face was heavily and rather badly made up, while her hair was expertly coiffured. To Rose, she seemed a woman of contradictions.

'How do you do, Lady Celia?' Rose said again, at a loss as to what else to say.

'I do very well as it happens.' Lady Celia gave Rose a particularly appraising look. 'I have to say you're not what I imagined. I thought you'd be prettier. No, there's no need to take umbrage. It's a compliment, you know. You obviously have something about you other than looks to have attracted young Cedric. He's rather a catch particularly for someone like you, not that I have to tell *you* that.'

There was an uncomfortable silence with Rose unsure how to respond and Madame Renard obviously of the view that this matter did not concern her. Having been duly scrutinised, Lady Celia appeared to have dismissed Rose from her thoughts for the woman's attention turned back to the unfortunate Marcel Girard, sitting across the desk from her still holding his head in his hands. She regarded him with an impatient and somewhat contemptuous stare.

'Really, this will not do, all this posturing,' Lady Celia snapped at the designer. 'I am not what you expected, I quite see that. You thought I'd look like Lavinia, all skin and bones, with a small waist and narrow hips. But how many women really look like that? Isn't that why you designers incorporate puff sleeves or butterfly sleeves, or whatever they're called, to create the illusion of slenderness? I mean to say, isn't that what you do?' She gave Monsieur Girard a particularly withering look, which was completely lost on him as he did not look up from the desk.

'Really, Madame Renard I can't imagine what all the fuss is about,' Lady Celia said, turning her attention to the proprietor. 'All these advertisements you see in magazines, why, they are quite unrealistic. There is a reason why they use drawings rather than photographs. The women they picture are always about three times as tall and thin as any woman I've ever come across. Except perhaps for Lavinia, but then she is rather waif like. But how many of your customers resemble her, I'd like to know.' She laughed rather dismissively. 'Not very many, I'd imagine, whereas I would hazard a guess that quite a few of them resemble me in profile, do they not?'

'Of course, what you say, it is true,' said Madame Renard, rallying a little. 'And had the fashion event been next week, there would have been no issue, I think.' She gave a quick glance at the designer as if she feared that he might contradict her. 'But it is not. It is tonight and the gowns, they have been made to fit Lady Lavinia.'

'Well, she's not here, is she?' snapped Lady Celia. 'And I am. Surely you can alter them? Let out a seam here, move a button there?'

'*Ce n'est pas pratique*,' cried Monsieur Girard, jumping up from his seat. 'The gowns, they are cut to the model's precise measurements. There are not the big seams with the great surplus of material that you imagine. We cannot let them out, as you say. And you cannot move a button from here,' he paused to point one hand flamboyantly to his left, 'to there.' He pointed to his right in an equally showy manner. 'It will not work. It will change how the garment looks, how the material hangs, the way it folds over the body, how it drapes.'

'Will it?' asked Lady Celia in a rather disinterested voice. 'I'm afraid that I don't know much about that sort of thing.'

'That, mademoiselle, is evident,' replied the designer. A lesser woman than Lady Celia might have recoiled from the look he gave her, but the woman in question did not flinch or even appear to notice. Certainly she did not fidget in her seat or look the least bit uncomfortable.

'The fact of the matter is, Lady Celia,' said Rose entering the conversation at last, 'the clothes that were made for Lady Lavinia will not fit you, and there is no time to make new ones to your measurements. We will have to find another model.'

'But –' wailed the proprietor.

'Madame Renard will of course desire your presence at the fashion event. Perhaps you could launch the event and endorse one or two of the outfits that you consider particularly becoming?'

'Becoming on someone else? And what, pray, am I to wear?' demanded Lady Celia. 'Surely you are not suggesting I wear one of my own gowns?' She turned and gave the designer a sweet smile, 'I fear they will overshadow your designs, monsieur. You see, my clothes come straight from the Paris fashion houses. Haute couture at its very best.'

'No, of course not,' said Rose quickly before Monsieur Girard could reply. 'I was going to –'

'You are surely not suggesting that Lady Celia wear one of our factory made garments?' cried Madame Renard.

'No, that's to say I was wondering whether Lady Celia might consider wearing one of the semi-made tailored outfits that you are introducing to the shop, Madame.'

'Goodness, whatever are semi-made outfits?' enquired Lady Celia.

'But of course!' exclaimed the proprietor. 'Lady Celia, they are expertly cut garments from manufacturers who tailor only the very finest retail outfits. These garments they have the same great attention to detail and workmanship that you would find with couture dresses, is that not so?'

Madame Renard had paused to glance at Monsieur Girard for confirmation, but it was Rose who answered: 'Oh, yes.' The designer himself looked inclined to disagree, but said nothing.

'All the difficult stitching, pleating and tucking is skilfully done by the manufacturer,' the proprietor went on. 'The dresses, they are virtually complete. The only seams that are left undone are those which will allow us to make your personal adjustments to ensure a precise fit. *Enfin!* A way out of our dilemma.'

'I hope you're not expecting me to wear something made out of one of those awful cheap materials like rayon,' complained Lady Celia.

'*Non.* Not at all,' Madame Renard said quickly. 'These garments, they are made from only the very finest materials like silk flat crepe.'

'And my gowns, the ones that I have designed, who is to wear them?' demanded Monsieur Girard. 'Is this to be a fashion event only of the factory made and semi-made garments? Perhaps I should go to another boutique who will appreciate my gowns.'

'No, please, monsieur, do not do that,' cried Madame Renard in a voice that threatened any moment to become shrill. 'Oh, Rose, who can we get to model monsieur's gowns? Oh, if only you were a little more slender you could do the job very well yourself. If only –'

'Sylvia,' said Rose. 'Sylvia can be your mannequin, Monsieur Girard.'

Chapter Four

'Sylvia?' Madame Renard looked taken aback as if she had been struck by lightning. 'Sylvia? That girl? Are you out of your mind, Rose?'

'Sylvia? Who's she?' demanded Lady Celia sharply, obviously intrigued by the proprietor's reaction. 'What's wrong with her?'

'Sylvia Beckett,' began Madame Renard, making a face and looking for all the world as if she had just eaten something rather unpleasant.

'Sylvia Beckett?' enquired Lady Celia raising her eyebrows. 'Sylvia Beckett?' She closed her eyes for a moment. 'Don't tell me she is one of your shop assistants? Not one of the girls out there, surely?'

'*Oui*. Really, Rose. *Quelle idée*. How can you suggest such a thing?' said the proprietor recovering her composure. 'The girl, she walks like a cart horse. And her manners. She will be scowling at the customers and frightening them away.'

'If that's the case,' said Lady Celia rather coldly, 'I'm rather surprised that you employ her. Although I have to admit that she does sound rather intriguing.'

Madame Renard turned scarlet and fiddled with a button on her blouse. 'It is true the girl has a few flaws. But she can be quite charming and attentive when she chooses, quite an addition to the shop.' She appealed to Rose. 'Is that not so, Miss Simpson?'

'Yes, indeed, Madame,' answered Rose, not wholly of that opinion herself. 'But I suggested Sylvia because of her physique not her disposition. She is as tall as Lavinia and thinner if anything so Lavinia's clothes should certainly fit her or require only very minor adjustment.'

'*C'est possible. Oui*. What you say, it may be correct,' said Madame Renard somewhat grudgingly, not sounding at all enthusiastic about the prospect.

'Sylvia?' Monsieur Girard said. It was the first time he had uttered a word regarding the proposal, and all eyes turned to him with interest. He looked up and stared at the wall as if he were looking into the distance and could picture the girl standing there before him swathed in one of his gowns. 'Sylvia.' He said the name again slowly to himself in a voice barely above a whisper, as if he were trying it out to see how it sounded on his tongue. '*Oui*. Yes. She has not the poise or temperament of Lady Lavinia, but the figure … yes … she has the silhouette.'

'Oh? I should like to see this girl,' Lady Celia said, clenching her hands together. 'You say she is in the shop now?'

'Yes. Miss Simpson will point her out to you if you like,' Madame Renard said. 'But I would rather you did not say anything to her about becoming the mannequin until I have spoken to her. She is a foolish girl, that one. It will go to her head, I think, if we are not careful.'

The two younger women ventured out into the shop with Rose wondering how she might discreetly point out Sylvia. To her relief both shop assistants were busy attending to customers and so their arrival went relatively unnoticed. Lady Celia walked immediately to one of the tables of accessories and picked up a hat which she pretended to study.

'I take it Sylvia is not that washed out looking girl over there?'

'No, that is Mary.'

'Ah, so she's the other one, is she? Pretty, yes. But rather a common little thing I would have said.' Lady Celia put down the hat and stopped all pretence at studying it. 'What, no word from you, Miss Simpson? Not even a frown and yet I can tell from your silence that you don't think much of me. I can't say I blame you. I daresay I come across as rather unkind. I don't mean to be, I assure you. I'm afraid I have a tendency to say the first thing that comes into my head. It is a great affliction.'

'Indeed?'

'I can see you don't believe me. You think I am making fun of you and your fellow shop assistants.'

'Aren't you?'

'As it happens, no, I'm not,' Lady Celia said, suddenly becoming serious. She gave Sylvia another glance and laughed. 'Why, I don't know what Madame Renard is making all the fuss about. The girl seems to be behaving quite charmingly to that customer. Really, I don't see how she could be more attentive if she tried.'

'Have you seen enough?' asked Rose. 'We had better go back to Madame's office so that you can be measured for your semi-made outfit. They will need to do the final seams. And Madame will want to speak with Sylvia. She will need to try on all Lavinia's outfits. It's likely to take quite a time. We'll be short staffed. I'll be needed back in the shop to serve.'

'Rose ... May I call you Rose? Let us not get off on the wrong foot. I daresay I have been rather unkind.' Lady Celia made an attempt at smiling sweetly. Instinctively Rose took a step backward.

'Oh, dear, what am I thinking?' sighed Lady Celia. 'I am going about this all the wrong way, aren't I? Have I made rather a mess at apologising? Really, I am not good at this sort of thing at all.'

No you're not, thought Rose, but she thought better than to say it out loud. Really, Lady Celia was the most objectionable of people. She longed to ask her the question that was on the tip of her tongue. Why are you here? For it was obvious even to the most casual of observers that Lady Celia was not at all interested in clothes let alone modelling them. So why had she volunteered to do so?

'How do you think I look in this, Rose?' asked Sylvia, admiring her reflection in a full length mirror. 'Don't you think it suits me very well?'

Sylvia was dressed in a black silk chiffon dress trimmed with a delicate Venise pattern collar. She swished this way and that to get the full effect, much to the annoyance of both Elsie, the seamstress undertaking the alterations to the garments, and Monsieur Girard, who was overseeing the proceedings.

'Mademoiselle, will you kindly keep still,' cried the designer throwing his arms up in the air for the umpteenth time. 'Do you want to be pricked by the pin? We have not the time for you to admire yourself in the glass. You look very fine, yes. But you will only wear these dresses tonight if Elsie can alter the gowns in time. You, mademoiselle, are not helping matters. The event, it is this evening, not next week. Elsie, she still has the seams to sew up on the semi-made gown for Lady Celia.'

Elsie, her mouth full of pins, made a rather strange humming sound to show that she concurred with what the designer was saying. For additional emphasis she yanked on the gown and grazed Sylvia's leg with a pin.

'Ow!' squealed Sylvia. 'You hateful girl. You did that on purpose.'

'She did not,' said Rose quickly. 'But do try and keep still and see sense. If nothing else we need you back in the shop as soon as possible. There are still customers to be served and a lot to do before tonight's event. You can't expect Mary and me to do it all ourselves, you know.'

'I don't see why Madame can't help you. It's her event and her shop after all.'

'Madame has a headache. I suggested that she go home for an hour or two to rest. No, don't look at me like that, Sylvia, it's for the best. It's her nerves. She's very anxious and worried about tonight. She's afraid it won't be a success.'

Sylvia sniffed, but remained still so that Elsie could pin her.

'Where's the marquis's daughter, I'd like to know?' she said after a while.

'If you're referring to Lady Celia, she's meeting a friend for lunch and then doing some shopping,' said Rose. 'She'll be back in a couple of hours to try on her outfit. So do be helpful and allow poor Elsie enough time to sew the seams.'

'Yes. It would be just awful, wouldn't it, if poor Lady Celia had to wait.'

'Really, Sylvia, I don't know what's got into you. Why are you being like this? Usually if a customer has a title you are all over them like a rash in the hope you might get a tip.'

'I am not!' protested Sylvia. 'You take that back. If you must know, I just don't like her, that's all,' she added sulkily, turning her gaze away from her reflection.

'I suppose you've taken against her because she's a friend of Lavinia's?' said Rose, aware that Sylvia had resented Lavinia when she had worked in the shop.

'All this playing at being a shop girl or playing at being a mannequin, it's enough to make an honest hardworking girl like me feel sick. Not for the likes of them the long hours and low pay,' moaned Sylvia. 'They think they're so above us, don't they, with all their money and titles and fine things? Still, I'm not sure why I'm saying all this to you. You'll be one of them soon, won't you?'

Rose felt herself blush and, much to her annoyance, she saw Sylvia smile.

'Well,' said Rose hurriedly. 'I doubt whether Lady Celia's that fond of you. But please, Sylvia, will you stop your complaining?' Rose sighed and tried a different approach. 'Oh, do cheer up, do. You should be pleased that Lady Celia hasn't your figure. You are getting to wear Monsieur's gorgeous gowns after all, and after tonight I doubt whether you will ever lay eyes on the lady again.'

Later Rose was to remember those very words spoken so casually and in haste, words designed to lift Sylvia's spirits and make her more accommodating. They were to prove true, but in such an awfully appalling way that had she had any inkling of the tragedy to come she would never have uttered them. They would have remained unsaid, instead of floating in the air in Madame Renard's little box room of an office already distinctly overcrowded with its disgruntled sales assistant, its anxious designer and the harassed seamstress pulling her hair out with it all.

'Darling, have you been waiting long?'

Lady Celia Goswell, not waiting for an answer to her question, arrived at the table in the Lyons Corner House in something of a rush. She deposited somewhat clumsily onto its surface a number of packages done up in brown paper and string which fought for space with the cutlery. A number of other parcels slipped from her grasp and rolled onto a convenient chair, while others still had toppled onto the floor. Evidence, if evidence was needed, of a successful shopping excursion. Lady Celia herself, seemingly oblivious or uncaring of the fate of her various purchases, sunk her large frame thankfully into a vacant chair, and in her enthusiasm and eagerness to do so, managed to upset the sugar bowl. Her companion, who was already well established at the table, had a look of weary resignation as he put aside the newspaper he had been reading and rose from his seat. He gave her a look which indicated that such an occurrence was not unusual, and set to retrieving the wayward packages and summoning the waitress to address the sugar bowl.

'Oh, it's so noisy and crowded in here, everyone jostling around and in an awful hurry. It's hard to make oneself heard or make any progress across the room. Downstairs is worse. I can't for the life of me think why you didn't choose somewhere else for us to have lunch.'

'You know very well why, my dear,' answered Bertram Thorpe, her companion. 'The prices here meet my pocket.' He regarded her with a touch of annoyance. 'And I say, did you have to be so late? You know full well that I have only an hour for lunch and I've been waiting for you nearly twenty minutes. I was about to order on your behalf.'

'Well, you may as well have done. Now what shall I have? I daresay the cold consommé followed by the stewed lamb will do me very well. And then, if we have time I'll have the pear tart ... although perhaps I'll abstain from having a pudding just this once. I want to fit into my dress. It took ages to be measured for it and really I don't know why they bothered, it was such a frightful thing. Now,' she regarded Bertram fondly, 'don't go on so, darling. I have so much to tell you. And it won't be the end of the world if you do go back a little bit late, will it? You do work for your uncle after all. Tell him I wanted to talk to you about changing my will or setting up a charitable trust or some such thing. That's what solicitors do, isn't it?'

'Amongst other things, yes,' Bertram said returning to his chair, the packages now in some sort of order. 'I'm not so very sure that the law is the life for me, you know, Celia,' he said, having regained some of his usual humour, 'I'm not certain that I'm cut out for it.'

'Well, after we're married you won't have to work at all, will you? Not if you don't want to.'

There followed an awkward silence which both parties were eager to break, but neither knew how, both being at a loss as to what to say. Celia cursed herself for having spoken of marriage, a subject which Bertram regrettably rarely mentioned. In the end it was Bertram who broke the silence by summoning the waitress. She weaved her way between the tables until she stood before them in her neat black, maid like uniform with its well laundered white collar, cuffs and apron. She tilted her head to take their order, which gave Celia the opportunity to study her cap which she noticed matched the apron and cuffs so perfectly. It was offset by thick black ribbon threaded through it. While Bertram gave their order Celia sat back in her chair and idly and with little interest regarded the orchestra. Her thoughts drifted back to the ground floor of the establishment with its large Food Hall and, as a means of occupying herself until the silence was broken, she set her mind to trying to recall the various delicacies that had been on display there. If she remembered correctly, they had included amongst other things hams, cakes, pastries, bespoke chocolates, fruit from the Empire, wines, cheeses and flowers.

'Celia –'

'I know, I'm sorry, I shouldn't have –'

'It's not that, darling. It's just that you know very well your father will never accept me as a son-in-law.'

'But of course he will. Why won't you understand? You'll suit him very well.'

'You're the daughter of a marquis, Celia, and I'm a humble solicitor in an unfashionable law firm. I have very few prospects.'

'I don't care. And it won't worry Daddy a jot,' Celia said, clasping Bertram's hand in hers. 'He wants me to be happy and if I'm completely honest, I think he'll be pleased just to get me off his hands. I'm almost thirty. He's given up on the idea that I'll ever be married off. He's afraid that I'm going to end up a dried up old spinster.'

'I can't imagine that you'll ever be dried up,' laughed Bertram. 'You're too full of life. Take just now. You came sailing into the room like a whirlwind upsetting everything in your path.'

Celia regarded him fondly. As always she thought that he cut quite a figure of a man, tall as he was, although his features were not spectacular or anything out of the ordinary. Perhaps, she thought that was why she liked him so very much. He was not a man to be intimidated by. His looks were not so much greater than hers, but he was comfortable in himself, not awkward as she was. She found his quiet composure reassuring. He was so unlike the other men of her acquaintance who were confident because of their status in society and their wealth. Unlike them he was not overwhelmed by her exuberant and ungainly manner. If anything, these qualities were what had attracted him to her.

'I really have had the most interesting of mornings, Bertram,' said Celia, leaning towards him and putting her hand lovingly on his arm. 'What would you say if I were to tell you that I am to be a mannequin this evening at a fashion event? It's to be held in the funniest little backstreet boutique you could imagine.'

'Good lord, Celia!' exclaimed Bertram. 'That doesn't sound like you at all.' He smiled and gave her an affectionate look as he spotted lipstick on her teeth. 'I say, is your lady's maid on strike? Your make-up looks a bit of a mess, darling, if you don't mind my saying. You've got the stuff on your teeth.'

'It's frightfully infuriating,' said Celia, dabbing at her mouth with the edge of her handkerchief. 'Betsy's ill and I've absolutely no idea how to apply the stuff myself. I thought I'd probably done it all right, but I can tell now from your expression that I haven't. No doubt Madame Renard and her awful little shop assistants were laughing at me behind my back.'

'Madame Renard?'

'Oh darling, do keep up. She's the proprietor of the boutique where I'm to be the mannequin. Now don't laugh,' Celia tapped Bertram's arm playfully. 'I daresay it sounds jolly funny and all that but really, I'm only helping Lavinia out.'

'Lavinia?'

'Lady Lavinia Sedgwick, sister of the Earl of Belvedere. I don't think you've met her. She's not a particular friend of mine.' Celia made a face. 'But I'm sure that I must have told you about that bet she had with her brother? Working in a dress shop for six months?'

'Now you come to mention it, I think I do remember you saying something of the sort. Did she stick it out? Good for her!'

'Yes. Well, as I was saying, she'd agreed to model some gowns for them this evening. There's to be a fashion show of sorts in the shop complete with French designer, would you believe? The shopkeeper has ideas of grandeur.' Celia laughed. 'But poor Lavinia's feeling rather poorly. She's had to cry off and doesn't want to leave the shop in the lurch.'

'I still don't understand how you came to volunteer your services, darling,' said Bertram, looking at her with interest. 'As I said before, it's not your sort of thing, is it? I never thought you were that interested in clothes. You always say that women spend far too much time preening themselves in front of a mirror for your liking.'

'Yes. Well, she telephoned Judith to tell her all about it. You know, Judith Musgrove? I happened to be having tea with the girl at the time. From what I could gather, Lavinia was in a dreadful state. She was hoping that Judith might be able to help her out, what with Judith being tall and slender and having a thing for dresses.'

'But she couldn't?'

'Couldn't or didn't want to. She said she had another engagement which she couldn't possibly put off. Judith's a dreadful snob, you know. She probably thought it was beneath her.' Celia laughed. 'So, much to everyone's surprise, I volunteered my services. You should have been there. Judith almost spilt her tea with the shock. I thought it would be a bit of a hoot.'

'Did you indeed?' Bertram raised an eyebrow and looked at her somewhat sceptically.

'Naturally Lavinia was rather disappointed. She tried to hide the fact, of course. She didn't think I was at all suitable, but she was desperate and I offered, so that was that.'

There was a moment or two of silence as Bertram tried to conjure up the image in his mind of Celia modelling a beautiful and elaborate gown made of some fine stuff, swishing gracefully this way and that. He laughed heartily.

'You are a good sport, darling. I suppose that's why I love you so.'

Celia beamed at him adoringly.

'So I'm to model a gown at Renard's tonight and have some frightful customers stare at me. Well, that's not quite true. I'm really only introducing the gowns, another –'

'Renard's?' enquired Bertram sharply.

'Yes, that's the name of the boutique. Didn't I tell you?'

'No, you mentioned that the proprietor was a Madame Renard. I suppose I should have put two and two together.'

'Why ... what do you mean?'

Celia, Bertram noticed, was watching him carefully. Was it his imagination, or was she holding her breath? He averted his gaze and fiddled with the cutlery on the table.

'No, of course ... I ... I mean to say that there was no reason why –'

'Have you heard of Renard's? Do you know of it?'

'No. Really, Celia, you do ask the strangest things. Why would I be familiar with a women's dress shop? Do you think I get my shirts there?'

'Of course not. It's just that you sounded surprised, that's all, when I said the name of the shop, as if you knew of it.'

'Well, I don't. And really, Celia, must you go on and on about it? I can't imagine why you are. Ah ... good, here's the consommé. Let's eat, shall we? I'm absolutely starving and I haven't much time.'

'Will you come tonight and see it?' asked Celia. The eager note in her voice was not lost on the young man.

'Come to see what?' Bertram looked up from his soup and turned pale. 'Surely you're not suggesting that I come to see this fashion show, are you? I'd be the only man there.'

'Nonsense. I expect quite a few of the customers will bring their husbands with them. They pay their wives' dress bills after all.'

'Well, I don't pay yours ... at least not yet.'

Celia stared for a moment at the crisp white tablecloth in front of her and clasped its comforting fabric between her fingers. She hardly dared look up and catch her companion's eye. She played back his words in her mind and wondered if she had misheard them. No … he had definitely hesitated and then insinuated that in future he might be responsible for paying for her clothes. If that was the case, then …

'I'd like you to come. Please, say you will. I'll only be wearing one gown and it is rather hideous. Why, it's not even as nice as that nippy's little uniform.' She paused to indicate the neatly clad waitress. 'But I'll be presenting the other outfits. Bertie, darling.' She leaned forward and grasped his arm. He found her hold surprisingly strong and possessive. Almost instinctively he had the urge to recoil from her clutches as if he were about to set foot into a trap.

'I'd like you to be there, really I would,' Celia persisted. 'You must be there, darling, you must be. I couldn't possibly do it if you're not.''

'I don't see why I must. It isn't my sort of thing at all, just as it isn't yours. Upon my word, Celia, I don't know why you're doing it at all.'

'Don't you?' Celia whispered the words so quietly that he was forced to lean forward to hear her.

There was another awkward silence between them as she awaited his response. He knew that if he looked up she would be watching him intently again. His thoughts went inadvertently to a cat waiting for an opportunity to pounce on its prey. He shivered.

'Oh, all right,' he said at last, shrugging his shoulders and staring gloomily at his cold consommé, which he all of a sudden found distinctly unappealing. 'If it means that much to you, darling, then of course I will.'

'Oh, it does.' Celia gave a sigh of relief and leaned forward. She held his hand for a moment in her large, gloved one. He felt the strength in her grip. 'You know I love you, Bertie, don't you? You know that I love you more than anything else in the world?'

Bertram gasped, somewhat taken aback. 'Of course,' he mumbled in an embarrassed sort of way. She let go his hand instantly and drew back in her seat so that the table, with its white starched tablecloth, was between them like some impenetrable barrier.'

'Now that's settled, let's eat, shall we?' Celia said in a completely different tone of voice. 'I've got to get back myself, for the fitting, you know. They'll be wondering what's become of me.'

Bertram felt resentment well up inside him. They had been playing some sort of game and he had lost. She had defeated him. He, weak and pathetic, had given in to her wishes. Now, why had he done that? It was so unlike him, and now he came to think of it, it was so unlike her to be so insistent. That was why he had given in to her. But there had been something else, another reason. It was only when the waitress had cleared away their bowls and brought them steaming plates of lamb stew that he realised what it was. He had felt afraid.

Chapter Five

Lady Celia returned to the shop at the allotted hour to try on the semi-made outfit that had been finished to her precise measurements. Madame Renard, her heavily ringed fingers knotted together, hovered at the door of her office, her face anxious.

'Ah, *parfaitement*,' exclaimed the proprietor as Lady Celia studied her reflection in the mirror. 'You see this skirt, it is of rippling flares and tiny pleats. See how it swirls when you move? *Voila*. It fits you perfectly.'

'Does it? Of course I'm sure you're right … but,' said Lady Celia. 'I think I may have preferred it in black rather than in royal blue.'

'In royal blue you will be seen, in black you may fade into the shadows. My customers, they want to see you.'

'They want to see Lady Lavinia,' Lady Celia corrected her. 'And I'm not at all sure about this column of bows down the front. There's rather a lot of them, the bows I mean. And it's all rather symmetrical, isn't it?'

'It is,' agreed Madame Renard. 'It is the style and it suits you to perfection.'

'I'm sure you are right,' said Lady Celia again, although she said it in such a way as to imply the opposite. 'But it's just a little fussier than what I usually wear. You don't think it looks a little common?'

Madame Renard gaped and said nothing. If truth be told, she was afraid that if she were to open her mouth she could not keep a civil tongue.

Lady Celia, apparently oblivious to the reaction her words had caused, toyed with the fabric of the dress, feeling it between her fingers. 'The material, it does not look or feel too cheap.' She sounded surprised.

'*Non, non, non*. It is not cheap. It is the very finest.'

Lady Celia raised her eyebrows and looked for a moment as if she were about to disagree. Instead she sighed and then all of a sudden looked distinctly bored.

Madame Renard breathed a sigh of relief. Her temper had passed. She put her hand to her head. The throbbing, nagging headache that had plagued her earlier in the day appeared to have retreated. Perhaps this evening would go well after all. But, just as these very thoughts were drifting through her mind, there was a knock on the door and Rose appeared.

'Madame? Oh, I am sorry. I thought you were alone. Lady Celia.'

'Come in, come in,' said Madame Renard ushering her in. 'Lady Celia, she looks very fine in her new frock, does she not, Rose? Very elegant. The style, it suits her, *oui*?'

'Indeed, it does,' concurred Rose, although privately she was of the view that, if anything, the dress rather accentuated Lady Celia's portly figure. 'Madame, Sylvia is outside wearing the silver gown. Monsieur Girard insisted that she come in and show you. He is quite beside himself with how well it looks on her.'

'Oh? He is adamant that we include that dress, is he? It was not decided. He knows I have my reservations –'

'On account of it being so expensive, yes. But he thinks when your customers set eyes on it the orders will come flooding in and I must admit I think he might be right.'

'Really?'

'Yes,' said Rose. 'I know –'

'This silver gown it sounds intriguing,' said Lady Celia, following the exchange with interest. 'Do bring the girl in so we can see it on her.'

Rose beckoned to Sylvia and then stood aside, standing in the narrow corridor, so that the girl might enter Madame Renard's office. With three occupants the room now appeared distinctly overcrowded and so Rose remained in the corridor looking on. This position afforded her the ideal opportunity to register the reactions on the two women's faces as Sylvia glided forward in the silver gown, a vision of loveliness.

As she had predicted, Madame Renard clapped her hands together and exclaimed loudly with delight, her voice shrill and her eyes bright. However it was Lady Celia's reaction that she found more interesting, unexpected as it was and in its own way no less intense than the proprietor's more effusive display of emotion. For, as Sylvia had walked forward and the sheen from the silk satin of her gown had seemed to brighten the room like the light emanating from a silver moon, the colour had drained from Lady Celia's face. Her jaw had dropped and she had gaped, mouth open, looking for a moment like a half-wit or a fish stranded and dying on a river bank.

Rose, from where she stood, was unable to see the expression on Sylvia's face. However she did not doubt that the girl was fully aware of the effect her appearance had caused and was basking in the afterglow, her lips upturned in a self-satisfied smile.

Rose had been similarly taken aback when she had first glimpsed Sylvia in the gown, for the girl had been transformed in appearance almost beyond belief. The dress had given Sylvia, almost impossibly thin, slender curves due to the softly draped bodice gathered at the waist by a large diamanté clasp. The front of the dress was covered in the most delicate of lace on which had been hand sewn the smallest of glass beads, hardly visibly from a distance, but the overall effect of which was to make the dress appear to glisten in the light.

Sylvia had slowly turned so that the two women could admire the low decollate back of the gown, set off by diamanté straps running across the back of the neck. The shoulders of the dress itself were formed of strings of silver and glass beads accentuated here and there with a smattering of diamanté which seemed to accentuate the plunging backline of the dress and the paleness of Sylvia's skin.

'It is magical,' cried Madame Renard. 'Sylvia, it makes you look like a princess from a fairy tale. Why, I think it looks even finer on you than it did on dear Lavinia if such a thing were possible. Perhaps, I think, because your hair, it is a little darker. Pale brown, mousy one calls it, yes? You permit me to say that I have always thought it looked a little drab. But here it is perfect. It softens and compliments the silver of the gown do you not think, Lady Celia?'

Madame Renard turned to regard her companion, who by this time had closed her mouth but was still staring, transfixed by the vision before her, as if she had seen a ghost or indeed a figure actually emerge from the pages of a book of fairy tales. She did not seem to have heard the proprietor, for she did not utter a word in reply or even nod her head.

'Rose, don't you think I look beautiful?' asked Sylvia. The spell was broken. Her posture followed. Gone was the straight back and the expression of quiet aloofness on her face as she caressed the lace of her gown and put a hand up to her shoulder to feel the beaded straps. 'Don't you think I look like one of those film stars?'

'Yes, you do …'

'Why, I think it's just the sort of dress that would make a man fall in love with a woman, don't you, Rose? Or propose marriage. If you have the figure for it, of course, like I do.'

'That dress,' said Lady Celia slowly. 'I want to wear it tonight. Not this rag.' She pointed dismissively to her own ensemble.

'But Lady Celia that is not possible. The dress, it takes hours to make, no, days to sew, it –'

'I want to wear that dress tonight, Madame,' said Lady Celia in a voice so final that no one said a word to contradict her no matter how absurd they thought her demand. The woman herself had turned back to the mirror and Rose fancied that she saw her hand shake.

Sylvia had taken advantage of Lady Celia having turned her back to them to roll her eyes at Rose and make a face. Momentarily it appeared that the girl had forgotten that Lady Celia could see their reflection in the mirror as clearly as if she had been facing them. Rose saw that Sylvia realised her mistake almost immediately, but it was too late. The damage had been done. Lady Celia had swung around, her face barely containing the fury that she must have felt at such a show of insolence.

'I shall wear *that* dress, not a copy or a replica, *that* one,' said Lady Celia very slowly and quietly as if she were speaking to a young child. 'You, Madame, will take it off the back of that wretched girl there and see that it is altered to fit me. I alone will wear that dress tonight.'

'But Lady Celia –'

'If you do not do as I ask, Madame, I shall not honour your event with my presence. Do you understand?'

Madame Renard's face crumbled and she clutched at the side of her desk as if for support. Sylvia cried and wailed as if she were fit to burst, her body shaking and trembling with each sob.

Rose put an arm around the distressed girl's shoulders, although the gesture seemed sadly inadequate and futile. She stared at Lady Celia finding it difficult to contain her own anger at the woman's spitefulness. It was only later that she wondered if matters might have turned out very differently had Lady Celia not caught sight of Sylvia's mocking gesture or indeed if there had been no exquisite silver gown of silk satin to stir up such emotion.

'Oh, don't go on so, Sylvia, please' said Rose for what seemed to her the umpteenth time. She sighed. 'There's nothing to be done about it, really there isn't.'

'But it isn't fair,' wailed the shop assistant, her eyes red and puffy from crying. 'Horrible, beastly woman.'

'Well, you only have yourself to blame. Whatever possessed you? Didn't it occur to you that she could see your reflection in the mirror?'

'I suppose I wasn't thinking,' sniffed Sylvia, drying her eyes on her sleeve.

'For goodness sake don't let Madame see you do that, Sylvia. Haven't you got a handkerchief about you? And do try and look on the bright side. This morning you weren't going to be modelling any of Monsieur Girard's outfits and now you'll be modelling all of them but one.'

'Yes, but the silver gown's the only one that matters.'

'Well, as I've said, it's all your own fault. You have no one to blame but yourself.'

'I know you're right. That makes it worse somehow. But I don't like the other dresses nearly so much, Rose. They're not a patch on the silver one. They're very commonplace, you know they are. But the silver gown … it made me look like a princess, Rose,' Sylvia said, a dreamy expression crossing her face for an instant, 'even Madame said so.'

Sylvia dabbed at her eyes again with her sleeve. There was a pause before she added: 'Do you think she was jealous of me, Rose? The way I looked in that dress? Do you think that's why Lady Celia was so very mean?''

'I daresay it had something to do with it,' agreed Rose, deciding that the best way to cheer the girl up was to appeal to her vanity.

'It's rather nice to think,' said Sylvia, a sly smile creeping over her face, 'that I have something that Lady Celia would love to have.'

Rose raised her eyebrows and looked up sharply. There was something in the girl's tone that had caught her attention.

'Beauty, Rose,' said Sylvia hurriedly, almost as if she were afraid that she had said too much. 'No matter how rich she is, it can't buy her a fine figure and good looks, can it?'

'No, I don't suppose it can,' agreed Rose, although she had the oddest impression that Sylvia was referring to something else entirely.

It seemed to Rose that she had done nothing that day but soothe ruffled feathers, calm tattered nerves and generally mollify all those involved with the fashion event. The arrangements were proving so annoyingly tiresome that she was beginning to feel heartily sick of it all and wishing that the occasion had never been mooted. It was only early afternoon and yet it felt as if she had already worked a full day and a half. The afternoon and evening stretched out long and unyielding before her. Undoubtedly there would be many more ups and downs along the way before the event was over and the day had reached its welcome conclusion. In time she knew the event would become a thing of the past to be looked back on with affection or relief depending on the outcome. She sighed. It was all very well to be philosophical but now she was faced with the present and, to make matters worse, she had the beginnings of a headache. How she wished that she could act on the advice she had given Madame Renard and lie down in a quiet room for an hour or so.

However, that was quite out of the question of course with so much to do and so many of the evening's key players out of sorts in one way or the other. Not for the first time did Rose curse Lavinia for her unfortunate and unexplained absence from the evening's festivities which seemed to be at the root of all the issues and problems that had occurred. What was her friend thinking, suggesting that Lady Celia take her place? Regardless of their different builds, the woman was arrogant and rude and decidedly unhelpful, almost as if she were intentionally going out of her way to be objectionable.

It suddenly occurred to Rose that only Mary had been relatively unaffected by the trials and tribulations of the day. Quiet, inoffensive Mary, with her washed out appearance as Lady Celia had so unkindly put it, and unobtrusive manner which made it all too easy to overlook her in the presence of more forceful personalities. Yet it was Mary who got on with the task in hand without fuss. Sylvia, as always, was scarce when there was work to be done, and yet here was Mary diligently rearranging the shop by herself in preparation for the evening's entertainment, clearing a space in the middle of the store, struggling with moving the overladen tables by herself to the very edges of the room, putting out the chairs in clusters and sweeping the floor.

'You have been busy, Mary. Here, let me give you a hand.' Rose rolled up her sleeves.

'Thank you. This table is rather heavy. I suppose I should have taken everything off it first before I tried to move it,' said Mary, stopping what she was doing and putting her hand to the small of her back as she straightened. 'I've tried to make sense of Monsieur Girard's diagram as best I could, but Madame has crossed one or two things out. I'm not entirely sure what she wants us to do with the counters. Do you by any chance know what is to happen with the Parisian one?'

The shop counter Mary was indicating was a large and impressive walnut one, which had a carved oval detailed front panel complete with a fluted frieze. It was Madame Renard's pride and joy, being one of only a very few items that she had brought with her from France.

'It's to go near the stairs. Monsieur Girard's intention was that Madame should stand behind it and use it as a sort of lectern when she introduces the outfits.' Rose sighed. 'I suppose she'll have to share it with Lady Celia now that she'll also be introducing one or two of the outfits instead of modelling them. The other one,' Rose paused to gesture towards a glass, oak framed counter, 'is to go against the wall there. We'll fill it with accessories to go with the various garments. It should hold quite a few.'

'So Sylvia wasn't boasting when she said she'd be modelling all the outfits,' Mary said quietly and rather miserably, Rose felt. 'I thought she meant just one or two. It'll mean there'll be more for us to do, won't it? Sylvia will be waltzing around showing off to the customers, while we'll be serving the drinks, writing out the orders and making all the appointments for the fittings.' She rubbed her aching back again. 'We'll be rushed off our feet while she'll be twirling this way and that in fine gowns. Some people get all the luck, don't they, Rose?' Mary did not wait for Rose to answer but went on in a rush: 'Even when they're horrible and hateful and don't deserve it.'

'Mary!' Rose looked at her sharply, considerably shocked. 'Whatever made you say such a thing? I always thought you and Sylvia were friends. Why, you're always huddled together in the corner whispering and giggling like a couple of school girls.'

'Oh ... oh ... we are,' Mary looked horrified as if she were taken aback by her own words. 'We are, friends I mean. I don't know why I said what I did. I suppose I was just a little jealous, that's all. It's only sometimes she can be ... well, rather beastly. I suppose I'm just tired and worried about tonight. But sometimes I … I … I wish Sylvia wasn't working here, Rose, I do really. Everything would be all right if she wasn't working here.'

Before Rose could ask Mary what precisely she meant by such a statement, the girl had turned tail and fled from the room on the pretext of getting some more water for a vase of flowers, as if she feared she had said too much and spoken too vehemently. Rose was left standing there, staring at the space where Mary had been, and pondering what Sylvia could possibly have done to have caused such an outburst from the usually placid and docile shop assistant.

Chapter Six

Rose acknowledged that the assumption had been made that Mary would be accommodating with regard to the additional work that would be landed on her shoulders following Sylvia's temporary elevation from shop assistant to mannequin. If truth be told, even Sylvia with her tearful and demonstrative outburst had quickly, if somewhat ungraciously, conceded defeat when faced with Lady Celia's unreasonable demands. The proprietor's anxieties had been more difficult to placate, the woman being torn as she was between having a member of the British aristocracy present to praise the gowns in front of her most favoured customers, and wanting the outfits to be modelled to their best advantage.

But it had been Monsieur Girard, however, who had proved the greatest challenge. On discovering that Lady Celia insisted on wearing his precious silver creation in place of Sylvia, the man had flown into an uncontrollable temper, waving his arms in the air and stomping around Madame Renard's little office like a man possessed. With little regard for what he was doing, he had bumped into the desk and upset a pile of papers onto the floor. Such action had caused Madame Renard to go scurrying around on the ground attempting to retrieve the documents while at the same time trying to navigate Monsieur Girard's ever pacing strides. For the designer was charging around the room so frantically and distractedly that he was giving not a care for what was beneath his feet.

Rose, fearing an accident, urged the proprietor to rise from the floor. She bent and gathered the remaining papers herself while keeping a watchful eye on Monsieur Girard's progress around the room. As she struggled to her feet, while at the same time trying to maintain hold of the large pile of bills and correspondence in her arms, almost unintentionally she allowed her eyes to glance absentmindedly over the various documents clutched in her hands. Odd words, alone and coupled, floated into her consciousness ... *festoon necklace ... Madame Aubert ... cotton pongette ... all silk flat crepe ... rayon ... scallop-edged collar ... brocaded ... finest materials ... silk satin ...*

Rose was roused from her idle perusal of the papers by having the pile snatched unceremoniously from her grasp with unexpected vigour by

Madame Renard, the bangles on her arms jangling noisily from the movement and her dark eyes blazing. Brought abruptly to her senses, what surprised Rose most was the expression on Madame Renard's face. For a moment she appeared strangely furtive as if it were the proprietor rather than the shop assistant who had been caught out doing something she shouldn't. Rose blushed and withdrew to the other side of the room. She had not given any thought as to what she was doing, motivated not even by idle curiosity. She had glanced at the topmost papers merely because they happened to be in her arms. Only now did she appreciate that what she had been so blatantly reading had included Madame Renard's private papers and correspondence. Little wonder then that the woman in question was put out.

Monsieur Girard meanwhile had worked himself into something of a fury and turned to face Madame Renard, visibly trembling with emotion.

'I will not allow it, do you hear me? I will withdraw all my gowns from this evening's event and go to a boutique who will appreciate my designs. *Oui*, one that will provide me with suitable mannequins and not, not …' The designer flung his arms up in the air as he paused, words having failed him as he tried to think of an appropriate description of Lady Celia's numerous inadequacies as a model.

'Marcel, you must do no such thing!' wailed Madame Renard. 'My shop, my reputation, it will be ruined. My clientele, they are expecting the most wonderful of evenings. And your clothes …' the proprietor paused to bring her fingers to her lips and kiss them, 'they are to die for, are they not? My dear customers, they will never have seen such fine garments, such attention to detail …'

Rose was amused to witness the designer pause in his pacing and, despite all his angry posturing of a moment before, begin to preen. He puffed out his chest and instantly he appeared taller, calmer and generally more in command of the situation.

'It is true what you say, Madame. Your customers, they are not used to seeing such fine clothes. It will take their breath away. But only if worn by Mademoiselle Sylvia. *Elle est jolie femme.* But by Lady Celia, *non!*' The designer flung his arms out theatrically and made a face. 'The silver gown, it is my greatest creation. It cannot be worn by that woman, it will be all wrong. She has not the figure. Your customers, they will see that dress on her and they will think how hideous it looks.'

'Monsieur Girard –' began Madame Renard weakly.

'They will not want to buy it, they will think it is a monstrosity.'

The designer banged his fist down on the desk and the paperwork threatened once more to topple onto the floor. Rose dived to the rescue just in time to stop it from falling.

'They will want to buy every dress but that one,' continued Monsieur Girard, apparently oblivious to everything but what he was saying, his face flushed and his manner becoming agitated again. 'No, worse than that, they will laugh. They will say have you ever seen a woman look so awful in a gown? It does nothing for her. It clings in all the wrong places. It makes her look stout and shapeless; that is a dress we will never want. Ah … but on Mademoiselle Sylvia ... *Oh là là*! They will see it for what it really is, this creation of mine. A dress fit for a princess.'

'Yes, Monsieur Girard, but –' interjected Madame Renard.

'They see the gown on Mademoiselle Sylvia and they think their daughters also can be transformed,' continued the designer as if there had been no interruption, '*Voilà*. Their daughters also can look like princesses if they wear this gown. That is what they will think, Madame. They will want to buy it, no, they will insist on buying it. They will push each other aside to be the first in the queue for a fitting. You see if they don't. It will fly off the shelves, my dress.'

'Of course you are right, Marcel. I do not disagree with what you are saying for one moment. You understand? I do not say what you are saying is incorrect. But Lady Celia, she is adamant,' cried Madame Renard. 'She will not yield. She will not see reason.'

'Then let us not have her at the event at all,' said the designer. 'We do not need her. It will not matter if she is upset and tells her friends. They do not shop here. You will lose no customers.'

'I can't do that,' wailed the proprietor. 'I promised my customers that Lady Lavinia would be there tonight. I said the daughter of an earl would be modelling the clothes and instead we have a shop assistant! Lady Celia must be here tonight to save my reputation. She is the daughter of a marquis. If I do not allow her to wear the gown instead of Sylvia, she will storm out. And Lady Lavinia, will she not be upset if I snub her friend?'

'I don't think Lavinia will mind so very much,' said Rose, contributing to the conversation for the first time. 'But I do see your dilemma,

Madame, and yours too, of course, Monsieur. If I might make a suggestion?'

'Please do,' cried Monsieur Girard. 'Anything to end this nightmare.'

'Lady Celia is only insisting on wearing the silver gown because she doesn't want Sylvia to wear it,' said Rose. 'The gown she herself was to wear does not compare favourably with it. She knows she will be overshadowed and she is used to being the centre of attention.'

'With her looks, she would be overshadowed if the girl were wearing a rag.'

'Marcel!' exclaimed the proprietor.

'I suggest, Monsieur,' Rose said hurriedly, 'that Lady Celia does wear your gown.' She held up her hand as the designer made to protest. 'But I suggest she wears a very simplified version of it. By that I mean a dress made in the same material. It could have some of the lace and glass beads sewn on it, but you could argue quite reasonably that you did not have sufficient time to include the diamanté straps at the back of the neck or strings of beads for the shoulders.'

'Then it will look nothing like my gown.'

'No. You are right. It will bear very little resemblance to it,' agreed Rose. 'But if you alter it as I suggest, the gown can be made to suit Lady Celia's figure.'

'But she will protest,' said the proprietor. 'It will not look like the gown that she saw on Sylvia.'

'I don't think that will trouble her, Madame,' said Rose. 'Her only concern, I think, is that Sylvia does not wear the dress.'

'But it will not be *my* dress,' protested Monsieur Girard. 'It will not be my design. It will be most ordinary. I shall not put my name to it.'

'I am not suggesting that you do, Monsieur. Have a dress made up for Lady Celia in a design that is ordinary, as you put it, but in the same material as your gown. No reference will be made to the dress during the fashion event. It will merely be the dress that Lady Celia wears this evening in place of the semi-made outfit.'

'But what of my creation,' cried the designer, 'is it not to be displayed?'

'No, Monsieur Girard. I am afraid not. At least not at this fashion event.'

There was an uncomfortable silence, broken at last by the proprietor.

'Well, perhaps that is just as well,' said Madame Renard rallying. 'It would have been a little too expensive for my customers, I think. Yes, and on reflection a little too grand. Alas, they do not have the budgets to buy such a dress or the occasions to wear it.'

Rose cast a look in the direction of Monsieur Girard. She fancied he was trembling slightly. His head was bowed as if in defeat and he was clutching at the top of the desk as if for support. Any moment now she thought he would scratch at the very surface with his nails. He had not uttered a single word since she had confirmed that they withdraw his gown from the show. His silence worried her. She sensed, as strongly if they had been her own emotions, his pent up fury beneath the surface, his feelings of powerlessness. Looking at the dejected figure, she saw clearly his unwillingness to concede to her proposal. He would fight against it if he thought any good would come of it, but acknowledged, however reluctantly, that there was no feasible alternative if Madame Renard was insistent that Lady Celia be present at the event.

'So be it,' Monsieur Girard said at last, raising his head. His voice sounded strangely flat and resigned when compared with the display of emotions he had expressed only minutes earlier.

Madame Renard at once looked relieved. The worried frown left her face, her composure was regained, and she was once again the matriarch in charge of her domain.

Rose was just about to give a sigh of relief herself when she noticed that, despite his words and the manner in which he had delivered them, there was a look of defiance in Monsieur Girard's eyes. Perhaps he was aware of her eyes on him, for the designer turned and looked at her. For a moment their eyes locked and Rose felt as if she could see into his very soul. She saw, as if in acknowledgment, his lips turn up into the briefest of smiles. It was not a pleasant smile. Rose hurriedly looked across at Madame Renard who, perhaps mercifully, had turned her attention to the papers on her desk and so was oblivious to the look that had passed between designer and shop assistant.

When Rose turned back to look at the designer, his face was expressionless and his eyes blank. For one moment she wondered if she had been mistaken. Perhaps she had imagined it after all. But she still felt his fury in the atmosphere as if it were a tangible thing, even if it had retreated to the very edges of the room; it still lurked in the shadows only partially obscured.

Madame Renard, on opening her office door, was immediately confronted with the spectacle of her son rifling through the papers on her desk in what could only be described as a furtive and frustrated fashion.

'Jacques, whatever are you doing here? *Mais qu'est-ce que vous faites là?*'

'Ah, Mama ...'

The young man had the decency to blush as he put down the papers he had been holding, his right hand still hovering over them as if he were reluctant to let them go. 'I thought you were having a lie down. Rose said you had a headache.'

'So you thought that you'd take the opportunity to go through my private correspondence?' admonished his mother, her dark eyes blazing.

'Of course not. I was doing nothing of the sort, Mother,' retorted her son. 'How can you think such a thing?'

'But I catch you in the very act,' cried Madame Renard, her voice rising. 'You pretend that I do not find you rummaging through the papers on my desk? You have the cheek, the nerve to suggest that I am imagining things? That what I see with my own eyes,' the proprietor paused to make a flamboyant gesture to emphasise the ridiculousness of it all, 'it is not true?'

'All right, Mother, for goodness sake don't go on so,' Jacques said hastily. He flung himself into a chair. 'But as it so happens, I was doing nothing of the sort. No,' he held up a hand as she made to protest, 'I daresay it did look as if I were going through your papers, but I wasn't. That's to say I was only glancing through them to make sure they weren't what I was looking for. My papers, I mean. I wasn't actually reading yours as such.'

'Whatever are you talking about? You make no sense. Why should there be your papers on my desk?'

'I thought I might have left something on your desk by mistake. The other day. You weren't here. I came in here to write a note for Marcel. I didn't think you'd mind, only I think I may have forgotten something. That's to say I may have put it down and not picked it up again.'

'And what is this thing of such significance that you put down on my desk and will not say what it is? Why so mysterious? It is important, yes? You sneak in here like a thief in the night. You scatter my papers this way and that –'

'I did nothing of the sort. And as to my … it was nothing.'

'*Non*. I do not believe that, Jacques. It was something and it was important, and you did not want me to find it. Why so secretive? What have you to hide, eh? You are in trouble, *oui*? You have got into a scrape, as they say? Out with it, my boy …' She paused and waited, clicking her fingers impatiently, her bangles jangling, but Jacques was silence.

'Ah,' she said at last, 'you say nothing, but you do not contradict me. I am right, am I not?'

'No, you're not as it happens,' replied Jacques rather sulkily. He searched his pocket for cigarettes. 'But it will do no good my telling you. You won't believe me, you never do. I could tell you until I'm blue in the face, but you'd never listen.' He looked away, his forehead furrowed and a sour look appearing for a moment on his face. 'You never take anything I say or do seriously. You do not take me as seriously as … as Marcel.'

'Marcel? Why do you choose him? But he is a good boy, yes. He makes his mother proud. Now, of course, if I thought you were telling me the truth,' retorted his mother. 'But no, you are lying … no … don't try and deny it, a mother always knows when her child is lying. I feel it here,' she paused to put her hand dramatically to her breast. 'You are trying to pull the wool over my eyes as they say, are you not?'

Jacques raised his eyebrows, but had the good sense not to protest. Instead he kept quiet, and there followed another uncomfortable silence.

'Ah, I thought as much. But what a fool I've been!' Madame Renard said suddenly, snapping her fingers in her enlightenment. 'There is no missing paper. You did not leave it on my desk. *Non*. For the simple reason that it does not exist. It is a figment of your imagination conjured up to explain why you are here.'

'I don't know what you're talking about. I was not rifling through your papers,' Jacques said hotly.

'No, you were not. I know that now. You came here to see that … that *girl*.' Madame Renard spat out the last word with some distaste.

'I take it by that you mean Sylvia?' Her son sighed and a look of weariness came over him.

'Of course I mean Sylvia. Who else could I mean? Unless of course you have developed a sudden passion for … Mary.'

'And so what if I came to see Sylvia? There's no crime against it, is there, Mother?' asked Jacques, having regained his composure.

'Huh! No crime as you say, except that it makes you lie to your mother and be sneaky.'

'I don't know why you've taken against her so. There's nothing wrong with Sylvia. I admit she gives herself airs and graces sometimes and can be a little rude to one or two of your customers, but I don't doubt that they deserve it.' Jacques laughed as his mother looked about to explode. 'But underneath it all she has a heart of gold, you know she does.'

'She has nothing of the sort! She has no heart at all, that one. She is a scheming little minx.'

'I say, that's rather hard,' Jacques said more seriously.

'Is it? I do not think so.'

'There's nothing wrong with Sylvia, as well you know.'

'I disagree.'

'Well, if that's how you feel about the girl, I'm surprised you employ her. Why haven't you given her her marching orders long before now?'

'You think I have not thought about it?' Madame Renard's eyes had lost their angry glint and her son fancied that she had turned rather pale.

'Why do you keep her on?' pried Jacques, interested by his mother's reaction.

Madame Renard appeared to tremble, certainly her bangles jangled in a hesitant and disjointed fashion.

'Mother, is anything wrong?' Jacques looked at his mother with concern.

'Wrong? No, why should there be?' With an effort Madame Renard rallied. 'I do not like the way the girl sets her cap at you. She wants you very much, I think. She wants to be proprietor of this shop when I am gone. I see it in her eyes, the way she looks around and surveys the shop as if it were her own, the way she speaks to customers … *Non*. You can do much better than her.'

'Oh, is that all?' Jacques looked distinctly bored, as if he had endured a similar lecture on numerous other occasions. 'I suppose that's why you sent me off to work at Harridges, to find a suitable bride amongst the staff. Well, I never, and here was I thinking that you sent me there to learn my trade.' He laughed, attempting to lighten the atmosphere. 'I say,' he added, changing the subject, 'do you mind awfully if I come to see the show tonight? I'd like to see the designs that Marcel's come up with?'

'But of course you must come.'

Madame Renard smiled affectionately and rather indulgently at him. Jacques returned her smile and left, whistling happily to himself in the knowledge that he had indeed pulled the wool over his mother's eyes. However, had he but seen her face as soon as his back was turned, he might have changed his mind and been under the misapprehension that Madame Renard had seen through his charade. But, as it happened, it was something else entirely that caused the look of anguish on his mother's face. The proprietor had worries enough of her own.

Chapter Seven

Rose took a step back to survey the results of her industry. Even to her own, overcritical eye, she had to admit that the shop had been transformed. The floor had been swept and polished to within an inch of its life. Not too polished, she hoped, for it would never do for one of the customers to slip and fall. She had visions suddenly of Sylvia tripping over the hem of one of her fine gowns and careering down the steps to land in an undignified heap at Lady Celia's feet. Rose tore her mind away from such musings and focused instead only on what was solid and tangible before her eyes.

The small clusters of chairs, which she had been afraid would appear rather a motley collection having been borrowed or purchased from various sources, looked reassuringly similar and coordinated now that large white satin bows had been tied to the backs of each. The chairs were arranged in a horseshoe fashion around the shop and were intermingled with a number of tables on which were artfully displayed numerous accessories for the gowns that were about to be modelled. These ranged from neckwear consisting of delicate lace triangles to hand painted scarfs. Also on display were: hats decorated with trimmings of fur, ribbon or satin, rhinestone and paste dress clips; soft calf leather handbags in black or brown sugar, delicate mesh and enamel evening bags; and fine crocheted or leather gloves in grey or tan or pastel hues. Costume jewellery was also on show boasting rich coloured enamel or vivid paste gem stones. Glass and mahogany counters jostled for space between the tables or else were positioned far back against the walls overladen and brimming with yet more accessories and wares. The overall effect was one of opulence, and not for the first time did Rose wonder if Madame Renard's purchase of stock had been somewhat excessive.

The proprietor herself wandered into the shop as the arrangements were nearing completion and clapped her hands in delight.

'*Ma foi!*' exclaimed Madame Renard. 'But you excel yourselves, Miss Simpson, Miss Jennings,' she said, giving an appreciative glance which encompassed both Rose and Mary. 'The glass, the mahogany, the very wood on this floor, I do not think I have ever seen it gleam so. It sparkles and shines like crystal. We have the electric lights, yes, that light up the room, but I have something else to add even more elegance. You wait, yes?'

She did not remain long enough for either one of them to answer, but darted from the room with surprising swiftness, leaving Rose and Mary to exchange bewildered glances. They had followed Monsieur Girard's plans to the letter. As far as both were concerned, all that was left to be done was to hang the great velvet curtains at the shop windows, which would add an air of exclusivity and warmth to the shop and prevent the general public from glancing in when the interior of the shop was lit up like a beacon in the night's sky. 'We do not want to look like a lighted fish bowl,' Madame Renard had said, 'for every Tom, Dick and Harry to look in and stare at us as if we are giving them some sort of spectacle. No, this event, it is by invitation only. It is for my particular friends and customers, that is all.'

Madame Renard returned from her office staggering somewhat under the weight of a tall, floor-standing silver candelabra, decorated with crystal glass. It appeared to be a good six feet in height, with nine arms; on each had been inserted a large cream candle.

'We will try it out, yes? It will look very grand will it not?'

'It looks very splendid indeed,' agreed Rose. 'But I am wondering whether we have the space to do it justice. Where are you proposing that it go, Madame?'

'Jacques, dear boy, has borrowed it from Harridges. I was thinking it should go by the counter over there behind which Lady Celia and I will be standing when we introduce the gowns. But I am wondering now,' said the proprietor putting her head on one side, 'whether the candles will cast a shadow on our faces. It will be very off putting for our audience, I think, if the flames splutter, or if one or two of the candles go out. Perhaps on second thoughts it would be better if it were to go by the window.'

'But the curtains,' protested Rose. 'We shall have to keep an eye on the candles to ensure that they don't set fire to the velvet. Madame, I really do not think there is the room … and Mary and I will be kept very busy with all –'

'We will manage very well,' said Madame Renard. She sounded annoyed. 'You have already said that we have not the space for someone to play the harp. If we are not to have music then we must have candles to create the ambience. The exhibition, it must be magical.'

'Yes, but perhaps we should not place the candelabra so near the door,' Rose said cautiously but quickly, in case her employer saw fit to object before she had made her point. 'Every time the door is opened to let in a customer it is likely to let in a gust of wind.'

'It must go there, there is nowhere else for it to go,' said Madame Renard firmly. 'But, yes, we do not want to set fire to the shop. We will not light the candles until everyone has arrived and the fashion show has started. Mary, if we have any latecomers you will have to be especially careful when opening the door.'

Mary nodded, and Rose could see clearly that the girl was thinking that it was yet one more thing to add to her list of things to do or to remember.

'Right, girls,' continued Madame Renard, 'hang the curtains and then we are ready, are we not? Wait, where is Sylvia? Surely she is not still being fitted for the dresses?' A frown appeared on her face. 'That one, she is so lazy. Get her for me please, Rose. She can hang the curtains.'

Anticipating the girl's protests, Rose made her way reluctantly to the storeroom where she supposed Sylvia was lurking out of the way until all the heavy and boring work had been done. It had been the only refuge available to Sylvia, Madame Renard having been in occupation of the office until recently.

Afterwards Rose realised she had approached the door too quietly. How much better it would have been to have in some way given advance notice of her imminent arrival. At the time, however, she had only wanted to hurriedly give the message, which she had known would be ill received, and be gone. The appeal of a cup of tea before the evening's proceedings had further enticed her to quicken her steps, so that she had opened the storeroom door all in a hurry and come upon not just Sylvia, as she had expected, but another also, before she had chance to take breath.

They had immediately pulled away from each other. It was as if they had been caught in some compromising position, although in truth Rose had had little opportunity to glimpse what they had been doing. Afterwards, she had difficulty determining in her mind whether she had seen them locked in a tight embrace or talking excitedly and earnestly in a conspiratorial way. When she did recall the event later, she was certain only that they had been huddled together in some capacity, their heads bent towards each other. She remembered too that they had spoken in whispers. On her entrance, both had looked up guiltily, Sylvia blushing a fetching shade of crimson, while her companion had turned pale. At once they had torn themselves apart so that they stood too far away from each other, which acted only to accentuate their previous closeness.

'Sylvia … Monsieur Girard … I'm sorry. I didn't mean to interrupt … I … I've a message from Madame. She would like you to hang up the velvet curtains over the windows, Sylvia,'

Rose had fled from the doorway and gone into the room next door, which served as a kitchen or scullery of sorts, although in reality it was equipped with little more than an old Belfast sink, a copper kettle standing on three Bakelite legs, and a cook's table with a porcelain-enamelled top and cutlery drawer. Thankful for some occupation, she began to fill the kettle from the sink. Somewhat to her surprise, she found that she was shaking. Looking up she was disappointed to discover that Sylvia had followed her out of the room and was now hovering awkwardly at the entrance to the kitchen.

'It's not what you think,' began Sylvia rather sulkily. 'You didn't see what you thought you saw.' She put a finger to her mouth and began to chew at the corner of her nail in an agitated fashion.

'And what do I think I saw?' asked Rose warily. She averted her gaze and passed a hand wearily over her forehead.

'That you disturbed some sort of a romantic tryst,' said Sylvia. She screwed up her face with a look of distaste. 'I daresay it may have looked like that, but it wasn't.'

'Well, what was it then?' Rose held up a hand. 'No, don't tell me, I don't want to know. It's none of my business what you do. But I wouldn't let Madame catch you, if I were you. She wouldn't take too kindly to you using her storeroom to embark on some clandestine affair with her designer while Mary and I are doing all the work getting ready for tonight's event.'

'I don't know what you take me for, Rose,' Sylvia said irritably. 'I can do better than the likes of Marcel Girard, I have you know. I expect a gentleman to show me a good time and treat me proper. A storeroom for goodness sake!' She arched an eyebrow and added slyly, 'You're not the only one who can do well for herself. There's many a man who'd like to take me out, I can tell you. And, an earl he might be, your Cedric, but I don't see no announcement in the newspaper concerning your engagement.'

Rose blushed and looked at the floor. She felt a surge of anger well up inside her. How gratifying it would be to slap the girl's face.

'Let you down, has he?' Sylvia gave her a sickly smile. 'Never you mind. Now come and help me with them curtains, they're too heavy for one person to hang, even if Madame does say different.'

'I say, Marcel, thank you for being such a good sport,' said Jacques, collapsing rather unceremoniously into a convenient armchair at his friend's lodgings.

Marcel Girard, in rolled up shirt sleeves and with a towel draped carelessly around his neck like a makeshift scarf, grunted rather irritably over his shoulder as he attacked his face with a razor. He was not in the best of moods having been obliged to answer the front door himself in a dressing gown, his landlady being otherwise engaged. Accordingly he did not feel inclined to engage in idle chatter when he had more pressing needs to attend to. The fashion event was due to start in less than an hour and he wanted to view the shop layout, to ensure that his instructions had been carried out to the letter, to say nothing of inspecting his gowns and reassuring himself with regard to Sylvia's appearance. He had a strong suspicion that the girl might try and overdo it with the rouge; that sort always did in his experience. Still, her deportment had been rather good earlier, when they had practiced how she should walk to show off the gowns. She had held herself surprising well he thought, chin up, head straight and with a sufficiently graceful walk such that had she happened to be balancing a book on her head at the time it would not have fallen off.

'A good sport?' Marcel queried without turning to look at his friend, his eyes screwed up in concentration as he scraped the blade across his cheek.

'Yes, I mean choosing Mama's humble little establishment to show your designs. It was awfully good of you. I mean to say, didn't you tell me that Thimbles were interested in exhibiting your work at one time?'

'Did I say that? Well, yes … yes, I suppose they were,' said Marcel, pausing in his shaving for a moment. He stared at his reflection in the little hand mirror, which he had propped up in front of him on a convenient ledge above the sink. 'But I thought your mother's boutique –'

'Oh, don't get me wrong, she's most grateful, as am I,' said Jacques quickly. 'All I'm saying is that it was jolly decent of you. You could have done a lot better for yourself than Mother's little shop.'

'Could I? I wonder.' The designer turned to survey his friend for the first time. 'I'm really not that good, Jacques. No, do not try to contradict me. I tell only you this. My designs, they are robust, I think you would say, yes. The outfits I sketch they produce garments that are well cut and well proportioned. But that is all. My dresses do not take one's breath away. They are simple.'

'You're too modest, Marcel, it's not like you at all,' Jacques said, chuckling. 'And it's certainly not what I've heard, about your frocks, I mean. You should hear Mother on the subject of your evening gowns.'

'You should hear what Miss Beckett says about my designs. I overheard her saying that she thought they weren't much better than factory made garments.'

'Pah! Ha-ha, did Sylvia say that?' said Jacques, his face quite red and his body doubled up in laughter. 'You shouldn't take any notice of what that girl says. Although I bet she changed her tune a bit when she found out she was to be your mannequin?'

'She did, yes,' conceded Marcel rather grudgingly. 'But that girl, I think she tells the truth.'

'She does nothing of the sort,' retorted Jacques. 'Why, she was probably jealous, that's all. She likes to be the centre of attention. I daresay she felt her nose had been out of joint when Mother started mooning over your gowns.'

'And yet she is, how do you say … your best girl?'

'She's nothing of the sort. I daresay she thinks she is. She'd certainly like to be. Although, if you'd heard her talk yesterday, you'd have discovered that she thinks she's too good for me. Told me she could do much better than the likes of me, would you believe? Cheeky little minx, I've a good mind –'

'Perhaps she can.'

'Oh, I say, that's a bit harsh.'

Jacques sat up in his chair and stared at his friend. It seemed to him that their conversation, which moments before had been light and easy, had suddenly taken another turn and become rather serious and cold.

There was an awkward silence as they met each other's eye. At length Marcel turned away to address his face.

'I suppose I did speak rather out of turn,' began Jacques in a conciliatory manner. 'There's nothing wrong with Sylvia as such. She's got a good head on her shoulders when she uses it, and she's quite a good looking girl in her own way.'

'Yes, she is.' Marcel turned and looked at his friend. 'I'm sorry, I am irritable, I know. I am anxious about this evening's event that is all.'

'Of course, old chap. I understand,' Jacques said more heartily than he felt. 'I shouldn't have just arrived as I did with no warning. It was damned inconsiderate of me. I should have known you'd be busy getting ready. I'll leave you to your ablutions.'

The young man got up hurriedly to go, anxious to be away. Something was wrong, but he couldn't quite put his finger on what it was. If he didn't know better, he'd think that his friend had formed an attachment to Sylvia. Of course, such a thought was absurd …

'Jacques …'

'Yes, what is it?' Jacques spoke more abruptly than he had intended, although all of a sudden he didn't feel minded to be civil.

'Tonight, you are coming to see the fashion event, yes?'

'I promised Mother that I'd be there. I might well miss the start of it as I have one or two things to do,' Jacques said nonchalantly, 'but I'll be there to see most of it.'

'Yes, you must be. Promise me, Jacques, if nothing else you'll be there for the finale.'

'How grand you make it sound, Marcel!' said Jacques, trying to lighten the atmosphere. 'Yes, I'll be there if only to see those designs of yours that you have been so damned secretive about showing me.'

'We are ready, are we not?' asked Madame Renard anxiously, looking around her shop. With the counters and occasional tables pushed back, the small groups of chairs dotted here and there, and the heavy, velvet drapes which covered the shop windows so effectively, it was as if she had been transported to another place entirely; a nightclub perhaps that was awaiting the band to arrive and the dancing to begin.

'Yes, I think so,' said Rose, adjusting a collection of silver plated compacts displayed in a basket on one of the counters. 'Mary has the list and will tick each name off as the customers arrive. We've set out enough chairs to accommodate every customer as well as one guest each. It's possible, of course, that one or two might bring more than one friend or relative with them, but others won't bring anyone, so hopefully it will even itself out one way or the other.'

'And the refreshments?'

'I've laid out the glasses in the scullery on top of the cook's table and put the bottles of wine and lemonade in the sink which I've filled with water to keep them cold. I'll pour out the drinks just before everyone arrives and carry them through on a tray.'

'Kitchenette, not scullery, please, Rose,' corrected Madame Renard. 'It sounds so much better, don't you think? I've read it's what they call those little kitchens that people have in flats where they get their own meals. Apparently they are so designed to make the utmost use of very small spaces.'

'Ours is certainly very small,' agreed Rose. Privately she thought that, however minute the kitchenettes to which the proprietor referred, they were doubtless much better equipped than their sad example with its chipped sink and cracked black-and-white check linoleum floor.

'I take it Sylvia is in the dressing room changing into her first frock? Good. Monsieur Girard will be here any moment. And Lady Celia, of course, and she will want to use my office after Sylvia so that she can change into her dress. I do hope it is ready and she will like the alterations.'

Madame Renard paused a moment wondering what was to be done if the dress did not meet that lady's very exacting requirements. She sighed and contemplated the tables instead, heavily laden as they were with every possible accessory to a woman's outfit. With satisfaction she acknowledged that they made rich and splendid displays that gleamed and glistened in the electric light and drew the eye. She imagined the light from the candles being reflected in their many polished and mirrored surfaces when the candelabra was lit. The atmosphere would be truly magical then, she thought, offset by the gentle clink of glasses as her guests sipped their wine …

'Rose.' A thought had suddenly occurred to her and she hastily took the girl's arm and drew her aside. It was such a quick and furtive movement that even Mary, engrossed as she was in giving the chairs one final polish with a feather duster, looked up in surprise.

'Sylvia will be kept occupied displaying the gowns, yes? You … you must keep an eye on the tables. The displays, they are so tantalising that one or two of our guests may be tempted to … but, no … not our customers …'

'I'm sorry,' said Rose, 'I don't quite understand what you are saying, Madame. Surely you don't think one or two of your customers might be tempted to take a piece of jewellery or suchlike from the displays without paying for it?'

'It is possible …' said the proprietor, not meeting her gaze.

'No, I don't think so,' Rose said firmly. 'It is only your favoured customers that are being invited to tonight's event after all, the ones that pay their bills on time and spend a great deal.'

'No, you are right. It is not my customers that cause me anguish,' admitted Madame Renard, 'It is not they that make me want to keep my wares under lock and key.'

'Who then?' persisted Rose, her curiosity aroused. For one ludicrous moment she wondered whether the proprietor harboured suspicions against Monsieur Girard, who had only recently taken to frequenting the shop.

At that very moment, a figure appeared at the top of the stairs. Both women looked up and a guilty glow crept over Madame Renard's visage, as if she feared she might have been overheard.

'Surely you can't suspect Sylvia of such a thing,' began Rose in a hurried whisper.

'Why not?' demanded Madame Renard. 'Someone has been helping themselves to the till. And items are going missing. The other day a pair of silk stockings. Of course, I am not accusing you, Rose. I know you are completely trustworthy, and that girl over there,' she indicated Mary by tilting her head in the other shop assistant's direction, 'she would never do such a thing. Why, the girl wouldn't say boo to a goose, you know she wouldn't.'

'So you think –'

'But of course. What else can I think? Who else could it be? There is no other explanation.' Madame Renard drew herself up to her full height and thrust out her chest indignantly. 'Sylvia is a thief. I know it here.' She thumped her heart. 'And what is more, I shall put a stop to her activities, see if I don't!'

Chapter Eight

At just after seven o'clock that evening the first customers had begun to arrive, lined up expectantly and excitedly at the street door until they were let in and greeted by an effusive, and particularly well dressed Madame Renard. The heavy drapes at the windows had given the occasion added mystery. More than a few of those queuing had craned their necks while waiting outside to catch a glimpse of the lighted interior as the door was opened and those in the line before them were admitted. The decision to permit only a few at a time had been Marcel Girard's idea to heighten the anticipation amongst the customers and to encourage them to feel they were privileged in being invited to attend such an exclusive event. Once inside the shop, they had been required to give up their invitations. These the proprietor had handed at once to Mary, positioned a little way from the door, whose task it was to cross off the names on the list of invitees, making a note if they had happened to bring with them a guest or two. It had soon become apparent that the number of guests was considerably more than had been anticipated or planned for, and the proprietor had endured a frantic and worrying quarter of an hour or so wondering whether there would be sufficient chairs. In the end, however, the matter had resolved itself quite satisfactorily. This was primarily due to the action taken by the men, many of whom appeared to have accompanied their wives under some duress. They appeared to prefer either to roam the room or stop and stand rather awkwardly and conspicuously at the edges rather than to avail themselves of the seats.

Rose had been kept busy going to and fro from kitchenette to shop bringing trays of wine and lemonade which the customers and guests had helped themselves to quite readily. She had weaved her way between the counters, tables and chairs; encouraging each person present to partake of refreshment, feeling all the while like one of the Lyons Corner House nippies. Some of the women had seen fit to find a chair at once, and stare fixedly forward waiting for the fashion event to begin. Others, on spotting one or two women of their acquaintance, had stopped to stand and gossip in small groups, while the men, initially self-conscious, had looked at each other in mutual commiseration, before striking up conversations to talk about more masculine pursuits.

Returning with yet another empty tray to the kitchen area, Rose realised that it had not occurred to her before how very noisy and busy the event was likely to be. The constant din was draining, verging on unbearable, and she was tempted to take sanctuary by the old Belfast sink where the noise from the shop was diminished to become only a gentle hum. She splashed her face with water. For a moment, she stood checking the number of bottles in the sink and took a deep breath. The cold water had refreshed her and brought her to her senses. It would do no good to have such thoughts of deserting. Madame Renard was depending on her and there was much work to be done. Not least of which was to ensure that Sylvia, who lingered in the storeroom, was dressed in the first garment to be displayed. There was also the matter of ensuring that Lady Celia, currently ensconced in the office-cum-dressing room, was suitably happy with her own rather inferior version of the silver gown. Now that she came to think of it, Rose was rather surprised that the lady in question had not yet seen fit to make an appearance in the shop.

With a growing feeling of trepidation, Rose abandoned her tray on the cook's table and made her way to the office. She tapped tentatively on the door, but did not wait for a reply, before opening it and going in. She found Lady Celia standing in front of a full length looking glass, which had been brought in from the shop for the occasion, gazing at her reflection critically. The woman did not turn around on Rose's entrance, but inclined her head slightly in front of the mirror to acknowledge her arrival.

'Is it that time already? Goodness, doesn't time fly?' exclaimed Lady Celia, still staring into the depths of the mirror. 'I say, it does sound rather noisy out there.' The sudden, anxious note in her voice was not lost on Rose. 'I thought this was going to be a relatively small affair.' The marquis's daughter clutched at the edge of the mirror as if for reassurance. 'I think I may have made a mistake. Tell me honestly, Miss Simpson, how do you find this dress on me? Do you think it suits me?'

'I do,' said Rose truthfully, privately considering it a vast improvement on the outfit she was to have worn, with its fussy, symmetrical pattern of bows. In addition given the time constraints, she thought Elsie, under

Monsieur Girard's guidance, had done a splendid effort in producing a gown that was more suiting to Lady Celia's fuller figure.

'It looks nothing at all like the dress that girl wore. There's hardly any lace on the bodice. And where are the glass beads? And,' Lady Celia half turned and stood at an angle, craning her neck to catch a glimpse of the back of the dress, 'the shoulders are all wrong. They're made out of material, not strings of beads.'

'But surely Monsieur Girard explained when you came for your fitting –'

'That it wouldn't look exactly like the dress that girl was wearing, yes, of course, I understood that. But I didn't think they'd finished altering it. I thought they just wanted to check how it fitted. It's so simple, so plain. Where is the diamanté?'

'I'm afraid there wasn't sufficient time –' began Rose.

'No, I suppose you're right. Oh, never mind,' Lady Celia said wearily, turning around to face Rose for the first time. She sounded suddenly as if she were distinctly bored with the subject, or else that her thoughts were preoccupied with other matters. 'Clothes really aren't my thing. I've made the most awful mistake. I shouldn't be here. If it wasn't for Bertie –'

'Bertie?'

'Bertram Thorpe.' Lady Celia fiddled with the material of her dress. 'I suppose one might say he's my young man. Is he here yet, do you know? I asked him to come.' Her face clouded over suddenly, as if an unpleasant thought had just struck her. 'I say, Madame Renard will let him in, won't she?'

'Yes, of course, if he says he's your guest. I can go and check with Mary now, if you like. She's making a note of everyone as they arrive.'

'No, don't trouble yourself. I expect he'll leave it until the very last moment to turn up.' Lady Celia bent towards Rose and lowered her voice as if about to divulge a secret. 'To tell you the truth, he didn't want to come. He won't be the only man here, will he? He'll be so dreadfully embarrassed if he is.'

'No, a few of the women have brought their husbands with them.'

Lady Celia's eyes drifted back to the looking glass, as if it held an irresistible fascination for her. 'This dress, it made the other girl look magical. It doesn't do anything for me at all, does it?'

'It makes you look very elegant,' said Rose, choosing her words carefully.

'But not beautiful, not like it did the other girl. It made her look like a princess. We all thought so, didn't we? Even Madame Renard said so.' She looked down at the floor. 'Bertie won't come, you know. He'll want to please me, of course he will, but at the very last minute he'll decide not to come. He'll make some excuse and I'll pretend to believe him, but he'll know that I see through him. He'll feel he's let me down and it will make him miserable. And then I'll feel upset. And it will all be for nothing. Because, I won't really know, will I? Even if he does come. Oh, if only I could leave things well alone. If only I wasn't so … so suspicious.'

'Suspicious?'

'No, I don't mean that exactly. Oh … I don't know what I mean. Only, I know I've made a dreadful mistake. I shouldn't be here. No good will come of it. If only I hadn't … And the awful thing is, it's too late to do anything about it.'

Lady Celia's face clouded over and she looked so unhappy that Rose was inclined to feel sorry for her, until she remembered the woman's spitefulness in demanding that Sylvia not wear the silver gown. The very same gown the woman was now deriding despite poor Elsie's very best efforts in getting it finished in time. All the same, Rose felt sufficiently moved by the woman's very obvious distress to offer some hope and encouragement.

'Let me go and check with Mary now. There's still time before the show starts. Mr Thorpe may well be here, and then you'll be worrying for nothing.'

'No, don't do that.' Lady Celia spoke the words quickly. She put out her hand and gripped Rose's arm surprisingly tightly, as if she feared the girl might disobey her request. Rose winced with pain.

'I'm sorry. I didn't mean to hurt you. It's only I'd just rather not know.' Lady Celia put her other hand to her head, as if she had a headache. When she next spoke, her words were uttered so quietly that Rose had to lean forward to hear her. 'I should never have asked him to come here. I'm afraid, you see. I don't really want to know if he's arrived or not because I have only just realised how much better it would be if he decided not to come after all.'

Before Rose could ask exactly what she meant by her words, Lady Celia had gathered up the skirt of her gown, cast one last, anguished look at her reflection in the mirror, and sailed out of the room, a fleeting vision in grey.

Rose made her way next door to the storeroom where Sylvia was pacing the floor in an agitated fashion, smoking a cigarette.

'Rose! Thank goodness. You've been ages.' Sylvia stubbed out her cigarette quickly on a saucer masquerading as a makeshift ashtray. 'Do tell me that dreadful woman's out of Madame's office by now? Really, I don't know why she had to change in there, while I had to make do with this awful storeroom. Why couldn't she have changed into her frock in here, I'd like to know? It's me who needs the dressing room most. I'm the mannequin after all, not her.'

'Oh, do be quiet, Sylvia. You should consider yourself lucky to be in here instead of out there, rushed off your feet attending to everyone. I've already had a broken glass to deal with and spilt wine to mop up. Honestly, I feel as if I were a waitress.'

'Well, that will all be behind you soon, won't it?' said Sylvia slyly. 'When you're a countess, I mean.' She laughed. 'Now, where's Marcel? Don't tell me Madame's parading him in front of everyone on her arm? That would be just like her.'

'Monsieur Girard went out into the street for one last smoke. Although I expect he'll be back in the shop by now. I must say I didn't expect him to be so nervous. Talking of cigarettes, whatever where you thinking, Sylvia, smoking one in here? The smell will linger like anything. And if Madame finds out what you've done –'

'She won't unless you tell her. If she says anything to me about it, I'll say it was Marcel. She won't reprimand him. He can't do a thing wrong in her eyes.'

Rose gave the girl a look, but said nothing. This was not the time to utter a suitable retort, but she still found it difficult to bite her tongue.

'Grab those outfits, will you, Rose, and help me carry them into Madame's office,' said Sylvia, idly pointing to some garments hanging up on wooden coat hangers around the room and to others draped on chairs. 'I'm not going to have much time between costume changes to come backwards and forwards between the storeroom and office.'

It soon became apparent that Sylvia's idea of Rose lending a hand was for Rose to carry all the garments herself, while Sylvia hurried out into the corridor to take up residence in Madame Renard's office. She walked quickly, almost as if she feared Lady Celia would return to claim the room for her own if it were to remain empty for a minute longer. Rose was sorely tempted to leave the outfits where they were. However, the show was scheduled to commence in a few minutes, so she bit her tongue and followed Sylvia out, almost staggering under the weight of the clothes.

'I suppose you'll ask me to hang them up for you as well?' began Rose, as soon as she was in the office. 'Look here, Sylvia, I'm not your servant. I –'

'No, don't worry, I'll do that,' said Sylvia quickly, much to Rose's surprise. 'Just leave them in a heap on that chair, will you? I'll sort them out in a minute.'

'There seems to be an awful lot of them,' said Rose, doing as she was bid before standing back to survey the pile of clothes. 'Surely you're not wearing all of these dresses in the fashion show? What's the outfit wrapped up in brown paper? It's awfully heavy. It'll be terribly crumpled folded up like that. Shouldn't one of us hang it up to get rid of any creases?'

'No, don't worry, I'll do it myself in a minute,' said Sylvia, almost snatching the parcel away from her. 'As you've just pointed out yourself, you're not my servant. And I expect Madame will want you out in the shop seeing to her customers. I didn't realise there'd be so many people, did you? I caught a glimpse of them when we were out in the corridor just now.'

'There are certainly more than we'd anticipated or provided chairs for,' agreed Rose. 'They have brought more guests with them than we thought they would. There are quite a lot of faces I don't recognise, which should please Madame.'

'Before you go, could you help me with my hair?' asked Sylvia, glancing at her reflection in the looking glass, as Lady Celia had done a short time before. 'It's just this little hair comb. It's awfully pretty, don't you think? Rhinestones and pearls. I thought it would look lovely with my first outfit, really set it off, so to speak. But I'm having a bit of trouble fixing it. It won't sit straight and keeps coming out. Would you have a go?

See if you can do any better. Look, I'll show you where I want it … oh …
no!'

'Whatever's the matter?'

Rose darted forward as Sylvia started to tug frantically at her hair,
pulling at it this way and that, so that Rose was afraid that she might tear
strands out, so frenzied were her actions.

'It's got caught on the lace collar of this dress. And I can't disentangle
it no matter how hard I try,' wailed Sylvia. 'The show's about to start any
minute now.'

'Let me see. I'll have a go at getting it … Sylvia, keep still, won't you?
If you keep wriggling about like a mad thing you'll only make it worse.'

'Ow! That hurt!'

'Well, what do you expect if you keep moving about?' cried Rose in
exasperation. 'No, it's no use. It's all twisted up in the lace. There's
nothing for it; we'll have to cut it out.'

'Not my hair!'

'Definitely not Monsieur Girard's lace,' said Rose firmly. 'There's no
need to look so worried, it'll only be a strand or two. It won't be
noticeable.'

'You wouldn't say that if it was your hair,' complained Sylvia
grumpily.

'There must be some dressmaking scissors here somewhere,' said
Rose, looking around. 'Is there a pair in the storeroom? Although really
we could do with a smaller and sharper pair of scissors.'

'Like a pair of embroidery scissors? Elsie left hers in the storeroom.
She uses them to cut the loose thread, so she was telling me. They're ever
so sharp.' Sylvia giggled. 'She'll be that cross when she realises she left
them here. She inherited them from her aunt and carries them around with
her everywhere. She's always going on about how valuable they are,
being gold. But if you ask me, they're only gold plated. Still, I have to
admit they're ever so pretty. In the shape of a bird, they are.'

'You stay here and I'll go and get them.'

'Well, I'm hardly going anywhere, am I? Not with my hair all tangled
up in my collar.'

It took Rose only a moment or two to locate the scissors in the
storeroom. She found them discarded on a wooden box, which had been
upturned and put on its end, serving as a table of sorts. When she picked

up the scissors and studied them more closely, she found that they were indeed gold in colour and were in the design of a bird, a stork or a heron perhaps, complete with fine tapered blades that formed the bird's beak.

'There,' said Rose, straightening up and regarding Sylvia, who was at last free of the tangled comb. 'All done, and I only had to cut a couple of strands of hair. You'd never notice.'

'Ouch. You needn't have been so rough,' said Sylvia ungratefully, patting the back of her head protectively. 'Well, I'm certainly not going to wear that thing now.' She pointed with disgust at the offending comb. 'And if any of Madame's customers show any interest in buying any, I'll discourage them, you just see if I don't!"

Having been unexpectedly delayed by Sylvia, Rose now turned her attention to the show and hurried out into the corridor, eager to be back in the shop before her absence was observed. Emerging from under the arch at the top of the steps, she took a moment or two to pause and take in the scene, making the most of her raised vantage point. The evening appeared in full swing with the women, having exhausted conversation, now milling around one display table or counter, before moving on to another. Every now and then they stopped to pick up a hat or silk scarf, holding it up to the light or trying it on and admiring their reflections in the conveniently placed mirrors that had been dotted around the room. The men had lost some of their reticence and shyness and now looked more at ease in their surroundings, although they still had a tendency to gather by the shop window, as if in readiness to make a hasty escape.

'Rose, where have you been?' Madame Renard appeared at her shoulder, a look of anxiety on her face. 'Tell me nothing is wrong. The wretched girl, she has not had second thoughts? She is not trembling like a leaf refusing to come out? Pah! That would not be Sylvia at all.'

'No, nothing like that. I was just helping her with her hair, that's all.'

As she was talking, Rose became aware of Monsieur Girard, who had positioned himself slightly behind the proprietor as if he were auditioning to play her shadow. She noticed that he was very pale and that all the time he was looking around nervously and rather furtively, as if he feared the reception his designs would receive. Rose sympathised with him, imagining that the men's attitude towards his gowns would be lukewarm at best, particularly when they were made aware of the amount of money required to obtain such couture. For a moment she wished that the outfits looked more out of the ordinary to justify their inflated prices, for she imagined that few amongst Madame Renard's clientele would fully appreciate the quality of the fabric, the expert cut of the cloth, and the extreme attention to detail that the designs entailed. It was a great pity, she thought, that the silver gown was not to be displayed that evening. Even the most disinterested and casual of observers, she felt sure, could not but marvel at the splendour of that garment and its overall effect. Unbidden, a vision of Sylvia as she had looked in the gown, fairylike and ethereal, appeared before her and suddenly she felt the girl's distress at being prevented from wearing the gown as acutely as if the disappointment had been her own.

Instinctively she looked beyond the stairs and into the crowded shop for Lady Celia, who in actual fact she discovered only a few feet away, standing behind the old mahogany counter that was to serve as the lectern in the evening's entertainment. Rose thought that for all the world she looked as if she were hiding or else holding onto the counter for support, clutching at its top with hands that trembled. Notwithstanding their earlier conversation, it had not occurred to her that the fashion event would hold any real dread for Lady Celia. Yet here was the woman staring nervously around, an unnatural and rather sickly smile fixed on her face. And as Rose studied her more closely, inexplicably drawn to watching her as she was, she realised that the woman appeared to be searching the sea of faces in front of her, as if looking for a particular one amongst the crowd. Bertram Thorpe, Rose thought. The woman's clearly agitated state suggested that a part of her wanted him to be there very much, and yet another part of her, anything but. I wonder why, pondered Rose. And at that very moment, as if to confirm the veracity of her thoughts, she witnessed the expression on Lady Celia's face change to one of pure joy, which lit up her eyes as well as bringing a smile to her lips. The woman went as far as to raise her hand and wave. But barely a moment later and the smile had vanished as quickly as it had appeared, supplanted by a pained look of apprehension. Lady Celia appeared to be waiting with bated breath for something to happen.

Rose followed the woman's gaze to ascertain the object of her fascination, and was surprised, and not a little disappointed, to find that it fell upon a bespectacled man of such ordinary appearance that he bordered on nondescript. She could not find one distinguishing factor about him to particularly merit a second glance. A feeling clearly not shared by Lady Celia, who was staring at him so intently and with such unconcealed devotion that Rose thought it a wonder that no knowing glances were being exchanged between Madame Renard's customers. The man himself appeared too busy surveying his surroundings to spot the woman worshipping him from afar behind her counter, who had so eagerly awaited his arrival with a heady mixture of trepidation and anticipation.

By the time he spotted her, it was too late for Rose to gauge his reaction fully for, having received a nod from Madame Renard, Mary had shut the shop door and ushered the last of the stragglers, of which he was one, further into the room. While the young man looked around in vain for an unoccupied chair, Mary lit the great candelabra. The proprietor took a deep breath, drew herself up to her full height and cleared her throat. A hush immediately overcame the audience, stopping in mid-sentence those who had been engaged in conversation. The silence, as a sea of expectant faces stared at Madame Renard, was complete, punctuated only by the odd cough or the sound of a person fidgeting in their seat. Madame Renard stepped up to the counter, flanked on one side by Lady Celia and on the other by Monsieur Girard, for all the world as if she were a queen and they her attendants.

'Ladies and gentlemen,' began Madame Renard, as soon as she was confident that she had everyone's full attention.

The show had truly begun.

Chapter Nine

The fashion event was in full swing. Rose stood beside one of the display tables at the side of the room, her legs tired and throbbing. The fashion display was taking far longer than she had anticipated and she had been on her feet all day. Momentarily, she wondered whether there was any possibility that she could perch or lean against the table to relieve her aching limbs, without such action being noticeable, but dismissed the thought almost immediately as being absurd. Instead she looked longingly at the seats occupied by Madame Renard's customers wishing that she too were a guest rather than an attendant. How wonderful it would be, not to be at the beck and call of all those who required further refreshment or details concerning one or other of the garments or accessories displayed.

Despite her own physical discomfort, she was honest enough to admit that the event was going rather well. The initial disappointment expressed by the audience at being informed that Lady Lavinia Sedgwick would not be attending due to illness had quickly subsided following the introduction of Lady Celia, who had done more than a passable job of singing the praises of the garments on display and the skill of the designer. She had drawn to their attention one or two of the outfits that she claimed looked particularly fetching, providing examples of when just such a gown should be worn. The audience, Rose noticed, was appreciative of her no nonsense approach to fashion, and she spotted more than a few of the women jotting down notes as Lady Celia gave forth, issuing her various pearls of wisdom.

However, it was Sylvia who had proved the greatest revelation. With a poise and style quite unlike her usual demeanour, she had appeared at the top of the steps, standing tall with her shoulders thrown back and her head straight, a curious and bewitching expression on her face. Almost effortlessly she had glided down the steps and paraded around the makeshift stage area; swishing, twirling, turning, first one way and then the other, holding out the fabric of the skirts so that the colour and intricacies of the design caught the light and were accentuated. She had then made her way to each cluster of chairs in turn and paused and chatted with the customers, answering their questions and allowing them to paw at the fabric of her garments as if she herself were on display. Even Madame Renard, Rose noticed, was impressed with the patient and tolerant manner in which Sylvia dealt with even the most annoying of customers. Rose supposed that it was due to the uniqueness of the situation and because, for one of the first times in Sylvia's existence, the girl was finding herself to be the centre and focus of attention.

'Who would have thought it?' whispered Marcel Girard.

It was all Rose could do not to jump out of her skin. Mesmerised by Sylvia's performance on the one hand, while keeping an eye out to see if any member of the audience required her attention, she had not observed the designer making his way stealthily towards her.

Marcel appeared amused and chuckled softly under his breath.

'My apologies, mademoiselle. I did not mean to alarm you. I wanted only to congratulate you on your suggestion. Miss Beckett, she is very good, is she not?'

'She is, yes,' replied Rose, having regained her composure.

'She does not look like the same girl who stands gloomily in the shop behind her counter, glaring at the customers,' continued the designer, his eyes half closed as he gazed at the subject of his reflections. 'No, she looks quite different. Lady Lavinia, she has the elegance, the breeding, the beauty, yes, but little Miss Sylvia, she has something else, yes?'

'There is certainly a naturalness about her performance,' agreed Rose, 'that I don't think Lavinia would have had.'

'A naturalness, certainly. *Oui*. But I think she has something more; an innocence, I think. And it is very alluring. Look at this audience, how it is drawn to her. They cannot take their eyes from her.'

Rose was secretly of the opinion that this was most probably because there was little else for the audience to look at. True, there was Madame Renard to stare at, hovering anxiously at the make-do lectern, trying to gauge the audience's reaction to each garment as it was displayed, wondering whether she would make any sales. Lady Celia, standing a little way from the proprietor, did not make much of a spectacle or compel a second glance. She instead looked awkward and uncomfortable in her new clothes, as if she found the material scratchy and irritating to her skin. She also looked a little bored, Rose thought, although every now and again she threw a glance at Sylvia. When she did so, her gaze was anything but indifferent. Her face expressed a mixture of emotions, and Rose found it hard to determine which sentiment was most dominant.

'The audience, they have seen how she is in the shop, how she looks and behaves. And they compare it with how she is now … transformed.' Marcel put his fingers to his lips and kissed them.

Rose tried hard to hide her smile. She found the designer's excitement touching, and reminded herself that this was the first time his work had been displayed. It was therefore inevitable that he was nervous and not a little relieved to find that his designs were receiving such gasps and murmurs of admiration, and that Sylvia was making a pretty good show at being a mannequin. While Rose thought that the designer's opinion of the girl's performance was a little exaggerated, she acknowledged that Sylvia had brought something to the role that Lavinia with her privileged upbringing could not have done. It was a sense of ordinariness, of being a real person, and showing what could be achieved by wearing good, well cut clothes. It was an understated quality, and yet Rose felt certain it would generate more sales amongst Madame Renard's clientele than a more polished performance by Lavinia. The shop assistant had shown what good designs and clothes could do to improve a woman's appearance and give her confidence. And the women in the audience, realising it was within their grasp, wanted to copy her example.

Rose found that Marcel, in his general excitement and enthusiasm, was finding it difficult to keep his voice below a whisper. The audience, she was relieved to see, showed no signs of being distracted by their murmured conversation. Indeed, the customers appeared engrossed in watching Sylvia's progress around the room or in sipping their wine. Some were even busily occupied with getting up from their seats to examine the items on display. But a few minutes later, as Sylvia emerged from the arch in a new outfit, those women standing and fiddling with accessories had returned to their seats and sat down, and it consequently became more obvious that she and the designer were engaged in conversation.

'And here we have a very elegant ensemble,' Madame Renard was saying. 'An all silk chiffon frock with foundation slip, complete with the most exquisite silk Georgette and Valenciennes patterned lace collar …'

Rose glanced quickly at the proprietor and was dismayed to find that she was looking at them intently, a frown creasing her forehead when she caught Rose's eye. Having made her point, she turned her attention to Sylvia, who at that very moment was twirling around the room. Madame Renard extolled the virtues of the garment the girl was wearing, speaking in a slightly louder voice than before, as if to emphasise her point that there were to be no distractions.

Rose turned to Marcel Girard to warn him that they had better stop talking, when she was arrested by the expression on his face, which indicated that such action would not be necessary. The colour had drained from his cheeks, and he now looked very pale indeed despite his olive complexion. Where moments before he had been chattering excitedly with gay abandonment, now he was silent, as if he would not permit a word to escape his lips. Rose was surprised to find the designer so affected by the reprimand, for it did not occur to her that they had done anything so very awful. Their voices, if they had carried at all, had caused a mild distraction at most, and it was more than likely that the proprietor would have forgotten the incident before the night was out. On closer inspection she became even more confused. The position that Marcel Girard had adopted, standing between a counter and a table, meant that he was facing neither Madame Renard nor the stage but instead staring out across the audience. It was doubtful therefore that he had witnessed the displeasure on the proprietor's face.

Before Rose had time to make any sense of this conundrum, the distinct noise was heard of the shop door being rattled from the outside. Mary scurried over and opened it to admit the latecomer, while both customers and their guests turned in their chairs and craned their necks to gain a glimpse of whoever it was who had the nerve to arrive so very late. Rose sneaked a glance at Madame Renard and saw that the woman looked about to explode at yet another distraction. However, her features almost immediately softened and her temper mellowed. Rose turned her attention back to determining the identity of the newcomer. Jacques Renard stood in the doorway, looking distinctly embarrassed at having caused a disturbance to the proceedings. Hurriedly he moved further into the room, and after looking about him, did his best to position himself away from the prying eyes of those seated in their clusters. In the end he sought refuge beside the heavy drapes and the candelabra, both of which partially obscured him from sight. Rose turned her focus back towards the stage area. It was only then that she discovered that Marcel Girard had taken the opportunity, with Madame Renard preoccupied with the arrival of her son, to retreat presumably to the sanctuary of the storeroom unobserved.

The fashion show was nearing its conclusion and Rose sighed with relief, safe in the knowledge that it would not be long before she could rest her aching feet. It had previously been decided that the shop would open its doors late the following morning to enable the shop to be cleaned and restored to its natural state. This meant that only the most cursory of clear ups would be required tonight, and Rose hoped therefore that she would be able to leave not long after the last customer had vacated the premises. Glancing over at her fellow shop assistant, she thought Mary looked equally done in, and even Madame Renard, basking in the knowledge that her first fashion event had been a success, looked tired. Only Sylvia, she knew, would be wanting the event to go on and on. The girl had undertaken so many costume changes and had tirelessly paraded around the room. Surprisingly, all the while, she had appeared unperturbed by the excessive attention. More than that, she had lapped it up, just as the proprietor was rejoicing in the knowledge that her order book was full.

Madame Renard had just finished making her closing remarks, and one or two of the customers and their guests had gone so far as to make their way to the shop door ahead of the crowd, when there was a gasp amongst the audience. The customers who had got up from their seats sat down again, and those who were at the door turned around and stared. Even the men loitering at the very edges of the room, supposedly disinterested in the evening's proceedings, looked up to ascertain what had caused such a reaction from the audience. Rose followed suit and stared beyond Madame Renard to the short flight of steps. Sylvia was standing on the top step, framed by the curve of the arch. It was a stance she had adopted frequently that evening, but it was not this that had drawn such a response from the crowd. It was what she was wearing. The glass beads and diamanté of her outfit glimmered and sparkled in the electric light, which also picked up the almost ghostly sheen of the silk satin, and seemed to accentuate the delicate and exquisite lace that draped the bodice.

Rose stared in disbelief. Sylvia was wearing the very same silver gown that Madame Renard, in no uncertain terms, had expressly forbidden her to wear. Yet here the girl was, standing before them as large as life in the very dress, and looking for all the world as if she had not a care in the world. Bewildered Rose could only wonder what had possessed Sylvia to do such a thing. Madame Renard was not a woman to put up with such disobedience amongst her staff. Sylvia had intentionally gone against her wishes. The girl could be in little doubt that, by so doing, she would forfeit her position. Had it really meant so much to her to wear the dress? Tonight she had been admired and been the focus of attention; tomorrow Sylvia would go unnoticed without a job.

Madame Renard, Rose considered, looked similarly astounded by the girl's behaviour. She stood there staring at Sylvia, quite at a loss as to what to say or do next. While her mouth fell open, no words came out, as if she had momentarily lost the capacity of speech.   Lady Celia, meanwhile, looked both shocked and furious. Her eyes blazed and for an awful moment Rose wondered if she was going to go over to Sylvia and tear the dress from her back.

'Sylvia!'

'Good lord!'

Rose turned around to see Jacques lurching forward, his face a mixture of puzzlement and something else that Rose could not quite put her finger on.

It was difficult to determine afterwards what would have happened without the unexpected intervention of the audience. Before either the proprietor or the aristocrat could decide how to act, the customers and guests took the matter into their own hands, surging forward like an uprising. For the most part, they wanted to know from whoever of the shopkeeper or her assistants happened to be nearest to them, why they had not been given the particulars of this gown or an opportunity to examine it in detail as they had the other outfits in the collection. Sylvia herself hovered for a moment on the top step, her face expressionless so that Rose could not tell whether she was delighted or alarmed by the reaction she had caused. On balance, Rose rather thought it might be the latter, which appeared confirmed when Sylvia abruptly turned tail and retreated from whence she came. While Rose and Mary were being besieged by customers and guests alike, the proprietor found that, before she had a chance to respond, Lady Celia had fought her way through the crowd to stand beside her. In a voice that was none too quiet, she demanded that Sylvia be sacked forthwith. Jacques, Rose noticed, had taken advantage of the confusion and mayhem to make his way to the arch and the rooms beyond. Monsieur Girard meanwhile, was nowhere in sight.

It did not seem possible that matters could get any further out of hand, and yet that is exactly what happened. A woman screamed, a high, shrill shriek, which had the effect of stopping everyone in their tracks. All eyes turned to face the front of the shop, which faced onto the street, from whence the cry had come. The cause of the wail at once became abundantly clear, together with the smell of burning fabric and smoke. The great candelabra, so precariously positioned beside the drapes, had toppled over and, in so doing, had set one of the velvet drapes alight. The drape in question was hung on the window beside the door, thereby temporarily preventing exit to the street. Fear filled the room, further fuelled by additional screams from various members of the audience until there was total panic. While some of the men had the good sense to tear the drapes from their hanging to prevent the flames from spreading, a considerable number of the audience tore around the room looking for a means of escape. In the confusion and panic that followed, a number of chairs and the makeshift lectern were knocked over.

Madame Renard, realising that her fashion event was threatening to end in disaster, was keen to take whatever measures were necessary to mitigate the damage. Accordingly, she sent Mary off to the kitchenette to get the key that hung on a hook under the sink. This unlocked a door off the storeroom which opened out onto the neighbouring street.

Rose, meanwhile, did her best to calm the frightened customers. Looking across at the window, she saw that some of the men were engaged in beating the flames into submission. Others had taken the initiative to locate the kitchen and were returning with all available receptacles, filled to the brim with water, so that they could drench the flames. The combined assault meant that the fire was soon put out and it was only the smell of scorched fabric and smoke that now pervaded the air. This did not stop a general exodus to the storeroom. The sight of flames had scared the customers and few were prepared to use the shop door. Instead they sought refuge through the door off the storeroom into the next street. The corridor and stairs soon became full of people jostling and pushing as they tried to fight their way through. The chaos was made worse by people falling and tripping on the steps. There also appeared some confusion as to where the door was located, some customers correctly favouring the storeroom, while others the kitchenette, so that there was considerable coming and going; the corridor itself became a sea of people going this way and that.

Jacques, Rose noticed, had now managed to open the shop door and clear a way through. A few brave souls, after hesitating for a moment as if afraid that the curtains might any moment reignite, made their exit to the street via this route. As they passed, they stared at the charred remains of what had once been the velvet drapes. Others slowly followed suit. Mary, meanwhile, ushered customers and guests out through the storeroom door. Rose stayed in the middle of the shop, at a loss as to whether to stay where she was and clear up or offer assistance elsewhere. An initial look at the damage suggested that, with the exception of the ruined curtains, the destruction to the shop was superficial and could be easily remedied by a lick of paint. Closer scrutiny would, of course, be required in the morning when they would have the benefit of daylight.

Madame Renard looked close to tears, surveying the now closed, deserted shop. Rose went over to her and put an arm rather awkwardly around her shaking shoulders. Such intimate an act towards her employer seemed strangely out of place despite the circumstances, for the proprietor often appeared aloof to her employees. However, at this moment she looked a shadow of her former self, needing all the support that was offered merely to function. Jacques soon appeared at his mother's side and, embracing her, offered his own words of comfort. The proprietor's sobbing subsided. For a moment there was silence as no one spoke, each lost in their own thoughts.

'Rose, where's Lady Celia?' Madame Renard said suddenly. 'I didn't see her go out, did you? Do you think she's still here in the shop?'

'I'm certain she went out with the others,' answered Rose reassuringly, 'although to tell you the truth, there was so much confusion, with people going backwards and forwards, that I couldn't tell you who left when.'

Somewhat reluctantly she mounted the stairs and accompanied her employer on a tour of the rooms off the corridor. The kitchenette was empty, as was the storeroom, although the latter had been left in chaos. In the eagerness to get out, boxes had been knocked over and parcels wrapped in brown paper had become undone. Their contents had mingled and sprawled out onto the floor to become trampled underfoot. A number of dresses also had fallen off their coat hangers as they had been bumped and knocked in the exodus. Madame Renard looked at the ruined clothes in dismay, and Rose wondered whether the greatest and most costly damage had not been done in this room. They made their way quickly to the office. As the room had been used that evening as a makeshift dressing room, Rose thought there was a vague possibility that Lady Celia might be here, although privately she considered it highly unlikely given the noise and kerfuffle that would surely have roused her attention. If nothing else, she thought that the woman would have made her presence known. She would not have been content to sit quietly in silence, while all about her were noise and the sounds of panic.

At the door, Madame Renard raised a hand as if to knock. Rose was fairly confident that they would find the room empty and, given the events of the evening, felt less inclined to observe the social niceties. Willing the evening to be over, she opened the door and went in.

The spectacle that greeted her was so awful and unexpected that for a moment Rose could hardly comprehend what she was seeing, and stood motionless, staring stupidly at the object that lay sprawled out on the floor in front of her at the far end of the little office which, due to the small size of the room, was in reality only a few feet away. She heard Madame Renard give a sharp intake of breath behind her as she took in the scene. The woman clasped at Rose's arm with fingers that dug into her flesh as if she feared she would slump to the floor without the younger woman's support.

Gently, but firmly, Rose unfastened the proprietor's fingers from her arm and made her way slowly over to the figure lying prostrate on the floor. It seemed to her that the proper thing to do was to feel for a pulse, and gingerly she knelt beside the figure to do just that, although the gesture appeared futile, for she already knew, without it being confirmed, that the woman was dead. Evidenced by, if nothing else, a small pair of scissors protruding from her neck. On further examination she found that the woman had also sustained an additional injury; a nasty gash on the side of her head.

'Is … is she dead?' whispered Madame Renard from across the room. So engrossed had Rose been in feeling the woman's body for signs of life that she had almost forgotten that the proprietor was there, and the sound of her voice made her start. The words themselves, however, brought her back to reality with a thud.

'Yes,' she said, her voice quite weary. 'I'm afraid there's no hope, she's quite dead.'

'Poor, poor Lady Celia!' wailed Madame Renard. 'I cannot believe it, I can't!' She began to weep bitterly. 'Tell me it's not true, Rose. And in my precious little shop too. My office of all places. Tell me that I am dreaming, that this is some ghastly nightmare and I will wake up and all this will be gone.'

Rose shook her head sadly and gave the dead woman one last glance before she got to her feet. Something, other than the obvious fact that the woman had undoubtedly been murdered did not make sense. Her attention was drawn to the woman's clothing, in particular the abundance of lace on the woman's bodice which could just be made out even though the woman was lying spread-eagled on her front. The shoulders of the dress should have been made of the same silk satin as the rest of the gown, but instead they were formed of silver and glass beads. She realised the woman's figure was all wrong too. With a sickening feeling growing up inside her stomach, Rose bent down and put her hand out and gingerly pushed away some of the woman's hair from her face.

'It's not Lady Celia,' Rose said finally. 'It's Sylvia.'

Chapter Ten

'Well, what have we here, Sergeant?' enquired the inspector joining his subordinate in the police motor vehicle.

Sergeant Perkins, rather a chipper young man, mirrored in his dress by the jaunty angle he wore his hat, cleared his throat, eager to make a good first impression. He had not worked with this particular inspector, although he did, of course, know of him by reputation. Nervously, he gathered together the papers on his lap. For a moment when he looked down at them he could see nothing but odd words that seemed to make no sense at all. He took a deep breath and tried to focus. He knew full well that, when he was nervous, he had a tendency to talk too much and often said the first thing that came into his head, appropriate or not.

'Take your time, Sergeant.'

The sergeant looked up anxiously to see if he could detect any signs of sarcasm on the other man's face. But the inspector, if anything, was looking at him kindly, and there had been no trace of sarcasm in his voice. The younger man visibly relaxed, sinking back a little in his seat so that he was no longer perched precariously on the very edge, in danger of falling off or, worse still, bumping into the inspector, should the police driver decide to take a corner rather fast.

'It's a murder in a dress shop, would you believe, sir? I know that they say some of the prices of dresses are criminal these days, but even so ...' The sergeant faltered as he saw the expression on the inspector's face. 'Yes ... ah, let me see, as I was saying, the deceased died in a dress shop, a small boutique, nothing very fancy, but quite nice all the same, I understand. Renard's. I don't expect that you've heard of it, have you, sir?'

'I can't say I have. Who was the deceased? The proprietor, I suppose? Did she live on the premises?'

'No, to both questions, sir. The deceased, as it happens, was one of the shop assistants.'

'Really?' The inspector raised his eyebrows in surprise. 'I say, that's a bit of a rum do, isn't it?'

'I don't think I quite follow, sir,' muttered Sergeant Perkins, looking confused.

'Well, it stands to reason she must have been dead for quite some hours. I'm surprised that's all, that the proprietor didn't come across her body before while she was shutting up shop for the night. Having said that, you'd have thought she'd have noticed one of her assistants was missing, wouldn't you?'

'Ah, I see what you're getting at now, sir,' said the sergeant, looking relieved. 'As it happens the murder took place between nine thirty and ten o'clock this evening.'

'Indeed? And what in heaven's name was the girl doing at the shop at that hour? Surely she wasn't stocktaking?'

'No, sir, the shop was hosting a fashion event of sorts. The girl was murdered in a backroom while the shop was full of people. And what's more, sir, the girl was the mannequin, which is why we can be pretty precise about the time of death. She'd not long gone back to the dressing room to change out of her last outfit.'

'Ah, I see. That's one mystery solved. But it'll mean we'll have a room full of people to interview tonight,' half groaned the inspector. 'Still, at least one or two of them should have seen something that will help us with our enquiries.'

'That's just it, sir. There was hardly anyone left in the shop when the body was found. There'd been a fire, you see, just about the time the girl was being murdered, or perhaps a little before. They'd covered the windows with heavy velvet curtains for the event, and the one nearest the door caught fire.'

'That was rather convenient for our murderer,' said the inspector, showing sudden interest.

'Wasn't it just, sir,' said the sergeant excitedly. 'The two things must be connected, don't you think? It can't be a coincidence. It created a damned useful diversion if you ask me. Apparently the place was in chaos with most people running all over the place trying to get out and a few trying to put the fire out. I'd be surprised if anyone saw anything.'

'Do we know what started the fire?'

'A candelabra, sir. Someone in their wisdom saw fit to place it near the curtains. A damned silly thing to do, if you ask me. Someone must have knocked it and one of the lighted candles happened to catch the curtain.

The shopkeeper swears blind that it couldn't have caught fire by itself. Most particular about it, she was.'

'It sounds as if it would have been easy to deliberately set the drape alight if anyone was so minded,' said the inspector. 'All someone would need to have done was pull up some of the fabric and hold the material over one of the candles.'

'Yes, and if the person positioned himself in front of the candelabra, it needn't have been obvious what he was doing,' agreed the sergeant.

'If they didn't think anyone was looking, they might even have taken a chance and moved the candelabra nearer to the curtains.'

'Wouldn't that have been a bit risky, sir? Surely someone would have spotted them doing that.'

'Not necessarily, not if all eyes were on the mannequin parade at the time.'

'Well, apparently the girl had just appeared in rather a spectacular gown by all accounts. Stayed there in the room for only a few minutes, she did, before disappearing, presumably back to the dressing room.'

'Well, we'll have a better idea what happened when we've seen the place and interviewed anyone who is still there. You never did give me the name of the deceased, by the way, Sergeant.'

'The deceased's a Sylvia Beckett, sir. She was one of the shop assistants, like I said. Bit of a shame really. Apparently she was very excited about modelling the gowns. It was a last minute decision, I understand. The mannequin was supposed to have been Lady Lavinia Sedgwick, but she pulled out at the last minute.'

'Lady Lavinia Sedgwick?' The inspector looked up, surprised.

'Yes, sir. Have you heard of her? Her photographs are always in the society pages. Quite a looker she is too. Her brother's the Earl of –'

'Belvedere, yes, I know. I've met her. Him too, come to that.'

'Have you really, sir? You'll be telling me next that they were suspects in one of your murder investigations.'

'As it happens, they were,' said the inspector, grinning at the expression on the sergeant's face. 'Now, who's still at the dress shop, the proprietor, I assume?'

'Yes, sir,' said the sergeant, perusing the papers on his lap. 'A Madame Renard, hence the name of the shop. Then there's her son, Jacques Renard, works at Harridges, he does. Then there's a Monsieur

Girard, he's the designer, whatever that is, and then the two shop assistants … now, what are their names? Ah, here we are, a Miss Jennings and a Miss Simpson.'

'Miss Simpson?' The inspector sat up in his seat with a start. 'What's her Christian name? It's not Rose by any chance, is it?'

'Let me see,' said Sergeant Perkins, studying his notes. 'Well, there's a thing. You're quite right, sir. Fancy you knowing that. The young lady is a Miss Rose Simpson. Don't say you're acquainted with her too, sir?'

'I am,' confirmed his superior. 'Or at least, I have been.' For a moment, he appeared to the sergeant to be lost in thought.

'You'll be telling me next, sir, that she's been involved in your murder investigations too.'

'She has. Now, don't gape at me like that, sergeant, it's far from becoming. Hello? We've stopped. We must be there. Bring your notes with you, will you, Perkins, there's a good fellow.'

The inspector climbed out of the car, followed by his sergeant, his notebook at the ready. Both policemen surveyed the exterior of the dress shop with interest.

'It doesn't look the sort of place there'd be a murder, does it, sir?' said Sergeant Perkins, pressing his nose against the window, trying to make out the interior of the shop through the gap left by the burnt drape. 'Still, I suppose you can never tell. My old man told me of a stabbing that had occurred in a tearoom once. Ever so respectable a place it was too. Full of little old ladies at the time having their afternoon cups of tea, it was …'

The sergeant's idle chatter faltered and dwindled into nothing, as he became increasingly aware that his superior was giving what he was saying absolutely no notice at all. Instead, he was staring intently at the shop, as if its very existence intrigued him. And when he spoke, it was so quietly, as if he were speaking to himself. The sergeant had to take a step or two towards him to catch his words.

'So this is where Rose works, is it? Well I never.'

Rose rubbed her eyes and tried to stifle a yawn. She was sitting on one of the chairs that, until an hour or so ago, had been occupied by a member of the audience. She dimly remembered that she had secretly coveted such a seat, standing as she had been with her aching feet. Now though, she longed to get up and stretch her legs. This sudden, overpowering tiredness she felt, she knew had nothing to do with the physical exertions of the day. It was something much deeper than that, which threatened to engulf her if she allowed herself to submit. It was the combination, she thought, of the shock and then the waiting. It seemed they had been waiting for ages, although in truth it had not been so very long at all.

They had given their preliminary statements to the first policemen on the scene, and now they were required to wait for the gentlemen from Scotland Yard to arrive to take more detailed statements. Only then would they be permitted to go home and sleep. However, bitter experience told her that, never mind how tired she was, sleep would elude her. She would not be able to close her eyes without seeing Sylvia as she had seen her last, sprawled out upon the floor, her hair dishevelled and matted by blood, a pair of small gold scissors protruding from her neck; the very same scissors that Rose had picked up and admired only a short time ago. She remembered Sylvia had liked the scissors too, had gone so far as to comment on how pretty they were with their bird design. It seemed even more awful somehow that she should have been killed with an object that she had praised and wished was her own. So much better if it had been something else, although Rose knew she was being stupid and sentimental. Because what was at issue was not the weapon that had been used to kill Sylvia, the salient point was that she was dead, and had been murdered at that. But who'd have thought, Rose mused, that such a dainty object could have caused such damage? It was almost unbelievable to think that such a delicate looking object could have been used for such a foul purpose as to take another person's life.

She glanced around the shop. The silence seemed eerie and unreal somehow after the noise and bustle associated with the fashion show. The shop itself showed signs that it had been hastily abandoned as a result of the audience fleeing from the fire. The small clusters of seats were now in disarray, with a number of the chairs on their sides where they had been knocked over in the ensuing rampage. The counters and occasional tables had also not gone unscathed. Some of their contents had scattered onto the floor, where they had been trampled and ruined or broken underfoot. The odd object remained intact, a brooch here, a scarf there, and such items seemed strangely out of place amid the destruction. The great drapes, which had contributed so much to the chaos of the evening, still adorned the windows. They succeeded in blocking out the night, although in places they had become detached from the hooks that secured them, and drooped and sagged like giant wilting flowers. The offending charred curtain itself lay torn and blackened on the floor, a sad reminder of how and when the evening had begun to deteriorate, although few if any could have imagined the devastating way it was to end.

Rose was roused from her reflections by the sound of whimpering, not dissimilar to that of a wounded animal. She looked up to see Mary, sitting a few chairs away from her, her eyes red and swollen from crying, and a general unkempt look about her, accentuated by her hair which had become undone from its fastenings. Strands of it fell across her eyes, and in places was plastered to her face by tears. The girl had her arms clasped tightly about her, her body rocking slightly in an involuntary movement. Every now and again she paused to sniff and wipe her nose on the sleeve of her blouse. Rose did not take the trouble or spare the time to dart a quick glance at Madame Renard, to see if the proprietor had noticed her employee's dishevelled appearance or erratic behaviour. Instinctively Rose took a woollen shawl from within the nearest counter and moved her chair so that she could sit beside the weeping girl. Putting an arm around her shoulders, she handed her one of the embroidered lace handkerchiefs lying on display on the nearest occasional table. Gently she stroked the girl's hair, while encouraging her to mop her eyes and blow her nose while she arranged the shawl around her.

'I'm sorry, Mary. I hadn't really thought what an awful shock all this must have been for you. It was frightful for us all, of course, but it must have been much worse for you.'

'Because we were particular friends, you mean?' said Mary between sniffs. Her voice sounded weary, as if she found it a struggle to talk, and was barely audible. 'Yes, I suppose it's the shock that makes me feel like this. I can't believe it's happened; it doesn't seem real. How can Sylvia be dead, Rose?' She tugged at the other woman's arm as if she believed Rose held the answer. 'And murdered too! Oh … it's all so horrible. And here of all places. Renard's! Rose, to think that it was only a few hours ago that she was ribbing me about having to wait on everyone while she pranced around the room, all eyes on her. I was that cross too, Rose. I said some spiteful things to her. Now I wish I hadn't. I wouldn't have said them if I'd known …' Mary's voice faded and a fresh bout of weeping overcame her.

'You weren't to know,' said Rose soothingly. 'And we all say things we regret. Sylvia could be very unkind at times.'

'Yes, she could,' agreed Mary. 'Sometimes she could be hateful. But that someone hated her so much they did more than just wish she was dead, they actually killed her.'

'Shush,' said Rose. 'Try not to think about it, Mary. It'll only upset you even more than you are already.'

'Can I tell you something, Rose? It's been eating away at me, and I know I can trust you. I didn't like her. I didn't like her one little bit. She thought I was her friend, but I wasn't. I pretended that I was, but I wasn't. I was always a little scared of her. I wanted her gone, but not like this. I hoped she'd get a better job and leave Renard's. Or perhaps get married. But sometimes, Rose I prayed that something … something awful would happen to her.'

'Whatever do you mean, Mary?' Rose gave the girl a sharp look and removed her arm from her shoulders.

'An accident, perhaps. I thought, if only she could fall down some stairs or be run over by an omnibus.'

'Mary!'

'I know, it's awful, isn't it, that I could have had such thoughts? But I couldn't help it, I tell you.' Mary bent her head towards Rose and whispered: 'Sometimes I even thought about killing her myself. I thought about the different ways I might do it. But I didn't think I'd have the nerve to go through with it. Don't look at me like that, Rose. I didn't do it, I swear I didn't. Because in the end I didn't need to; because someone else did it for me.' She laughed, and to Rose, who looked at her appalled, she sounded a little insane.

Madame Renard, herself distraught, looked across at her two employees. Mary, she thought, looked especially distressed, as well she might, Sylvia being her particular friend. Like the two girls, the proprietor was sitting on one of the chairs vacated by the audience, although her instinct was to get up and pace the floor, her bangles jangling on her arms in a comforting manner, as she wrung her hands to express her agitation. The presence of her son, however, sitting beside her, holding one of her hands absentmindedly in his while he stared at the floor, was enough to restrain her from rising from her seat. It would have been futile anyway, she reasoned, for there was nowhere to go other than walk back and forward in this one room. Even had she been permitted to leave the shop, she could not have done so, for it was as much a part of her as her son.

No, that wasn't quite true, of course. Nothing was as dear to her as her own beloved Jacques. Everything she had done, she had done for him. And what hadn't she done? She could not bring herself to dwell too long on the measures that she had taken to protect him, the steps she had put in place so that he would never know. She stared around the shop, her own dear shop that she had built up from nothing to be his inheritance. It had taken every ounce of her strength and determination, and she had suffered setback after setback, but in the end she had succeeded and made it what it was. It was difficult to look about her now and not feel a sense of repulsion because of what had taken place tonight. Yet she knew that she must overcome the urge to retch and recoil from it. This shop was her sanctuary after all, her little kingdom, even if it was now contaminated and tainted by the girl's death. In time, she hoped she would feel nothing, or very little, but how long would it take until she reached that feeling? Would she ever be able to bring herself to sit at her desk, in her office, in the very knowledge that it was there that Sylvia had met her violent death? She shuddered. She must not think of it; if necessary she could change the layout of the shop and place her office somewhere else. Perhaps that would be for the best anyway, regardless of her personal feelings. It would be far better for business if her customers could not visualise the crime every time they entered her shop. How awful would it be to catch them whispering and pointing to the door of her office and hear them saying: 'That's where it happened!'

The proprietor stifled a sob, whether for Sylvia's plight or for her own potentially ruined business, she could not say. She looked instead out of the corner of her eye, beneath heavily blackened eyelashes, at her son. She wondered how he was taking Sylvia's death. She could not deceive herself. She was distinctly worried about him. It was not helped by it being so difficult to ascertain how fond of Sylvia he had been. There had been a time when she had been sure he loved her, but that was some time ago. His mouth, she noticed, was set in a grim straight line, and he was very quiet, which was not at all like him. In fact he had barely uttered a word on being informed of Sylvia's death. Instead he had pushed past herself and Rose, in the rudest of fashions, to check the girl's pulse as if he doubted their word or did not think them capable of undertaking such a task themselves. One look at the girl's face, however, had been enough to tell him she was dead. How unfortunate that he had now averted his gaze and she could not see his eyes. She wondered whether they were moist with unshed tears. Perhaps more importantly, she wondered if he was afraid.

She looked up and saw Marcel Girard doing what she longed to do, pacing the room in an absentminded, dejected fashion, every now and then coming back to lean a hand on the back of Jacques' chair and bending down, as if to enquire how he was, but saying nothing. Perhaps the designer thought he would be intruding on his friend's grief. Madame Renard stared at him and tried to ascertain his emotions from the expression on his face. But his visage was strangely blank, devoid of any tangible sentiment, his feelings hidden.

She closed her eyes and her thoughts floated back unbidden to the moment when they had first discovered Sylvia's body spread-eagled on the floor. She remembered how initially she had not comprehended what she was seeing, and for one blissful moment even wondered whether the figure was merely sleeping and not dead. She remembered too the horror she had felt on believing it to be Lady Celia lying murdered on her floor, and the momentary relief she had experienced on discovering that it was the shop assistant's body she was staring at. She had made a mistake, such an awful mistake, and she blushed now from the memory, although surely it was impossible for anyone to guess her thoughts.

Thinking of the body made her think of Rose, in particular, the way she had admonished Jacques for pushing past them, telling him in vain that he must not touch anything until the police had arrived ... Rose! How very stupid of her not to have thought of it before. Madame Renard chided herself for her own stupidity. Why hadn't it occurred to her? This was not the first time that the girl had experienced violent death. Why, to her knowledge, Rose had been involved in at least three murder investigations and, unless the bits of gossip she had gleaned were untrue, had played a pivotal role in solving each case. Madame Renard sat up in her seat. For a moment she did not know whether to be relieved or afraid. She must decide what to do.

However, before the proprietor had the opportunity to do anything, the uniformed constable, who all this time had been present, standing discreetly at the very edge of the room, leapt forward from his position by the window and opened the shop door. Out of the darkness emerged two men. Madame Renard assumed from their appearance, and by the deferential way the constable spoke to the older of the two in particular, that these were the gentlemen from Scotland Yard. As if to confirm the accuracy of her reasoning, she saw Rose jump up from her seat so hurriedly that she almost overturned her chair. The girl ran forward, her arms outstretched, as if she meant to embrace the older of the policemen. Perhaps at the last minute she thought better of it, for suddenly she stopped and hesitated. She remained where she was, hovering rather awkwardly. Her face, however, had erupted into a smile and her eyes were shining.

'Detective Inspector Deacon,' Rose cried. 'I'm so glad it's you.'

Chapter Eleven

It had been only a few months since Rose had last seen Inspector Deacon, and yet the thought struck her most forcibly that he had aged considerably in that time. Dark-haired and tall, he was still a rather handsome man, but his face was paler than she remembered, and there were lines at the corner of his eyes and etched out on his forehead that had not been there before. It was to be expected, she told herself, after what had happened. For she knew for a fact that the inspector had been shot during the course of investigating a burglary. It had been feared that his wounds would prove fatal, but he had pulled through and undergone a lengthy period of recuperation. It stood to reason, therefore, that he had only recently returned to his duties. Was it surprising then if he was not fully recovered and was finding his work tiring?

'Miss Simpson,' said Inspector Deacon, his face brightening. 'It is a pleasure to meet you again, although I would have wished that it might have been under more agreeable circumstances.'

'Yes, indeed, Inspector,' said Rose, rallying, 'but I'm awfully glad you're here. And I'm frightfully pleased to see that you've fully recovered from … from your injuries.' She wanted to add that it had been an awful shock to hear what had happened to him. However, she bit her tongue. It didn't seem fair somehow to rake up the past.

It was only when the two policemen ventured further into the room, the constable closing the door behind them, shutting out the night sky, that she became aware of the extent of the inspector's injuries. She saw at once that he was holding a cane. With a sickening feeling, but nevertheless fascinated, she found that she could not tear her eyes away from the stick. Appalled by herself as much as anything, she watched as the inspector all but shuffled further into the room, using the cane for support. He walked with a pronounced limp. She remembered that Sergeant Lane had said as much during the incident at Sedgwick Court, and yet she found it difficult to reconcile the image of the limping man before her with the picture of the upright policeman she knew. She stood staring at the cane stupidly before she could recollect herself. When she did come to her senses, she saw that the inspector was eyeing her curiously. For a moment he held her gaze. She wondered what emotions her look conveyed. She wondered at the look in his eyes which she could not quite fathom; she hoped vehemently that it was not disgust. Before she could analyse it further, he had dropped his gaze and passed a hand over his forehead, for a moment concealing the expression on his face. Rose, ashamed, her cheeks crimson, fought in vain for something to say.

'Alas, not quite fully recovered, Miss Simpson,' Inspector Deacon said finally. He spoke quietly so that she had to take a step forward to hear him. 'I am told that this limp is here to stay, I'm afraid. But I must be thankful for small mercies. Had one of the bullets been a fraction lower I should have been in the mortuary, so I can't complain.'

He smiled at her, but she saw what she took to be hurt in his eyes. She cursed herself for having stared so very obviously at both his stick and the way he had walked.

'Well, I'm so very pleased that you're all right,' Rose said hurriedly. 'It was the most frightful shock when Sergeant Lane told us what had happened.'

As soon as Rose said the words, she thought them a dreadful understatement. For a moment she was back there at Sedgwick Court hearing the news of Inspector Deacon's shooting for the first time. Like now, it had had come in the wake of a murder, and she recalled it had made her feel suddenly lightheaded. She remembered that she had slumped to the ground and that when she had regained her senses, Sergeant Lane's face had been peering over her, full of concern. His voice, as he said her name, had sounded anxious. She recollected it all so completely that the incident might have occurred yesterday rather than a few months ago. She prayed heartily that the sergeant had disclosed none of this to the inspector.

'Thank you for your best wishes,' the inspector was saying, seemingly unaware that her thoughts had returned to the past. 'And those of Lord Belvedere, of course. Lane was as good as to pass them on. I can tell you they were very much appreciated.'

'I'm so glad. And I'm so glad you're all right,' Rose said. She realised that she was repeating herself and stared at the floor, awkwardly. She didn't know what else to say.

'And now I see you have got yourself involved in another murder inquiry. Dear me, Miss Simpson, this will never do. You do seem rather to attract them, murders, I mean.'

Rose knew that the inspector was trying to lighten the atmosphere and make her feel better, not just about his injury and her own reaction to it, but also about what had happened at Renard's that evening to necessitate his arrival. It didn't work. With a jolt she was recalled to the present. If anything, the policeman's words seemed to have had the opposite effect to his intention. If anything she felt worse. The previous murder inquiries in which she had been associated had involved the violent deaths of people with whom she had been little acquainted. They had occurred at stately homes and grand mansions, and been as far removed from her everyday existence as was possible. This time, she realised, it was different. The incident had happened so much nearer to home. The dead girl was someone she had known for a number of years. The murder had occurred at the very place where she worked, where she came almost every day; a place she considered her second home, almost as if it were an extension of her mother's house.

Perhaps something of what she was feeling showed itself on her face, for she was aware that the inspector was staring at her with a look of concern. He made as if to lean forward and take her hand, and then apparently thought better of it.

'I'm sorry, Miss Simpson. Forgive me, I was being flippant. I had no right to jest.' He looked embarrassed and not a little annoyed with himself. 'I can only imagine how awful this must be for you, and I feel for you terribly.'

'Where is Sergeant Lane?' said Rose, trying to regain her composure. 'Why isn't he here with you?' There was something so entirely comforting about the sergeant, she thought. His presence would restore the situation to normality. Somehow she and Inspector Deacon had got off on the wrong foot, and try as they might, they couldn't do anything about it. Instead, the two of them appeared to be walking on eggshells, afraid of saying anything to offend or hurt the other. She couldn't try to understand it. How she wished that they could go back to the easy familiarity that they had previously enjoyed.

'He's employed on another case with Inspector Bramwell,' answered the inspector. 'I don't doubt that we'll be working together again before long. As soon as the present case they are engaged in is closed, I imagine. In the meantime, may I introduce you to Sergeant Perkins? He'll be working with me on this investigation.'

The sergeant moved forward and grinned at her. He was considerably younger than the inspector's usual associate, and there was an eagerness about him that Rose found almost endearing. But all at once, she missed Sergeant Lane dreadfully. Of all the murder investigations in which she had found herself embroiled, he had been the one constant factor, besides Cedric, of course. And neither of them were here with her now. She was comforted in the knowledge that should she choose to telephone Cedric, neither hell nor high water would keep him from her side. It was a comforting feeling and gave her renewed hope that everything would come out all right in the end. She visibly brightened and Inspector Deacon was encouraged to go on.

'I understand you made the acquaintance of Inspector Bramwell at Sedgwick Court,' the inspector said. 'That was a very sorry business, I must say. What happened at the earl's residence, I mean. Lord Belvedere must have found it most upsetting.'

'Yes … yes, it was.'

'Now, what was I saying? Yes, you made quite an impression on Inspector Bramwell, so I believe. Not an easy thing to do by any means, but he was quite taken with you, so I've heard.'

'Well, he didn't take to me at first,' said Rose, remembering that her first encounter with the policeman had been far from promising. 'Actually, he was rather against me at the beginning. Sergeant Lane told me that the inspector didn't hold with amateur sleuths,' she blushed. 'Not that I am one, of course.'

Inspector Deacon gave her what she could only describe as rather a strange look. She had never consciously thought of herself as an amateur detective, no matter how many times Cedric and Lavinia had referred to her sleuthing skills and abilities. Even so, she was a little taken aback, and not a little hurt that the inspector remained silent. She would have expected him of all people to say that she had proved useful in helping to solve the murder investigations that they had shared. After all, if one were to listen to Cedric, anyone would have been forgiven for thinking she had solved the cases singlehandedly.

If she was disappointed by the inspector's failure to endorse or appreciate her detective skills and contribution, then she was more than compensated by Sergeant Perkin's reaction.

'Ah! So you're *that* Miss Simpson, are you?' the young sergeant exclaimed, looking at Rose with renewed interest. Until then, she realised, he had looked a little bored, no doubt impatient to proceed with the investigation proper. 'I knew I recognised the name from somewhere. Couldn't quite place it. I've heard all about you, so I have, Miss Simpson. From Sergeant Lane, of course. You and your achievements. You've made quite a name for yourself and no mistake.' He bent forward and spoke in a conspiratorial manner, although he neglected to lower his voice. 'Holds you in very high esteem, Sergeant Lane does. Very useful he says you've been. Why, he says, if it hadn't been for you, one or two of the cases might never have been solved, least not so quickly anyhow. Well I never! He'll be that disappointed to have missed you, I can tell you. And I don't envy him where he is, stuck on a case with old Bramwell.'

In his excitement, the sergeant's voice had risen and one or two of the others in the room had looked up and were now staring in their direction. In particular, Marcel Girard and Jacques Renard appeared to be looking at them rather quizzically. As if aware that the policemen were drawing attention to themselves, without having first addressed those present or made any reference to the current murder inquiry, Inspector Deacon hurriedly intervened.

'That'll do, Sergeant. I don't doubt that you'll have a chance to reminisce with Miss Simpson before this murder investigation is out, but right now we've better things to do.' He took a step or two forward and surveyed the shop.

Rose wondered whether the inspector was conscious that he now stood with his back to her so that he appeared to be addressing everyone in the room apart from herself. Perhaps he considered her complicit in distracting his sergeant from the task in hand although, in all honesty, she did not feel that she had given him any encouragement. If anything, to be praised so gushingly by a stranger had embarrassed her, not least because it had contrasted so sharply with the inspector's apparent indifference.

'If I might have your attention, please,' Inspector Deacon began in a clear voice. 'Firstly, I should like to introduce myself and my sergeant.'

He had an air of authority about him which commanded attention. Marcel Girard and Jacques Renard had been engaged in a hurried, whispered conversation, the former every now and again gesturing with his hand for added emphasis, reminiscent of Madame Renard. The latter had said little and looked miserable. Their conversation had stopped abruptly, however, as soon as the inspector had begun speaking, and they now stared at him with a mixture of wariness and confusion and fear. The expression on Madame Renard's face, Rose thought, was one of hopelessness. She also looked scared.

Only Mary seemed unaffected by the arrival of the policemen from Scotland Yard. Unlike the others, she had not turned in her chair to face them, but continued instead to look into the far distance, as if something there held her attention, or at the very least was of more importance to her than the officers of the law. Rose was brought up sharp. With dismay she realised the girl was staring at the closed door of the office, behind which still lay the lifeless body of Sylvia, waiting to be viewed dispassionately by the representatives from Scotland Yard, before being taken away to the mortuary, and from there to its final resting place.

It suddenly occurred to Rose that she would never see Sylvia again. Never again would the girl flounce into the room giving herself airs and graces. She would never giggle again with Mary behind the counter, to be admonished with a frown from Madame Renard. Rose would never have the opportunity to look on as Sylvia alternated between being overly polite to those customers she favoured and objectionably rude to those she disliked. She would never flirt with Jacques Renard when his mother's back was turned. And she would never glide so effortlessly around the room showing off Marcel Girard's designs to an enraptured audience. For the first time that evening, Rose fully took in what had happened. To her surprise, considering she had never particularly liked the girl, she realised that she would miss Sylvia Beckett. The shop would be a different place without her.

'I fully understand that what has happened must have come as a very great shock to you all,' continued Inspector Deacon, 'and you have my deepest sympathy. I am aware also that it is rather late.'

The inspector paused to glance at his wristwatch as if to familiarise himself with the precise time, and one or two of those present did likewise including Rose. Much to her surprise she discovered it was a little before half past eleven. It seemed to her that it had been hours and hours ago that they had discovered Sylvia's body and yet conversely also only minutes, so vivid was the image in her mind as if it had been drawn there in indelible ink.

'But as I am sure you will appreciate,' the inspector was saying, 'it is imperative that we get to work as soon as possible. I'm afraid that will mean that we will need to interview each and every one of you this evening.' A collective groan was heard. Madame Renard looked close to tears. 'I can tell you, though,' added Inspector Deacon quickly, 'that as soon as you have been interviewed, you will be free to leave. All I ask is that you give the constable here your details before you go. We will no doubt wish to interview you again tomorrow.'

'I say,' protested Jacques. 'It is awfully late, Inspector. My mother's quite done in. It's been the most frightful shock for her, what with it happening in her shop, and Sylvia being her employee and all. Couldn't your questions wait until morning? I'm sure that I speak for us all when I say that what we all need is a good night's sleep. I don't think you'll get much sense out of us otherwise.'

'That may very well be so, sir,' replied the inspector rather gravely. 'Monsieur Renard, isn't it?' Jacques nodded. 'But it's just possible that one or two of you may have some vital piece of information or may remember something that you may well have forgotten in the morning. We need to interview you all while everything is still fresh in your minds.'

Jacques grimaced, but did not attempt to protest further. He did, however, look distinctly put out. Marcel Girard likewise began to fidget in his seat and bite his beautifully manicured fingernails.

'I say,' said Inspector Deacon, turning slightly so that he could whisper in Rose's ear, 'that girl over there, is she all right? She looks as if she might faint any minute. And what's she staring at? I don't think she's heard a word I've said.'

'Mary Jennings,' answered Rose. 'She's another shop assistant. She and Sylvia were good friends. She's not bearing up well under the shock, I'm afraid. I was trying to comfort her and make sure she was all right when you arrived. I really don't think she's in a fit state to be interviewed tonight.'

'That's as may be, but we'll have to speak to her all the same,' said the inspector grimly. 'Even if the poor girl's gone to pieces. We'll be gentle with her though, I promise. She looks a timid little thing.'

Rose's mind drifted back to Mary's earlier worrying and disjointed ramblings. The girl had sounded upset and confused. She had spoken of wishing Sylvia harm, of praying that something awful would happen to her even. Rose felt the colour drain from her face. Hadn't she also talked about killing Sylvia? Hadn't she said that it was something that she had considered doing? She hadn't meant it, of course, Rose was certain of that, but even so, it wouldn't do for Mary to say such things to the policemen. She was such an innocent that she might. And they wouldn't understand. The police would be bound to take what the girl said at face value, and that would never do. They didn't know Mary as she did, didn't know that even if she were minded to contemplate such a hideous act in theory, she would not have had the necessary courage or wherewithal or wickedness to put it into practice. Besides, she was essentially kind and good, at least Rose had always considered her to be so. And what was it Madame Renard had said about the girl? Yes … that was it … that she wouldn't say boo to a goose.

Rose gave a sigh. She put a hand up to her eyes and rubbed them. What was she thinking? Perhaps she was going half mad herself with all that had happened. That was one of the unfortunate indirect consequences of murder. It made you think irrational thoughts and suspect everyone, even people you had known for years and years and knew full well could never be capable of such a thing. And this case *was* different from the other murder investigations in which she had been involved. She knew the potential suspects, in some cases very well. She must take a deep, hard breath, and when she did so, she'd realise that Mary was no more a murderer than she was herself. Mary hadn't really wanted the girl dead. She was delirious with grief that was all.

It was rather disconcerting to find that Inspector Deacon had been watching her closely throughout her musings. Much to her annoyance she felt her cheeks colour under his impenetrable gaze.

'I do hope, Miss Simpson, that you are not contemplating trying to protect someone you think innocent,' the inspector said very quietly. 'I had hoped you'd have learnt your lesson after what happened last time.

You know as well as I do that it won't do any good. It'll only muddy the waters. The truth will out in the end, you know full well it will.'

'I was thinking no such thing,' said Rose indignantly, while simultaneously wondering whether that was exactly what she had been doing even if she hadn't put it into words as such.

'And yet I cannot forget that when last we met you went as far as to suggest a possible alibi to someone you wished to shield.' Rose looked about to protest. 'No, forgive me, I believe you went further than that. Do correct me if I am wrong, but I think you went so far as to suggest that that person lie to the police.'

'I did, you know I did,' admitted Rose. 'And I've regretted my actions ever since. But whatever you may think of my motives at the time, I meant well.'

'I don't doubt it for one moment.'

'You don't?'

She could hardly bring herself to look him in the eye. She remembered now how she had felt at the time, how she knew that she had let him down and most probably herself. Certainly she had gone down in his estimations and she remembered that it had mattered awfully to her what he thought of her.

'No, I don't doubt it. But you must promise me one thing, Rose, to tell me everything this time. Don't hold anything back.'

'I promise,' Rose said, aware of nothing else for a moment other than that he had called her by her Christian name.

The sound of renewed whimpering brought her back to her senses. Mary was crying softly to herself again. She did indeed look a pathetic sight. Rose's heart went out to her. In all conscience Rose knew she ought to disclose to the inspector what the girl had said, that it was her duty to do so; and yet looking at Mary, the pitiful way that she mopped at her eyes with her tear sodden handkerchief, her plain little face blurred and distorted from crying, she could not bring herself to do so. For the time being at least, she knew that she would not say a word.

Chapter Twelve

'She's very young,' muttered Sergeant Perkins.

They had entered the makeshift dressing room to view the body. The inspector was of the opinion that the sergeant sounded very young himself, and not a little scared. He supposed it was the effect of coming face to face with violent death. Certainly any sign of the young man's usual cheeriness had deserted him, and he held back near the door, as if afraid or reluctant to go any further into the room. The detective inspector thought the better of him because of it.

'Isn't she?' said Inspector Deacon, staring with compassion at the prostrate figure on the floor, which had once been Sylvia and now looked anything but a living, breathing woman. He took in his surroundings, with its full length looking glass which commanded a central position at the back of the room, the desk that usually stood there having been consigned to one side. It had been pushed up to the wall near the door, so that it was the first thing that greeted a person as they entered. It had apparently been employed during the fashion parade as a table or sideboard, as on its surface were littered the remnants of accessories and suchlike used to add the finishing touches to the garments worn by the model. There was also a selection of cosmetics, and a hairbrush and comb. The latter two items looked strangely out of place amongst the finery because of their very ordinariness. They both sat at an angle where they had been hastily put down and discarded, to be picked up and used again and again between costume changes as required. Now of course they were surplus to requirements, and because of it they looked forlorn. Never again would they be picked up and used by their owner. The inspector wondered if the murdered girl had had any inkling that she was brushing and combing her hair for the very last time.

With these thoughts at the forefront of his mind, the inspector slowly knelt beside the body.

'All right to turn her over?'

Sergeant Perkins nodded. 'Yes, sir, our chaps have done their stuff with dusting for fingerprints and the like and they've taken that many photographs you wouldn't believe.'

'Good. I'll be careful not to dislodge the scissors. It's awful somehow to imagine that such a very pretty pair should have been the murder weapon. They look harmless enough, don't they? More like a decoration than a tool of death. What's the design supposed to be, a bird of some sort?'

'A stork, sir. My mother's got a pair just like them, although they're made from brass, not gold like these are. And I'd hazard a guess these are solid gold, not the usual gold plate. But the doctor doesn't think that's what killed her though, sir, the scissors, I mean.'

'Oh? You don't say. What did then?' Ah, hello? No need to answer that, Sergeant, I think I can guess. Looks as if the girl hit the side of her head on something when she fell or was pushed. Now ... let me see. Yes ... here we are, there's blood on the top of this chair back. She must have fallen forward at a slight angle and caught the edge of the chair. How does old Hodges say it happened? I know he likes to play it out in his mind. Never knew a fellow quite like him who could visualise a murder so exactly.'

'Well, sir, just as you said. His theory is that the girl was struck from behind with the scissors. They're wedged in her neck as you see. She wouldn't have died instantly, if at all, if it had just been for the scissors.'

'Wouldn't she, by Jove?'

'No, sir. It's a damned nasty business, that's what it is, sir. Doctor Hodges, he says she'd have been conscious after being stabbed and may even have had time to crawl out of the room and get help if it hadn't been her misfortune to go and get that bump on her forehead. That's what actually killed her. The blessing is that after that, her death would have been very quick.'

'So, if what you're saying is correct, after the deceased was struck with the scissors she was either pushed or happened to topple forwards of her own accord and hit her head on the back of that chair back, the one that's been drawn up to the mirror.' The inspector stared at the offending article of furniture.

'It would all have happened very quickly, so the doctor says,' said the sergeant. 'She'd hardly have known anything about it, if at all.'

'Well. I suppose we should be thankful for small mercies.'

'She might not even have been aware she'd been stabbed with the scissors before she hit her head and died.'

'By the same logic,' said the inspector, 'one could argue that she might not even have known the identity of her assailant, unless she happened to catch sight of his reflection in the mirror of course. She was struck from behind, wasn't she? So in all probability she was looking at herself in the mirror.'

Inspector Deacon wrinkled his brow, bowed his head slightly as if in prayer, and passed a hand over his forehead. He then stared into the depths of the mirror, as if he imagined he might catch the murderer's reflection in the glass looking back at him.

'You have a point there, sir,' agreed the sergeant. 'The young lady might have been too engrossed in powdering her face or hooking her frock to have noticed the murderer come into the room if he had happened to sneak in, ever so quick like.'

'Of course, she could just as easily have been in the middle of having a conversation with him and then was unwise enough to turn her back on him for a moment and he took his chance. She might not have realised that she was in any danger. She might have trusted the fellow.'

'We keep saying 'he', sir, but Doctor Hodges says the murder could just as easily have been done by a woman, especially if she happened to catch the girl off guard.'

'Does he, indeed? It stands to reason, I suppose. No great force was required. And the girl would probably have felt perfectly safe with a woman. She wouldn't have anticipated such an attack.'

'She was a pretty little thing, wasn't she, sir?' Sergeant Perkins sounded close to tears.

'She was,' said the inspector gently. 'It oughtn't to matter, but it does somehow. It makes it seem all the more tragic. Such a needless waste of a life. It doesn't seem right that such a death should befall a girl like her, that's what you're thinking, aren't you, Sergeant?'

'Yes, sir. It's a crying shame, that's what it is.' The young man hung his head.

'Well, the best thing we can do is to channel those feelings of yours constructively, Sergeant. Find out who murdered the girl and see that he is brought to justice. That's all we can do for the girl now.'

'You know that man? He is a friend of yours, I think?' demanded Marcel, as soon as the two policemen were safely ensconced in the office-cum-dressing room, the door shut tightly behind them. He gave Rose a sharp sideways glance, before peering quickly around the shop, as if to ascertain the precise whereabouts of the lone constable. With a flick of his head, he satisfied himself that the man in question had removed himself back to his favourite position by the street door. He was therefore out of earshot.

With the exception of Mary, who remained both emotionally distant and physically apart, the others were huddled together on the vacated chairs, forming their own individual little cluster as the various groups of customers had done before them. Had the chairs not been positioned at odd angles, with some facing the street door while others overlooked the back of the shop with its makeshift lectern and stage, it might almost have been supposed that they were expecting the fashion show to be reprised. It was a sobering thought, however, that the only persons who would be emerging from the corridor and descending the stairs in the immediate future would be the two policemen. And instead of parading gowns they would be returning from viewing the body of a brutally murdered woman.

'Yes … No … that's to say we are acquainted,' said Rose, wondering how best to describe her relationship with Inspector Deacon and whether she could describe him as a friend.

'You seemed awfully pleased to see him though,' remarked Jacques, taking up the thread of the conversation. She noticed he was looking at her with renewed interest and she visibly coloured under such close scrutiny.

'But of course!' exclaimed Madame Renard. 'You have met him before. How stupid of me not to think it might be a possibility. Ha! How many inspectors are there at Scotland Yard who investigate these murders?'

'A great many I would have thought,' said Jacques drily. His mother chose to ignore him and carried on with her train of thought.

'The other murders you have been a part of, he was present, was he not, this young man?' She stared disapprovingly at Rose, as if the girl, in knowing the detective, had somehow brought about the death on her premises.

'Yes … that's to say, he was not present at all the investigations –'

'*All* of the investigations? But what are you saying? How many murders have you been involved with?' Marcel cried, looking at Rose incredulously.

'I'd quite forgotten with all the excitement,' said Jacques, butting in quickly, a slightly bitter edge to his voice. 'Our Miss Simpson is something of an amateur sleuth, aren't you, Rose?'

'Well –' began Rose, but he did not let her finish.

'Let me see, there was that little business at Ashgrove last summer, followed closely on its heels by that incident at Daresmore Hall … that's what that great house was called, wasn't it?' said Jacques, counting off each location on his fingers in a slow, laboured fashion with the aim of achieving maximum effect. 'And then of course, who could forget the murder that happened a couple of months or so ago at that most grandiose of establishments, Sedgwick Court? Dear old Lavinia's place, if I'm not mistaken?'

'Dareswick Hall,' corrected Rose. Mortified she stared at Jacques. She could feel herself trembling slightly from the shock of it all. It was so unlike him to speak to her in such a hurtful, spiteful way. His tone had frightened her, the way he had spoken the words with such hostility, almost as if he were spitting them out. She wondered if he was overcome with grief, or was it something else. Did he feel, as his mother seemed inclined to believe, that in some way she, Rose, was responsible for bringing death to Renard's? Embarrassed, she stared at Jacques stupidly, tempted to say something, yet at a loss as to exactly what.

'You're more at home investigating murders that happen amongst the highest classes, aren't you, Rose?' continued Jacques in the same vein. 'Aristocrats and all that. Didn't I even hear mention of a foreign count being present in your last case? Not just our British aristocracy, huh? But you've come down a bit in the world, haven't you? To be embroiled in a murder that's happened here in a dress shop of all places. Not a stately home or butler in sight. Still, I have it on the good authority of Mama that we are a very good class of people.'

'Jacques!' cried his mother, horrified. All through this tirade, Rose had noticed Madame Renard staring at her son anxiously, opening and shutting her mouth as if about to protest but thinking better of it. Or perhaps she could not believe her ears.

It occurred to Rose that both she and his mother were trying to ascertain what lay behind the man's sullen façade. At a loss she made do with looking at him reproachfully, as if he had behaved like a disobedient child. Perhaps it was this, or his mother's exclamation, that returned him to reason. Certainly he must have been aware of the intensity of each woman's gaze as they regarded him earnestly. Or conceivably he acknowledged the strangeness of his own behaviour and caught himself up. Whatever it was, he hurriedly mumbled an apology and returned to stare forlornly at the floor.

'Are you going to find out who the murderer is, Rose? Are you going to find out who killed Sylvia?'

The voice, quiet and unassuming as it was, nevertheless seemed to fill the room. The bluntness of the question and the urgency in which the words were spoken made them all turn around as one to determine the identity of the questioner. Rose realised then that Mary had been all but forgotten, sitting apart from the rest as she had been. It had probably not occurred to any one of them that she had given their conversation much heed, even less that she intended to contribute to their discussion. In addition she had managed somehow to creep up to them unobtrusively and unobserved, so that her sudden appearance standing beside them as she now was, made them all start and catch their breath quickly.

Initially met with silence as she was, Mary repeated her question. Her voice now had a strange quality to it, being both dispassionate and innocent in equal measure.

'For goodness sake, Mary,' exclaimed Madame Renard, being the first of them to recover her wits. 'Must you creep up on us like that, like … like a thief in the night? My nerves, they are already on edge, they –'

'Are you going to find out who did it?' Mary persisted, cutting through the proprietor's words with never a glance at her employer. It was almost as if she were unaware that she had spoken, so fixed was her gaze upon Rose. This, together with the way Mary's voice had risen as she had repeated her question for the second time, had an unsettling effect on her audience. Jacques stared at her open mouthed, Madame Renard put a hand to her chest, which rose and fell more rapidly than was natural, and Marcel looked distinctly ill at ease. Rose, to whom the question had been addressed, felt obliged to give an answer, inadequate though it might be. She opened her mouth to speak, but was saved from the necessity of so doing by the proprietor's son jumping out of his seat in an agitated manner.

'I say,' said Jacques, 'isn't it best to leave that sort of thing to the police?'

Madame Renard gave her son a sharp look. 'But of course,' she agreed. 'It is what they are paid for. It is nonsense to ask Rose to do anything of the sort. The girl, she is not qualified or trained to do such a thing.'

'But you said this girl is a sleuth,' objected Marcel. It seemed to Rose that they spoke of her as if she were not present. 'If that is so, then she must investigate Sylvia's death.' The designer turned to address the proprietor. 'Surely you agree, Madame?'

'You are seemingly present whenever a murder is committed in a great house, is that not so, Rose?' admitted Madame Renard, rather grudgingly.

'Yes, she is,' said Jacques. 'And I happened to catch what that sergeant fellow was saying just now when the inspector was glaring at him so ferociously, for speaking out of turn. He was speaking very highly of Miss Simpson, he was.' He turned and smiled at Rose, and this time his words held some sincerity. 'It seems you have gained yourself a bit of a reputation with the police, Rose. That sergeant chappie spoke of you in the most glowing of terms.'

'If what you say is true, then that is even more reason to ask Miss Simpson to investigate Sylvia's death,' persisted Marcel, his face suddenly becoming animated. 'We can sit here and wait for the police,' he paused to stare at Madame Renard before continuing, 'who will decide in their wisdom that it must be one of us. You or I, Madame, because we are foreigners.'

He was prevented from continuing what he was saying by a string of protests from the others, who spoke in quick succession along the following lines:

'What?' exclaimed Madame Renard, 'but that is ridiculous! It is obvious to anyone that the murderer came in here pretending to be one of my customers. Or perhaps he was one of their guests. Yes … now, that I consider, I think that is more likely. The murderer, this wicked man, he seizes the opportunity to do away with poor Sylvia. Her death, it is most sad and tragic, but it has nothing to do with any one of us.'

'Look here, Marcel, you're talking a lot of old rot,' protested Jacques. 'I happen to have a better opinion of our British police force than you do. And even if, as you claim, they'll be looking to fix this crime on a foreigner, which is a ridiculous thought in the extreme, well, why not include me in your equation? I'm as much of a Frenchman as you are.'

'Yes, in so much as you were born in France and have a French name,' said the designer disparagingly. 'But you have lived most of your life in this country. Your manners, the way you think, and the way you talk; it is like an Englishman, is it not?'

'I don't think you need have any concerns on that score,' Rose said quickly, before Jacques had a chance to respond. 'Inspector Deacon is not a bit like that. He'll want to make a proper arrest. Those who are innocent have nothing to fear.'

'Are we all innocent?' asked Mary. She spoke very quietly, almost as if she were talking to herself.

The others turned and stared at her, clearly unnerved by the girl's words. Rose wondered whether they were thinking what she herself was beginning to fear; that the murderer might very likely be one of them, in fact, in all probability was. For it seemed to her highly unlikely, no matter how desirable the notion might be, that the murderer was a stranger who had taken advantage of Madame Renard's fashion event to undertake his ghastly deed.

Jacques Renard was the first to recover his composure and break the silence.

'Of course we're all innocent. It's a nonsense to suggest that we aren't. And on reflection, I think Marcel's idea may be a good one.' He rose from his chair and began pacing the room as if to emphasise his point. 'We should ask Rose to investigate Sylvia's murder for us. And I don't know about any of you, but I for one don't want to sit around here feeling I'm doing nothing, waiting for the police to interview each and every one of us one at a time. They'll draw their own conclusions and we won't know what they're thinking. We'll have no idea where their line of enquiry or the evidence is taking them. They'll keep us all in the dark and I don't think I could bear it, the waiting I mean. Not knowing what is happening or who they suspect.'

'You feel that, yes?' enquired Madame Renard of her son. Rose thought that, although the proprietor still looked anxious, she detected a glimmer of hope in the woman's eyes. Certainly, she seemed to relax a little, her breathing becoming more regular. She even went so far as to permit the shadow of a smile to cross her lips.

'Yes, I do, Mother, most sincerely.'

'Then it is settled? It makes sense, does it not?' argued Marcel. 'We have in our midst a girl who can investigate and, what is more, she is one of us.' He turned to address his next words exclusively to the proprietor. 'She will be mindful of our reputations and she will protect Renard's name for you, Madame. And besides, we owe it to Miss Beckett, you and I. She was in your employ and killed in your shop. And she was my mannequin and died while parading my designs. The game, it is afoot, as you English say, and Rose is our Holmes.'

'What say you, Rose? Will you investigate Sylvia's murder for us?'

The words had been uttered by Jacques, but it was as if he had spoken for them all, become their nominated representative so to speak. They all turned to look at her, and she noticed as she gazed at their expectant, upturned faces, that the expressions revealed to the world on their faces were mixed, although she had difficulty in deciphering or determining any individual emotion. For instance, she did not know if it was fear or hope that showed itself so visibly on Marcel's face. Likewise, she felt uneasily that Jacques was as much daring her to investigate Sylvia's death as wishing that she do so. Madame Renard seemed to look both eager and apprehensive at the same time if that were possible. And Mary, what was the expression on her face? She had been the first to suggest that Rose take an active role in the proceedings, and yet now she looked unsure of herself, as if she might have made a mistake.

Of only one thing was Rose certain. They all held their breath, as if as one, while they awaited her answer. And in response she found that the words sprung from her own lips before she had time to consider them.

'Yes, of course I'll investigate Sylvia's death,' said Rose.

Chapter Thirteen

The question arose as to where the interviews should take place. It would have suited Inspector Deacon's intentions very well to have used one of the backrooms for this purpose. However, the kitchenette was far too small and conversely the storeroom, while considerable in size, was filled fit to bursting with stock and packaging as to prove quite useless. The office-cum-dressing room would have sufficed had it not been the very room where the murder had occurred. For although the gathering and documentation of evidence had now been concluded and the body safely removed to the mortuary, the inspector surmised that the room was unlikely to be conducive to the holding of interviews. The temptation was too great, he reasoned, to permit one's eyes to glance at the very spot where it could be imagined the body had lain, and then it would be all too easy to allow one's mind to drift off and visualise the awful deed being done. With all these preoccupations, his questions would fall on deaf ears. And there would be some reluctance in voicing anything distasteful regarding the deceased's character, for the girl's presence would still be felt in that little, claustrophobic room, almost as if she were still lying on the floor beneath their feet. No, no one would feel comfortable speaking ill of the dead. It was never easy at the best of times or in the most accommodating of locations, but made that much worse if one could imagine that the murdered girl was there in spirit, if not in body, overhearing every word uttered against her character.

It was therefore decided, in the end, to use Madame Renard's flat for the purpose, it being so conveniently located close to the shop, and yet also discreetly removed from it as to be another dwelling. Sergeant Perkins, who did not normally consider himself to be of a particularly nervous disposition, breathed a sigh of relief. For he had found himself momentarily rattled and unsettled on emerging through the arch after viewing the body. The reason for this was ludicrous in the extreme, his rational self knew very well, but still he could not rid himself of the troubling impression that the dead girl was physically in the room before him, lurking in the shadows. The explanation was a simple one. He had chanced to catch a glimpse through the space where the ruined drape had hung of a wax mannequin that formed part of the window display. A shaft of light from the room had happened to fall upon the glass eyes, which had looked as dead and expressionless as those of a fish. The fur eyelashes and painted lips had only added to the notion that he was looking at some oversized grotesque doll. In all it reminded him uncomfortably of the body he had only moments before left in the dressing room, which looked no more human than did its wax equivalent.

Borrowing the keys from the proprietor, inspector and sergeant made their way to Madame Renard's flat. It was situated above Renard's at the top of a long flight of stairs, boasting its own front door at the foot of the stairs, which opened out directly onto the street. The flat itself consisted of little more than two rooms, the largest of which, square in design, appeared to be used both for meals and as a sitting room. There was little furniture in the room, the sofa looked tired and in need of upholstering, and the small jade green dresser that hugged the wall looked inexpensive and flimsy. The furniture was completed by two wooden chairs, painted to match the colour of the dresser, and a plain, round oak table, covered with a white cotton tablecloth edged with lace.

Both walls and ceiling were painted in distempered cream and further examination revealed that the rug, which covered the walnut spirit stained floor, was threadbare in places. Sergeant Perkins was unable to stop himself from emitting a gasp of surprise. For the flat, with its stark and meagre decoration, was at such complete variance with the opulent surroundings and overstuffed and overladen counters and tables in the shop downstairs as to be staggering. That the shop's proprietor and the occupier of this little, wretched flat could be one and the same person seemed beyond belief. He turned to his superior to determine his reaction. But if the inspector was of the same opinion, he kept it to himself, for he gave no sign of it. Rather he showed an impatience to know what was beyond the sitting-cum-dining room, and hurried on.

This square room opened out directly onto a rectangle room of disappointing proportions purporting to be a bedroom, although the divan bed was disguised as a sofa by way of a piped cover with box pleat frills which fitted snugly over the mattress and bedclothes. Further camouflage of its night-time use was provided by a number of brightly covered cushions, arranged as a sofa back. The room was also furnished with a small writing table and two bookcases so that in appearance it resembled more keenly a study than a bedroom. Compared with the sitting room, this room appeared cluttered despite the scarcity of furniture. On further scrutiny, this was due not only to the room's smaller dimensions, but also to the fact that one side of the room had been partitioned off and given over to a combined kitchen and bathroom area, curtained off from the main room by drapes of dark red imitation linen, strangely reminiscent of the dark velvet drapes in the shop downstairs.

'This will do well enough for our interview room,' said Inspector Deacon, looking around the room with something akin to satisfaction. 'We'll use the chair there that's drawn up to the writing desk and we can bring up a couple of the chairs from downstairs. The others can sit on the settee and the chairs in the other room while they're waiting to be interviewed.'

'It seems a mean little flat, doesn't it?' ventured the sergeant. 'It reminds me of the flat my sister shares with another girl. They earn their own living, they do. Call themselves bachelor girls. But it doesn't seem quite the thing for our Madame Renard, does it? I mean to say, she seems to have every sort of accessory downstairs, and it's cluttered as anything there, but this flat has no knick knacks of any description that I can see. And next to no furniture. What there is is pretty cheap and awful looking. And the walls! Don't know that I've ever seen anything look so drab, my own lodgings put it to shame. I'd have had her down as having a great deal of pink and flowers on the walls and about the place, rose chintzes and pink lampshades and the like, but not a bit of it.'

'I would imagine,' said the inspector, 'that the better part of her income has been spent on furnishing and stocking her shop. Not much left over to lavish on this place, I'd say. Right, go and bring up the chairs, will you, Perkins. We'd better start interviewing everyone, otherwise we'll still be at it at dawn. Tell the others to give us a moment or two and then they can come up.'

'Yes, sir. Who do you want to start with? I expect Miss Simpson could tell us a thing or two, don't you? Tell us the lay of the land so to speak, and all the suspects' various peculiarities if she so chose.'

Inspector Deacon raised an eyebrow and gave him a sardonic look, but said nothing.

Sergeant Perkins hurried out. Really that Inspector Deacon was a strange fellow. He couldn't make the man out at all. He could have sworn that Lane had told him that the inspector had a soft spot for the Simpson girl on account of how helpful she'd been with his inquiries. Thought a great deal of her, Lane had said, even if the inspector didn't quite know it himself. And the girl had an earl of all people for a young man; well I never, and she just being a shop girl. You'd have thought that old Deacon would have been as pleased as punch to have her here, but if looks could kill. Why, when he'd mentioned just now about her being something of a sleuth, well, that hadn't gone down at all well. He'd have to watch his step in future, and no mistake.

The others had been glad enough to leave the shop behind, with its sad associations with death, and decamp to Madame Renard's flat, cramped though it was. The proprietor had appeared relieved to be home, and had sunk back into the settee as if its very familiarity provided comfort. Mary had perched on the other end of the settee looking conspicuous, while Marcel had chosen one of the jade green chairs, placed his elbows on the table and buried his head in his hands, presumably resigned to a long and arduous night. Only Jacques had paced the room as if he felt hemmed in by his surroundings.

Rose, eager to have something with which to occupy herself, had gone in search of the kettle. Realising that there was no separate kitchen as such, she had tentatively knocked on the door of the other room and been admitted by an inquisitive Sergeant Perkins. Inspector Deacon, on hearing her voice, had looked up briefly before returning to study his notes. Feeling vaguely admonished, Rose had retreated behind the curtains where, somewhat to her surprise she found a bath covered by a polished lid, which presumably doubled as a work surface for the preparation of food. Beside it was a small enamelled hand basin, and above the sink on one side was a shelf on which was placed a tiny gas griller. Directly above the sink was a small window, and above that a meat safe.

This was the first time that Rose had ever set foot in her employer's flat, and the rudimentary layout and décor, not to mention the limited occupation of just two main rooms, surprised her. It was now apparent that her employer lived more frugally than she had thought. She discovered that this revelation made her admire Madame Renard even more than she had done previously. The fashion parade had ended disastrously and tragically in respect of both Sylvia's death and also the fire, which had sent the customers fleeing, mostly before they had placed an order or arranged a fitting. Awareness of the proprietor's individual sacrifice made the situation seem even more poignant. It also gave Rose additional resolve, if indeed she had needed any, to solve the case. Not only did she believe she had a responsibility to Sylvia to determine the identity of her murderer and see that he be brought to justice, but now she felt she also had the same responsibility to her employer in order to restore Renard's ruined reputation.

Whatever Inspector Deacon's various misgivings, he had complied with his sergeant's suggestion and summoned Rose to be interviewed first. Rose had taken a deep breath as she left the square room, aware that the eyes of the others were upon her, and also that she held in her hands their hopes for a quick and easy resolution to the catastrophe that had befallen them. As she walked, she felt she carried their anxieties about her like a heavy, cumbersome bag.

It seemed remarkable now to think that the fashion event was supposed to have been a joyous occasion, signalling a new direction for Renard's as it extended its horizon; the move from ready-to-wear clothes to couture. It was to have played a part in launching a new designer on the London world. But instead it had all come to nothing. Worse than that, it had resulted in a girl's death and more than likely had destroyed Madame Renard's very livelihood. Only time would tell whether Sylvia's death would affect the long term fortunes of Renard's. Once news of the murder was out, it was hard not to imagine that at least some of Madame Renard's most favoured customers would be tempted to abandon her establishment and take their custom elsewhere. And what of Marcel Girard and his fledgling design career? Sylvia had been killed wearing one of his gowns. Who would want to own such a creation, magical though it was, knowing that just such a dress had been a girl's shroud?

Rose entered the rectangle room and noticed at once that the Inspector had shifted the writing desk from its position against the wall. Now it stood in the middle of the room and he himself was seated at the desk as if it was his own. One of the chairs from downstairs had been drawn up directly opposite him and he gestured that she sit on this as he rose from his chair. As Rose seated herself in the empty chair and the inspector resumed his seat, she realised that the desk created a physical barrier between them, the roles of interviewer and interviewee being clearly established. So close was her chair to the desk, that if she were minded to lean forward she might possibly be able to make out the scribbled words on the paper, which the inspector had been perusing as she entered the room. She sat back resolutely in her chair and waited for him to begin. Familiar with the interview process, she was aware that behind her at a little distance sat Sergeant Perkins, his pencil poised to take down her every word.

'Right, Miss Simpson, now, where to begin?' Inspector Deacon smiled at her and Rose noticed that this time his smile reached his eyes. 'We have a great deal of ground to cover and not much time in which to do it, if any of us is to get any sleep tonight.'

'I shall be as helpful and concise as I can be,' said Rose rather primly.

'Glad to hear it. Now, perhaps you'll be as good as to tell me something of the people next door and the deceased of course. We'll need to find out everything we can about her character, if we are to find out who killed her.'

'Very well,' Rose said, but even so she hesitated. She had never much enjoyed this part of the interview process. It had always made her feel as if she were being asked to speak out of turn somehow. In this particular instance it felt worse. She was being asked to be disloyal to those she had worked with and known for years, to take apart their characters and highlight their foibles and peculiarities.

'I appreciate that this is very difficult for you, they being friends of yours so to speak. But it is necessary that we find out all we can about the people involved with this tragedy,' Inspector Deacon said, looking at her keenly. She was relieved that he acknowledged her divided loyalties.

'Well, there's Madame Renard of course,' said Rose, rallying a little. 'As you know she's the shop's proprietor and my employer. I've worked for her for a number of years, as has Mary and as had Sylvia, come to that. They were both working in the shop before me, but only by a few months or so.'

'You were telling me about Madame Renard,' prompted the inspector.

'Yes, I was. Well, she came to England over twenty years ago, bringing her child with her. She had been widowed when her son was only a few months old. From what she's told me, it was her intention from the very start to set up her own dress shop.' Rose sighed. 'I don't think her husband left her very well provided for, and from what I gathered, although she didn't say as much, she had to scrimp and save and do without to build up her business.'

'Very admirable.'

'Yes, isn't it? It can't have been easy for her, what with having Jacques to look after and no maid to speak of. That's one of the reasons I feel so awful about what's happened. It's the first fashion parade she's held and now it looks as if her life's work is falling down around her ears. I only hope that she hasn't lost many customers. They can be jolly fickle, you know.' Rose passed her hand over her hair. 'Oh, just listen to me! I sound so dreadfully heartless and callous, don't I? When one thinks of poor Sylvia everything else pales into insignificance.'

'Doesn't it just,' agreed the inspector. 'But it is only natural to think such things. You'll have all sorts of strange and irrational thoughts. It's the shock, you know. You knew the deceased, and you knew her well. She was part of your everyday existence. And you found her body as well, didn't you? You mustn't forget that.'

'Yes, it was awful. Although sadly I'm rather used to murder. Only this … it was so unexpected. Even now I can't quite get my head around it. I can't quite believe she's dead, you see. I keep expecting her to walk in here any moment and glare at us as she would at an objectionable customer.'

'That is only to be expected. It takes a while for a thing like this to sink in.'

'You're being awfully kind,' Rose said softly.

Inspector Deacon coughed and looked taken aback. Rose went crimson. There was an awkward pause. She found herself speaking hurriedly to break the uncomfortable silence and hide her own embarrassment, hardly giving a thought to what she said or its significance.

'To make matters worse, we didn't think it was her at first,' Rose said, putting a hand to her forehead and rubbing it. It was a relief to blot out the inspector's face. 'We thought it was Lady Celia.'

'Oh?'

Inspector Deacon's head shot up. Rose imagined that Sergeant Perkins was equally interested by this fact. Certainly she sensed, although of course she could not see the expression on the sergeant's face having her back to him as she did, that a look passed between the two policemen.

Now that she had uttered the words out loud, she saw the significance of what she had said. Why hadn't she thought of it before?

'We were looking for Lady Celia. Madame Renard had not noticed her leave and we thought she might still be in the shop and unaware of the fire. So you see, when we opened the office door we were expecting to see her and not Sylvia.'

'When did you notice your mistake?'

'Not until I bent over the body and felt for a pulse.'

'Did they look alike, then, Lady Celia and Miss Beckett?'

Despite everything, Rose was tempted to laugh.

'Oh, not at all but for their colouring. Other than that, Sylvia was as thin as a rake and Lady Celia is … well, rather plump.'

'I see. But in that case I don't quite understand how you didn't recognise it was Miss Beckett at once, if physically they looked so very different as you say.'

'They were wearing the same dress. That's to say, they were both wearing evening dresses made out of the same material, a silver silk satin. Lady Celia's was a very inferior version having been put together at the last minute. It didn't have all the fine attention to detail and embellishments of Sylvia's dress. But it was only when I was bent over her body and noticed the strings of silver and glass beads, that I realised I wasn't looking at Lady Celia's dress, I was looking at Sylvia's.'

'Miss Beckett was killed from behind,' mused the inspector. 'It's just possible that the murderer never saw the girl's face. One would have thought that he would have caught a glimpse of her reflection in the mirror, but suppose he didn't …'

'And Sylvia was only wearing that dress in the shop for a few minutes,' Rose said excitedly. 'She wasn't supposed to be wearing it at all tonight.'

'So it's just possible that the murderer didn't see her in the dress at all,' said Inspector Deacon.

'Whereas Lady Celia wore her version of the dress all evening. And for most of the time the back of her dress was hidden from the audience, because she was standing facing them. She was behind the lectern.'

'Let me get this straight in my mind,' said Inspector Deacon. 'The back of Lady Celia's dress didn't have any strings of silver and glass beads on it?' Rose nodded and he continued. 'But if the murderer was one of Madame Renard's customers, or a guest of theirs come to that, they might not have been aware of that fact.'

'And they would have been in a hurry, wouldn't they?' volunteered Sergeant Perkins suddenly from his seat behind Rose, making her start. 'They would have wanted to get the business over and done with as quickly as possible. They wouldn't have wanted to stay in the dressing room for any longer than was absolutely necessary in case they were caught in there with the body.'

'So what we are saying,' said the inspector slowly, 'is that Miss Beckett may not have been the intended victim.'

'No,' agreed Rose, 'it might have been Lady Celia. And if we're right, it's just possible that the murderer doesn't know he's made a mistake. He might still believe that the body he left to be discovered is that of Lady Celia.'

'And unfortunately for Miss Beckett,' said the inspector, 'he killed her by mistake.'

Chapter Fourteen

'Do you really think it could have happened that way, sir?' asked Sergeant Perkins. He had given up all pretence of being an unseen scribe and was now standing beside the inspector, his fingers drumming on the desk top in a mixture of impatience and excitement.

'I don't know, but we certainly can't rule it out.' Inspector Deacon looked quizzically at Rose. 'Where is Lady Celia now, do you know?'

'No. I'm afraid not. After the shock of finding Sylvia's body ... well, we all rather forgot about her,' admitted Rose. 'I daresay she left with the others when the fire broke out. There was rather a panic. Everyone was trying to get out of the shop as quickly as possible. It was all rather silly because the fire didn't really catch hold. It was soon put out. Some of the men beat it out, you see, and there really was not much damage done.'

'Perkins, I want you to telephone Lady Celia's residence without delay. Use the telephone in Madame Renard's office downstairs. You needn't frighten her ladyship. Speak to her butler and see if she's there. Get him to check that she's safe and well. Then I want you to put a call through to the station. Arrange for a uniformed officer to go to the house, will you? He's to satisfy himself that everything's all right. And he's to stay on duty outside the house until I tell him to do otherwise, is that clear?'

'Yes, sir', said the sergeant, his eyes bulging with eagerness. 'Do you really think the young lady may be in danger, sir?'

'I honestly couldn't say, but I'm not taking any chances. It's possible that the murderer has realised his mistake. If he has, he may try again. Now, what's the time?' The inspector paused to glance at his wristwatch. 'If it wasn't so damned late, and I didn't already have a room full of people to interview next door, we'd go and interview her tonight. Instead it'll have to wait until the morning when we've snatched a few hours' sleep.'

The inspector rubbed his eyes and looked back at the notes on the desk before him. It was going to be a very long night for them both. After a moment's reflection he said:

'Of course, it's only one line of inquiry. There's nothing to say Miss Beckett wasn't the intended victim. We mustn't lose sight of that.'

'But if she wasn't, if Lady Celia was the intended victim, then the murderer might not be one of the people in the room next door,' said Rose eagerly.

Perhaps she was clutching at straws. She had assumed, perhaps wrongly as it might well turn out, that one of the people in the room next door must be the murderer. It had seemed too far-fetched to believe that some stranger had decided to murder Sylvia in Madame Renard's dress shop. Not only to select such a strange location for the murder, but to choose a time when the shop would be full to bursting with people so that there was an array of potential witnesses, made no sense at all. It would have been far easier, she thought, to have killed Sylvia on her way to or from work on an isolated stretch of road. Yet if the murderer had intended to kill Lady Celia, then the whole thing made much more sense. Lady Celia, she assumed, was either usually chaperoned or at the very least more often than not in the company of others. A mean feat indeed to make an attempt on her life under those circumstances. Far easier to try and do away with her in the shop. Although it couldn't be forgotten that the murderer had taken a considerable risk. He could easily have been spotted going to and from the dressing room. Or someone might have decided to go into the dressing room while he was doing the deed itself. Rose shivered. It didn't bear thinking about. But it still begged the question, who knew Lady Celia would be there? Most of the audience had been expecting to see Lavinia. Lady Celia's presence had come to many of them as a complete surprise.

In which case, wasn't it more likely that Sylvia was the intended victim after all? They had all known that she would be there, even if everybody had assumed that she would be donning the mantle of shop assistant rather than that of mannequin. When one came to think of it, it really had been most fortunate for the murderer that she had taken on the role of model, for it had meant that at various times during the course of the evening she had been alone. If she had been attending to the customers and guests, then she would hardly have had a moment to herself.

The more she thought about it, turning each scenario over and over in her head, the more she did not know what to think. It seemed to Rose that the whole thing might be argued either way. When all was said and done, the murderer had seized the opportunity on finding Sylvia alone in the dressing room and also taken a very great risk. How very fortunate it had been for the murderer that the curtain had caught fire when it had done and everyone had therefore been distracted and preoccupied either with putting it out or with fleeing the scene. It had been complete chaos with people going this way and that, and the murderer had taken full advantage of the situation for his own awful purposes. Of course, there was always the possibility that it had not been a coincidence, that the murder and the fire were somehow connected. And if that was so, then was it not logical to assume that the person who had committed the murder had also set fire to the curtains? It was not conclusive of course, but worthy of consideration all the same …

If Lady Celia turned out to be the intended victim, then it was unlikely that the murderer would prove to be one of them. It would be a relief to know that none of those she held dear were guilty of Sylvia's murder, and yet somehow it would seem more tragic still if the girl had been killed needlessly in mistake for another. And Lady Celia at that. It was wrong to feel like that, of course. She didn't really know Lady Celia. For all she knew, she might be very pleasant. And when all was said and done, murder was murder, and it was awful whoever was dead. But still …

'While we're waiting for Perkins to come back,' said the inspector breaking in on her thoughts, 'I'd like you to carry on giving me chapter and verse on the people next door. I'll take my own notes. We'll come to Miss Beckett's character in a moment if we may. First, what can you tell me about … eh,' he paused to consult his notes, 'Ah, yes … Miss Jennings? She's a frightened little creature if ever I saw one. Is it her natural way, or do you think she has something to hide?'

'Well, as I said just now, Mary was working in the shop before I started,' began Rose, wondering how she was going to answer the inspector's second question. 'She's a very pleasant sort of a girl, if frightfully timid. She's always afraid of doing the wrong thing, if that makes any sense. Sylvia always used to say she was afraid of her own shadow and Madame says that she wouldn't say boo to a goose. They were right. She is painfully shy and lacking in self-confidence, but very diligent and kind all the same. Too placid and easily led perhaps. If I'm honest, I rather thought Sylvia sometimes took advantage of her good nature.'

'Oh?'

'Oh, it was nothing really. It's only a feeling I had,' said Rose quickly, fearing that, despite her best intentions, she had said too much.

She heard again the words Mary had spoken a few hours before the fashion show, how she had described Sylvia as being horrible and hateful. She was reminded also of how badly the girl seemed to have taken Sylvia's death, turning in on herself and keeping the others at a distance. It probably meant nothing. It was so easy to read too much into everything, to think everyone a suspect and guilty of something. But what then of the awful things she had said? The confession she'd made …

'Miss Simpson. Miss Simpson? Are you all right?'

Inspector Deacon spoke urgently and leaned forward, a concerned look upon his face. Too late Rose realised he had been watching her closely. She wondered if he had an inkling as to what she'd been thinking, whether her thoughts were blazoned across her own face as clearly as if they had been written there. She blushed under such scrutiny and saw his expression harden, as if he were aware that she was consciously trying to keep something from him.

'I'm sorry, I was just thinking how upset poor Mary is by what has happened. Why, you commented on it yourself,' said Rose, rallying a little. 'I told you that she and Sylvia were by way of being friends. It's been the most awful shock to her.'

'If that's all it is,' said the inspector gravely. 'Please don't keep anything from me this time, Miss Simpson. It'll all come out in the end, you know it will. Much better to tell me all now.'

Rose took a deep breath. She wasn't quite sure what to say, how to put it into words. The inspector's manner had returned to brusque and she felt less minded to confide in him or speak aloud her fears. Really, his behaviour was very contrary. One moment he was the Inspector Deacon of old, the man she liked immensely. And next moment he was cold, as if they were strangers who had never met before. It was hard to believe that in the recent past he had respected her contributions to his investigations, encouraged them even.

'This Miss Jennings, she didn't by any chance happen to say anything to you, anything incriminating, that is? Or anything that might throw some light on to this matter?'

'No … that's to say, yes,' began Rose reluctantly, before hurrying on so very fast with her words that she barely had time to think. 'But it's only because she was so upset by it all. I don't think she knew what she was saying, or at least she didn't mean anything by it. People behave like that sometimes, don't they? When they've had a shock?'

'Some do and some don't,' said the inspector dryly. 'And if you please, it is up to us police to determine, rather than for you to decide, what has any bearing on this case. What did Miss Jennings say exactly that worries you so? Something to the detriment of Miss Beckett, I'll wager?'

'She said Sylvia was horrible and hateful and that people like her didn't deserve any luck. '

'My, my, that doesn't sound very friendly, does it? When did she say this?'

'A couple of hours before the fashion event. I think she was rather put out that Sylvia would be modelling Monsieur Girard's designs. It meant much more work for the two of us, you see, and Sylvia didn't help matters. She would insist on showing off about it.'

'Is that all? It doesn't sound overly incriminating. It sounds to me as if her nose was put out of joint and she understandably was feeling a little bitter about it.'

'Well, Mary said a little bit more than that,' admitted Rose. 'She wished that Sylvia would leave Renard's.' Rose played with the fabric of her skirt before adding rather hesitantly, 'Mary said that, when Sylvia was being particularly hateful, she sometimes wished that something awful might happen to her.'

'Did she indeed?'

'Yes, but of course she didn't mean anything by it. It's just one of those things that one says, isn't it?'

'Is it?'

'Yes … no. Well, I suppose it isn't something one would normally say about someone. I daresay you think it sounds frightfully bad. A point against Mary, you might say. But in Mary's case it's different. It's so hard to explain how she is, to put it into words.'

'Why don't you try? You'd be surprised how very many strange things a policeman hears and is asked to believe.'

'She said it out of frustration, because there was nothing else she could do. She wouldn't have had the nerve to say anything to Sylvia. That's why she said what she said to me. Once it was said it was over and done with. And I could tell that she regretted it immediately, that she had said what she did, I mean. Don't you see? She was very upset by it all. She never meant to say such a thing. She had shocked herself as much as she had shocked me. From then on, she wouldn't have said or done anything to Sylvia, at least not this evening when everything was still so fresh in her mind. She'd have been too embarrassed by it all. Why, she'd have gone out of her way to be nice to Sylvia. You do see that, don't you?' Rose was aware that she had been verbose and that a pleading note had crept into her voice, which she didn't much like.

'I don't think much of your reasoning,' said Inspector Deacon, looking rather sceptical. 'And if what you say about her character is true, then it seems to me that she's just the sort of girl to fly off the handle and pick up a conveniently placed pair of scissors and stab someone with them. Yes, just the sort to do that, I'd say, and then regret it like anything afterwards.'

'Well, I don't think she did it,' said Rose stubbornly. 'She hasn't got it in her to do something like that.'

'There we might have to disagree. Is there anything else you'd like to tell me?'

Of course, now was the time to confess that Mary had said much more than that. The girl's words, spoken so carelessly, floated up into Rose's mind. She had admitted that she had thought about killing her friend, had even gone so far as to contemplate the different ways she might do it. Rose could say as much to the inspector. But what would he think then? He already thought her view of Mary was rose tinted. He did not know Mary as she did. He wasn't to know that Mary was incapable of doing anything so frightful. Or was she? Might the inspector be right after all? Was it not possible that Mary, on the spur of the moment and if sufficiently provoked, picked up the little golden scissors and thrust them at Sylvia's neck? The poor girl would hardly have been aware of what she was doing. Certainty she wouldn't have meant to hurt her friend, Rose was sure of it, would stake her life on it if necessary. Mary would only have wanted to put a stop to Sylvia saying something particularly hateful and spiteful …

At last, she was aware of the inspector's eyes upon her, as if he were monitoring her every blink of the eye and change of expression. The very intensity of his look was willing her to speak, begging her to utter the truth. In this little room, with only the two of them present, she found his expression oddly hypnotic, as if she could tell him everything. Worse than that perhaps, as if she could tell him nothing but the absolute truth, wrenched from her though it might be. Before she could even think what she was saying, or the impact her words might have, she said miserably:

'Mary told me that sometimes she wished Sylvia was dead, that she had even thought of the various ways in which she might kill her.'

She heard Inspector Deacon take a sharp intake of breath. Clearly this was not what he had expected her to say. Other than that, there was a moment of complete silence in the room. If there had been a clock on the mantelpiece, she would surely have heard it tick. She could hear her own heartbeat, not only feel it. If she listened carefully and strained her ears, she could just make out the hum of voices in the room next door. She found herself in a state of expectation, whether waiting for Inspector Deacon to say something, or to hear something from outside this claustrophobic and confined little room, she did not know. All she knew was that she shouldn't have spoken so freely, that by doing so she had let Mary down. Mary, who she remembered suddenly, had first raised the suggestion that she investigate Sylvia's murder. Perhaps she should say as much to Inspector Deacon.

She opened her mouth as if to say something to that effect. But, just at that very moment, she heard the clatter of feet, the sound of shoes on wood. Someone was running up the flight of stairs two at a time. The door to the square room was opened. They heard the person stride across the floor with its threadbare carpet, and the door to their own little rectangle room was unceremoniously thrown open. Inspector Deacon, she noticed, had risen from his seat, and Rose, without thinking, found that she had followed suit.

Sergeant Perkins stood before them. He looked flushed, whether from his physical exhaustions or the news he had to impart, it was hard to tell. Rose sneaked a glance at Inspector Deacon. He appeared to be as apprehensive as she was herself.

'Out with it, man,' demanded the inspector. 'How is Lady Celia? Pray, don't tell me she's lying there with her throat cut in the drawing room?'

'Not a bit of it, sir,' answered the sergeant cheerily. 'She's as right as rain, so she is. The butler sent her lady's maid to check up on her. Sleeping like a new-born babe, she is.'

'The maid was quite sure her mistress was only sleeping?' said the inspector sharply.

'Yes, sir. Quite sure. She was snoring fit to wake the house, so the maid told the butler. Although I understand there was nothing unusual in that. I thought the butler was going to keel over with the shock of it all when I told him her ladyship might be in danger. He went very quiet and dropped the telephone apparatus, so he did.'

'I'm not surprised,' said the inspector, thinking that his sergeant was enjoying his dramatic retelling of events a trifle too much. 'Did he say what time she arrived home?'

'Yes, sir. About a quarter past ten, give or take a few minutes, he thought. And she wasn't alone. She was escorted home by a gentleman. I've written his name down here.' He paused to glance at his notebook. 'Ah … here we are … a Mr Bertram Thorpe.'

'He's her young man,' said Rose quickly. 'He was at the fashion event this evening. She'd asked him to attend.'

'I see. Well, we'll need to speak to both of them in the morning. Anything else to report, Sergeant?'

'The butler was that anxious when he heard a murderer was about. He's stationed a footman to stand all night outside her ladyship's bedroom door and positioned another to stand outside her window. Poor fellow. Let's hope it doesn't rain.'

'Well, that's made our job easier,' said the inspector looking relieved. 'What about the uniformed officer?'

'I waited downstairs by the telephone so that he could report back to me, sir,' said the sergeant. 'He's confirmed the butler's story. Lady Celia's safe and well. He could hear her snoring when he stood outside her bedroom door. He's staying on duty outside the house as you requested. They'll be that many people watching over the lady, sir, no harm will come to her tonight, and that's a fact.'

'Let's hope you are right,' said Inspector Deacon grimly.

Chapter Fifteen

'Now, let me see if I understand the situation correctly,' said Inspector Deacon. 'Jacques Renard is the proprietor's son, works at Harridges and lives out in lodgings?' He looked about his surroundings. 'Goodness knows there's hardly enough room for him to live here with his mother.'

'Yes, Madame Renard sent him to work in Harridges to learn the shop trade. She wants to prepare him for the day when he takes over the management of Renard's.'

Rose might have added that it was her own personal view that another reason her employer had dispatched her son to work at the department store had been an eagerness to keep Jacques and Sylvia apart. The words came readily enough to her lips, but on refection she thought better of it. It might surely only serve to muddy the waters unnecessarily. It would suggest a possible motive for murder which she herself thought highly implausible.

If Inspector Deacon had noticed her intention to add anything further, then he gave no sign of it. Indeed, given by what he asked next, it appeared that his thoughts had moved on from the proprietor's son entirely.

'I see. And how does Monsieur Girard come into the picture?' He asked, getting up to stretch his legs and arms before taking his seat again.

It was with some effort that Rose did not allow her gaze to fall on the inspector's injured leg. She wondered whether it gave him pain. A part of her rebelled at the notion that, as the investigation progressed, she would become accustomed to seeing his reliance on the cane. It occurred to her to speculate whether he felt the same. Did he awake each morning and remember his dependence on his stick, or for one blessed moment did he forget?

'He also works at Harridges,' said Rose, tearing her thoughts away from consideration of the inspector's injury. 'That's where Jacques met him. Monsieur Girard arranges their window displays.'

'Oh?' Inspector Deacon sounded surprised. 'Then he doesn't design clothes for a living? It's not his profession?'

'No. I believe it's by way of being a bit of a hobby with him. He hasn't shown any of his designs before. Tonight was the first time he had put them on display.' Rose sighed. 'This evening's fashion event was being held both to launch Monsieur Girard's clothes collection and to illustrate Madame Renard's intention to start offering haute couture to her customers. A departure for her from selling only factory made clothing.'

'I see, so the success of this event was important to the both of them?' said the inspector. 'Is he any good, this Monsieur Girard, as a clothes designer, I mean?'

'Yes, he is rather, in a quiet sort of a way. By that I mean he has a good eye for the cut of fabric and how it drapes around the body. His outfits are well made and fit beautifully,' said Rose. 'His clothes have a subtle style about them. There is nothing flamboyant about them in any way, which was part of the attraction of them for Madame Renard. They were very wearable. She could picture in her mind our customers dressed in them.'

'It sounds as if they differ a bit from his window displays. Quite spectacular some of them are at Harridges,' volunteered Sergeant Perkins from his seat behind Rose. 'You could stop and stare at one for hours trying to take in all the little details. The things they think of to put in the windows, you'd never believe it. Quite a bit of art they are, those windows displays, as good as any picture in one of those picture galleries.'

'Thank you, Sergeant,' said the inspector, sounding none too pleased at his subordinate's interruption.

'Yes, he specialises in beautifully dressed displays,' said Rose, amused by the young man's enthusiasm. 'They tend to be themed.' She had half turned in her seat to include the sergeant in the conversation. 'Although I'm not sure our customers appreciate such attention to detail. Or should I say the price that is associated with such clothes? From a distance it's difficult to see all the work that has gone in to producing such garments.' Rose turned back to face the inspector. 'The one exception of course was the satin silk gown.'

'Ah, that was the silver dress the girl was wearing when she was killed?' said Inspector Deacon. Rose nodded. 'It was hard to tell what it looked like when we saw it.' He paused a moment to dwell with some reluctance on the image of the body on the floor conjured up in his mind's eye. 'But from the way you were describing it earlier, with the strings of glass and silver beads and all, it sounds as if it were a grand dress, spectacular even?'

'Yes, it was. There were a lot of gasps and sighs from the audience when Sylvia emerged in that dress. It's hard to put in words how magnificent the gown was. It sounds silly, but it had almost a magical quality to it. It so totally transformed her appearance, you see. I think that was one of the reasons the audience were so taken with it. They were familiar with seeing Sylvia dressed in her shop habiliments, of blouse and skirt. It's a smart ensemble, but jolly plain. When Sylvia appeared in that silver dress, she looked like a princess. We were literally besieged by the audience; everyone wanted to arrange fittings for the dress.' She gave a half smile, which only emphasised the sadness in the room. If the evening had not ended so tragically, she would have been tempted to laugh. Unbidden, a vision of Sylvia as she had looked in the dress appeared in her mind's eye. She blinked back her tears. How very wretched all this was. 'Poor Monsieur Girard. No one will want to buy his silver gown now that it has such a sad association.'

'It's difficult ever to predict how the general public is going to react to such a thing. It might well give the gown a morbid fascination for some, particularly if it was as magnificent as you say it was. Now, tell me about Sylvia Beckett. What sort of a girl was she? Were you by way of being friends?'

'I wouldn't say we were particularly friendly,' said Rose, brought abruptly back to the present and picking her words with care. 'We knew each other well, of course, working in the shop together as we did. But I don't think she liked me very much and I didn't particularly take to her. She could be rather temperamental. One moment she would be as nice as anything, the next rather sulky and insolent. She could be dreadfully rude to customers she didn't like. And she rather took against me after Lavinia and I became friends. She resented Lavinia when she worked in the shop, you see. If I'm honest, I can't say I blame her. Lavinia was just playing at working after all, and Madame Renard would insist on giving her the less onerous tasks to do, the ones that we enjoyed doing. And she did rather fawn over her. She thought Lavinia would be good for business, you see, It didn't surprise me in the least that Sylvia was jealous of her. Had I not liked Lavinia, I might well have felt the same.'

'So, the young lady didn't like Lady Lavinia? Well, I won't hold that against her,' said Inspector Deacon, not being particularly fond of the lady in question himself. For she had not made a very favourable impression on him when they had chanced to meet during a previous murder investigation.

'Lavinia is all right,' said Rose smiling. 'I think you got off on the wrong foot, that's all. She's not nearly as bad and selfish as she likes to make out. Really, she's rather a dear.'

'I'll take your word for it, Miss Simpson,' said Inspector Deacon, sounding far from convinced.

'It's rather funny in a sad sort of way,' said Rose. 'But Sylvia rather reminded me of Lavinia in a manner of speaking.'

'Oh? I would have thought them very dissimilar.'

'Sylvia thought rather a lot of herself, you know, gave herself airs and graces. She always thought herself rather above us, Mary and me, as if she were intended for far better things than to be a shop assistant. The way she used to talk, one would be excused for imagining that she had a string of eligible young gentlemen lining up to marry her.'

'Oh, anyone in particular?'

'She and Jacques Renard used to be rather taken with each other, although I fancy things may have cooled between them lately. It's only an impression I had, that they weren't so close. Monsieur Renard had spent less time at Renard's since he started working at Harridges a few months' ago. And Sylvia talked about him less often.' Rose sighed. 'I don't think there was ever anything very serious between them anyway, certainly not on Jacques' part at least.'

'You were saying that the deceased reminded you of Lady Lavinia,' prompted Inspector Deacon.

'Yes, she liked having people wait on her. She would have loved to have had her own servants. This evening she even had me carry her outfits for her from the storeroom to the dressing room. I offered to hang them up for her, but she was most insistent that she do that herself. Now I come to think about it, I suppose she didn't want me to see that she'd brought the silver gown into the dressing room. She wasn't supposed to wear it this evening, you see.'

'Oh, why was that?'

'Well it was her own fault really. Lady Celia caught Sylvia making a face in the mirror when she, Lady Celia that is, said that she would like to wear the same dress herself. She took against Sylvia over that and insisted that she not be allowed to wear the dress. It was all so silly and unnecessary. Sylvia was awfully upset about it, as was Monsieur Girard because Lady Celia really did not have the figure to carry off the dress. In the end he and the seamstress created a simplified version of the dress for her to wear.'

'And yet Miss Beckett decided to wear the dress after all?'

'Yes, I can't understand what possessed her to do so. She risked incurring Madame Renard's fury and Lady Celia flew into quite a rage about it and insisted on her immediate dismissal.'

'Did she indeed? Now, where were we? Yes, you were saying that Sylvia Beckett reminded you of Lady Lavinia in character. Do you have anything else to say on that?'

'Yes. She asked me to help her with her hair this evening. It's just the sort of thing Lavinia would ask me to do for her … oh!'

'What is it?'

'The golden scissors! It was me who brought them into the dressing room. They were in the storeroom and I went and got them. Sylvia was trying to fix a hair comb in her hair and her hair got all tangled up with the lace collar of the outfit she was wearing. Try as we might we couldn't free it. She was dreadfully impatient and would refuse to keep still, you see. In the end I went and got the scissors and cut out the bit of hair. I didn't know Elsie had left her scissors in the storeroom; she was always very precious about them. It was Sylvia who remembered that they were there. If only she hadn't! But it's all my fault because I forgot to return them. I put them down on the desk beside the door and forgot all about them. We were in the most awful rush, you see.'

All colour had drained from Rose's face and a mist of dizziness rose up before her. She clutched at the seat of her chair with both hands to steady herself. Out of the corner of her eye, she was vaguely aware that Inspector Deacon had risen from his seat and was standing in front of her, as if to be in readiness to catch her should she slide from her chair. She heard the scrape of a chair behind her and assumed that Sergeant Perkins had also risen to come to her aid if required. With a tremendous effort of will, not least driven by the desire not to make a fool of herself by fainting, she fought through the mist and regained her senses.

'If I hadn't left them there … the scissors, I mean, the murderer wouldn't have had anything to hand to stab Sylvia with. I provided him with the weapon! It hadn't occurred to me before, even when I found Sylvia's body stretched out on the floor and saw them sticking out of her… They were on the desk right by the door … the scissors, I mean. He hardly had to come into the room to see them lying there. Perhaps they gave him the idea to do what he did. If only –'

'If they hadn't been there, then the murderer would have used something else,' Inspector Deacon said quickly. 'I daresay there was a letter opener on the desk. He could have used that instead. It would have been just as effective. It's not your fault, Rose. You mustn't blame yourself.'

'It's all very well to say that, and of course I know you're right but –'

'Don't think any more about it,' said the inspector. 'It doesn't do to dwell on such things. The best thing you can do for Miss Beckett now is to help us catch her murderer. Now, let's go through the events of today leading up to the fashion show itself, shall we?'

'Very well,' said Rose wearily. 'It's rather difficult to know where exactly to begin. I think it is perhaps worth mentioning something that happened yesterday.'

'Oh, and what was that?'

'I telephoned Sedgwick Court to speak to Lavinia. As you may, or may not, know it was originally intended that she should model Monsieur Girard's outfits not Sylvia.'

'Yes, I was aware of that. Lady Lavinia pulled out at the last minute, didn't she? And Miss Beckett stepped in to be the mannequin.'

'She didn't pull out as such. Lavinia is unwell,' said Rose rather defensively. 'She would never have let Madame Renard down if she could possibly have helped it. And she did try and find someone to replace her.'

'Are you saying that her intention was that Lady Celia should model the gowns in her place?' Inspector Deacon sat back in his chair looking interested.

'Yes, only of course it wasn't possible. Lady Celia's figure is quite different to Lavinia's. There wasn't time to make the necessary alterations to the outfits. But we only knew that this morning when she came into the shop to be fitted.'

'So it was then decided that Miss Beckett should model the outfits instead because she had a similar figure to Lady Lavinia?'

'Yes. It was decided that Lady Celia would present one or two of the outfits instead. Madame Renard was most particular that a member of the aristocracy should preside over the proceedings.'

'I see. Would I be right in assuming that had this evening's event gone as originally planned, with Lady Lavinia modelling the gowns, Lady Celia would not have been present?'

'Yes. She wouldn't have been there.'

Rose heard Sergeant Perkins cough behind her and saw Inspector Deacon look up. She imagined the inspector and the sergeant exchanging a knowing look. She was not surprised. The significance of what she had just said was not lost on her. She had thought as much earlier, but now that she had articulated the facts, spelled them out for all to see, she felt more certain than before that her suspicions had proved correct. Lady Celia had not been the intended victim. There had been no mistake. The murderer had planned to murder Sylvia all along. And more likely than not, unless the killer was revealed to be a disgruntled customer, the murderer was currently waiting to be interviewed in the very next room.

Momentarily, she had toyed with the idea that the intended victim might even have been Lavinia, but had rejected the thought almost immediately. Madame Renard had announced at the very start of the event that Lavinia would not be present. The murderer would therefore have been aware of her absence regardless of whether or not he was currently residing in the room next door. Also, although similar in build, Sylvia and Lavinia had been different in colouring. She therefore had considered it highly unlikely that Sylvia had been mistaken for Lavinia.

She could see the inspector becoming impatient. Perhaps he thought that he had wasted valuable time by interviewing her first when he had more important people to interrogate in the other room. In all likelihood, the murderer was sitting quietly with the others. He might well be there concocting an alibi or working out what to say when he was interviewed.

'There are a number of questions I should like to put to you, Miss Simpson. If I had more time, I would put them all to you now. But it is very late and I wish to speak to the others in the room next door before I call it a day.'

'Or should that be a night?' quipped the sergeant from his corner.

Inspector Deacon ignored the interruption other than to make a slight grimace. It occurred to Rose that he might be missing the reliable Sergeant Lane very much.

'So I will put only a very few more questions to you tonight. The other things that I have to ask you can wait until tomorrow. Now, tell me this. Was a record taken of all those who attended the fashion show this evening?'

'Yes, the event was by invitation only. Those invited to attend were our most favoured and affluent customers. The invitations themselves were handed in as people entered the shop. Mary … Miss Jennings marked off the names of those attending on a register. Each customer was permitted to bring a guest. Positively encouraged to, I should say. Madame Renard hoped it might be a way to attract what she referred to as "the right sort of people" to her establishment. As it happened, in some cases the customers brought more than one guest with them, which created a bit of a problem with the chairs. We hadn't provided enough.'

'I see. Perhaps you will now tell me in your own words just what happened this evening. I would particularly like to know if you noticed anything out of the ordinary. Suppose we start when the first customers arrived.'

'That would have been a little after seven o'clock,' said Rose. 'There was quite a queue of them waiting outside when we came to open the door. It was the first such event Renard's had put on, and I remember everyone was excited, not knowing quite what to expect.'

'Where were you while the customers were coming in?'

'I was kept busy going backwards and forwards between the kitchen area and the shop bringing in trays of wine and lemonade. The customers were encouraged to help themselves to the drinks, which I must say they did quite readily.'

'So the customers were strolling around helping themselves to drinks, and chatting as well, I daresay?'

'Yes, there was a lot of noise. An almost unbelievable amount. I could hardly think let alone make myself heard. I kept having to say: "excuse me" as I made my way between the customers with the trays, but hardly anyone heard me. That's to say, they didn't get out of my way. I thought it was only a matter of time before someone knocked into me and I dropped the tray I was carrying. I had visions of wine and glass going all over the floor. But if I recollect correctly, we only had one actual breakage.'

'What happened next?'

'I went to check up on Lady Celia. The fashion event was due to start and I realised she had not made an appearance. I wanted to make sure she was all right.'

'Where was she?'

'In the dressing room.'

'And how did she seem to you?'

'Rather apprehensive. I think her nerves had got the better of her. She was having second thoughts about the whole thing, not helped by the fact that she didn't much like the dress she was to wear. And she was awfully anxious about whether her young man had arrived or not. I think she was rather afraid that he wouldn't turn up.' Rose sat back in her chair and gave a half laugh. 'I know this sounds rather ridiculous, but I had the oddest impression that his attending the event or not was some sort of a test that she had set for him, to determine his affection for her.'

'It doesn't sound so very strange to me,' said Sergeant Perkins. 'It's just the sort of thing my girl would ask of me. You know, get me to do something she knew I wasn't fond of to show how much I cared for her. In her case it's me going to have tea with her parents. Her mother can't abide me on account of me being a bobby, and she doesn't try and hide the fact neither. She –'

'Thank you, Sergeant,' said Inspector Deacon rather irritably. 'Do go on, Miss Simpson.'

'Well, she left the dressing room and I went to see Sylvia. She was waiting in the storeroom next door for the dressing room to become vacant so that she could go in there and hang up her outfits.'

'Was she alone?'

'Yes. Monsieur Girard had gone outside to have a last cigarette before the show. Sylvia, as it happens, had taken it upon herself to smoke in the storeroom. I had words with her about it because I knew Madame Renard would be furious if she found out, but Sylvia didn't seem to care.'

'How did she seem to you generally?'

'Excited and nervous in equal measure, I would have said. Both she and Lady Celia were rather anxious about the number of people. It was not what they had been expecting.'

'And that is when you helped Miss Beckett carry her outfits to the dressing room and gave a hand with her hair?' Rose nodded. "What happened next?'

'I went back into the shop. The show was about to start. Most of the audience had taken their seats by then. As I said before, there was a shortage of chairs. Most of the men had chosen to stand by the door. Madame Renard was standing behind the counter that was being used as the lectern, and Lady Celia and Monsieur Girard were standing on either side of her. Bertram Thorpe, Lady Celia's young man, arrived just as the show was about to start. He went and stood next to the other gentlemen.'

'And where was Jacques Renard during all of this? Was he standing with the other men?'

'No. He wasn't there. He didn't arrive until the middle of the fashion show and rather drew attention to the fact. I doubt anyone could have failed to have noticed his arrival. You see, the door to the street was locked. He had to rattle it from outside to get anyone's attention. Mary had to hurry over and unlock the door for him.'

'Where did he go once he'd gained admittance?'

'I think he was rather embarrassed at having caused a disturbance,' said Rose. 'I remember he went to stand between the drapes and the candelabra. They obscured him from view a little, you see, from the audience. People would insist on turning around in their seats and staring at him. One woman even went so far as to point him out to her friend as being the latecomer who had disrupted the proceedings and another one tut-tutted.'

'Very embarrassing for him, I'm sure,' said Inspector Deacon. 'But rather enlightening for us, I would say.'

'I'm not sure that I follow you, Inspector.'

'Oh, I think you will, Miss Simpson. If what you are saying is correct.' He paused and held up his hand as Rose looked about to protest. 'I have no reason to doubt your word, I assure you. But you must see, don't you, that both where Monsieur Renard had chosen to stand, and being partially obscured from view as he was, placed him in an ideal positon to set light to the curtain without being observed?'

Chapter Sixteen

'As it happens, Inspector, I don't see that at all,' said Rose.

'Why not? You have just told us that Jacques Renard was standing partially hidden between the candelabra and the drape. I would have thought that placed him in a very good position to start the fire.'

'Of course it would have done,' agreed Rose, 'if he happened to be standing there when the curtain caught fire.'

'You mean he wasn't?' asked the inspector rather abruptly, looking more than a little disappointed that his theory had come to nothing. 'Are you certain of that? Where was he?'

'Yes, I am quite sure. He was nowhere near either the candelabra or the curtains when the fire broke out.'

'Where had he gone?'

Again the inspector's tone was offhand, as if he considered it her fault that there were deficiencies with his reasoning. Perhaps not irrationally, Rose found herself irritated by his manner, which meant that she spoke more smugly than she had intended.

'I saw Jacques Renard go through the arch a few minutes before the curtain caught fire. I assumed he was going to one of the rooms leading off it. I thought …' Rose hesitated, before allowing her voice to drift off and come to a rather unsatisfactory stop. Better that Jacques should have remained by the curtains than to have gone in search of Sylvia.

'Indeed? Did you see to which room he went?'

Perhaps her own senses were overly heightened. Certainly Rose felt she could feel and sense every emotion in that small, overcrowded room. Foremost, she was aware of the barely concealed excitement that hung in the air as if it were a real, tangible thing. She imagined the sergeant learning forward in his chair behind her, perhaps even biting the end of his pencil in nervous anticipation of what she would say next. The inspector, though from practise and bitter experience better able to conceal his emotions, was nevertheless looking at her with interest. The frown disappeared completely from his forehead as if it had never been there. Perhaps he thought that instead of thwarting his enquires she might after all hold the key to the mystery.

'No, I didn't,' said Rose, finally. Even to her own ears, the word sounded sadly inadequate.

The tension in the room disintegrated. She heard the sergeant's sharp intake of breath behind her, and saw a flicker of disappointment appear for a moment on Inspector Deacon's face. Instinctively she felt the need to explain.

'I didn't see where Monsieur Renard went,' Rose said, 'for the simple reason that everything became rather chaotic, I'm afraid. Sylvia had just appeared in the silver dress. It had an enormous effect on the audience. Everyone wanted to have a better look at the dress, and then of course Sylvia disappeared quickly and they couldn't. That only made matters worse. They were demanding to know why the gown hadn't been included in the fashion show and why they hadn't been provided with any details, as if it were all our fault. I've never known our customers behave like that. They were so indignant, so insistent. Really, they were most unreasonable. And it was all the more frightening because it was so unexpected. They crowded around us and we felt quite hemmed in. We didn't know what to say because of course the gown wasn't to have been shown. We tried to explain but it only served to make them more annoyed.'

'Where was Miss Beckett during all of this?' demanded Inspector Deacon. 'You said that she had disappeared. Had she gone back to the dressing room?'

'Yes. At least I assumed so at the time. I think she was as taken aback by the reaction to the dress as we were, to say nothing of the look on Madame Renard's face. I remember that Madame looked quite dumbfounded, as if she could not make sense of it all. She was simply staring at Sylvia in disbelief. And then of course the situation was exacerbated by Lady Celia's outburst. She was absolutely furious and demanded that the girl be sacked immediately. She wasn't very quiet about it and created quite a spectacle. I imagine a lot of the customers heard what she was saying. It was all very embarrassing for poor Madame Renard.'

'Are you sure Miss Beckett vanished before Monsieur Renard set off through the arch?'

'Yes.'

'There are three rooms that lead off the corridor through that arch, aren't there? The dressing room, the storeroom and the kitchen area. That's right, isn't it?'

'Yes.' Rose hesitated for a moment before continuing. She reasoned it would make things worse for the proprietor's son if she were to hold anything back; far better, she thought, to tackle and confront the suspicions head on. 'I know what you are going to ask me next,' she said hurriedly, 'and you are quite right. As I have said, I didn't actually see where Jacques went, but I assumed at the time he had gone to see Sylvia.'

'On account of him being rather fond of her?'

'Yes that, and also on account of what Monsieur Renard said just before he set off. And the expression on his face,' said Rose. 'He looked quite taken aback as if something had startled him badly. I assumed at the time that he could not quite recognise that the girl in the dress was Sylvia.'

'Ah, because she looked like a princess in that silver gown,' interjected Sergeant Perkins. 'I know how he must have felt. When I first saw my Agnes dressed in her best frock for me to take her to the tea dance. Well, she looked as pretty as a picture, so she did, and if my heart hadn't already –'

'What did he say?' interrupted Inspector Deacon rather roughly, as if his sergeant had not spoken.

'I don't remember exactly. It was something like: "Sylvia! Good Lord!" It made me turn around to see who had spoken, and Monsieur Renard was standing there behind me. I remember he had such a peculiar look on his face.'

'Then I think we can safely assume that he went to see Miss Beckett. If he did, he must have been one of the last people to see Miss Beckett alive.'

'Or the very last, sir, if he was the murderer,' said Sergeant Perkins rather smugly.

'Quite so, Sergeant. Either way, it's something that we will raise with Monsieur Renard when we interview him. I would be grateful if you would not forewarn him, Miss Simpson, when you return to the other room. It's possible that he believes he was not observed leaving the shop and going through the arch. I will be interested to know if he volunteers the information. Now,' the inspector looked down at his notes, 'I should like to go back a few steps, if I may. Or perhaps it is forward? I am interested in that fire. Its occurrence was very timely for our murderer. When precisely did the fire break out?'

'I've told you already,' said Rose, putting a hand to her forehead, which was starting to throb. She suddenly felt very tired indeed. 'It was a few minutes after Monsieur Renard had gone through the arch, and when the audience was crowded around us demanding details of Sylvia's dress.'

'Can you tell me exactly what happened?'

'A woman screamed. Everyone turned around to see what had made her scream and they immediately saw that the curtain was alight. It's strange … now I come to think about it, it was the scream that made everyone panic. If the woman hadn't screamed, I think the fire would have been put out very quickly with little inconvenience to anyone.'

'Do you know the identity of the person who screamed?'

'No, I'm afraid not. But I'm certain it was a woman. It was a rather ghastly and high pitched scream. However, one thing I do know, Inspector, is who it couldn't have been.'

'Oh? And who couldn't it have been?' said Inspector Deacon, with renewed interest.

Rose imagined Sergeant Perkins seated behind her, looking up from his notebook, his pencil hovering in mid-air in preparation for scribbling down the names as they fell from her lips.

'Madame Renard, Lady Celia or Mary. And Sylvia of course, on account of her being in the dressing room.'

'None of the three women?' Inspector Deacon looked taken aback. 'Are you quite sure?'

'Yes, Inspector, I'm quite certain. You see Lady Celia was fully occupied with berating Madame Renard on account of Sylvia wearing the silver gown. Madame Renard was wondering how to respond, and Mary and I were surrounded by members of the audience demanding details of the dress.'

'Where was Monsieur Girard during all of this?'

'He disappeared before Sylvia appeared in the gown. I imagine he had gone back to the storeroom. But it couldn't have been him. It was definitely a woman who screamed.'

'So let me get this straight in my mind,' said Inspector Deacon. 'When the fire broke out, Madame Renard, Lady Celia and Miss Jennings were engaged elsewhere in the room, and Miss Beckett was in the dressing room. Monsieur Renard had gone through the arch and had most probably joined Miss Beckett in the dressing room. And lastly, Monsieur Girard was in all likelihood in the storeroom. But wherever he was, he was nowhere near the candelabra or the drapes?'

'Yes, that's right' agreed Rose. 'So you see, Inspector, none of them could have screamed. And if, as I have no doubt you imagine, the drapes were deliberately set alight, none of them could have done that either.'

There was a moment or two of silence.

'Well, perhaps it was Lady Celia's companion,' piped up the Sergeant. 'Now what's his name … ah, yes … Mr Bertram Thorpe.'

'No, I think that unlikely,' said Rose, before the inspector had a chance to respond. 'For the same reason it could not have been Monsieur Girard. Bertram Thorpe is a man. It was a woman who screamed, I'm certain of it. And it's also my theory, for what it is worth, that the woman who screamed and the person who set the curtains alight are one and the same person.'

'What?' The inspector looked aghast.

'Nothing else makes any sense. The scream was too loud. It was far too theatrical to be a proper scream.'

'But if what you say is true,' said Inspector Deacon slowly, 'either the fire and the murder are unconnected, although it seems a remarkable coincidence that the fire should break out at the very same moment our murderer contemplates murder, or – '

'The murderer isn't any one of our suspects,' said Sergeant Perkins.

They had all taken a moment or two to digest the possibility that the murderer was some shadowy figure from outside the shop, who had taken advantage of the fashion event to undertake his ghastly deed. If the murderer and the arsonist were indeed one and the same, it was also to be realised that a disturbing degree of planning had been undertaken to facilitate Sylvia's murder. The notion that her death had been a spur of the moment act, carried out in a moment of fury, was diminished. There was something rather comforting about the thought and yet also frightening, if that made any sense at all, which Rose supposed it didn't. And yet, could it equally be possible that the fire and the murder were not linked as it was now supposed? Could the arsonist and the murderer be no more connected than two strangers in the street? In which case, the fire would have had no more bearing on Sylvia's death than providing a useful distraction, which the murderer had exploited, by making full use of the ensuing panic and disturbance for his own ends.

The question foremost in Rose's own thoughts, and to a degree in those of the two policemen who shared with her the little partially cluttered, closed in room, was why anyone, not intent on murder, should have wished to set fire to Madame Renard's establishment. To confuse the issue further, it had been no serious act of arson. The fire had been quickly put out and the damage to property had been minimal, so that the physical destruction of the shop had not been the goal. It appeared then that the aim had been only to ruin the fashion event, to have it live on in the minds of those who had attended as having been something of a disaster, never to be repeated. But why? Who could have been so against the event as to take such physical action? Of course that question in itself opened up other motives, motives that must be explored and investigated almost as keenly as the murder itself.

In the end, it was Inspector Deacon who summed up all their thoughts.

'We need to find out who set light to the shop and why. It is as imperative to this inquiry as finding out the identity of the murderer, whether or not the two acts are linked.' He gave a sigh. 'If what you say is correct, Miss Simpson, it very much looks as if the fire was started by a member of the audience.'

'I think, Inspector, that finding the arsonist may be easier said than done,' said Rose, after a further moment of reflection. 'You see, almost everyone would have been facing the other way. I suppose that is why the person chose the very moment that they did to do it. Lady Celia was creating a scene; she was making no attempt to speak quietly despite Madame Renard's desperate attempts to encourage her to do so. Believe me, many of those present would have been fascinated by watching such a spectacle. And the remainder of the audience would have been crowding around Mary and myself trying to get details of the elusive silver gown. So you see, my point is this, no one would have been looking in the direction of the candelabra or the curtains.'

'That said, there is always a chance someone might have seen something. Some of the men, for instance. I doubt they were particularly interested in that dress, no matter how magnificent it was, even if their womenfolk were. We will need to have a look at Miss Jennings' register and interview everyone whom attended this evening's event and was still at the shop when the fire broke out.'

'Mary did make a note of each customer as they left,' Rose agreed, 'or rather, those who left before the fire. She made a note against their name as to whether or not they had made an appointment for a fitting or wanted to have another look at the outfits on their next visit. So from Mary's list we should be able to gather who was still here when the curtain caught alight. I should perhaps warn you that we are talking of a great many people, particularly when one includes the various guests of customers. You see, the vast majority of the people stayed on until the end. Very few of them left in the middle of the show.'

There was a faint but audible groan from Sergeant Perkins.

'Yes, I know, Sergeant, a boring and laborious task which might quite well prove fruitless, but necessary all the same,' said his superior.

'I know that we have all but dismissed the idea, but I suppose there is no possibility that it was an accident, the fire I mean?' Rose asked.

'None whatsoever, I'm afraid. We haven't left that possibility to chance either. Our men have tested it. There is no way, given where the candelabra was positioned, that the curtains could have caught alight other than that one of the drapes was deliberately held over the flame of at least one of the candles. But cheer up, Perkins.' The inspector paused to grin at his sergeant. 'We'll need to interview the customers and their guests anyway about the murder, unless we happen to stumble on the culprit before, that is. It's just possible that one of them may have noticed someone going into, or coming out of, the dressing room at around about the time Miss Beckett was killed.'

'It's unfortunate that so many people congregated in the corridor while they were waiting for Mary to unlock the storeroom door, the one that backed onto the street,' said Rose. 'It would have been easy enough for the murderer to choose his moment to slip out of the dressing room unobserved and join the queue.'

'Our murderer was rather fortunate that no one chose to go into the dressing room to see if that room had a door backing out onto the street,' said the inspector.

'Yes, he was. I suppose that was in part due to Madame Renard's quick thinking. She acted almost immediately when the fire broke out. I think it may have come as a welcome relief. By that I mean it was a means of getting herself away from Lady Celia and her anger. When Madame Renard asked Mary to get the key from the kitchen, she deliberately spoke very loudly so that her voice could be heard over the din. I suppose that she hoped it would bring some calm to the proceedings. But it did mean that everyone was more interested in following Mary around than looking for an alternative exit. Why, one or two of our more impatient customers even followed her into the kitchen in search of the key, would you believe?'

'That girl, Miss Simpson, she has been in with the policemen a very long time,' said Marcel Girard, eyeing the door to the next room suspiciously.

'Well, that inspector fellow's a friend of hers, isn't he?' said Jacques, half sitting, half reclining, languidly on the settee. All of a sudden he was feeling tired and lethargic.

He was beginning to find his friend's endless pacing of the room irritating in the extreme. For one thing, to watch him was boringly repetitive. Due to the modest dimensions of the room, the designer was compelled to repeatedly walk around the room's perimeter, which meant that he trod on the same bit of well-worn carpet again and again. At first Jacques had found this oddly mesmerising, predicting which precise bit of rug his friend's foot would tread on each time he passed. Now though he found it merely tedious. His annoyance and frustration came out in his words.

'What did you expect, Marcel? She's probably telling that police inspector this very minute about all our little weaknesses and defects, everything we have ever done wrong, reciting verbatim every word that we've ever spoken against poor Sylvia. I am surprised your ears aren't burning, Mama, given all the times you've called Sylvia insolent and lazy.'

'Jacques!' exclaimed his mother clearly horrified. 'How can you say such awful things and at a time like this? To be so cruel, so heartless, to treat this like a game put on for your entertainment when that poor, dear girl is lying dead, I do not know where.'

'In the mortuary, I imagine, and I'm doing no such thing, Mother,' said Jacques, nevertheless righting himself so that he was sitting up straight and now all but perched on the very edge of the sofa. He passed a hand over his eyes so that his expression was partially hidden, although his voice took on a serious note. 'I suppose it's because I don't know what else to say or do, or how best to answer Marcel's damn fool of a question. They don't tell you, do they, how utterly boring and unbearable this waiting around to be interviewed is?' He threw a glance at his mother who looked no less appalled than before. His voice softened, although a look of anguish appeared on his face. 'Do you not think I feel Sylvia's death as deeply as any of you? Perhaps more so.'

'I do not know what to believe,' said Madame Renard miserably. She stared at her hands and played with a ring on the middle finger of her right hand. The bangles on her arm jingled albeit rather more sedately than was their custom. 'It is all so unreal. It is like a bad dream. I keep expecting to wake up any moment, but I know that I won't. What will this all look like tomorrow in the daylight, I wonder? Will I find Sylvia's blood on the floor? And this waiting, yes, it is almost the worst part of it all.'

'Well, I shouldn't worry, Madame,' said Marcel from his position in the corner of the room. He had been watching the exchange between mother and son with some interest. 'The policemen, they will want to speak to you next, yes? It is your shop and Miss Beckett, she was your employee.'

If the designer had intended that his words should provide the proprietor with some comfort, then he was to be disappointed. Madame Renard went pale and visibly shuddered. Her arms, bedecked in their bangles, clattered noisily against the sofa's armrest, while her fingernails tapped the polished wood restlessly. Her eyes, almost impossibly large, looked frightened, reminding Marcel of a rabbit caught in the headlights of a motor car. Dark smudges had appeared under her eyes like badly applied make up, contrasting starkly with her deathly pallor. He found himself moved by the woman's wretched state and, looking across at his friend, saw that her son looked equally concerned. Jacques felt a stab of compassion for his mother which, not surprisingly, exceeded his friend's feelings. It was not only that she was his mother, but that he alone knew how much Renard's meant to her; it was as much her child as he was himself, and he felt her suffering as keenly as if it had been his own.

For now at least Renard's had become soiled and tainted. It was impossible for any one of them not to feel that. A sense of evil permeated the shop as strongly as the smell of smoke from the ruined drape. It was not hard to imagine that his mother had recoiled, if only temporarily, from her once cherished establishment. He stretched out a hand and clasped one of her hands in his. He was surprised how very cold it was; he might have been touching the hand of a ghost.

As it happened Madame Renard was thinking about a ghost of sorts. She was wondering if she would ever be able to rid her mind of the dreadful image of the dead girl that had greeted her so forcefully when she had peered into the room and looked beyond Rose's kneeling form. She had lingered awkwardly in the doorway, too afraid to go any further into the room and yet reluctant to leave, for appearance's sake if nothing else. Even in a highly agitated state faced with the worst catastrophe that could be imagined, Madame Renard had been conscious that it would not be considered the done thing at all for a proprietor to leave her shop assistant to deal with a dead body, even a shop assistant with as much experience of murder as Rose Simpson. It was upon such thoughts that Madame Renard became vaguely aware that her son was talking to her and, as she listened carefully, the words floated towards her as if they were coming from a long way away.

'You must request that Rose be there with you, when you are interviewed,' Jacques was saying. 'I would accompany you myself, only they wouldn't allow it. The inspector will want to interview us separately. They won't want our answers to be influenced by what others say.'

He might well have added that the police would be hoping to find contradictions in their statements that they could use to their advantage, to trip up the guilty party, making them slip and stumble into a confession. He thought these things, but refrained from saying them out loud.

'And Rose?' mumbled his mother, through lips that barely moved.

'They must have asked her all the questions they intend to by now. She'll have told them everything she knows.'

'And she is one of them, is she not?' said Marcel with something akin to distaste.

'She is one of *us*,' corrected Jacques firmly. 'You said so yourself. And it was you who insisted that she should investigate on our behalf, or have you forgotten that?'

'No, of course not;' said the designer defensively. 'But I am wondering now whether we can trust her.'

'Trust her to do what?' asked Jacques. He sounded irritated, as if he had had enough of it all.

'To portray us in a good light. To not tell them anything that we rather she didn't.'

'I think it's rather late for all that, don't you?' said Jacques rather wearily. 'Knowing Rose as I do, she will try to be as fair to us as possible. She won't say things just for the sake of it. But I should warn you that she will approach this case with the object of discovering the truth.'

'The truth,' said Marcel, 'is perhaps what we do not want.'

Before Jacques had an opportunity to ask precisely what his friend meant, Mary, who all the while had remained wretched and silent where she sat, drawn up to the old wooden table, chose that very moment to speak.

'Will she tell them everything, do you think? Everything that we have told her even if it's not relevant, even …' she paused, '… if it's quite awful?'

It was like a feeling of *déjà vu*. They all experienced it. Mary had been so quiet and withdrawn that they had again all but forgotten her existence. Her entry now into the conversation had the effect of rousing them all from their lethargy. Madame Renard in particular, who had all but slumped back in her seat, as if retreating from the world around her, now looked up not a little perplexed. As it happened, it was fortuitous that they should at that moment have become awakened and alert. For only seconds later the door, which obscured the policemen from their sight, opened and Rose Simpson came out.

Chapter Seventeen

Rose Simpson's interview could not be said to have ended well. She did not think so and neither did Inspector Deacon, or even young Sergeant Perkins come to that. True, it had started promisingly enough, even if the inspector appeared slightly more formal towards her than she would have liked, or was strictly necessary, given their past association. As the interview had unfolded, she felt that they had reverted to their usual positons albeit rather grudgingly on the inspector's part. He had started to include her in a review of the case, had shared his thoughts and had considered her opinions. They might have been back at Dareswick Hall with all its grandeur and finery, instead of Madame Renard's pokey and suffocating little flat. Instead of sipping lukewarm tea made by herself on a stove in an area that resembled more a cupboard than a kitchen, hot tea and biscuits might have been brought in to them by an attentive footman. It was these memories, she realised thinking back on it that had perhaps lulled her into a false sense of security, her thoughts dwelling too much in the past than in the present.

Certainly she had not expected him to have spoken as he had done at the conclusion of the interview, a cold edge to his voice and his face unbearably solemn, as if suddenly encased by a mask.

'Now, I want you to promise me something, Miss Simpson,' he had said.

'Oh? And what is that?' Immediately she had been on her guard, reluctant to promise him anything until she knew what it was that he asked of her.

'I want you to promise me that you will go home now, the very moment this interview is finished. I don't want you to harbour any notions that you will undertake an investigation of your own into this murder. I don't want you to start asking all sorts of questions of goodness knows who. I don't want – '

'You can't possibility ask me to promise you all that,' protested Rose.

'I don't see why not, Miss Simpson,' said Inspector Deacon rather curtly. A frown had appeared on his forehead distorting his rather handsome features. It suddenly occurred to Rose that he had scowled at her rather a lot during the course of the interview. 'It makes perfect sense that the investigation of a murder should be left to the police to carry out. It is our job to gather the evidence and to see that the guilty person is brought to justice. We are the experts in the matter and we can do without having to – '

'To do what exactly?' demanded Rose. 'Why, you sound just like Inspector Bramwell! You'll be patting me on top of my head next and telling me to go off and be a good girl or some such thing equally frightful.'

Rose heard a noise behind her which sounded very much like Sergeant Perkins desperately trying not to laugh. The thought of the sergeant doubled up with suppressed laughter brought a smile to her lips. She stole a glance at the inspector to determine his reaction to the turn of events. To his credit, she thought he was doing his upmost to conceal a smile himself. Certainly he coloured as she stared at him.

'If I do sound like Inspector Bramwell, well, then all well and good. Perhaps, Miss Simpson, it is no bad thing,' said Inspector Deacon. 'I know that in the past I have been rather indulgent in allowing you to help us with our investigations, encouraged you even, but now it is quite different, don't you see that?'

'To be perfectly honest, no I don't,' said Rose.

'Then I shall set it out for you very clearly. You have earned something of a reputation for being a bit of an amateur sleuth. I won't say it isn't justified, because of course it is. Your help has been invaluable to us in the past.'

'Well, then I don't understand – '

'If you would only let me finish than I will explain,' snapped the inspector.

Admonished, Rose sat back in her chair and stared at the floor. Inappropriate though it was, given the circumstances, she had an overwhelming desire to laugh. The only thing that restrained her from doing so was being awfully afraid it would not be well received. She wished she could turn around and see how the sergeant was taking it all. Surely witnesses and suspects weren't usually spoken to like this. Instead she could only but imagine what the sergeant must be thinking.

'It is for that very reason that I ask you not to involve yourself in this case,' Inspector Deacon was saying, cutting through her meditations. His voice had lost its cold edge. Now, if anything, it held a quiet sincerity, which encouraged Rose to look up. All of a sudden she no longer felt a wish to laugh.

'The suspects in this case are your friends and colleagues. They will be fully acquainted with your successes. Don't you see what that means? The murderer will perceive you as an undoubtable threat. A threat that might require being dealt with. I not only want you to promise me that you won't try and investigate, I want you to say as much to the people outside this room. I'm sure that you can think of something to say. Perhaps that the murder is too close to home and you would feel uncomfortable investigating it. Yes … something along those lines, I think.'

'I am afraid, Inspector, that is quite out of the question,' said Rose.

'Oh, do be reasonable, Rose,' Inspector Deacon said, beginning to lose his temper. 'Why must you insist on being so difficult? Don't you see that what I am saying is only for your own good? It's for your safety. Surely you see that? And for our convenience, I hasten to add. I do not wish to find myself investigating another murder.' His expression softened, and traces of the Inspector Deacon she knew appeared. 'Look here. I daresay you feel a moral obligation to investigate Miss Beckett's murder, what with her being a work colleague of yours.'

'Yes, I do. But I'm afraid it's not just that,' said Rose quickly. 'They've all asked me, you see, to investigate Sylvia's murder, I mean. And I said I would. And really, I can't go back on my word, even if I wanted to, which I don't. So it's no good asking me to tell them that I have changed my mind, because I simply won't.' She hurriedly pushed back her chair, making a scraping noise on the floor as she did so, and got to her feet. Quickly she made for the door before she lost her nerve, or the inspector tried to appeal further to her better judgment. 'And even if they hadn't asked me, I wouldn't have been able to stop myself. How could I possibly justify it to myself? How could I in all conscience investigate the murders of people I don't know in grand houses, and yet not investigate the murder of someone I have known for a number of years in a place I consider to be almost my second home?'

The inspector looked as if he was taking a moment or two to consider his response. Aware that she had the stage but that the time afforded her would be brief, she ploughed on, desperately trying to avoid looking at

Sergeant Perkins. How she wished he wouldn't sit there with his mouth wide open. It really was rather unbecoming for a sergeant.

'And if it's my safety you're concerned about,' she said, pressing her advantage, 'well, it would make much more sense, wouldn't it, if we combined our knowledge and worked together? We'd probably solve this case much more quickly and I'd spend less time being in danger.'

Anxious looks greeted her return to the sitting room-cum-dining room. Rose gave a nod and a brief smile of encouragement, but received very little for her efforts. Every person seemed to turn away from her, as if she carried the stench of death about her. She had expected them to crowd around her and ask numerous questions. What was the inspector like? Did he have a particular suspect in mind? How long would they be expected to wait in this room? Surely, given the hour, the rest of the interviews could wait until morning? But instead there was an uneasy silence, like the quiet before a storm.

'The inspector would like to speak with you in a few minutes,' she said, bending over the seated figure of Madame Renard. The proprietor looked up at her apprehensively, almost as if she expected some sort of a trap.

Rose had spoken softly. Jacques, perhaps realising that she wished to have a few quiet words with his mother, relinquished his seat on the sofa with a backwards glance and joined Marcel Girard at the window. It seemed a futile action for neither man was able to see out into the street; the curtains had been pulled hastily across some time earlier to shut out the night's sky. Instead of giving the room a cosy feel, as might have been expected, the shutting out of the world beyond the window sought only to add to the feeling of isolation and confinement.

'He'll want you to tell him everything,' said Rose, seating herself on the sofa beside her employer. 'He will want to know the sort of relationship you had with Sylvia, whether you were on friendly terms and all that.'

'The girl was my employee,' the proprietor said rather coldly. 'Of course we were on friendly terms. Yes, I know what you are going to say, that the girl could be difficult and rude. Do you not think I know that? But the police, they do not need to know this. It is most unfair to the poor girl, this speaking ill of the dead. And there is no point to it, no point at all. It had nothing to do with her death.'

'Very likely, but even so you will need to tell them what she was like. They will want to know her character and whether she had any enemies or anyone who might have wished to do her harm. You see, anything we tell them, no matter how irrelevant or unimportant we might think it, may prove frightfully valuable in helping them to build up a picture of her. You do see that, don't you?'

'If you say so.' Madame Renard sounded distinctly uninterested. She went as far as moving an inch or so closer to her end of the sofa. 'But I do not know why you say this only to me. What about Mary? She was Sylvia's particular friend. If anyone knew the girl's character, it is she.'

'And the inspector will be asking her too. He will want you to run through the events of the evening as you perceived them,' continued Rose. 'And he'll want you to tell him if you saw anything suspicious.'

'How could I?' snapped Madame Renard. 'My hands, they were too full. I did not have the time to see anything suspicious.'

'Well, you may have seen something and not realised it was significant.'

Madame Renard's only response was to sniff, as if something distasteful had been placed under her nose.

'The police will be asking the same questions of everyone,' continued Rose. 'Please, you mustn't withhold any information.'

Madame Renard gave her such a look as to infer that she had nothing to suppress even if she had been so minded.

Rose paused a moment before proceeding. She had been thinking about how best to moot what was on the tip of her tongue to ask. She had known that it would not be an easy matter, but it was further hindered by Madame Renard's current mood, which appeared to be neither very accommodating nor particularly agreeable. She was unlikely to suffer Rose putting questions or suggestions to her, particularly if she considered them of a distasteful nature. And of course what Rose had to say was unpalatable and, in the grand scheme of things, likely to have little relevance to the murder. But ask it she must. If nothing else it had been troubling her ever since Madame Renard had first mentioned it earlier that evening.

'You will need to tell the inspector what you told me just before the fashion show. Do you remember what you said? You will need to tell him that you suspected Sylvia of being a thief.'

Madame Renard's jaw dropped and her eyes bulged. For a moment she gaped helplessly at Rose like a fish out of water, stranded and defenceless, unsure what to say or do next. She clasped her hands together in her lap and looked down at them almost as if she were surprised that they were there. Rose meanwhile waited, almost with bated breath. She had anticipated that her employer would show some resistance to the suggestion that she volunteer information on Sylvia's criminal activities to the police. What she had not expected, however, was that Madame Renard should react in this exaggerated fashion. It betokened a woman driven more by fear than by a natural reluctance to divulge something unpleasant about the deceased.

While Rose waited for Madame Renard to voice her objection at the very least, her mind returned to the conversation that had been alluded to. What had been said exactly? It was difficult to recollect anything but Madame Renard's righteous indignation at the fact that one of her employees was a thief. She had decided, indeed spoken with absolute certainty, that Sylvia must be the thief. But she had not mentioned being in possession of any proof, only having an unwavering feeling of the fact. What was it she had said exactly? Rose knew it had made her feel uneasy at the time. Of course, if it hadn't been for the fashion event she would have pressed her further, demanded that her employer tell her how she was so sure and what she intended to do …

'You said you would put a stop to her activities,' Rose said, the words flooding back suddenly into her mind. She remembered the determined and resolute way that Madame Renard had spoken. An awful thought crossed her mind unbidden. It remained there only briefly, but nevertheless she felt compelled to give it voice. '"See if I don't!" That is what you said. I didn't think anything of it at the time. But … please, tell me you didn't. …no, I …'

She broke off from what she was saying and stared at her employer, unable to bring herself to proceed with such an accusation. How she wished that she had not felt compelled to articulate her thoughts. However, it had the desired effect. Something of the horror of what she felt must have shown itself on her face. For it seemed to provide the necessary impetus the proprietor needed to throw off her indifference and take a hold of herself.

'Don't be stupid, Rose. I meant nothing by it. You think I stabbed the girl with the scissors because she stole a couple of pairs of silk stockings? Pah! It is ludicrous, what you are suggesting.'

'I know. Of course it is. I'm sorry ... it was stupid of me to think ... I just remembered how very angry you were, that's all ...'

'That is not surprising, eh? Anyway, you do not need to concern yourself. It does not matter. I made a mistake,' said Madame Renard. 'Sylvia was not the thief.'

But you said – '

'Yes, but I was wrong. I know that now.'

'But you were so sure. And if Sylvia wasn't the thief, then that means – '

'I don't want you to say another word about it, do you hear me?' The words were said so forcefully and with such abruptness that they invited no contradiction. To remove any further doubt, if indeed it were needed showing that the matter was now closed and should not be referred to again, Madame Renard looked at her so coldly that it was all Rose could do not to retreat to her end of the settee. For the second time within half an hour she felt herself thoroughly admonished. But if nothing else, it was proof at least that she had touched a nerve and she felt duty bound to worry at it, like a dog with a bone, in order to uncover the truth. She was in danger of incurring her employer's wrath by so doing, but really there was no alternative. Still she hesitated.

Before she was required to make a definite decision as to whether to pursue the subject or not, it was perhaps fortunate that at that very moment the door opened to admit Sergeant Perkins come to summon Madame Renard for interview. Everyone turned to stare at the newcomer; not one of them looked away. The room became restive with suppressed anticipation. The proprietor did not move. After a moment in which no one did anything except look rather guiltily at the sergeant, as if they all had secrets to hide, Madame Renard roused herself. She took a deep breath and seemed to collect herself, as if she were preparing to engage with a difficult customer. As she got to her feet, she put her hand out and clutched at Rose's sleeve. The gesture was something of a desperate one, revealing an anxiety that Rose had not imagined the woman possessed.

156

Even so there was nothing weak about the grasp which felt strong and insistent. Madame Renard clearly had no intention of letting go her grip until she had got her own way.

'You will come in with me, Rose,' she said. The proprietor spoke as if it were a statement rather than a question. She might have been asking Rose to tidy one of the counters or help a customer with her purchases. Rose herself had some reservations in complying with the request. If nothing else, she was reluctant to face Inspector Deacon so soon after their last encounter. He had made it quite clear that he did not wish her to investigate Sylvia's murder. She had made it equally plain that she had every intention of doing just that. Barely more than a few minutes had elapsed for him to reconcile himself to the fact. For all she knew, he had just been complaining about her to that sergeant of his. Certainly Sergeant Perkins was regarding her with interest. If she did not know better, she would have sworn there was a twinkle in his eye. The inspector might be none too pleased to see her enter the room with Madame Renard but, she reasoned, he would not be unduly surprised.

It took a moment for Rose to realise that Madame Renard was still speaking to her, probably because she had lowered her voice so considerably that when she spoke it was barely above a whisper.

'You won't mention the thefts, will you? Sylvia wasn't the thief. It had nothing to do with her death.'

Chapter Eighteen

'If you don't mind my saying, sir,' said Sergeant Perkins, as soon as the door had closed behind the retreating form of Rose Simpson, 'I think the young lady has a bit of a point.' He glanced over at his superior officer and took his silence to signal a willingness to hear what his subordinate had to say. 'What I mean, sir, is that it stands to reason, doesn't it, that if we work together, we'll go further forward? And Miss Simpson, I reckon she has a way with her. Sergeant Lane told me people open up to her as they wouldn't do to us. They confide in her, like. She's such an ordinary looking young lady, but there's something about her all the same, at least there must be for that young earl of hers to be so taken with her.'

Inspector Deacon gave his sergeant something of an exasperated look. Sergeant Perkins, fearing that the inspector was likely to interrupt him before he had made his point, hurriedly ploughed on.

'These people, they're friends of hers, aren't they? They'll confide in her and even if they don't she'll know if they're lying or if they're hiding something.'

'But that is part of the trouble, Perkins. Miss Simpson has a tendency to form an opinion regarding someone's innocence early on in an investigation. And when she does, she goes all out to protect them, even if it's obvious to the most casual observer that they're hiding something which may, or may not, have something to do with the case in hand. I'm not saying that they necessarily turn out to be the murderer, but she lets her feelings intervene. She can't look at the position dispassionately as we can. She can't be objective. And I hasten to add that's with people she hardly knows, one's with whom she has only the briefest of acquaintance. Can you imagine what she'll be like in this investigation?'

'I daresay you're right, sir, but you heard what she said just now. Whatever we say, even if you talk to her until you're quite blue in the face, you won't be able to persuade her to leave this case to us to investigate.'

'You're right, Sergeant, she'll investigate regardless of what we say,' said Inspector Deacon emitting a sigh. 'And, if I'm honest, I can't say I blame her. Not entirely anyway.'

A picture of the defiant Rose appeared in his mind's eye, and he did his best to suppress a smile lest his sergeant should see. Rose Simpson in a dress shop was rather different from Rose Simpson in a sprawling country estate, the surroundings in which he had encountered her before. Then, despite knowing her profession, her social standing had seemed considerably beyond his own, as if the social class of her friends and acquaintances had somehow rubbed off onto her so that in his eyes she too was an aristocrat. Now he saw her for what she truly was, in her own environment. The shop, with all its pretentions of grandeur, was still little more than a backstreet boutique. It was not the sort of establishment to be frequented by the likes of Lady Lavinia Sedgwick or Lady Celia Goswell. It was also possible that the house Rose shared with her mother was no more furnished than Madame Renard's flat. In the same way, he remembered that she had not appeared disconcerted by the meanness of her employer's kitchen facilities and had apparently thought nothing of waiting on them with cups of tea as the servants, employed in the grand establishments in which she had been a houseguest, had attended on her.

A spasm of pain from his injured leg brought him to his senses. He rose from his seat and made a turn of the room as best he could given its limited dimensions. He was further hindered by both his stick and the abundance of furniture, the latter partially due to the addition of the two chairs from the shop. Unless he was mistaken, it was likely that another chair would be required, which would only make the room more cluttered and confined.

'This damned thing,' he said, stopping and pointing to his injured leg, 'it has made me more cautious. It's made me realise how very dangerous police work can be. But for a bad shot, I might have been killed. Someone like Miss Simpson, she plays at investigating a murder almost as if it were a game – '

'I say, sir, I don't think that's quite fair,' interjected the sergeant.

'You are quite right, Perkins, my choice of words was not good. But what I mean is someone like Miss Simpson will not be cautious in her investigations. She will want to arrive at the truth, and she won't mind much if she takes some risks to achieve it, because she won't be convinced that there is any peril. If the murderer is found to be one of her friends or colleagues, then that is how she will view them, as a friend rather than as a murderer. She will expect them to behave to her as they always have, whereas you and I know how dangerous a cornered animal can be. After all the murderer will have nothing to lose if he were to do her harm and potentially much to gain. Remember, he can only be hung once.'

'What you're saying, sir, is the girl's a bit naïve. I daresay you're right, and of course you know her better than I do, but I reckon she'll be all right. It's not as if this is her first murder case, is it?'

'No, it isn't, more's the pity. It would seem that our Miss Simpson has got rather a knack for attracting murder wherever she goes.'

Before Madame Renard's interview could begin, Sergeant Perkins was dispatched to the shop to acquire an additional chair. Much to Rose's relief, Inspector Deacon gave no sign that he considered her an interloper in the proceedings. Instead, while they awaited the sergeant's return, he made much of shuffling the papers on the desk in front of him. He had risen on their entrance and remained standing as did Rose, who stood at her employer's shoulder in the guise of some guardian angel. Madame Renard had seated herself warily in the chair opposite the inspector, her back as straight as a rod. She was perched right on the chair's edge as if ready for flight.

Waiting afforded Inspector Deacon an opportunity to scrutinise the woman before him. She had on a long, black velvet dress over which she had thrown a silk shawl seemingly effortlessly, which had the effect only of accentuating her foreignness. Despite its finery, it seemed appropriate in the circumstances, reminding him of funeral garb as it did. Small and petite, and anything between forty and forty-five, in complexion Madame Renard inclined to Mediterranean, her olive skin smooth and unlined, her eyes dark. He could appreciate that there was a certain presence about the woman that belied her diminutive physique. Even as she entered the room, he noted that she carried herself well. To the inspector, she epitomised the typical Frenchwoman. He had the impression also of someone consumed with a pent up energy, which he assumed usually presented itself in expressive and flamboyant physical gestures and loud exclamations. This evening, however, the woman's demeanour was quiet. He imagined the energy bubbling under the surface, creating an inner turmoil. He knew the type well. The interview would more than likely proceed in one of two ways. The woman could be sullen and restive, fiddling with those great bangles of hers, but giving only monosyllabic answers. In which case the exchange was likely to be laboured and unfruitful. The inspector groaned inwardly. Conversely, there was also the possibility that Madame Renard might fly off the handle for little reason and become verbose. He knew the trick to achieving this was to touch a nerve or a subject on which the woman felt so strongly that she was unable to keep her emotions contained.

The sergeant returned and the chair was put in place. Rose sat down next to Madame Renard and the policemen resumed their seats.

'I understand that this is a very distressing time for you, Madame Renard, and that the hour is very late,' began Inspector Deacon. 'I shall try to keep my questions as brief as possible. It may therefore be necessary for me to speak to you again tomorrow.'

The proprietor gave him the briefest of nods to indicate that she understood what he was saying. There then followed the preliminary routine questions regarding Madame Renard's particulars, and Rose found her thoughts drifting off. She tried to visualise in her mind where this room was positioned in relation to the shop below. Were they directly above the kitchenette and storeroom, or above the storeroom and office-cum-dressing room? Perhaps part of their room edged over the shop floor itself. What a dismal little room this was. It felt intrusive to be in what was after all Madame Renard's bedroom of sorts, even if it did also serve the function of a study. She stared at the dark red curtain and thought of the bath and sink hidden behind it, nudging shoulders with the mean little cooking facilities, if one could even call them that. She looked up at the walls and ceiling and saw signs of damp and peeling paint. Her eyes focused next on the desk before her, which constituted so effective a physical barrier between policeman and suspects. The desk itself was a poor imitation of the one downstairs in Madame Renard's office, the latter piled so high with bills and correspondence that they had scattered on the floor when Marcel Girard had inadvertently knocked the desk while pacing the room …

'Now, I should like you to tell me about the doors to your shop, Madame,' the inspector was saying when Rose returned her attention to the conversation in hand. 'There are only the two, I understand, the main entrance, which is the shop door facing onto the street and used by your customers, and the door at the back of the storeroom opening out onto the next street?'

'Yes.'

'Now, just to help me get this straight in my own mind, am I right in thinking that no one could have come through the main door this evening without being admitted by you or one of your staff, that's to say a person could not just have walked in off the street?'

'No, they could not. The door, it was kept locked. No one could enter unless they were admitted. The event, it was by invitation only, you understand? The door was opened to let each person in and they were only admitted if they had an invitation.'

'And the guests? By that I mean your customers were allowed to have a guest or two accompany them, weren't they? I assume these guests didn't also have an invitation?'

'No. It was not necessary. They accompanied the customers.'

The proprietor gave the policeman a look which suggested that she thought he had asked a remarkably stupid question.

'What would happen if someone were to claim to be a guest of one of your customers and the customer in question did not happen to be there?'

'They would not be admitted.'

'You are quite sure of that?'

'Perfectly, Inspector.'

'Right, let's talk about this other door, the one in the storeroom opening onto the next street. Was it locked?'

'But of course. Mary had to get the key to let everyone out. That door, it is always kept locked. My stock, it is stored in that room.'

'And the key, it is kept in the kitchen under the sink, I believe?'

'Yes. And if you are thinking one of my customers got the key and let in some accomplice through the storeroom, you are wrong, Inspector. The key, where it is hidden, it is not obvious.'

'So what you are saying, Madame, if your scenario is correct, that's to say someone was let in, it could only have been done by one of your staff?'

'Or by a member of your family?' piped up Sergeant Perkins. 'Your son perhaps? I'll wager he knew where you kept that key. I daresay even that Monsieur Girard had a fair idea, didn't he?'

There was an awkward silence. Rose stole a sideways glance at her employer. The proprietor had not turned around to face the sergeant, and yet the woman had been clearly affected by the interruption. She might well have forgotten that the sergeant was there, positioned out of their sight, as he was. Or perhaps it was what he had said that had disturbed her so deeply. Madame Renard had her hands clasped tightly in her lap, yet they were not still. There was a nervous movement to them which betrayed her emotions, accentuated by the slow jangling of the bangles, which created an odd music in the stillness. Madame Renard looked down at those hands as if she were trying to entreat them to be motionless.

Rose, who knew her employer well, and was fully versant with how she was likely to react given almost any situation was nevertheless perplexed. This was not because of what the young and rather tactless sergeant had said, for the inspector had implied as much. It was rather how the proprietor was reacting, not only in this interview, but to the whole situation. Madame Renard was a woman who expressed herself in dramatic and flamboyant gestures, who threw up her arms and spoke in exaggerated terms on almost every subject. Why, look how she had reacted when informed that Lavinia could not attend the fashion event. She had said something along the lines that it was a disaster, no less than a catastrophe and that her reputation would be ruined. All nonsense of course, because at worse it had been an inconvenience and something of an embarrassment. And yet with a murder on her premises, and the victim a member of her staff no less, her reaction had been remarkably subdued. One would have been forgiven for expecting histrionics on a grand scale. If Rose had been asked before how she anticipated Madame Renard would react in the event of such an occurrence, she would have said that her employer would be wailing the place down and literally tearing out her hair. She would certainly not have expected that she would be sitting quietly as she was now, albeit clearly agitated. One could put it all down to shock, of course. Perhaps everything was yet to register clearly in her mind. Perhaps the histrionics had merely been postponed or deferred, and when they did materialise they would be even more dramatic than could ever be imagined.

'What exactly are you suggesting, Inspector?' asked Rose, more to break the silence than anything else. 'There was no need to unlock the storeroom door. We were all in the shop when Sylvia was murdered. Or are you proposing that one of us unlocked the door during the course of the evening to admit the murderer?'

'We are looking at all possible avenues, Miss Simpson. That is just one of many we must consider. At this stage we want to know only if such a thing would be feasible.'

'I suppose it would be. But it's rather unlikely, isn't it? For one thing, Monsieur Girard was going backwards and forwards between the storeroom and the shop all evening. If the murderer did come in that way, he would be taking an awful risk of being discovered, unless of course Monsieur Girard was the person who unlocked the door for him. You had better talk to Mary. She'll be able to tell you whether the storeroom door was unlocked when she tried the key.'

'Thank you, Miss Simpson, for your words of wisdom. We will naturally be speaking to Miss Jennings in due course, and of course Monsieur Girard himself. Now, if you don't mind,' the inspector paused to bestow on her a particularly stern look, 'I would be grateful if you would refrain from interrupting for the rest of this interview. Otherwise I will have no alternative but to ask you to leave.'

'In which case I would refuse to answer any more of your questions,' said Madame Renard.

This was so unexpected that without exception they all turned to stare at her.

'That is of course your prerogative, Madame. But I don't think I need to tell you that you would be taking a very grave risk if you refused to answer our questions. By that I mean the conclusions that we would be bound to draw from your refusal to answer would not be favourable. If you are innocent of this murder, you would not be going the right way to make us think so.'

'You think I murdered Sylvia? That is ridiculous!'

A flush of colour appeared on Madame Renard's neck and crept up across her face. Her eyes which had been dull and half veiled by drooping lids and heavily blackened lashes, opened wide and bright. For a moment she even looked as if she might get up and wave her arms about, but presumably on reflection she thought better of it. Her attitude of listless, sullen indifference was replaced by an animated being. This was the Madame Renard with whom Rose was better acquainted. She had been concerned by her employer's withdrawn and dispirited state. Really, she should have been pleased at the change. Instead she felt inexplicably afraid.

Having provoked a reaction, the inspector showed no signs of relinquishing his advantage.

'We must investigate every possibility and until we have eliminated a person from our enquiries, they remain a suspect,' Inspector Deacon said rather coldly. 'Now, I should like you to tell me about Miss Beckett if you will, Madame. What sort of an employee was she?'

'Sylvia … ah, she was the sweetest of girls. My customers, they were very fond of her.'

'Indeed? I was told she could be difficult and uncooperative.'

'I do not need to ask from whom you heard such stories.' The proprietor paused to glare at Rose, who herself coloured visibly.

'It doesn't matter who told us,' said the inspector rather abruptly. 'Are you saying it wasn't true?'

'The girl had her moments, like everyone, when she was not on top form as you English say. She could be a little rude sometimes. When this happened I took her aside and had a quiet word with her. The girl, she was receptive.'

'Was she indeed? I am glad to hear it. I understand she was very fond of your son, and he of her.'

What? *Non*! Who has told you such lies?'

Madame Renard looked indignant. Her eyes blazed and she leant forward in her seat so that she appeared to loom over the desk towards the inspector. Any moment now, Rose thought, she is going to wag a finger at him.

'It was a mild flirtation that is all. My son, he is a very handsome man and of course he has the good prospects, yes. He could have any girl he likes and he will set his sights high. Higher than poor Sylvia. Jacques, he was pleasant to the girl, nothing more. I am not saying she did not read more into it than there was. She was that silly sort of girl who attributes serious intentions where there are none. She went about with idle young men whose idea was only to amuse themselves. I will not speak ill of the dead, Inspector.' Madame Renard paused a moment before, having started on a subject on which she had very strong views, she did just that. 'Poor Sylvia was not at all a satisfactory girl when it came to boys. She was young and pretty and very popular with men. She was one of those girls who get themselves talked about.'

'I see. But your son, he was not particularly fond of her, you say? It has been suggested to us that you were afraid Miss Beckett and your son had formed an attachment.'

'Nonsense! I have told you he did not like the girl.'

'You said no such thing. Isn't it correct that your main reason for securing your son a job at Harridges was to get him away from the clutches of Miss Beckett?'

'No! He needs to learn the trade.'

'Shall I tell you what I think, Madame Renard? I think your son and Miss Beckett were very fond of each other. I also think that you did not consider the girl to be good enough for him, your words I think, and did your best to distance them from one another. Unfortunately for you, Monsieur Renard came to the fashion event this evening and saw Miss Beckett wearing a dress which, I have been reliably informed, made her look like a princess. He was so taken by her appearance that he uttered an exclamation that was sufficiently loud that it made people turn around and stare at him.'

'That is not right. He was not fond of her. She … yes, as I have said she may have been fond of him, but what girl wouldn't have been? But she was not going to marry Jacques. My son, he could see the sort of girl she was. Pah! She gave herself airs and graces that one. The way that she glanced around my shop as if it were already hers; I saw it in her eyes. The way she put her nose in the air and looked at the mannequins and the displays. I could see what was going on in her mind. She was thinking, when this is my shop, I shall put this there, I will have different mannequins, I will sell only couture, I will be mistress of this shop that is what she thought. She was a simple girl. She thought she was too clever for me, but no, I saw through her, her "Madame" this and her "Madame" that. I see what she is after. She would not get it, my shop … my son. She would not get them at all.'

All the while she had been talking, the proprietor's voice had been rising in both volume and pitch. Her tone had begun measured, but as she had worked herself up into more and more of a state, her words had come out tumbling over each other until she was speaking very fast indeed. Rose thought the whole thing the most awful spectacle. More than once she had been tempted to put out a hand in an attempt to stem the flow. She knew, however, from bitter experience it would not have done any good. Madame Renard was determined to have her say, and nothing would stop her. If possible, Rose did not wish to draw any more attention to Madame Renard's outburst. In particular, she did not want the policemen to realise how alarmed she had been by it. Far better to pretend it was a regular occurrence and that the proprietor meant nothing by it. It was only words after all.

'Over my dead body,' added Madame Renard, as if to avoid any lingering doubt regarding how strongly she felt on the matter.

'Perhaps it would be more apt to say over *her* dead body,' said Inspector Deacon quietly.

Behind them Rose heard the sergeant suppress a chuckle.

Chapter Nineteen

The colour that had risen so vividly in Madame Renard's cheeks disappeared, replaced by a chalky pallor. The eyes that only moments before had been alert and bright, became dull and clouded. The hands went back in her lap, clenched tightly together and held fast, as if she were afraid that they had a will of their own. She sat there with her head bowed, as if she knew she had said too much. Looking at her now, Inspector Deacon was certain that he would obtain little more information from her this evening. She would hold him alone responsible for goading her into a temper, so that her words had come cascading out of her mouth almost of their own accord, with little thought given to what she was saying.

'I would like you to tell me something, Madame,' said the inspector after a while. 'We are particularly interested in the time between Miss Beckett returning to the dressing room in that silver gown of hers, which seems to have sparked such a reaction, and when the woman screamed drawing everyone's attention to the fact that the curtain was alight.'

'I can't tell you anything, Inspector. I saw nothing. Lady Celia, she was very angry. She clawed at my arm. Look, you can see the bruises where her fingers dug into my flesh.' She pushed up the sleeve of her dress to the elbow reveal two angry black smudges on her forearm. 'It was not my fault if the girl, Sylvia, chose to defy my orders. Yet to hear her talk you would have thought that I'd worn the dress myself. I did my best to stop her making a scene. That woman, Lady Celia, yes? She spoke so loudly, everyone could hear. I saw nothing because I was trying to placate her.'

'But I am right in thinking that, where you were standing, you would have been facing the curtains and the candelabra? You didn't perhaps look up for a moment and see something?'

'I told you. I saw nothing.'

'It might have been something very small,' persisted the inspector. 'Perhaps someone standing rather close to the candles, or perhaps holding the curtain in their hands? They might have been pretending to admire the fabric.'

'No. The first I was aware of anything was when I heard the woman scream.'

'Did you see who screamed?'

'No, I did not. And I am quite, quite sure, Inspector. You do not need to ask me again. My answer, it will not change. My head, it was turned towards Lady Celia all the time.'

'What about after the scream? Did you by chance see anyone walk over to the corridor in, shall we say, a deliberate fashion?'

'No, I don't think so. It is hard to tell. People were running all over the place. It was not possible to say where they were going.'

'And what about before the scream? Let us say the time between Miss Beckett returning to the dressing room and the scream itself. Did you see anyone walk across the shop and disappear under the arch then?'

'No.'

There had been a slight hesitation before Madame Renard had given her monosyllabic answer. Rose had picked up on it immediately, and she felt certain the policemen had also. It had been another trap, set to see if the proprietor would answer truthfully. And it was a test that, without a doubt, she had failed.

Rose walked out of the room with Madame Renard. It was possible that Inspector Deacon would have permitted her to remain and discuss the proprietor's interview with them, drawing conclusions from the answers given. However, she felt little would be achieved by this, for she knew what they would be saying, as clearly as if she were in the room with them now.

Madame Renard had not given a good account of herself. She had come across as highly strung and volatile. When the need arose she had shown herself capable of a violent temper. The police would consider her just the sort of person to pick up a convenient pair of scissors, which just happened to be lying close at hand, and stab Sylvia in a moment of anger. To make matters worse, she had made it very clear how much she had despised the murdered girl, particularly regarding the supposed relationship between Sylvia and her son. It was clear to the most casual observer, and Inspector Deacon was far from being that, that Madame Renard adored her son and would stop at nothing to protect him. And if that wasn't enough in itself, she had appeared to lie about seeing her son go through the arch into the corridor. Or was it possible that she might not have seen him, deeply embroiled as she had been in discussions with Lady Celia? They might have thought no more of it, or at least given her the benefit of the doubt, had that slight hesitation not given her away.

All this and more passed through Rose's head. It would have been enough to engross her thoughts, but there was something else that was on her mind. An additional reason for not wanting to remain in the room at the back, huddled in its close confines with the policemen. She must have a word with Jacques Renard. It might well be her only opportunity. She surveyed the room. Madame Renard had resumed her seat on the sofa and, always the attentive son, Jacques was bent over his mother now ascertaining how she had fared and whether or not she required any further refreshment. While she awaited a suitable opening to draw the young man aside, Rose was provided with an opportunity to consider further something that had been worrying her throughout the interview. She thought how fortunate it was that the inspector had not picked up upon it. It seemed to her so very obvious a point, it was almost remiss of him not to have done so. Thinking about it now, she realised this matter had been troubling her for a while. Why, even Lady Celia had enquired about it during the very brief time she had spent in the shop earlier that day. If Rose remembered rightly, the proprietor had been moaning about the way Sylvia behaved towards her customers. She had made her complaints following Rose's suggestion that the girl be the mannequin in Lavinia's absence. Madame Renard had referred to the girl's bad manners and said that she would scowl at the customers and frighten them away. It had been an exaggeration of course, but it had prompted Lady Celia to make the observation that if that was the case, she was surprised Madame Renard employed the girl. And hadn't Rose herself often wondered that? Why had Madame Renard continued to employ Sylvia as a shop assistant when she found the girl so unsatisfactory and wanting?

Rose would once have believed it was because the proprietor wished to keep an eye on the relationship developing between her son and Sylvia. But Jacques had effectively been removed from contact with Sylvia following his employment at Harridges. She recalled how Madame Renard had responded to Lady Celia. She remembered how the proprietor had appealed to her to reinforce her claim that Sylvia possessed some redeeming qualities. At the same time, Madame Renard had turned scarlet and fiddled with a button on her blouse. Why hadn't it occurred to Rose before? It was all so obvious when one thought about it now. There really could only be one logical explanation, one that fitted all the pieces. Sylvia had had a hold over Madame Renard, the possible nature of which for the moment alluded her.

It was with this thought foremost in her mind that she became aware that Jacques had left off his attentions to his mother and now seemed intent on drawing Rose aside.

'How did it go? My mother's interview, I mean?' he said, speaking quietly.

'I'm afraid it could have gone better. At first she appeared rather uncooperative and then … well, she as good as lost her temper with the inspector.'

'Did she indeed?' Jacques frowned. 'We thought we could hear raised voices, Marcel and I.'

'Jacques, quickly, I must ask you something,' said Rose pulling at his arm. He could not fail to notice the urgency in her voice. 'The sergeant will be coming out any moment now asking for you to go in and be interviewed. We haven't much time, so please just answer my question. Don't, whatever you do, become all indignant and say you won't answer such a question. You'll just be wasting time. And you needn't bother asking me why I want to know.'

'Very well,' said Jacques, looking more than a little apprehensive. 'I should tell you, however, that you are beginning to alarm me very much.'

'That certainly isn't my intention. Listen to me. Earlier this evening, just before the fashion show, your mother told me that she thought Sylvia was a thief. She accused Sylvia of having stolen from the shop. She didn't say it to Sylvia's face. She said it to me. She told me that Sylvia had stolen from the till and had also taken some items, silk stockings, I think your mother said. As you can imagine, she was very upset about it. I daresay a few more items had gone missing than those she told me about.'

'I say, that's pretty rum. Poor Mama. I'd have thought better of Sylvia than that. Well, it just goes to show … We needn't say anything about this to the Inspector. I wouldn't want him to think badly of the girl. I say,' said Jacques, a sudden thought having struck him, 'you're not going to tell me that my mother tackled Sylvia about it this evening, are you?' His face had gone quite ashen.

'No, I don't think so. For one thing, she wouldn't have had the chance. But she did say that she would put a stop to Sylvia's activities.'

'Surely you don't mean – '

'No, I don't mean she killed her. As it happens, I think she changed her mind about Sylvia's guilt.'

'What do you mean?'

'I think she decided that the thief was someone else entirely. Your mother said as much to me this evening.'

'I take it she didn't say whom she suspected?'

'No, but I've got a pretty good idea.'

'Oh?'

'I think it was you.'

'Me? I say, Rose, that's a bit rich. I – '

'Shush! Keep your voice down. I am not saying the thief *is* you, only that I think your mother thinks it's you. Something must have happened to make her think so. Cheer up. For what it's worth, I don't think it was you.'

'Good. Because I mean to say, if I was going to steal from anyone it would be from Harridges, not from my own mother. For one thing they have a much better selection –'

'Do be quiet and take this seriously,' said Rose. 'I want to know why your mother changed her mind about Sylvia being the thief and decided it was you instead. What happened to make her suspect you? Have you any ideas? I think it would have had to have been something you did today. Up until just before the fashion show, she still thought Sylvia was the thief. But she subsequently changed her mind. That's to say after the murder, she definitely thought it was you. She must have thought things through during the fashion show.'

'Today, you say?' said Jacques, racking his brain. 'Well, all I can think is that it must be connected with when she caught me going through the papers on her desk. I was looking for something of mine that I thought I might have left there by mistake. Now I come to think of it, she did accuse me of acting like a thief in the night. You know how my mother is one to overreact. I suppose it didn't help matters that I refused to tell her what I was looking for.'

'What were you looking for?'

'Never you mind. It doesn't matter now. I've found out what happened to it.'

'That doesn't answer my question, Jacques.'

'No it doesn't, does it? It's funny,' said Jacques, 'at the time I thought she was more concerned with the idea that I had been rifling through her private correspondence than anything else. She didn't mention anything about money. I suppose she must have kept some in the office?'

Rose didn't reply. She was suddenly thinking about something else entirely.

Chapter Twenty

The door opened and Inspector Deacon studied Jacques Renard with interest. It was unlikely that the young man himself was aware that he was being so closely scrutinised, the inspector having perfected the art of appearing nonchalant when in reality he was feeling nothing short of a pent up excitement. The line 'the woman doth protest too much' had sprung unbidden to his mind at Madame Renard's fervent denial of an attachment between her son and the deceased. Sergeant Perkins, he noticed, seemed not to be so expert in the matter of concealing his own emotions. The inspector was therefore thankful that, for the most part, the young man would have his back to the sergeant, and that the inspector alone would be witness to Sergeant Perkins' assortment of smirks and grimaces. Good heavens, the man had already stubbed his pencil on his notebook and snapped the lead.

As Jacques Renard came into the room, the inspector was somewhat surprised to find Rose Simpson following in his wake. He had expected that she would accompany Mary Jennings, but not the proprietor's son. Inspector Deacon took in the young man's appearance. Dark-haired and bespectacled, there were the first tell-tale signs of a dark shadow around his mouth and cheeks that gave him something of a dishevelled look, at odds with his clothes, which were both good and fashionable in cut but somewhat creased. This, together with his hair, which stuck up in tufts, was the consequence of lounging so indifferently on the sofa. Yet the inspector noted that his eyes were bright and his shoes well-polished and tended to the view that, under normal circumstances, Jacques Renard would lean towards being well turned out.

However, this was anything but a usual situation in which Jacques Renard found himself. Generally of a cheery and affable disposition, due in part to an inner confidence, it was now obvious that he was ill at ease. As if to illustrate the point, beads of sweat had appeared on his forehead and the skin above his upper lip was also moist and glistened in the electric light.

Inspector Deacon began by asking the usual routine questions. When Monsieur Renard replied, his voice was something of a surprise to both policemen. Sergeant Perkins, in particular, had expected to hear heavily accented English fall from the man's lips, similar to that which they had heard spoken by his mother. Instead they discovered his voice was more that of a man who had been to Oxford rather than that of a Parisian. Inspector Deacon, in full view of Jacques Renard as he was, hid his astonishment well. Sergeant Perkins, not hindered by the same constraints, sat for a moment or two with his mouth wide open. The inspector was reminded of some words of wisdom that a great aunt had once bestowed upon his younger self. Something along the lines of it being rude to stare, but if one really must, at least close one's mouth to prevent the possibility of swallowing a fly.

'I understand that this must be distressing for you, Monsieur Renard. The deceased was a particular friend of yours, I believe.'

'Was she?' Jacques Renard looked first surprised and then decidedly flustered. 'Oh, I suppose she was in a way.'

'I was led to believe that you and Miss Beckett were rather fond of each other.'

'Well, I suppose we were after a fashion,' Jacques said rallying. 'I took her to the pictures once or twice, but we weren't really courting. We made each other laugh, that's all. I liked her because she spoke her mind and didn't care a jot what people thought of her, even my mother. You don't know how refreshing it is to find a girl like that.'

'So the two of you had formed an attachment of sorts?'

'Oh, nothing as grand as all that, Inspector. A little flirtation, that's all it added up to. No great love affair. I wasn't the least in love with Miss Beckett and she wasn't the least in love with me. When she wasn't putting on an act or sulking, she was a cheeky, fun sort of a girl to pass the time of day with. You needn't read any more into it than that.'

The inspector remained silent. Jacques fidgeted in his chair. He looked first at the ceiling, then at the floor, following which he decide to appeal to Rose.

'You tell the inspector, how it was, Rose. I daresay he'll listen to you.'

'Miss Simpson is here on sufferance, Monsieur Renard,' Inspector Deacon said sharply. 'She will not be contributing to this interview, will you Miss Simpson?' He bestowed on Rose a look which suggested that he was not to be tested on this issue. She returned his gaze with an affected look of innocence.

'I say, I think that's a bit harsh, Inspector. Much better to let Rose say a word or two. She'll be able to confirm that I'm telling you the truth. I mean to say, it seems an awful shame you wasting your time on me when you've got a murderer to catch.'

'How we choose to go about our enquiries is up to us, Monsieur Renard.'

'Oh, absolutely, Inspector,' Jacques said quickly. 'You know best of course. I'm not trying to teach my grandmother to suck eggs.'

'I'm glad we are agreed on that point. Now, if we may proceed, I – '

'Look here, Inspector, I think we may have started off on the wrong foot. It's my fault, I know, and I'd like to put it right if I can. What say, we start again?'

'All right, as you wish.' The inspector concealed a sigh. Jacques Renard was beginning to try his patience. The fellow probably meant well, but in his experience they were often the type to prove the most infuriating to interview.

'Well, there was a time when I had been rather fond of Miss Beckett, and she of me. It all came about more by chance than anything else. It sounds rather awful to say it now, but at the time we, that's to say, she and I thought it would be frightfully funny to see how Mama reacted to her darling boy to all intents and purposes stepping out with one of her employees. And not her favourite employee either, but one that was quite happy to give her a bit of cheek. You've met my mother, Inspector. She holds me on something of a pedestal. Nothing is too good for her son, and certainly no woman. It really is frightfully draining to be worshiped in such a way. I could do no wrong. So I suppose I was tempted to put it to the test. Sylvia … Miss Beckett and I thought it would be a dreadful hoot to see how Mama reacted if she knew we'd gone to the pictures together. But then, as it happened, we found that we rubbed along quite well.'

'I see, so at the time of her death – '

'I had seen very little of Sylvia for some time. My mother had packed me off to Harridges on the pretext of learning the trade, although I think it had rather more to do with keeping me away from what she perceived as Miss Beckett's clutches. Luckily for my mother and all her machinations, I found that I rather enjoyed it at Harridges. I still do, come to that. The people are a jolly decent crowd. We get up to no end of fun, I can tell you.' Jacques bent forward and lowered his voice in a conspiratorial

176

manner. 'If I'm honest, I much prefer working in a grand department store like Harridges to working in a small boutique like this one. It's rather nice not having my mother watch my every move, it gets a bit much for a chap. But you'd better not let my mother hear me say that. There would be all hell to pay.'

'And Miss Beckett, how did she take the prospect of not seeing you so often?'

'Rather well, Inspector. I thought she'd give me no end of grief. I'd been putting off telling her that I had … well … met another young lady as it happens. What Sylvia and I had …well, it was all only a bit of fun when all was said and done, as I've just been telling you. But I was dreadfully afraid that she might not see it quite like that. I thought she might have been bitterly disappointed that there had been a falling off of my affections, so to speak. I knew that she'd more than likely give me the rough end of her tongue and, to tell the truth, I'd rather worked myself up into a blue funk over the whole business.'

'I see. But when you told Miss Beckett, you discovered that she wasn't overly upset by the news?'

'That's right. It was yesterday as it happens, or should I say the day before yesterday, as it's passed the witching hour?' Jacques said, glancing at a rather splendid gold pocket watch, which Inspector Deacon could not help but think must have cost a pretty penny.

'The day before the fashion event?'

'Yes, that's the one. I was out on an errand and decided to pop in to see how Mama was faring, getting ready for the grand event and all. Miss Beckett was in the shop alone. I didn't notice that at first, otherwise I might have turned tail and not gone in. Anyway, she said her bit about me neglecting her, but I had the impression that she said it because she thought she ought to, rather than because she was particularly annoyed. It was all rather good humoured, our conversation. We teased and ribbed one another something rotten.' Jacques paused a moment and stared into the distance. 'You know, I'd forgotten how much fun Sylvia could be. I remember thinking it at the time. Then she said something that rather took the wind out of my sails.'

'Oh? And what was that?'

'She said something about having got herself a proper young man, one that was up in the world and had prospects. I can't say I fully believed her at the time. She was a one for exaggerating and … well, I supposed she was trying to make me feel jealous. Now I come to think of it, I suppose I was a bit. Of course, I know I had no right to feel like that. But it was the way she said it, it had me feeling a little intrigued. I do remember her saying that she could do better than the likes of me and no mistake, which riled me rather.'

Inspector Deacon inclined to the view that the young man had got what he deserved. A suitable retort sprung readily enough to his lips, but he refrained from uttering it. Instead he said:

'But you believed she might have been telling the truth? Well, it's certainly worth investigating. Make a note of that if you will, Sergeant.'

'If anyone knows if she had a young man, it would be Miss Jennings,' said Rose, contributing to the conversation for the first time. 'I'm inclined to think she may have done. Something she said to me last night makes me think – '

'Good heavens, I almost forgot you were there, Miss Simpson, you were so quiet. Not like you at all.' There was a twinkle in the inspector's eye, which was not lost on Rose. Much to her embarrassment, she felt herself blush. 'Now, what was that you were saying, Miss Simpson? Miss Beckett spoke of her young man to you?'

'No, Inspector, not as such. It's just thinking back, I remembered something she said.'

'Well, out with it. It's not like you to hold back, Miss Simpson.'

'Thank you, Inspector, you are very kind,' replied Rose rather primly. 'I think on second thoughts I might try and work things out in my own mind before I say anything. I should so hate to waste your time.'

Inspector Deacon raised his eyebrows and gave her a suspicious look. That he suspected that she wanted to investigate the matter further on her own, Rose had little doubt. It was contrary to his wishes and expressly what he had asked her not to do. She wondered if he would take umbrage. There was a moment or two of an uncomfortable silence while it seemed that they all awaited the inspector's response. Fortunately for Rose, Inspector Deacon decided not to press her, and returned his attention instead to Jacques Renard.

'Monsieur Renard, by you own admission, you knew the deceased well. Did she have any enemies, do you know? Can you think of anyone who may have wished to do her harm?'

'No, I can't, Inspector. I've been racking my brains all evening. I can't imagine who'd have wanted to kill Sylvia. She could be damned disagreeable when she put her mind to it, but to ....' He passed a hand over his hair in an agitated fashion. 'I feel pretty shaken up by it all, I can tell you.'

'I'd like you to take me through the events of this evening, if you will,' said Inspector Deacon, changing tack. 'I think I'm correct in saying that you arrived late to the event?'

'Yes. I didn't mean to be quite so late. It hadn't occurred to me that they'd lock the shop door. I caused quite a racket, I can tell you, banging on it. Mary ... Miss Jennings had to come and open it for me. It was frightfully embarrassing having everyone turn around in their seats and stare at me. Damned humiliating, I can tell you. I scurried off and as good as hid behind one of those frightful curtains.'

'You stood beside one of the drapes,' said Inspector Deacon slowly. 'And the candelabra, where was that in relation to where you were standing?'

'Next to me, as good as,' admitted Jacques rather guardedly. 'Look here, Inspector, if you're trying to insinuate that I had anything to do with that fire – '

'I was suggesting no such thing,' the inspector said rather curtly. 'Pray, do go on.'

'Well, I stayed where I was for the rest of the show. There was a shortage of chairs, so I couldn't have sat down, even if I'd wanted to. Anyway, I had a good enough view. For what it's worth, I thought Sylvia was making a jolly good stab at being a mannequin. She was certainly showing off Marcel's outfits to their best advantage. Mary handed me a glass of wine, and I remember thinking that the evening was proving far more enjoyable than I thought it would be. I tried to get Marcel ... Monsieur Girard's attention to let him know I thought it was all going well and that the audience liked his outfits. I hoped that I'd have the chance to say a few words to him, but he kept going backwards and forwards from the shop to the storeroom. I remember thinking he couldn't seem to settle. I daresay he was rather anxious. I know I would have been in his place. It was the first time he had shown any of his designs, you know.'

'Let's go on to when Miss Beckett appeared in that silver gown, shall we?'

'Oh, I wondered when you were going to mention that.'

'Did you, Monsieur Renard? Now why was that, I wonder?' Inspector Deacon shifted slightly in his seat. It was clear to Rose that he was trying to contain an inner excitement. After an unpromising start, the interview had suddenly become more interesting. Sergeant Perkins, she was sure, was sitting with his pencil poised. Even she was wondering what Jacques would say next.

'Miss Beckett appeared in the silver gown,' said Inspector Deacon, keen to move the interview forward. 'That made quite an impression on you, didn't it, Monsieur Renard?'

'It did, as it happens, but how did you know?' Jacques raised his eyebrows in surprise.

Rose had an overwhelming desire to tell him to think very carefully before he answered the inspector's next questions. She threw him a warning glance. Unfortunately, he was not looking in her direction, but staring at the inspector. From what little she could see by looking at his profile, he looked confused but not unduly distressed by the line of questioning.

'You were heard to give a loud exclamation.'

'Was I, by Jove? I suppose I might have done.'

'Yes, you were heard to say "Sylvia! Good Lord!'

'Was I? I can't say I remember saying it, but it wouldn't surprise me in the least if I had said something to that effect. It was such a surprise, you see.'

'To see Miss Beckett in that dress? Yes, I think I can understand how you must have felt. From what I hear the dress made her look like a princess.'

'It did, didn't it, Rose?' said Jacques, turning his attention to her. 'Everyone thought so. The audience was so excited. I couldn't quite believe it. It didn't seem real. More like a dream.'

'At which point Miss Beckett turned tail and retreated to the dressing room. And you, Monsieur Renard went after her.'

'No, I didn't, Inspector.'

'You were seen going through the arch. Monsieur Renard. Are you denying that you did that?'

'No. I went through the arch all right. But I wasn't going to the dressing room to see Sylvia. I went to the storeroom to see Marcel … Monsieur Girard.'

'Oh?'

'If you must know, I wanted to have it out with him.'

'Have what out with him, Monsieur Renard? Did you perhaps think he might be Miss Beckett's new young man, the one she referred to as having prospects? We've been looking into Monsieur Girard's background. It appears that his father is the owner of a large department store in Paris. Archambault's. You may have heard of it? Suffice to say his family is not short of money. Monsieur Girard can definitely be said to be a man of wealth.'

While Jacques and the Inspector were speaking, Rose allowed her mind to wander. A vision floated up before her eyes. She was opening the storeroom door and Sylvia and Marcel were pulling away from each other, as if they had been caught in some compromising position …

'Is he indeed? I never knew that. But you don't understand, Inspector I – '

'Oh, I think I understand quite well, Monsieur Renard. You went to confront Monsieur Girard about his relationship with Miss Beckett and then you went to see the deceased, to have it out with her as you put it.'

'No. I never saw Sylvia. And it's not what you think, Inspector. It's about the dress. I went to confront Marcel about the dress, not about Sylvia.'

'I don't understand –' began Inspector Deacon.

'Really, Inspector, it's all very simple if you'd just let me speak. I wanted to know why Sylvia was wearing that gown. My gown. You see, Marcel Girard did not design that dress, I did!'

Chapter Twenty-one

There was a moment or two of stunned silence where no one said anything at all. Jacques, having made his declaration seemed content to sit back in his chair as if drained of all energy, and merely to watch the effect of his words. A bright spot of a crimson shade had appeared on each of his cheeks like hastily applied rouge, giving him something of a toy soldier look. It occurred to Rose that the admission had cost him dear. She wondered if he doubted his ability as a designer and whether his dabbling in that field was something of a close guarded secret, which he would be rather embarrassed about should his work be criticised and found wanting.

Inspector Deacon looked as if he were having difficulty digesting this new piece of information. In truth, he was trying to determine what impact, if any, it had on his murder investigation. Rose could only imagine how the news had affected Sergeant Perkins. She conjured up in her mind various pictures of his astonished face.

'Let me get this straight in my mind,' said Inspector Deacon at last. 'Are you saying that you designed the silver gown that we've heard so much about, the one that the deceased was wearing when she died?'

Jacques nodded.

'Of course, we only have your word for that at this stage, Monsieur Renard. Monsieur Girard, when we ask him, will of course be able to collaborate your claim, or not, as the case may be.'

'It isn't his design,' said Rose, 'Monsieur Girard's I mean. It is Jacques'. As I told you earlier, Marcel's designs are good in a quiet sort of a way. They demonstrate a good eye for the cut of the fabric and how it's draped around the body. But the silver gown wasn't a bit like that. It was remarkable. Oh … it's so hard to describe. Words don't do it justice. There was something almost magical about it. I don't know why I didn't see it before. What a fool I've been.'

'See what?' asked Inspector Deacon.

'That the person who designed the silver gown could not possibly have been the same person who designed the other outfits.'

'I say, Rose, that's awfully good of you to describe my design as magical. Do you really think so?' A beam had spread across Jacques' face.

'In which case, you are suggesting are you not that Monsieur Girard was trying to pass off the gown as his own design?' Inspector Deacon did not give either Rose or the proprietor's son an opportunity to answer. 'Miss Simpson, I am right in thinking, am I not, that until now you all thought that Monsieur Girard had designed that dress?'

'Yes, of course.'

'If that's the case, Monsieur Girard was taking something of a risk. If nothing else, it was more than likely that you,' he paused to nod in Jacques' direction, 'as Madame Renard's son, would be attending the event. And he could hardly have expected you to hold your tongue while he implied that the gown was his own creation. Wouldn't he have been afraid that you'd create a scene?'

'The dress wasn't to be worn if you remember rightly, sir,' piped up Sergeant Perkins from his corner, making them all jump. 'That Lady Celia had seen to that. It wasn't to have been displayed at all.'

'Yes, but that was rather a late development in the proceedings. Up to the day of the event, the garment was definitely to have formed part of the display. If I am not mistaken, it was to be the *pièce de résistance*. I am right, am I not, Miss Simpson?'

'Yes, but –', began Rose

'Really, Inspector, you've got it all wrong,' protested Jacques, looking decidedly flustered. 'I do wish you'd permit me to say a word or two before you go accusing people of doing things they haven't done.'

'But you said just now that you went to confront Monsieur Girard over the dress,' protested Inspector Deacon.

'And so I did. I really had no idea that Marcel had arranged for my design to be made up. Even less that he had planned to show it at the fashion event. But he had no intention of pretending that it was his own work. He was going to present it this evening and announce that I was the designer.'

'He told you that, did he?' asked the inspector. He made no effort to keep the scepticism from his voice.

'Yes, he did. And whatever you may think, Inspector, I happen to believe him. Why, he was most insistent that I come to the event. He even went so far as to make me promise I would be there. He stressed that I must, at the very least, be there for the end. And, as you surmise, I suppose that's when he meant to unveil the silver gown.'

'When was this?' asked Rose.

'When was what?' asked Jacques.

'When did Marcel Girard make you promise you would attend this evening's event?'

'Miss Simpson, if you please, you are not here to ask questions,' protested Inspector Deacon.

'Shortly before the event. I went to Marcel's lodgings. He was getting ready, shaving and the like. He was none too pleased at being disturbed in his ablutions, I can tell you. He was rather preoccupied, to tell the truth. I don't think he much liked my arriving unannounced. I didn't stay long on account of it. I made my excuses and left.'

'What I don't understand,' said the inspector, 'is why Monsieur Girard went to all the trouble of having your design made up into a gown.'

'He did it because I don't have any belief in my own designs. He'd told me that he thought them very good. But ... well, I suppose I didn't really believe him. I certainly would never have had the confidence to display them in public. I didn't take them seriously, my designs. You see, I regarded them as a bit of a hobby. I remember Marcel telling me I had a talent and that it was an awful waste not to use it. He was quite cross about it, that I wasn't intending to exhibit my work, I mean.' Jacques paused for a moment or two and appeared to be looking at something in the distance far above the inspector's head. It was almost as if the wall had opened up and he was looking out far beyond at the stars. 'I couldn't quite believe it when I saw Sylvia in that gown. It took me a few moments to realise that it was my dress. As well as showing him my design, Marcel had made me describe it to him in the minutest detail, and suddenly I understood why.'

'You said he had the dress made up without your knowledge. How did he get hold of your design? Did you give it to him?' asked Inspector Deacon. 'I take it he wasn't just working from memory?'

'No. of course not. I showed it to him, my sketch, I mean. Although it was a bit more than a drawing. I'd written down all the details about material and embellishments and the like. We happened to be in my mother's office downstairs, and ... well, I must have put it down on the desk and forgotten to pick it up. That's when Marcel must have pocketed it. I couldn't remember when I had last had the design and have been frantically looking for it everywhere ever since. It's quite a relief, I must say, to know it isn't lost. I'm not sure I could have recreated it.'

'That is what you were looking for in your mother's office when she caught you going through her papers,' said Rose.

'Yes, it was. I felt damned embarrassed about it, I can tell you. Of course she wanted to know what I was doing. I couldn't bring myself to tell her. But I say, I have never known her be so angry.'

'Why didn't you just tell your mother the truth?' asked the inspector.

'I wanted to, really I did. But … well, she assumed I'd got myself into trouble. She probably thought I'd been gambling or something and owed someone some money. It rather put my back up, I can tell you. I accused her of not taking me seriously, always assuming the worse, that sort of thing.'

'All right. I'm glad we've got that settled,' said Inspector Deacon, 'It seems to me we have spent more than enough time talking about that gown of yours. Let's get back to the business in hand. You went to see Monsieur Girard in the storeroom. Go on from there if you will.'

'Righto. I went to see Marcel, as you say. I wanted to ask him what he was playing at. I was in a pretty foul mood, I don't mind telling you.' Jacques looked a little sheepish. 'He explained that the only reason he'd agreed to take part in the event was so he could show the world my gown. Thimbles, that rather grand boutique, were interested in showing his designs, you know. But he chose Mama's shop over them. He knew I'd never have had the courage to do it myself. Even so, I think he was a bit worried what I might do. He wasn't in the shop to see how the audience reacted, but he could certainly hear them through the door. He told me my mother would have to take my designs seriously now. Then he handed me a glass of wine that he had procured and we both drank to my future career. I can't tell you how happy I felt. If only Sylvia …' Jacques' voice faltered.

'Quite,' said Inspector Deacon. 'What happened next?'

'I went back into the shop.'

'Wait a minute. Surely you went to see Miss Beckett first? You'd have wanted to see how the dress looked close up, wouldn't you? And you would probably have wanted to tell the girl you'd designed the gown she was wearing, if she didn't already know.'

'You're quite right, Inspector. I intended to do just that. She was only in the room next door, after all. I went as far as to stand outside the door and raise my hand to knock. But I didn't go in for the simple reason that I could hear that she already had someone in there with her.'

'Did she indeed! Who was it?' Inspector Deacon leaned forward in his seat. He had lost all pretence at casual indifference now.

'I don't know. I didn't hear them speak. I wish to God that I had. It was Sylvia's voice that I heard. It was obvious that she was talking to someone. I didn't catch what she was saying but, from the tone of her voice, I remember thinking at the time that she sounded excited.'

'Do you believe him, sir? That he didn't go and see Miss Beckett, I mean?' asked Sergeant Perkins as soon as the door had closed behind Jacques and Rose.

'Well, we only have his word for it. He may have been lying about hearing her talking to someone else,' said Inspector Deacon.

'Yes, sir, that's what I thought. It's a bit convenient that. He might just have wanted to throw suspicion away from himself.'

'You may well be right, Sergeant. On balance, however, I think I'm inclined to believe him.' The inspector got up from his chair to stretch his legs. He proceeded to make a circuit of the chamber as best he could, given the cluttered nature of the room. 'The fellow could just as easily have said that he wanted to tell his mother about the gown first. That would have been natural enough. There was no need for him to admit that he had been intending to go and see Miss Beckett.'

'I'll be interested to see what that designer fellow has to say about the gown,' said Sergeant Perkins, closing his notebook. 'I don't mind telling you, sir, I didn't take to that Monsieur Renard chap one bit. He's a handsome devil and no mistake, but he's a bit too full of himself, I'd say. One for the ladies, I'd wager. And that accent of his, it's like they talk on the wireless. And him being a Frenchman too, it's not natural!'

'The policemen, they want to see me next?' demanded Marcel Girard of Rose, as soon as she and Jacques appeared in the outer room.

'Yes, but I'm afraid there'll be a bit of a delay. Jacques is taking his mother to stay at his lodgings tonight. Naturally he doesn't want her to stay here alone. If nothing else, it's not convenient with the policemen using her flat to interview everyone. Madame Renard has just gone in to them now to gather together a few bits and pieces to take with her.'

'This flat, it is very wretched, yes?'

'It is very modest,' said Rose, choosing her words with care. She did not much like the way the young man glanced around him with a look of very obvious disdain. 'Monsieur Girard, there is something I should like to ask you.'

'Oh? And what is it that the sleuth would like to know?' said the designer looking at her quizzically. 'Shall I guess, perhaps? Let me see. When you came upon Miss Beckett and myself in the storeroom, was it what you call a compromising position, in which you caught us? That is the question is it not, that is on the tip of your tongue?'

'No. I daresay it might have been one of the questions that I would have put to you earlier if I'd had the opportunity. But, as it happens, I know the answer to that question now.'

'Do you, indeed? How very intriguing. Well, what is this question that you have to ask me?'

'I should like to know what startled you.'

'What startled me?'

'Yes. Something startled you during the fashion event.'

'No, I don't think so.'

'I think it involved a member of the audience,' said Rose. 'I think you saw someone sitting there whom you were not expecting to see.'

Marcel Girard visibly paled. He gave Rose what she could only describe as a penetrating look, as if he were trying to ascertain how much she knew as opposed to guesswork. He swallowed hard. For a moment he appeared in two minds as to whether or not to say anything. The slightly mocking, somewhat patronising, demeanour had forsaken him. If nothing else, he was clearly shaken.

Whether he would have remained silent or spoken and either confirmed her suspicions or fervently denied them, Rose was never to know. For, at the precise moment he appeared about to speak, the door to the other room opened and Madame Renard and her son emerged, the latter carrying a small leather suitcase which, although of good quality, had clearly seen better days.

'Monsieur Girard if you could come this way please, sir,' said Sergeant Perkins appearing in the doorway. 'The inspector will see you now.'

Marcel stared at the sergeant a moment and then returned his gaze to Rose. Before she had sensed a feeling of hostility about him, as if he considered she was prying into matters that did not concern her. Now she felt his sense of apprehension as clearly as if it had been her own. Before there had been something rather defiant about him. She had expected him to refuse her offer to accompany him into the other room, to sneer even at the very suggestion. Now it did not surprise her when he grabbed her arm.

'You will come with me, like you did the others, yes?'

'All right,' said Rose. 'But a word of advice. You need to tell the truth. The policemen, they'll want all the facts. If you give them the facts, you'll have nothing to worry about.' Unless of course you murdered Sylvia, said a voice inside Rose's head, but she decided not to say that bit aloud.

Chapter Twenty-two

If Sergeant Perkins had been disappointed by the very Englishness of Monsieur Renard, then any similar reservations he may have had with regard to Monsieur Marcel Girard were quickly dispelled. To the sergeant, Marcel looked every inch the classic Frenchman. Although lacking Jacques' physique, being a good few inches shorter and considerably below what was generally considered average height, he was slender and lean in build and immaculately turned out. His clothes, which were of a good quality and obviously made by a first-class tailor, fitted him well and became him to perfection. In appearance, he had very finely drawn features, with eyes that were a particularly delicate shade of grey and a rosebud mouth that was surprisingly sensual. This latter feature, coupled with the fact that Marcel Girard wore his hair a little long, which gave him something of a Bohemian air, made Sergeant Perkins consider him rather effeminate. This impression was not disbursed by the man's apparent fondness for wearing what the sergeant later referred to as a woman's perfume.

'Monsieur Girard, please take a seat,' said Inspector Deacon who, Rose noted, was eyeing the designer with some interest.

'Before we begin, I'd be grateful if you'd tell me about this silver gown that I've heard so much about.'

'I take it that you are referring to the gown designed by Jacques Renard?' the designer said slyly. He was staring at the inspector a little warily. 'You try to catch me out, I think? You want me to say I designed the dress and that Jacques Renard, he is talking nonsense?'

'I'm not trying to set traps for you to fall into, if that's what you're afraid of,' the inspector said a little brusquely. 'You needn't think I am. I'm merely trying to arrive at the truth. I was keen to see if your and Monsieur Renard's accounts reconciled, that's all.'

'Jacques, he told you that he designed the dress, yes? Me, I do not deny it. I do not pretend it is my work.'

'Except that you did. Madame Renard, she thought you designed the dress, didn't she?'

'*Oui.*' Marcel Girard sounded exasperated. He threw his arms rather flamboyantly in the air as if to illustrate his frustration, the effect of which was to make Sergeant Perkins think him even more foreign than before. 'I have explained it all to Jacques, why I did what I did. He is happy. I do not need to explain it to you. It doesn't concern you.'

'It does if it has anything to do with this investigation. Fortunately for you, Monsieur Renard has already given us a very full account on that score. Now, tell me, how well did you know the deceased?'

'Not at all.' Marcel Girard turned to glare at Rose, a fact that was not lost on Inspector Deacon. She wondered if the designer suspected her of having spoken of finding them in a compromising position. 'Until today I did not know the girl other than being aware she was one of Madame Renard's assistants. It was only when Lady Lavinia, she became ill, and sent that odious, monstrosity of a woman –'

'I take it you are referring to Lady Celia?'

'Yes, that woman. A mannequin, huh! Far better that I should wear the outfits than that she should. I would have looked better in them than her, I think.'

Rose heard a noise behind her which sounded very much like Sergeant Perkins trying to suppress a chuckle. She imagined his face bright red as he did his best to stuff his mouth with a handkerchief or his fist.

'You laugh, yes. You think it funny, but it wasn't,' spat Monsieur Girard, his eyes flashing dangerously. 'This event, I did it for Jacques. Do I want to show my designs in a little boutique like this when I have Thimbles snapping at my ankles, as you say? No, I did it for him. And that woman was not going to spoil it. But Miss Simpson, here. She had the good idea that Miss Beckett be the mannequin. Me, I would not have thought of it. But it was a brilliant choice. She looked magnificent. My designs, they made her look beautiful. And the audience, they knew what she looked like ordinarily in that drab little uniform of hers. They saw that when she wore my garments she could be transformed into something of loveliness.'

There was a brief silence as those present conjured up for themselves a vision of Sylvia being magically transformed from a Cinderella type creature clad in rags to the belle of the ball who had won the prince's heart. Rose was secretly of the view that Marcel's claims were grossly exaggerated. She wondered whether he was mixing up in his mind the

190

effect the silver gown had produced with his own inferior designs. Something niggled at the back of Rose's mind if only she could put a finger upon it. Something that Sylvia had said to her that night when she had talked about the silver gown … Yes, she remembered now … *I think it's just the sort of dress that would make a man fall in love with a woman, don't you… or propose marriage* … Sylvia had been speaking of Jacques Renard's dress, not Marcel's lesser ones.

'Did she know? Sylvia, I mean, that Jacques had designed the silver gown? Did you tell her?' asked Rose.

'Miss Simpson –' protested Inspector Deacon.

'No, of course not. It was a secret. That girl, do you think I would tell her? Why, she could never have held her tongue. She would have been telling everyone. Little Miss Jennings and even Madame Renard herself. *Non*. Marcel Girard, he keeps it to himself.'

'But when Lady Celia demanded that Sylvia didn't wear the dress, what then?' persisted Rose. 'You needed to persuade her to go against Lady Celia's and Madame Renard's wishes and still wear the gown. I caught you trying to persuade her in the storeroom, didn't I? That's why you were both looking so guilty and Sylvia refused to tell me what you had been doing.'

'Yes. You thought you had disturbed a romantic tryst. We did not disillusion you, I think.'

'But whatever did you say to Sylvia to make her wear the dress?'

'Miss Simpson, please,' protested Inspector Deacon.

'I'm sorry, Inspector. But I think it could be very important,' implored Rose. 'Sylvia fell in love with the silver gown and wanted to wear it. She knew it made her look marvellous. But she also knew that if she did wear it, it was more than possible that she'd lose her job. It was too great a risk for her to have taken just to satisfy her own vanity. Don't you see? There must have been more to it than that.'

'She was fond of Jacques, was she not?' said Marcel, looking a little flustered. 'I thought she decided to wear it because of him. He had been neglecting her a little and well, she wanted him to see her in the dress and come to his senses. That is what I thought at the time. I was certain of it.'

'Why do you say that?' asked Rose.

'Because it took so very little persuasion,' said Marcel. 'I asked her to wear the dress and she said yes. Just like that. She did not hesitate, she did not argue. She did not sulk and make a face as I expected. She did not get me to promise to secure her a positon at Harridges if she lost her job because of it. Of course I told her I would speak to her employer, reason with the woman. But really, Madame Renard, she would not have listened to me. But Miss Beckett, she did not care. I was surprised, I remember that. I felt a little guilty, yes, at what I was asking her to do.'

'Well, I think we've spent enough time on this subject,' said Inspector Deacon wearily. 'It may be we will never know why Miss Beckett went against her better judgement and wore the dress. I want to focus on the murder investigation. Likely as not, the dress has nothing at all to do with it.'

'I think it has,' said Rose.

'Miss Simpson, if you please. If you interrupt one more time, or try to steer the questions as you have done, I shall have no alternative but to ask you to leave. Do you understand what I am saying?'

'Perfectly, thank you,' answered Rose rather primly. She looked at her hands clasped in her lap, her cheeks flushed.

'Now, where to start, Monsieur Girard. I understand you were going backwards and forwards between the shop and the storeroom all evening?'

'Yes, I was very nervous, you understand. A part of me, it wanted to see how the audience would receive my designs. Would they be bewitched, or would they be bored? Another part of me, it wanted to go and hide until it was all over. I was worried too, that Jacques he would not come. I made him promise that he would, but even so … I could not feel happy until I knew he was there. And he left it so very late to arrive. Oh, you cannot imagine how pleased I was to see him rattling the door. It disrupted the proceedings of course, but I didn't care.'

'Did you go over and speak to him when he arrived?'

'No, I went back to the storeroom. I was afraid of giving myself away. He had arrived and that was all that mattered. I could now retreat to my sanctuary in the happy knowledge that he was there. I had only to wait.'

'You didn't come back out into the shop?'

'No.'

'Do you happen to know whether the storeroom door, the one that led out onto the next street, was locked?'

'But of course it was. Madame Renard insisted it be kept locked at all times. All her stock, it was kept in the room. Anyway, I know it was locked because I locked it myself when I came back from having a last cigarette in the street. That was just before the event started.'

'Did you unlock that door at any time to admit anyone else, anyone who came in that way rather than using the shop entrance?'

'No, of course not. Why would I?' He had a sudden flash of inspiration. 'I did not admit the murderer, if that is what you are thinking. Yes, that would be easy for you, wouldn't it? The murderer, he is some lunatic that no one knows and he was let in by the stupid foreigner.'

'Now, now, Monsieur Girard, there is no need for that,' said Inspector Deacon rather gruffly. 'We should like to know, that's all, whether it's possible that someone could have come into the shop other than through the front door. You have just told us that you didn't let anyone in through the storeroom door. You were also going backwards and forwards between the shop and storeroom all evening. It therefore seems unlikely that the murderer entered by that way.'

'I could have told you that, Inspector.'

'Perhaps you can tell me if you can think of anyone who may have wished to do Miss Beckett any harm?'

'No. I can think of no one. Why would any person wish to kill a shop girl? I can think of no reason.'

'It is possible that they may have mistaken her for Lady Celia,' volunteered Sergeant Perkins from his corner. 'They were wearing similar dresses and had almost identical colouring.'

'Ah, now that I can imagine,' said Marcel excitedly. 'She is an awful woman, that one. I can understand quite a few people wishing to do her in, as you say.'

'Monsieur Renard told us that he came to see you in the storeroom after Miss Beckett had appeared in the silver gown.'

'Yes, he did. I was expecting him, Inspector. He wanted an explanation for what I had done. I handed him a glass of wine and told him that I knew he would never show his work himself, so I had done it for him. He has such talent, it is hard to put it into words. Me, I may be a little successful. My father, I think he will display my designs in his department store in Paris. But Jacques, he is an exceptional designer. He has the vision. I think he could become a very famous designer like Jeanne

Lanvin or Jean Patou. His name could be on the lips of the best dressed women in the world, if only he believed in his own ability. Why, he puts my designs to shame.' Marcel leaned towards Inspector Deacon and lowered his voice. 'It is his mother, you know, that is the problem. He is afraid of disappointing her. Everything she has done, it is for him. She has built up this little shop from nothing to leave to him. But Jacques, a shop proprietor? *Non*. His talents, they would be wasted. She dreams of the House of Renard. And Jacques, he could create that for her with his designs.'

'So, it was a friendly conversation that the two of you had?'

'But of course. Once I had explained everything, Jacques, he laughed, he joked, he was very happy.'

'What happened when he left you? Did you stay in the storeroom?'

'No, of course not. There was no need. Jacques, he said he wanted to see Miss Beckett in the dress. He had not had the opportunity to look at the gown closely. And of course, I thought he was fond of the girl ...'

'So what did you do?'

'I would have gone out into the shop and spoken to Madame Renard, told her what a clever and talented son she had. But Jacques, he had told me about that awful woman –'

'Lady Celia?'

'Yes. He told me how she made a scene, how she went almost mad with anger. She is a hateful, spiteful woman, I think. Poor little Miss Beckett, she did not often have the opportunity to wear nice clothes. That awful woman, she wears the very best clothes all the time and still she looks –'

'Yes, yes,' said Inspector Deacon quickly. 'I think I understand how you must have felt. But what did you do?'

'I could not go into the shop because of Lady Celia. She would have started shouting at me, I think, if I had dared to show my face. Jacques, he had been gone a few minutes. I thought to myself, he has had time to embrace the girl, to whisper the sweet nothings in her ear. They will not mind if I join them now. We can laugh together about Lady Celia. Jacques, he will make sure Sylvia does not lose her job.'

'Well?'

'I opened the door and went into the corridor. I looked through the arch and the first thing I saw was Jacques trying to put out a fire. Madame

Renard, she was shouting instructions to Miss Jennings. I looked around for Miss Beckett. She was not there. I thought, she is still in the dressing room.'

'Did you go into the dressing room?' demanded Inspector Deacon.

There could be no mistake this time that the inspector was leaning forward in his chair. Rose suddenly realised that she had been half conscious all the time of Sergeant Perkins scribbling in his notebook. Now she was aware only of the silence. It seemed that he too was waiting with bated breath.

'No,' said Marcel Girard. 'I did not. You see, I could hear that Sylvia had someone in the room with her.'

'How did you know someone was in the room with her? Did you hear them talking?'

'No, not as such. I might have been tempted to go in if it had only been that. I would have thought it was only Miss Jennings or Miss Simpson here. Rose would not have minded me disturbing them. But I heard a laugh. A frightful, awful laugh. It wasn't a nice laugh at all. It sounded malicious. It chilled my blood, as you say.'

'Was it a man's laugh or a woman's? Could you tell?'

'Yes, it was a woman's laugh.'

'Did you recognise the woman from her laugh?'

'Yes, it was Sylvia.'

Chapter Twenty-three

As soon as Marcel Girard came out of the room, he left with exaggerated haste for his own lodgings. Rose remained in the square room, which looked oddly forlorn and empty now that it had only two occupants. Rose longed to sink onto the settee which, while far from being snug, offered a degree of comfort lacking in the rigid straight back chairs of the other room. It was past two o'clock in the morning. The long hours and laborious activities of the day, coupled with the shock of the murder, were having their toll. She was feeling distinctly weary and desired nothing more than to sink between sheets and sleep. This, however, was not a possibility. For one thing, sleep may very well have eluded her, given that her brain was still trying to process and digest all the information she had received during the course of the various interviews she had attended. Her mind was busily attempting to separate the useful facts and comments from those that could be disregarded. It was a particularly difficult thing to do, Rose felt, when one was not certain what was, or was not, a relevant detail. But more importantly, Mary was still to be interviewed, and she had a feeling the girl would require her assistance.

Mary's interview may well have been the last, yet in Rose's mind it was one of the most frightening. For one thing, she was scared about what Mary might say. She herself had paved the way with the policemen as best she could. She had warned them not to take what Mary said too seriously, had as good as told them that the girl would not hurt a fly. Even so, Rose was apprehensive as to how the interview would unfold.

Mary, who had been so very self-contained and removed from them since the discovery of Sylvia's death, as if she were an isolated being, looked up at Rose now with eyes heavy and red from weeping. It was painfully obvious that while Rose and Marcel had been in the other room with the policemen, by the look on her face, the girl had taken the opportunity to cry almost to distraction. Whether she had wept for herself or for Sylvia, it was impossible to say. Rose felt a tinge of guilt. She should have insisted that Mary be one of the first to be interviewed. She really did not look fit to have been left alone with all her troubles given freedom to race around in her head and fester.

'Mary, I'm sorry. Come with me now into the other room. They're waiting for you,' said Rose, taking her hand. It felt as cold as ice and she was reminded again of death and Sylvia lying spread-eagled on the floor. Inadvertently she shuddered. 'They'll get the questioning over and done with quickly, see if they don't.'

'They've left me to last to be interviewed. They've waited until everyone else has left. Why? Is it because they are going to arrest me? They think I'm guilty, don't they? I've been sitting here watching people come and go and I've been feeling more and more afraid.'

'There's no need to be scared,' said Rose, adopting a brisk manner. 'And as to seeing you last, it's because the police don't think that you will have very much, if anything, to tell them. So you see, it was silly of you to worry.'

'You're only saying that.' Mary reminded Rose of a sulky child who couldn't make up its mind whether or not to allow itself to be comforted. 'I could tell them a great deal if I chose to, which I don't,' Mary added. She spoke so quietly, barely above a whisper that Rose wondered if she was talking to herself. Perhaps she had not meant to utter the words out loud.

Rose hesitated, wondering whether to say anything. A part of her was afraid to ask Mary to elaborate on what she meant. She decided instead to focus only on the first bit of Mary's answer.

'No, I'm not just saying that. It's the truth. But you will need to pull yourself together, Mary, or the police will think the worst.'

Mary sniffed and mopped at her eyes with the back of her hand. It made an ineffectual handkerchief and Rose handed her a lace edged cotton one from her own wrist, which had been tucked into the strap of her watch.

'Mary, there is something you must do.' Rose knelt beside the girl so that she could speak quietly. 'Promise me you will. You must tell the policemen what Sylvia had done to upset you so.'

'No, I can't,' cried Mary, drawing away from her with one swift movement. A fresh set of tears threatened to spill. 'I can't, Rose, I can't. Please don't make me.'

'It can't be as bad as all that,' Rose said soothingly. Despite her reassuring words, she felt afraid. It was so easy to think of Mary as meek and mild, rather like a lamb. The nursery rhyme 'Mary had a little lamb' came as if from nowhere into her head. Even timid people can be provoked into doing something truly dreadful, she thought. If they are pushed too far, they can snap. Sylvia was just the sort of girl who would have teased and goaded Mary to distraction. She would have thought it fun, like a game. She wouldn't have minded very much that Mary hadn't been laughing, and she wouldn't have noticed if she had pushed Mary too far. Rose took a deep breath. She mustn't think such things. She was allowing her thoughts to run away with themselves and become fanciful. She put it down to tiredness and the events of the day. Surely Sylvia had not been as bad as all that, and Mary … well, Mary wasn't really so very weak, was she?

'I'd rather die than tell them. I'd rather throw myself out of that window there.' Mary threw a desperate gesture at the velvet curtained window, the one which Jacques and Marcel had been standing in front of earlier in the evening.

'Stop it! Stop it now!' Rose spoke more forcefully and angrily than she had intended. 'Don't you dare talk such nonsense. Don't you think the police are used to hearing all sorts of things? There is nothing you can tell them that will shock them so very much, or that they haven't heard a good many times before.'

'Do sit down, Miss Jennings. I am very sorry to have kept you waiting, but I'm afraid it couldn't be helped,' said Inspector Deacon. 'Would you like a glass of water perhaps?'

The girl's deathly pallor alarmed him. She really was as pale as anything. Her skin was so very white as to be almost translucent. He half expected her at any moment to pitch sideways off the chair and fall into a dead faint. He wondered whether she always looked so delicate and fragile, the word insipid sprung to mind. The same great aunt that he had had recourse to think of earlier would have said the girl looked washed-out. He stared at the hands lying in her lap. They were making quite a mess of the handkerchief she had clutched between them. She had wrapped it up into a messy sort of ball which she held fast in one fist, while the fingers of the other hand pulled at the flimsy material. She was hardly looking at what she was doing, quite unaware of the fact that she was pulling away the lace edging from the handkerchief. In a moment it would be completely ruined.

198

It occurred to the inspector, as it had done to Rose, that they had been foolish to leave interviewing Mary to last. In Inspector Deacon's case, it was because he remembered what Rose had said about the girl's friendship with the deceased. There had been a falling off of affection, and the girl's words that evening before the murder had been a cause for alarm. Now that Mary sat before him, wringing the handkerchief between her hands and all but shaking, it was also very apparent to his practised eye that the girl was hiding something. He had encountered many nervous suspects and witnesses in his time, and this girl appeared to him utterly wretched and close to despair. Perhaps due to the lateness of the hour, or because the girl obviously had some information to impart, or even because he felt that he had made so little headway in the investigation so far, he found himself minded to go less gently with her than he might have done.

'Now, Miss Jennings, I understand that you and Miss Beckett were by way of being friends?'

Mary gave the briefest of nods, so slight in fact that Sergeant Perkins was compelled to lean forward in his seat to catch it. Even then he looked at the back of her head rather hesitantly, as if he were not certain.

'For the benefit of my sergeant who is taking notes, you indicated in the affirmative, did you not?'

'Yes,' said Mary, through lips that barely moved.

'You would know if she had a particular young man.' Inspector Deacon phrased this more as a statement than a question. 'I understand that the young lady was rather keen on Monsieur Renard?'

'She used to be. But recently she talked of another young man, one with better prospects.'

'Oh?'

'She said he was mortal fond of her. I didn't know whether to believe her. Sylvia liked to exaggerate, you see. She was awful jealous of Rose … Miss Simpson, on account of her walking out with the gentry as she put it.' Mary stole a glance at Rose, who smiled encouragingly.

'Did she happen to mention the young man's name?'

'No. She could be frightfully secretive when she put her mind to it. She liked to feel she knew something that other people didn't. She thought it made her important,' said Mary, a look of disdain on her face.

'Did she know something about Madame Renard that no one else knew?' interjected Rose quickly, before the inspector had the opportunity to put another question.

'Miss Simpson, please –'

'Yes, she did, Rose,' said Mary excitedly, the colour flooding back to her cheeks. 'At least she hinted at it. She went on something terrible about it. Said Madame was no better than she ought to be, and there she was giving herself airs and graces when if her customers knew the truth about her, why they wouldn't touch Renard's with a bargepole, let alone give her their custom.'

'Do you know what it was that she knew about Madame?'

'No, but it must have been something frightful, mustn't it, for her to go on like that? I didn't encourage her, Rose, I swear I didn't. Whatever she knew, I didn't want to know. Madame's been awful good to me. Whenever Sylvia mentioned it, I pretended I wasn't listening.'

'Thank you. Miss Simpson. Now, perhaps you will kindly let me get back to asking the questions,' said the inspector. Nevertheless, Rose thought he looked interested in what Mary had had to say on the subject.

'Miss Jennings, I understand that there had been some sort of a disagreement between you and the deceased. That you were on less friendly terms than you had been previously?'

'No. No, I don't think so,' said Mary, quickly, looking worried. The lost look had returned to her eyes.

'Come, Miss Jennings, we have it on good authority, Miss Simpson's in fact, that this very evening you said you thought Miss Beckett was horrible and hateful. I think you even went so far as to say that you wished that she was dead. You had even thought of the various ways in which you might kill her, I believe.'

'Don't!' sobbed Mary. 'Don't, it's too awful. It was frightful of me. You don't know how much I've regretted thinking it and saying it after what happened.' She turned and glared at Rose, her face screwed up and distorted with something akin to loathing. 'Did you have to tell them I said that? How could you, Rose? How could you be so hateful? I didn't mean anything by it. I thought you were my friend.'

'I am your friend, Mary,' said Rose gently. 'I'm not surprised that you don't think well of me. I didn't mean to tell so much. But it is very important now that you tell us what Sylvia did to upset you so much.'

'I can't. I can't. I've told you, I'd rather die than do that.'

'Come, Miss Jennings, it can't be as bad as all that.' This was Inspector Deacon, at rather a loss as to what to say. 'Suppose you tell us what is worrying you.'

'Madame Renard, she will hate me. She'll never trust me again. She'll dismiss me without a reference, and you know how much this job means to me, Rose.'

'I do,' said Rose. 'But no one will help you if you will not allow yourself to be helped.' She paused and picked up the girl's hand. 'Tell me, is it anything to do with stealing from Renard's?'

'Oh!' The word uttered involuntarily, was mirrored in the look upon Mary's face, her mouth surprised and forming the letter 'o', her eyes wide and consumed with a haunted look.

'How did you know?'

'It was a guess, that's all. Madame Renard told me this evening that she suspected Sylvia of being a thief. She had found money missing from the till and other things as well. She mentioned only one or two pairs of stockings, but I got the distinct impression that more had been taken.'

'And she suspected Sylvia?' whispered Mary.

'Yes, but she didn't have any proof. Today she caught Jacques rifling through her papers, or so she assumed. In actual fact he was looking for a sketch which he thought he might have left in her office. I don't think she thought anything more of the incident at the time, but afterwards I think she wondered whether Jacques was the thief, instead of Sylvia.'

'She never suspected me?'

'No.'

'Oh, Rose, I didn't mean to do it. I didn't want to, really I didn't. I lost my purse in the street, and I didn't have enough to pay my week's rent. Mrs Daley, my landlady, she's awfully strict about that sort of thing. I knew she wouldn't understand, that she'd think I'd spent it and give me my marching orders. I was wondering what to do when I happened to notice that the drawer to the cash till hadn't been closed properly. Sylvia, I expect. You know how slapdash she was over that sort of thing. Anyway, it got me to thinking. I could borrow some money to tide me over for a couple of days. I'd scrimp and save like anything and then put it back as soon as I'd been paid.'

'But Sylvia caught you?' said Rose.

'Yes. She came out of the storeroom and caught me literally with my hand in the till withdrawing some money. I'm not very quick or I might have thought up something.' Mary dropped her head upon her hand to screen her eyes. Her embarrassment, however, was clearly visible in the colour of her cheeks. 'I tried to explain, that I only needed the money for a couple of days and fully intended replacing it in full, but she wouldn't listen. She threatened to tell Madame. I pleaded and pleaded with her not to.'

'And she agreed, providing you stole some items for her?'

'Yes. At first it was just the odd pair of stockings. But then it was bigger, more expensive things. She wanted me to steal her a dress. I didn't want to do it. But I didn't know what else to do. I have been so worried. I thought it was only a matter of time before Madame caught me in the act.'

'You should have told me,' said Rose. 'I could have helped you.'

'Miss Jennings, if what you are saying is correct, you had a very strong motive for wishing Sylvia dead,' said Inspector Deacon.

'Yes, I know. I did. But I didn't kill her, Inspector, I swear I didn't.'

For a minute or two no one said a word. It appeared, however, that the silence was more than Mary could bear, for she rushed in on it with nervous speech.

'I knew you wouldn't believe me. I knew you'd think me guilty of Sylvia's murder.' She gulped back a sob.

'The inspector thinks nothing of the sort,' said Rose firmly. She gave the policeman an imploring look. Perhaps he took pity on her, for he seemingly changed tack.

'Now, Miss Jennings, I understand that, after Miss Beckett had appeared in the silver gown, you were all quite overcome by the audience crowding around you trying to obtain details of the dress?'

'Yes. It was quite frightening.'

'And where were you facing when this happened?'

'Do you mean in which direction was I looking?'

'Yes.'

'In the direction of the street. I remember looking at the shop door and wishing everyone would leave.'

'Then you must have seen the woman who screamed?' said Inspector Deacon leaning forward.

'Oh, yes, I did. It was after the drape caught fire. I remember thinking it rather odd because it looked as if she deliberately set the curtain alight. But of course I must have been mistaken, mustn't I, because why would anyone have wanted to do such a thing?'

'Miss Jennings,' said Inspector Deacon very slowly. 'This is desperately important. Who did you see set the curtain alight and scream?'

'I don't want to get anyone into any trouble,' Mary said rather fretfully. 'They might not have set the curtain alight on purpose. It might have been an accident. It –'

'Miss Jennings, please.'

'Oh, all right. It was Mrs Milton's guest. I don't know her name.'

'A guest of Mrs Milton's?' said Rose. 'But Mrs Milton wasn't there this evening.'

'Are you quite sure, Miss Simpson? There were a lot of people. You may not have spotted her in the crowd.'

'Quite sure, Inspector. We were looking out for Mrs Milton, you see. She likes to finger the fabric of the clothes and we didn't want her pulling the model this way and that. We made a joke of it. She rather likes a tipple and we decided we'd ensure that her glass was kept topped up.'

'I remember now,' said Mary. 'The woman, she handed me Mrs Milton's invitation. She said that Mrs Milton couldn't come and that she was attending in her place.'

'But the guests of customers were only to be admitted if the customers were also present,' said Rose.

'I know. I shouldn't really have let her in. But she had Mrs Milton's invitation, and she was most insistent. Really, she was a most respectable looking woman. I didn't think there'd be any harm if I let her in.'

'Never mind.' The inspector shrugged. 'I daresay Mrs Milton will be able to tell us to whom she gave her invitation. If you could furnish my sergeant with her details before you go.'

Rose opened the door for the two of them to leave, and almost collided with Madame Renard and Jacques. It transpired that, on reaching her son's lodgings, the proprietor had suddenly realised that she had left behind some essential item necessary for her night's sleep. Much to the annoyance of Jacques, and amid his loud protestations, the two of them had returned to Madame Renard's flat. It had taken Madame Renard but a few moments to locate and procure the item she had in mind. Jacques Renard had already turned tail and was taking the stairs two at a time. Madame Renard was on his heels. As she looked on, something suddenly occurred to Rose, a piece of the jigsaw that might fit. It was ridiculous of course to try and test her theory now, but try as she might, she couldn't let it go. Madame Renard was at the top of the steps. Rose ran up to her, her breath pounding in her ears. Somewhat startled, the proprietor half turned to face her employee.

'Yes, Rose, what is it? Can it not wait until tomorrow? It is very late.'

'Aubert,' Rose said. 'Madame Aubert.'

For a moment Madame Renard remained motionless. It was as if she had been turned to stone. The colour had drained from her face, replaced by a mask of an almost white, waxy substance. There was a wild look about her eyes and horror on her face. Rose, who had instinctively stretched out her hand to clutch the woman's arm, found herself recoiling back into the shadows of the room. Time stood still. For a moment it seemed likely that Madame Renard would drop down in a faint. When it seemed almost a foregone conclusion, she rallied and, before Rose had the opportunity to say another word, the proprietor was stumbling back down the stairs in pursuit of her son.

Chapter Twenty-four

Rose laid her head upon her pillow and tried to get some sleep. Her attempts so far had been rather half-hearted, for she had allowed her memories of the evening to play out in her mind. There was a part of her that wanted the night to end, to wake up and find that it had all been some awful dream. The amateur detective in her, however, would insist on clinging to her recollections of the interviews, playing them over and over in her mind lest she should forget something that would later prove a vital piece of information.

The mattress on the floor which, for that night at least, constituted her bed was not conducive to sleep. For one thing the mattress itself was lumpy and missing a spring or two, and for another Rose found herself lying in a draught. She looked enviously towards her bed, on which lay the sleeping form of Mary. Mental exhaustion had overtaken the girl as soon as her head had touched the pillow and now Rose watched her as she enjoyed a sleep untroubled by insomnia.

It had not seemed right to send Mary off to spend the night alone at her lodgings, with only the unsympathetic and disagreeable Mrs Daley for company. Far better that she should stay the night at the house that Rose occupied with her mother. It was a modest establishment, for the Simpsons had come down in the world following the return of Rose's father from the Great War and his subsequent death, but it was preferable to Mrs Daley's lodging house. If nothing else, Mrs Simpson had been on hand to fuss over them and insist that they partake of a little hot milk and bread and butter before retiring to bed. She had at once been affected by the girls' sombre moods, sensing immediately that something dreadful had occurred, not least because of their very late return from the event. However, she had not pried or shown the least signs of being inquisitive, seeming to realise that it was not to be spoken of until later that morning once the girls' had enjoyed a few hours' sleep. Rose, however, had felt an obligation to give her a very brief account of the events of the evening. Mrs Simpson, her mouth set in a thin line, had raised her eyebrows but said very little. If the thought occurred to her that her daughter had developed quite a habit of becoming involved in murder investigations, she did not express it.

It was no good, Rose could not fall asleep. Certainly not while everyone's words were flying around in her consciousness, perching for a moment at the forefront of her mind before retreating and being replaced by another phrase uttered by a different person. If only she could switch off her mind as one did a wireless set. The fractured sentences seemed to be tearing and spinning around her head faster and faster, so that she became afraid that, if she did not listen to her thoughts more carefully, they would mingle and become integrated to such an extent that she would not remember whom had said what.

There was only one obvious solution. She must get up and write it all down. Only then would her tired and exhausted mind, freed from the information it held, surrender to the sleep that deserted her. Quietly, so as not to wake Mary, Rose pulled her sensible wool flannel negligee over her cotton nightdress and crept downstairs. Opening the sitting room door, she was soon established at her mother's writing desk. Taking up notepaper and pen, she proceeded to write a summary of each interview, paying particular attention to the facts gleaned and the theories put forward.

The room was silent save for the ticking of the old clock on the mantelpiece and the scraping of the pen nib as Rose's firm hand covered page after page in good clear script. Every now and then she paused as she tried to recollect a certain phrase or the expression on someone's face as they had imparted a particular piece of information. Time marched on and still she wrote, emptying her mind with each stroke of the pen. Sometimes she paused a moment to look back through her notes in order to compare the details obtained from each interview to ascertain if a particular statement or impression could be verified. Slowly she found that a picture was beginning to emerge, not the one of which she was familiar, but a secondary one which had played out in the shadows and of which she had not been a participant. At first it was just the vaguest of outlines, but as she compared the narratives of what had actually been said or hinted at, the more vivid the picture became.

There were various questions in her mind that required resolution. Only now did she find that one or two of the answers appeared as if of their own accord with each stroke of her pen. It was as if they had been summoned from her scribbled notes. She was fairly certain now that she knew the secret that Madame Renard had been so desperate to keep hidden. As time progressed, Rose also formed a view regarding the identity of the woman who had set fire to the curtain. It was an easy task to ascertain if she was indeed correct, and she drummed her fingers on the top of the desk, frustrated with impatient anticipation.

Of all else, it was the identity of the murderer that was utmost in her thoughts and still eluded her. It was as if he hovered in the shadows waiting with bated breath to see if she would find some clue to unmask him. Why was it so very difficult to determine the murderer's identity? The murder had occurred broadly within a half hour timeframe. Perhaps less, for if they were to be believed, both Jacques Renard and Marcel Girard had overheard Sylvia engaging with someone in her room, presumably only a handful of minutes at most prior to her death.

A vision of Sylvia, emerging in the silver gown, sprung before her eyes. An ethereal figure that had hovered for a moment at the top of the steps commanding every eye. She remembered how the silk satin had shimmered and glistened in the light as the girl had descended the stairs before gliding effortlessly across the floor to be admired anew. Again she heard Jacques' cry of surprise. So vivid was the recollection that for a moment, crouched over the desk in her mother's little sitting room as she was, Rose was almost tempted to turn her head and look over her shoulder. For the fancy took her that if she were to do so, she might see again the look of astonishment on the young man's face. She remembered his explanation for why he had been so affected by the spectacle of Sylvia in the gown, which had in part been corroborated by Marcel's account. It was while she was pondering on this that she suddenly realised something she had previously overlooked. She had made a mistake because she had not remembered something quite correctly. As if to confirm that she was on the right track at last, various things that the murdered girl had said, to which she had paid little notice or attention at the time, came trickling into her mind. All along Sylvia had been providing her with little clues if only she had known it. Sylvia had not foreseen her own death, but various things she had hinted at and done would help identify her murderer.

As dawn approached it was a tired and weary Rose who returned to her mattress on the floor. She must snatch a few hours' sleep. Although a part of her did not want to rest at all. For she had information of the utmost importance to impart, if Inspector Deacon would but be prepared to listen to her reasoning. She had the answer within her grasp, having narrowed down the field considerably. For now she knew that the murderer could be one of only two people. She felt certain of it. Now all she had to do was to find out which one.

They had caught two buses and were now walking swiftly along the pavement. The shops on either side of the road were already heaving with early morning shoppers and Mary, distracted by the hustle and bustle of it all, together with the appetising smells and splendour of the window displays, was stumbling to keep up with Rose's quick strides.

'I don't understand why we had to set off so early, Rose,' she grumbled in her quiet, unassuming way. 'I feel as if I've hardly slept a wink. And I say, must you walk so fast? I'm having difficulty keeping up.'

'I've told you, Mary. I need to see Inspector Deacon as soon as possible. He's most probably at Lady Celia's house by now. He was intending to interview her this morning, if you remember. But first there is something we need to do.'

'What?'

'Go shopping.'

'Rose, how can you possibly suggest such a thing? I shouldn't be able to bring myself to buy anything today given the circumstances, even if I had the money, which I don't.'

'I'm not suggesting that we buy anything. I'm wanting to test out a theory, that's all. Tell me, Mary, do you think you would recognise the woman who set fire to the curtain if you happened to see her again?'

'Yes, I'm sure I would.' said Mary. 'She was very nicely turned out. Knew what clothes suited her, I'd say. She made quite an impression on me, I don't mind telling you. She looked ever so respectable. That's why I couldn't believe my eyes when I saw her hold that curtain over the flame.'

'Here we are,' said Rose, stopping outside a large boutique, the proportions of which put Madame Renard's little shop to shame, to say nothing of the splendour of its window display with mannequins of the finest quality draped with clothes that far outshone those offered at Renard's.

'Thimbles!' exclaimed Mary. 'Whatever are we doing here, Rose?'

'You'll see,' said Rose, opening the door and walking inside.

Mary hesitated for a moment before following. She had only ventured inside the shop once before and had found the experience rather intimidating. For one thing, the assistants looked so immaculate and well groomed, and for another she had felt that her own modest attire had been heavily scrutinised and found wanting. The prospect of reliving the experience therefore was one she did not particularly relish. There again were the perfect shop assistants, their outfits seemingly freshly laundered and they themselves with not a hair out of place. Instinctively she patted her own rather mousey locks. She wished she hadn't worn her drab little brown hat, with its rather tatty satin trimming, which did very little for her complexion. Oh, to be like Rose, who seemed quite oblivious to the rather disapproving glances their arrival had produced. For if the girl were aware that the shop assistants looked at them down their noses, and sneered behind their hands, then she gave no sign of it. Instead she strode resolutely on as if she had some purpose that exceeded all other considerations.

Weaving their way between the occasional early morning shoppers and counters filled with an array of beautiful accessories, and warding off the advances made by the shop assistants to ascertain their business, they reached the far end of the boutique. The proprietor was standing there, her back to them. She was speaking in polite and interested tones to an obviously favoured customer. They stood and watched as if transfixed. Perhaps the proprietor could feel their eyes on the back of her neck, or perhaps the customer, standing at an angle to her, had alerted her to their presence. Whatever it was, after a moment or two the proprietor paused amid her conversation and turned around.

Mary all but dropped her bag as her hand flew up to her mouth to stifle a scream. Her eyes large and bright looked imploringly at Rose, who answered her with a look of understanding. Her theory had been realised. Along with Mary, she stared at the woman who in turn was looking at them dumbfounded. Rose fancied there was a look of fear in her eyes. And so there should be. For she and Mary were staring at the very woman who had set Madame Renard's curtain alight. The very same who had subsequently uttered a high pitched scream.

Chapter Twenty-five

'Celia, are you all right? There's a constable standing outside your house. I had the most awful job persuading him to allow me to pass. I thought he was about to arrest me on the spot.'

Lady Celia Goswell looked down at Bertram Thorpe, from her elevated positon on the grand staircase rising above him, with a renewed sense of adoration. She had so rarely seen him look anything other than composed. Now, though, he looked anything but calm and collected. He looked positively haggard as if he had been up all night, or spent a sleepless night tossing and turning in his bed. And it was obvious by his appearance that he had dressed hastily. His collar didn't sit quite right and his hair appeared innocent of any pomade, sticking up this way and that in the most endearing of fashions, she thought. Although it was with a feeling of growing irritation that she noticed how he looked around the grand entrance hall of the Goswells' London residence, with its deeply coved and coffered ceiling supported by fine columns and panelling of English alabaster. Granted, this was his first visit to the establishment and the hall often had the effect of taking a visitor's breath away, modelled directly on ancient Roman buildings as it was. But did Bertram really have to stare about him quite so obviously with his mouth wipe open, quite agog with the splendour of it all?

She stole a sideways glance at Beeswick, the butler, a faithful family retainer if ever there was one. Good. He was managing to keep a straight face and remain dignified. It was a pity that the new, young footman was unable to do so. Why, he was positively smirking, and making no effort at all to conceal the fact. Well, he would have nothing to smile about soon after she had spoken to the old butler and demanded the footman's dismissal. It would jolly well serve him right. Who did he think he was to pass judgement on how her guests conducted themselves?

Her first thought was to allay Bertram's fears. She took a deep breath and said in a high sing-song voice, which sounded false and artificial even to her own ears, purporting as it did a gaiety that she did not feel: 'Oh, Bertram. How quick you were in coming here. I wasn't expecting to see you for at least half an hour or so.'

'You sounded so anxious and mysterious on the telephone. I knew at once that something must be the matter. And seeing that constable just now … well, it only confirms that I was right to be worried, doesn't it? For goodness sake, Celia, tell me what's happened.'

With a wave of her hand, Celia dismissed both butler and footman from her presence. She was left alone at last with Bertram in the magnificent hall. All in a rush she ran down the last few stairs of the grand staircase, as eagerly to greet him as any child a favoured parent. She took his outstretched hands in her own. To see him look so anxiously at her, to notice the concerned look upon his face, it revealed to her as nothing else would have done his regard for her safety. Even so, to her annoyance he continued to look about him apprehensively, as if he felt that he did not belong there beside her in such grand a place.

'It's all right. Father's at our country estate if that's what's worrying you. Really, Bertram, you'll have to meet him one of these days.'

'What's worrying me,' said Bertram, regaining his composure somewhat, 'is why there is a policeman positioned outside your house and why you telephoned me to come over to see you at the crack of dawn.'

'It's hardly that, Bertie,' said Celia, now resting her head upon his shoulder. How comforting it was to lean one's head against such a tall and solid man. It was quite idiotic, of course, given the circumstances in which she found herself, but she could almost believe she had not a care in the world.

'It's half past eight,' she said, lifting her head and meeting his gaze. 'Hardly early at all.'

Really, she didn't care a bit what the servants thought. Let them gossip amongst themselves if they wanted to. Heaven knew she had given them little enough to chatter about in the past. She would have smiled up at Bertram now, if he hadn't looked so very worried and out of sorts. She hoped fervently that his apparent ill humour was a reflection of his concern for her wellbeing rather than the result of feeling ill at ease in her father's palatial home.

Of course she knew she was putting off the awful moment when she must tell all. She could hardly bear to see the look of horror, which would surely appear upon his face once she told him. She did so hope that he would rise to the occasion and not crumble, that he was the man she hoped he was.

'Darling, something dreadful has happened. Now, I don't want you to get upset. I didn't myself when they told me. I've tried to be very brave, and you must be too.'

'Celia, for goodness sake what's happened?' demanded Bertram.

He didn't look particularly concerned now, only irritated at her refusal to answer his question directly and succinctly. As if to illustrate the fact, he put his hands roughly upon her shoulders and pushed her away from him so that now he held her at arms' length and could scrutinise her face. Celia found herself forced to forsake her own daydreaming. Really, the way he clung to her shoulders, it rather hurt. She winced and he immediately let her go. She massaged her injured skin with her fingers in an exaggerated fashion, and was rewarded by a mortified look on Bertram's face.

'I say, Celia, I'm awfully –'

'You forget how very strong you are, darling,' said Celia reproachfully. 'Now, listen very carefully to what I have to say. The reason there's a constable outside the house is because the police think I am in danger.'

'In danger of what?'

'Of being hurt, silly. To be precise, of being murdered.'

'What?' Bertram looked appalled.

'A girl was murdered last night, and the police think the murderer mistook her for me.'

'Celia, what on earth are you talking about? You're making no sense at all. Why should anyone wish to murder you?'

Bertram was staring at her with a look of complete puzzlement upon his face. 'And who was this girl who got herself murdered anyway? What had she to do with you?'

'Very little, as it happens. It was one of the shop assistants from that awful little dress shop we went to last night.'

'The dress shop? You can't mean Renard's?'

How very irritating Bertram was being, querying and questioning everything she said as if he were simple. Really, she didn't see how she could make it any easier for him to understand.

'Well, of course I do, darling. We didn't go to any other dress shop last night, did we?'

'Celia, tell me who was murdered? It was one of the shop assistants, I think you said?'

'Yes, a girl called Sylvia Beckett. She was the one modelling all the clothes. A pretty little thing, if a little common.'

'Celia!'

'Oh, I know, darling, I'm being a little heartless, and I don't mean to be. I think it's the shock, that's all. I really am so terribly frightened to think it could have been me, instead of her, I mean. I suppose that's why I'm being so ghastly about it. Bertram?'

'I … I'm sorry, it hasn't quite sunk in.' Bertram dropped his forehead to his hand in such a manner as to screen his eyes. 'I think I should like to sit down, if I may, and you can explain it all to me properly.'

'Of course, darling. It took me a while to digest it all myself when they initially told me about it first thing this morning. I thought it was all some sort of beastly joke. Poor old Beeswick. I think he was quite beside himself when the police telephoned him last night. The dear old thing insisted on positioning a footman outside my bedroom door and another outside my window. Have you ever heard of anything so adorable?'

'Celia … You are being quite –'

'Yes, I know darling, I'm being absolutely horrid or silly or both. I just don't want to think about that poor girl, particularly after I was so beastly to her. I'm not saying that she didn't deserve it, because she did, but if I'd known then … There now, let's not talk any more about it until you've sat down and had some sweet tea. I believe that's just the thing for shock, isn't it? Hot tea with heaps of sugar. Or perhaps you'd prefer brandy?'

'Tea will be fine,' Bertram said firmly enough, although he allowed himself to be led into the breakfast room where Celia rang the bell for tea. He sank into one of the chairs drawn up to the table. He put his elbows on the table top, and rested his head in his hands so that the expression on his face was once again obscured from view.

'Of course it is very sad,' Celia was saying. 'And to think we saw the poor girl only last night. Apparently, would you believe, she was killed a very short time after we left.'

'Oh?' Bertram looked up, with something akin to interest.

'Yes. The police think the girl was killed sometime between returning to her dressing room after showing the last dress and that ridiculous fire breaking out. Really, I wonder whose idea it was to position that dreadful candelabra so close to the curtains. If any servant of mine did that, they'd soon find themselves without a positon. Now, what was I saying ...? Oh, yes, the girl's body was discovered in the dressing room by the proprietor shortly after all the customers had left the shop. She was looking for me apparently, the proprietor I mean, not the girl. Madame Renard hadn't seen me leave and she was concerned that I might not know anything about the fire.'

'But if it happened when you say it did,' Bertram said, slowly and with deliberation, removing his hand from his face as he did so, 'we would more than likely have still been in the shop when the girl was killed.'

'You might be right,' said Celia sounding rather doubtful. 'But we would definitely have been on our way out.'

'But would we?'

'Really, darling, does it matter? We didn't see anything, nothing that could help the police anyway.'

'Celia, there's something I must tell you, I –'

'No!' Celia said forcefully and so quickly, she hardly had time to draw breath.

It was only when she saw the way Bertram flinched that she realised that she must have raised her voice. Certainly he looked quite taken aback. She looked down at her hands, and realised she was shaking. Quickly she hid them in her lap and clasped them together to try and keep them still. She must recover her equanimity.

'Please,' she said quickly, with an urgency she had not experienced before. 'Please don't say anything more. I don't want to know, do you hear? I couldn't bear it. And besides, it's in the past. Don't go over it, it doesn't do any good.'

'Celia, I have –'

'There's nothing either one of us can do about it. So let's not talk about it. No good will come of it. We must look to the future. And, darling,' she bent forward and took his hand, 'I forgive you.'

'But Celia –'

'No! Don't you understand, Bertie?' She had risen from her seat and was now kneeling beside him. She realised she was holding his hand so tightly, she didn't think she would ever let it go. 'Look at me, darling. Nothing would stop me loving you. But if you tell me something now, something that you have done that is awful and despicable I won't be able to keep it to myself, even if I want to. I'll be obliged, you see, to tell the police everything I know. I won't want to, of course. If I know it will do you harm, I should rather die. But I won't be able to keep quiet about it, no matter how much I want to. You do see that, don't you, darling?'

'Yes ... I suppose so.'

Bertram spoke so quietly that she had to bend her head even more closely towards him. He looked so very deflated and miserable, that she almost relented. But that would never do, it was too dangerous. Instead she squeezed his hand and was relieved when he answered by squeezing hers, if a little reluctantly.

Reassured, Celia got up and resumed her seat. It was not a moment too soon, for the insolent footman immediately entered with the tea and for a moment or two she busied herself pouring English breakfast tea into the most delicate of porcelain cups, the clatter of teaspoons on china resounding comfortably throughout the room. It might have been the most ordinary of mornings. Bertram might have been another one of the frequent houseguests who enjoyed the Goswells' hospitality, sitting enjoying a cup of tea after breakfast. If he had been one of the usual men of her acquaintance, they might have been about to discuss the weather or how they intended to spend the day which stretched out before them. Instead, Bertram said, as soon as the servant had departed:

'I say, what makes the police think you might have been the intended victim and not the girl?'

'We were wearing the same dress.'

'Were you?' Bertram sounded surprised. 'I must say I didn't notice.'

'Didn't you?' There was a slight chilliness to Celia's voice. 'No, I suppose you wouldn't. It was only for a very short while that we were wearing the same frock. It was the last gown she came out in. Don't you remember what she was wearing?'

'I can't say I do.'

'A silver satin evening gown with lace and glass and silver beads. She wore it for a few minutes at most. I was wearing a dress in the very same material. It was similar to it in style too, but not quite as nice or as decorative. It didn't have all the little embellishments that were on her dress.'

'You looked very becoming in your dress,' said Bertram, rather weakly. 'I thought that the moment I saw you this evening.'

'Did you really? But the girl's dress suited her even better,' added Celia. 'It was much more elaborate and … well, she had the figure for it.'

There was an awkward silence. It was only of a few moments' duration, but it seemed nevertheless to fill the room, creating a physical gulf between them. Celia hurried on. She could not bear the thought that Bertram might be that very moment conjuring up a vision of the mannequin in his mind's eye. She feared she would compare unfavourably in comparison. And he could almost be forgiven if he was wondering how the murderer could possibly have mistaken the two women for one another.

'The girl apparently had her back to the door of the dressing room,' she said, as if an explanation was required. 'So it's possible that the murderer did not see her face. Not only was she wearing the same sort of dress that I had on, if I remember correctly, the colour of her hair was a similar shade to mine.'

'But even so –' protested Bertram.

'The constable told me the murderer would have been at pains to carry out the deed as quickly as possible so as not to be caught in the act.'

'Well, it still seems to me highly unlikely that the murderer made a mistake,' said Bertram. 'If nothing else, who on earth would want to kill you, Celia?'

'Lots of people I expect,' said Celia rather flippantly. 'I have been known to ruffle one or two feathers.'

'You don't believe that any more than I do!' retorted Bertram.

'Well, whoever would want to kill a shop girl?' replied Celia rather haughtily. 'But, whatever you and I might think, the police will be coming here shortly to interview me. I expect they'll want to interview you too, what with you being there and then escorting me home afterwards.'

'I say, do you really think so?' Bertram paled.

'Well of course they will, not that we have anything to tell them. We didn't see anything that will help them with their investigations. Now, as I recollect,' said Celia speaking slowly and deliberately, 'the girl came out in the silver gown. Both the proprietor and I were rather taken aback as we had not expected her to do such a thing. If the truth be told, I had expressly forbidden her to wear the dress because I had chosen to wear it myself. Oh, don't look at me like that, Bertram. You don't understand.

She had been particularly rude to me in front of everyone else and I just wanted to get my own back.'

Celia began to pace the room as she recounted her version of events. She stopped every so often to steal a glance at Bertram to ensure that he was following her narrative. He in turn looked a little appalled, as if he found the whole business distasteful. She ignored him, having got into her stride, and went on, the words escaping from her lips until they seemed to fill the room.

'The girl realised at once what she had done. I daresay she had second thoughts, because she soon turned tail and retreated to the dressing room. Do you remember?' Bertram said nothing. He looked so dazed by it all that she wondered if he realised what she was saying. 'I was extremely annoyed, and said as much to Madame Renard when I managed to fight my way through the audience to her. I was rather ungracious, I'm afraid. I demanded that the poor girl be sacked. You must remember my saying that? You caught my eye and looked at me reprovingly.'

'Did I? I don't remember doing that.'

'Well, you did, darling. And you were quite right of course. Only, I couldn't stop myself. Now ... where was I? Oh, yes. The fire broke out. There was a lot of yelling and shrieking, chairs and tables toppled over and people were going in all sorts of directions to try and get out of the shop. So silly when one thinks that it was such a very little fire and so quickly put out. I lost sight of you for a few moments and then I saw you. You were with the other men beating out the fire. You looked so strong and brave that I fell in love with you all over again.'

'Celia –'

'Please don't interrupt, darling, I want to go through what happened while it's still fresh in my mind. You caught my eye and smiled. You mouthed some words to me. I think you said something to the effect that I was not to worry.'

'Celia, I did no such thing.'

'Yes, you did.' said Celia firmly. 'You stayed to help put the fire out and then we decided to slip out into the street. You do remember that, don't you?'

'Celia, let me think for a moment,' said Bertram. 'The fire had put paid to the evening. The fashion show had as good as finished before the drape caught fire. We decided there was no need to stay. You thought it only polite to say goodbye to the proprietor, but she and her assistants had their hands full trying to calm the crowd.'

'Yes,' agreed Celia. 'We thought the best thing we could do in the circumstances was to leave. We didn't wish to add to Madame Renard's burden, did we?'

'Most of the people were fearful of passing the smoking drapes and were trying to make their way out through the back of the shop. We thought it jolly silly. It was easy enough to leave the shop through the main shop door that faced the street.'

'And so that is just what we did,' said Celia almost gaily. 'We must have been amongst the very first to leave, because when I happened to look back over my shoulder, there was a queue of people trying to leave the premises through the storeroom. It had a door that came out onto the street at the back of the shop. '

'And so that is what we shall tell the police when they interview us?' said Bertram.

'But of course, darling. It's the truth after all.'

Bertram frowned and averted his gaze.

'Not the whole truth,' he mumbled, although he spoke so quietly that it was doubtful whether his companion was even aware that he had spoken. 'We've omitted one or two things.'

Chapter Twenty-six

'We need to speak with you,' said Rose quietly but briskly. 'I suggest you may wish to take us somewhere private to have this conversation, unless of course you'd like your customers and assistants to hear what we have to say.'

'I don't know what you're talking about. Now, please go away.' There was no doubt now that the woman was frightened, fear tinged her voice.

'You know full well what we are talking about,' said Rose speaking a little louder. 'You were seen setting fire to one of the curtains at the fashion event held at Renard's last night.' The women made a gesture to protest. 'No, please don't try and deny it. If you do, I shall shout it out so that the whole shop can hear. I am sure your assistants would be most interested to know. Why, I must say, that customer who you were talking to just now looks rather interested in our conversation. I daresay she'd like me to speak up a little so that she can hear what I'm saying. Excuse me,' Rose said raising her voice considerably as she addressed the woman in question, 'would you like to –'

'Shush!' implored the proprietor. She put a hand up to her face as if she were trying to hide behind it. 'Come into my office quickly and say whatever it is you have to say to me there, if you must. I warn you though that I shall deny everything.'

The proprietor hurried over to the customer and made her excuses, summoning one of the shop assistants to tend to the woman's needs. It was not lost on any of them that various sets of eyes followed their progress as they made their way to the office.

'You've no right accusing a respectable, law abiding person like myself of anything so improper,' began the proprietor, as soon as she had closed the door firmly behind them.

'Mrs ...'

'Mrs Berry,' said the proprietor.

'Mrs Berry, please hear me out before you say anything,' said Rose firmly. 'We know full well that you set fire to the drape. There really is no use denying the fact. You were spotted doing it and I am fairly sure I know why you did it.' The proprietor made to protest again. 'No, please don't try and deny it,' Rose said quickly. 'No good will come of it. I think I can speak truthfully when I say that, if you were to arrange to pay for the damage caused, Madame Renard is unlikely to bring any criminal charges against you. We really do have far more pressing things to concern ourselves with at the moment than a ruined curtain.'

There was an awkward silence while Mrs Berry appeared to be considering her options.

'Please make your mind up quickly whether or not you intend to tell us the truth,' Rose said. 'If you'd rather speak to the police, I am sure that can be arranged. Mary, perhaps you'd like to telephone Scotland Yard and ask to speak to Inspector Deacon. I am sure that gentleman will be most interested to hear what Mrs Berry has to say for herself.'

Mary was slow to respond, staring at the telephone on the desk. Rose's words had however had the desired effect on the proprietor who almost threw herself on the telephone so that the instrument could not be used.

'No … wait. Do you promise me I shan't get into any trouble?' Rose nodded, although she doubted if she was qualified to give that assurance. 'I shall tell you everything if you promise not to tell my staff or customers. I don't really know where to begin,' added Mrs Berry sounding flustered.

'Suppose I tell you what I know or rather what I've surmised,' said Rose. 'I think Marcel Girard had arranged with you to exhibit his designs at Thimbles, am I right?'

'Yes, he hadn't shown them before, so he said, and they really were rather good. We were planning our own fashion event at which to unveil them,' said Mrs Berry. She leant forward. 'Of course, it would have been a far superior event to the one held at Renard's last night.'

'Jacques Renard mentioned that Thimbles were interested in showing Monsieur Girard's designs,' said Rose. 'Marcel must have mentioned it to him. He told me that you were snapping at his heels to exhibit his work.'

'Did he indeed?' said Mrs Berry with a look of disgust. 'Well he needn't think we'll be showing his designs now, not now he's showing them in every Tom, Dick or Harry dress shop. Exclusive to Thimbles, they were to have been, his designs.'

'But you found out about the Renard's fashion event?'

'Yes. Purely by chance, I might add. One of my customers, she also shops at Renard's. Not that she ever finds anything there worth buying of course. Much prefers my garments, I can tell you. '

'That would have been Mrs Milton?'

'Yes. I was telling her all about our fashion event and then blow me if she doesn't tell me there's going to be one held at Renard's and of the same designer, would I believe? Well, I certainly didn't believe it until she produced that invitation of hers and showed me. There was his name, bold as brass. You could have knocked me down with a feather.'

'What did you do?'

'Well, I tell you, I was minded to go straight to Harridges and have it out with Monsieur Girard, I can tell you,' said Mrs Berry. 'But then I said to myself, no Ivy, don't be too hasty. Because I remembered, you see, that Mrs Milton had left her invitation in the shop. I'd put it in a drawer of my desk meaning to give it to her when she next frequented Thimbles. Not that she needed it as such, having told me that she wouldn't be going as she had a prior engagement. Well, I decided I'd go in her place, that's what I'd do. A nice shock it would be for young Monsieur Girard to see me there, I thought. It would serve him right.'

'It was a shock to him,' said Rose. 'I saw his face when he spotted you in the audience. He kept mainly to the storeroom after that. I expect he was afraid that you'd make your way over to him and make a scene.'

'Well,' continued Mrs Berry. 'I'm not so sure I'd have done that seeing as some of Madame Renard's customers are also mine. I wouldn't have wanted them to think I was some sort of fishwife. Wouldn't have been the done thing at all, me making a spectacle of myself. No, I said to myself, Ivy, you bide your time, and that's what I did. Those designs Monsieur Girard showed at Renard's, they weren't particularly good. Not his best work, I'd have said. The ones he was going to show at Thimbles, why, they were far superior.'

'So you had forgiven him for the deception?' prompted Rose.

'Well I had and I hadn't,' answered Mrs Berry. 'But then of course he ruined it all by having that girl come out in that silver gown. The show had all but finished and when she made her entrance I saw at once what he was doing. Leaving his best designs to last. You should have seen the audience, mesmerised by that dress, they were. I thought, hello Ivy, that's just the first of many, that is. He'll have her parading out in a number of gowns like that one and who'll want to come and see the fashion event at Thimbles? Because I can tell you that he hadn't shown me any designs like that.'

'What did you do?' asked Rose, although she already knew.

'I wasn't going to let him get away with that, not likely,' said Mrs Berry. 'I know it was very wrong of me, but I had to do something to stop him. I was standing by the candelabra and it gave me the idea. Only the fire took hold rather more than I thought it would. I screamed. It did the trick all right. Everyone was running here and there and Monsieur Girard couldn't show any more of his gowns. They were putting the fire out quickly, I'll say that for them, but the place smelled of smoke and burnt cloth. If he's contrite I daresay I might let him show those evening gowns at Thimbles after all.' Mrs Berry crossed her arms and looked rather smug. 'Anyway, no harm's been done has it? I'll pay Madame Renard for the curtain, of course I will. I'll give her a bit more to show goodwill. But if it's all the same to you I'd rather you didn't tell her –'

'You really don't know what you've done, do you?' said Rose. She found that she was trembling. 'You did cause harm. Far more than you could ever have imagined. A woman is dead. Don't you see? You caused a distraction and someone took advantage of that opportunity to commit a murder. They killed the girl that was the mannequin. If it hadn't been for you, she would most probably still be alive today.'

Chapter Twenty-seven

'Miss Simpson, fancy seeing you here,' said Sergeant Perkins with genuine warmth as Rose and Mary were ushered into the drawing room of the Goswells' London residence. 'And you too, Miss Jennings. I'd have thought you'd both be still tucked up in bed, what with the night you've had. Me, I could hardly open my eyes this morning. It seemed as if I'd just shut them for a few seconds and I had to get up again.'

'Where is Inspector Deacon, Sergeant? I've something awfully important to tell him,' said Rose hurriedly.

'He's having a quiet word with Beeswick, miss. He's the butler here, you know. The inspector, he's asking him a few questions such as the time Lady Celia returned here last night and the like … ah, here he is now. Sir, we have a couple of visitors.'

'So I see. Miss Simpson, what on earth are you doing here?' said Inspector Deacon, in a not altogether friendly tone. It somewhat amused Rose to note that his annoyance did not appear to extend to Mary, who was watching their exchange with interest.

'It's nice to see you too, Inspector,' said Rose, giving him something of an indignant look. 'I thought you might be interested in knowing that I've discovered the identity of the person who set fire to Madame Renard's curtain.'

'The woman who screamed?' asked Sergeant Perkins earnestly.

'Yes, that's the one, Sergeant,' said Rose cheerily. 'But if the inspector would rather not know or perhaps, being a policeman, has found out already for himself, then we'll be on our way. Come on, Mary. It appears that all our efforts this morning have been wasted.'

'Rose … Miss Simpson, wait a minute.'

'Oh, have you changed your mind, Inspector? I'm so glad,' said Rose, taking a seat and smiling sweetly. 'You see, I'd like to be present when you interview Lady Celia, if you have no objections of course.'

'We'll have to see about that,' said Inspector Deacon. 'But first I'd like to hear what you have to tell us about the woman who set fire to the curtain.'

Rose proceeded to give a brief summary of their excursion that morning, including her reasoning for undertaking the journey, and what Mrs Berry had to say for herself when confronted.

'Well, I never!' exclaimed Sergeant Perkins. 'And you deduced all that from those interviews with Mr Renard and Mr Girard, did you? She must have been worried, that proprietor woman, when you accused her of starting the fire. I bet she thought she'd got away with it. Well, I would have put the fear of God into her myself, I can tell you. A wilful bit of damage that was, to say nothing of being damned dangerous.'

'Rose did,' said Mary. 'Put the fear of god into her, I mean. Mrs Berry looked ever so worried.'

'Just right. It was a nasty, spiteful thing she did,' said the sergeant. 'I think she should be prosecuted, so I do.'

'I promised her I wouldn't tell Madame Renard,' said Rose. 'She's going to pay for the damage, and … well, I thought it was more important to find out whether the fire and the murder were connected. Mrs Berry wouldn't have told us anything if she had thought it would get her into trouble. At least we now know there wasn't any connection other than that the murderer took advantage of the distraction caused by the fire.'

'Well done, Miss Simpson. It seems you've put us all to shame,' said Inspector Deacon quietly. Unless she was mistaken, there was a touch of coldness to his voice.

'I didn't mean …' began Rose, her cheeks burning. Although quite what she didn't mean, she didn't know.

'We shall have to interview the woman ourselves of course. I'm afraid that we can't just take your word for it. We'll have to satisfy ourselves, but it won't be the first thing to do on our list.'

There was an uncomfortable silence, which was thankfully interrupted by Inspector Deacon being called into the hall by the butler.

'Don't worry, miss,' said Sergeant Perkins sympathetically. 'By all accounts the inspector's not quite himself. Hasn't been ever since the shooting. Sergeant Lane's been that worried about him, I can't tell you. The inspector, he does appreciate your efforts though, whatever he says, but he doesn't feel he can let on. Doesn't think it would be professional like. We're not in the habit of encouraging amateur sleuths, they'd put us out of business! All joking aside, miss, he's only concerned for your safety. I reckon myself he holds you in pretty high esteem.'

The sergeant was very tempted to say a bit more, but rather unusually for him he thought better of it, and held his tongue. He didn't want to be responsible after all for letting the cat out of the bag. He wouldn't be thanked for doing that. And by all accounts Miss Simpson had a nice young man, although whether anything would come of it, he really wouldn't like to say. It wasn't often that you heard of a member of the British aristocracy marrying a shop girl, was it? Although that was not to say it was unheard of. Some of them had married chorus girls and actresses in the past, hadn't they? Created quite a scandal if everything he had heard about them was to be believed.

'Sergeant Perkins,' said Rose, 'didn't you hear me?'

'I'm sorry, miss, you caught me daydreaming. I told you how I hadn't had enough sleep, didn't I? Now, what were you saying?'

'I was saying how frightfully important it is that I be present at the interviews of Lady Celia and Mr Thorpe. He's still here, isn't he, Mr Thorpe, I mean? The footman said he was.'

'Yes, he's still here. Her ladyship summoned him first thing this morning.'

'You see, I'm pretty sure that I know who the murderer is. That's to say I think it's one of two people, and ... well, as I've been fortunate enough to attend all the other interviews, I'd like to be present for Lady Celia's and Mr Thorpe's also. You do understand, don't you, Sergeant?'

'I do indeed, miss. And all I can say is, well I never. You knowing who the murderer is and all.' Sergeant Perkins' eyes were as large as saucers. 'And I don't doubt for a minute you're right. If you're half as good as you were over that fire business, well, the case will be as good as solved by lunchtime.'

'I don't think the inspector will appreciate you saying so,' said Rose. 'I'd be grateful if you wouldn't mind being quiet about it until after the interviews. But I was wondering whether you could help me. You see, if I could have a quick word with Lady Celia before she is interviewed, I think she'll agree to me accompanying her and then Inspector Deacon ... well, he really won't be able to object, will he? Not if Lady Celia requests it.'

'You'll get me into trouble, miss. I'd like to help you, of course I would but –' began Sergeant Perkins. Rather fortunately for him, he was interrupted by the sound of the door being opened. Lady Celia walked into the room.

'Hello Rose. Beeswick said you were here. Don't tell me, you're doing some investigating, aren't you? How wonderful.'

'Yes, I am, Lady Celia,' said Rose quickly. 'I've attended all the interviews and I should like to be present at your interview and Mr Thorpe's as well, if you don't have any objections of course.'

'Oh, absolutely, why should we possibly object? I should hate it if you were to leave us out,' cried Celia. 'Gosh, I've never seen an amateur detective detecting, so to speak. How thrilling.'

'Lady Celia … ah, Miss Simpson, still here?' enquired Inspector Deacon, appearing at the door.

'Yes, Inspector. Lady Celia would like me to accompany her when you interview her. I'm sure you understand?'

'Perfectly, Miss Simpson. How very foolish of me to have made the mistake of leaving you in here alone.' Rose wondered whether he had forgotten the presence of the sergeant lurking in the corner, or whether his choice of words was intentional. Certainly Sergeant Perkins looked rather sheepish.

'Oh, rather,' said Lady Celia. 'That's to say, I should like Miss Simpson to be with me. I should hate to feel singled out. She was only just telling me how she had been present at all the other interviews.' She turned and smiled at Rose. 'I've heard Lavinia thinks very highly of your abilities, my dear. Now I shall have the opportunity to see if she's right. Where would you like us to go, Inspector? I was thinking of the library. That seems rather fitting don't you think?'

The library proved very satisfactory with its abundance of straight back chairs, a large desk for the inspector to sit behind and a small writing table on which the sergeant was able to take down his shorthand.

Once the preliminary questions were dealt with, Inspector Deacon proceeded to get down to the business in hand. Lady Celia, he noticed, was sitting very erect in her chair, her hands held daintily in her lap. That she was trying to give the impression of a thoroughly attentive witness, happy to answer all the questions he had to ask, he had little doubt. If he were to be uncharitable, he would say she was regarding the whole business as a bit of a game. And yet her smile was a little too fixed and, unless he was mistaken, she looked genuinely anxious. There was nothing uncommon about that, of course. People generally were nervous of being interviewed by the police as part of a murder investigation. It was expected and, had she behaved differently, it would have aroused his suspicions. Nevertheless, for the first time he wondered if she had something to hide. Rose too, he noticed, was watching the woman very closely.

'Lady Celia, I appreciate that this must be distressing for you.'

'No, Inspector, not really. You see, I didn't know the girl. It's very sad and all that, but not distressing. Unless of course ...' she paused so that she might lean forward slightly towards the inspector; he could almost feel her breath upon him, '... you are going to tell me that the murderer meant to kill me after all.'

'No. We now have no reason to believe that Miss Beckett was not the intended victim. I'm sorry if we caused you alarm.'

'Oh, I see,' she sounded slightly disappointed. 'But Beeswick told me –'

'Yes,' said the inspector quickly. 'It was a possible line of enquiry that we were investigating. I should like to put your mind at rest that we are now satisfied that in all probability Miss Beckett was the intended victim. Now, perhaps you could tell me how you came to be at Renard's last night.'

'I'm sure Miss Simpson has already told you. I happened to be having tea with a friend of mine, Judith Musgrove, when Lady Lavinia telephoned to enquire if Judith could stand in for her as a mannequin. Judith couldn't and so I offered to do so in her place. There's no more to it than that, Inspector. I was just trying to do a good turn.'

'You are a good friend of Lady Lavinia's?'

'I wouldn't say that, Inspector. But it sounded as if it might be frightfully fun.'

'Why?' asked Rose. 'You're not a bit interested in clothes. You find them rather boring. You said so to me yourself.'

'Oh, I say, that's a bit harsh,' said Lady Celia, colouring visibly. 'And I have to say, I didn't realise that you would be asking me questions as well as the inspector, Rose. Is this what is referred to as a two pronged approach? I'm not sure I like it. I don't know which one of you to look at.'

'Miss Simpson is merely here in an observational capacity,' said Inspector Deacon. 'She won't be asking any more questions, will you, Miss Simpson?' He gave her a warning look.

'Oh, I don't really blame her, Inspector. I suppose it's what amateur detectives do, isn't it?

'Did you happen to know the deceased at all, Lady Celia?' continued the inspector.

'No, of course not. We didn't move in the same social circles, as I'm sure you will appreciate, and I would never go shopping in a shop like Renard's.' She lowered her voice. 'It sells ghastly ready-to-wear clothes, Inspector, and between you and me, the material they use is frightfully cheap, artificial silk and rayon, and that sort of thing.'

Rose, her cheeks burning as if the insult had been directed towards herself rather than Madame Renard's shop, focused her attention on a row of books on the far wall considerably above the inspector's head. It was all she could do not to give some sort of a retort. Words flew readily enough to her lips, but she did not utter them. If she had, she would undoubtedly have been sent packing. Really, she had quite forgotten how very unpleasant and contrary Lady Celia could be.

'So you had not met Miss Beckett until yesterday?'

'No.'

'I understand that you had what one might call a bit of a falling out,' said Inspector Deacon.

'Oh, that. Really it was nothing, Inspector.' Lady Celia laughed a high, artificial little laugh. 'The girl was a little impertinent, that's all, and understandably I took great exception to her attitude.'

'I believe it had something to do with the silver gown?'

'Yes.' There was a cold edge to the woman's voice as she called the incident to mind. 'The girl, she looked very pretty in it and ... well, I wanted to wear it too. I knew that I wouldn't look as beautiful in it as she did, because I didn't have her figure, but I thought it might be quite fetching on me. The girl, she was dreadfully unkind about it. She made a face behind my back. I saw her reflection. Silly girl, she'd forgotten that I was looking in the mirror. Well, I'm afraid it made me act in rather a beastly way towards her.'

'You insisted that she didn't wear the dress, I believe?'

'Yes. It sounds so spiteful and mean-spirited when you say it now. But really she was dreadfully unkind and I was very angry about it. Of course if I'd known then …. But I didn't … If I could turn back the clock … But whatever you think of me, Inspector, I wouldn't kill someone because I had caught them making a face at me.'

'According to a number of witnesses, you were quite livid when Miss Beckett appeared in the dress at the end of the show. I've been led to believe that you demanded that Madame Renard dismiss her on the spot.'

'Again, Inspector, not my finest hour. But it appeared to me at the time that the girl was deliberately trying to upset me. But as I've said, I bitterly regret the way I behaved towards her. I should have risen above it, as my old governess would say.'

'Perhaps you would be so good as to tell me your movements from … let's see, the point when Miss Beckett returned to the dressing room and you spoke to Madame Renard about the girl losing her job.'

'Well, I was very annoyed, I have you know. So I'm afraid I gave Madame Renard rather a talking to. I had to fight my way through the crowd to get to her, even though she was standing fairly near me. I was none too pleased, I can tell you. I'm afraid I wasn't very quiet about it, giving Madame Renard a piece of my mind, so to speak. Taking her to task and all that. Bertram … Mr Thorpe, caught my eye and looked at me rather disapprovingly, but I couldn't stop myself.'

'What did you do next?'

'Well, I think that was when the fire broke out. Everybody was awfully frightened, I remember. It was such a silly little fire, but people will panic, won't they? Anyway, it was soon put out. Mr Thorpe and some of the other men saw to that. Bertram mouthed to me that I wasn't to worry, that everything was in hand. But the evening was completely ruined, so we decided that it was time for us to take our leave.'

'Did you say anything to Madame Renard about your going?'

'Oh, no. She had her hands completely full. I intended to send her a little note today.'

'By which door did you leave?'

'The shop door. The one that faces the street. I expect we were two of the first to leave. Most of the people were trying to get out through the storeroom. They were afraid of passing the curtains, I think. Awfully silly of them.'

229

'And you came straight here?'

'Oh, yes. Mr Thorpe escorted me home and then left for his service flat. It had been quite an eventful evening and we were both tired. Of course we didn't realise at the time how eventful it had been. Poor girl. I didn't particularly take to her, but even so it's a frightful shame. Now, Inspector, is that all? May I go now?'

Lady Celia was already up out of her chair and halfway across the room before the inspector had a chance to reply.

Chapter Twenty-eight

'Well, I can't say we've learned very much from Lady Celia,' said Inspector Deacon as soon as the door had closed behind the retreating figure of the woman in question.

'No,' said Rose slowly. 'It was rather disappointing. I should like to stay here for Mr Thorpe's interview if I may. He might be a little more forthcoming.'

'It will be up to him whether or not you stay,' said Inspector Deacon rather gruffly. 'Sergeant, go and ask the fellow to step in now, will you?'

'Yes, sir,' said Sergeant Perkins, although it was with some reluctance that he left the room.

How he'd have liked to have been a fly on the wall listening to those two. Miss Simpson would put her case pretty well, he thought. Yes, and she was liable to be even more outspoken without him there. He'd like to see that, so he would. As to the inspector, he thought he'd give in to her demands. Anyone could see that he wanted to, he just didn't think it was proper to do so. And of course he was concerned about her. He didn't want her to go investigating by herself. Who knew what sort of trouble she'd get herself into? It wasn't so much this case, it was the ones that would follow when he might not be there. Why, according to Miss Simpson, this case was almost done and dusted, although he personally hadn't a clue who the murderer was and thought it unlikely he ever would have, no matter how many more interviews they had. He thought not one of them had been enlightening or produced anything of particular significance. The inspector now, he'd probably got a better idea of it all. Quite as bright as Miss Simpson, he was. Now where was this Thorpe fellow? The last he'd heard he was in the breakfast room, wherever that was. He'd ask one of those fancy footmen …

It might have surprised the sergeant to know that, following his immediate departure from the room, there was an uncomfortable silence. The inspector went to the far side of the room, ostensibly to look out of the window. Rose fiddled with the catch on her bag as if she were looking for something within. A few moments passed and still they were both employed in their self-imposed, rather useless occupations. When the silence was more than either of them could bear, it was Rose who rushed in on it with nervous speech.

'Please don't be against me,' cried Rose, tugging at the inspector's arm, before stopping short and colouring visibly.

Inspector Deacon turned. He had not heard her approach, and now he did not know quite what to say.

'I'm not against you,' he mumbled. However, he would not look her in the eye.

'Yes, you are. But we haven't got time to discuss it now. We must hurry. Don't you see? Bertram Thorpe will be here any moment and I need your assurance that you'll let me speak. I need to ask him one or two questions. You must permit me to do so without interrupting, or asking me to be quiet, or threatening to evict me from the room if I so much as open my mouth to breathe.'

'Miss Simpson,' began the inspector. To her horror she saw that he was desperately trying to keep a straight face.

'This is no laughing matter, Inspector. I am being deadly serious. I need to be allowed to ask a few questions and then … well, I shall know who the murderer is.'

The look on the inspector's face turned from laughter to surprise. He stared at her in earnest for a moment. She herself could hardly breathe. What would have happened next, what the inspector would have said, if anything, Rose was never to know. For the door opened and in walked Bertram Thorpe, with Sergeant Perkins following behind.

'Ah, Mr Thorpe,' said Inspector Deacon rallying. 'Do take a seat. This is Miss Simpson. You may remember her from last night's fashion event? I wonder, would you have any objection to her remaining? She is something of an amateur sleuth who has been engaged by Madame Renard to investigate this sad affair.'

With the inspector's words ringing in her ears and the look of utter astonishment on the sergeant's face, Rose rushed in to make the most of her advantage.

'I hope you don't mind, Mr Thorpe? Lady Celia was most eager that I be present at your interview. I was present at hers. She absolutely insisted upon it.' She gave him her most charming smile.

'Well … I don't know. I'm not sure,' said Bertram Thorpe rather hesitantly. 'But If Lady Celia thought it was all right, then I daresay –'

'Thank you so much, Mr Thorpe.'

Rose was very tempted to position herself opposite Bertram, in order to catch any change of expression on his face as he answered the questions put to him. She decided, however, that it was best not to test the inspector's patience and tolerance too far. Instead, she opted to sit a little away from the inspector, which provided her with a good view of Bertram's profile. She was reminded again of how very ordinary in appearance she had thought him when she had first laid her eyes on him the previous evening. Having a better view of him as she did now, she realised that she had been doing him a disservice. True, there was nothing particularly distinguished about his features, but he was above average in height and slender in build. There was also a quiet composure about him, even now when he was clearly frightened. Only his hands betrayed any signs of nervousness, picking at imaginary bits of fluff on the top of his trouser leg. It occurred to Rose that he had much to be frightened of.

The preliminary questions began, and Rose found her mind drifting off to a vision of a woman in a silver gown, her head held high, and a smile playing about her lips in acknowledgment of the appreciative glances bestowed upon her. She was descending the stairs and parading around the room with a poise and elegance that Rose had not known Sylvia to possess. *I think it's just the sort of dress that would make a man fall in love with a woman, don't you… or propose marriage…*

'Had you ever met the deceased before, Mr Thorpe?' asked Inspector Deacon, cutting into her thoughts.

'The deceased?'

'Yes. The girl who was the mannequin. You may remember her? Her name was Sylvia Beckett.'

'I'd never met her before, Inspector.' Bertram said, averting his gaze slightly.

'Well –' began the inspector.

'You're lying, Mr Thorpe,' said Rose. 'You happened to know her very well indeed. You were her young man, weren't you?'

'I don't know what you can be talking about.' Bertram's eyes were darting around the room. He looked wildly at Rose and then at the inspector and the sergeant, as if he were trying to find an ally amongst them. 'How can you think …? It is madness what she's saying –'

'No, it's not,' said Rose sharply. 'It's no use denying it. You are the young man of whom Sylvia spoke of to all of us. To Mary, Jacques and myself. The young man with prospects.'

'It's all nonsense, what you are saying,' said Bertram. 'Why, I'm all but engaged to Lady Celia.'

'And that I think,' said Rose, 'was the issue.'

'Come, Mr Thorpe, it would be far better if you were to tell us the truth,' said Inspector Deacon, making a good attempt at concealing his own surprise. 'We'll find it out anyway, you know we will. It's a habit we have. It would be much better if you were to tell us in your own words.'

'I ... oh, all right. What's the use of my denying it?' Bertram put his hand to his head. For a moment it looked as if he might weep. 'What I will say in my own defence is that I had ceased to be her young man ... I'd broken off our relationship. I did so as soon as I met Lady Celia but ... well, the girl, she wouldn't accept it.'

'Mr Thorpe, I should warn you –'

'No need, Inspector. I know my rights. I'm a solicitor after all. I had fully intended to lie about knowing Sylvia, only I can't, not really. It seems rather a rum sort of thing to do to the girl, don't you think? She deserved better than that.'

'Yes, she did. Now, sir, initially you said there was no attachment. Now you would have us believe that an attachment of sorts had existed but that you had subsequently ended your relationship with Miss Beckett. Is that correct?'

'Yes. Sylvia ... she was being very difficult about it. It was all my own fault of course. We had talked of marriage. But then I met Lady Celia.'

'Whom you considered a much better marriage proposition?' suggested Inspector Deacon. There was a slight coldness to his voice that was not lost on Rose.

'You needn't look at me like that, Inspector,' said Bertram indignantly, his colour rising. 'It had nothing to do with Lady Celia's title or money, if that's what you're thinking. I happened to like her better, that's all. She didn't ask or expect anything of me, and she wasn't at all vain. After Miss Beckett, you have no idea how refreshing that was.'

'Perhaps that's because she didn't need to be,' said Rose.

'You're quite right, Miss Simpson, she didn't. But what I found quite remarkable was that she was quite happy to settle for someone like me.

She'd had a whole host of other suitors, but she had turned them all down. What she saw in me, I can't imagine.'

Neither can I, thought Rose, but she decided not to voice her thoughts out loud. Instead she said:

'You must have given Sylvia some hope. You still saw something of her, didn't you?'

'How did you –'

'She was making someone steal clothes for her from Renard's. She wanted to look her best when she saw you.'

'I told you. She was being damned difficult about it. I had to see her. I tried to make her see reason, but she wouldn't. You know what her sort are like, Inspector, easy to acquire but damned impossible to get rid of.'

'No, I'm not at all familiar with that sort as you put it,' said Inspector Deacon. There was no mistaking the coldness in his voice now. 'But it would suffice to say for our purposes that you treated Miss Beckett rather shabbily and she had become something of an inconvenience to you?'

'Yes,' said Bertram rather sulkily. 'You could put it like that.'

'I do. You knew where she worked, I suppose?'

'Of course.'

'It must have come as quite a shock then to find that Lady Celia intended to go there last night to model some gowns?'

'Of course it was the most frightful shock. I didn't know what to do.'

'Under the circumstances, I would have thought it rather unwise for you to go to the event yourself.'

'I didn't want to, but Celia insisted. I couldn't think of an excuse why not to go. She put me on the spot rather. She announced it at lunch yesterday. It did occur to me later simply not to turn up. I nearly did just that. But I knew there'd be no end of trouble if I didn't show up. As it was, I left it until the very last minute to arrive. If I'm honest … well, I was rather afraid that Sylvia might take the opportunity to speak to Celia about her and me if I wasn't there to stop her.'

There was a brief pause while the others digested Bertram's remarks. If the man in question realised that he had said something potentially incriminating, then he made no sign of it. Instead he looked at the inspector rather pathetically, as if he hoped the man might be sympathetic to the predicament in which he had found himself. But Inspector Deacon was not such a man. He did, however, take the view not to pursue this particular line of questioning, much to Rose's surprise.

'I'd like you to tell me about last night. What you did, whom you talked to, that sort of thing.'

'Oh, very well, Inspector. Where would you like me to begin, from the moment I arrived?'

'No, I don't think that will be necessary. Let us go from when Miss Beckett appeared in that silver gown, shall we? Unless of course you spoke to her earlier in the evening?'

'No. of course not. I didn't speak to her at all.'

'Are you sure about that, Mr Thorpe? You have an unfortunate habit of averting your gaze when you're lying,' said the inspector.

'I tell you I didn't speak to her.'

'I'm afraid I don't believe you, sir.'

'Neither do I,' said Rose. 'I think you went and saw her as soon as she had returned to the dressing room in that dress. You haven't asked me how I knew you were Sylvia's young man with prospects. There were one or two things that Sylvia did which suggested it. But you also gave yourself away.'

'Did I?' Bertram looked surprised.

'Yes. You called out Sylvia's name when you saw her in the silver gown. I suppose it was an involuntary action on your part. At first I thought Jacques had said it. But he didn't. He spoke immediately after you did which confused me. Particularly when I turned around and saw him standing there behind me. But you were there too. You were standing next to him.'

'Excuse me for interrupting,' piped up Sergeant Perkins, 'but I'm not sure I follow … for my notes –'

'When Miss Beckett appeared in the dress, Mr Thorpe exclaimed "Sylvia!" and Monsieur Renard immediate followed with "Good lord!"' clarified Rose. 'I thought Jacques had said both sentences. It was only when I was thinking back on things early this morning that I realised that they had in fact been said by two different people speaking consecutively.'

'You're right, Miss Simpson. I did go and see Miss Beckett. Her appearing in the gown like that … well, it rather took the wind out of my sails, I can tell you. I wanted to see her. Celia was busy taking that poor proprietor to task as if it were all her fault. I remember standing there wondering whether Celia would notice if I went across the floor and through the arch. I was weighing up the risk of doing such a thing when the audience suddenly surged forward. Everything became rather chaotic and I decided to take my chance. I was almost deterred when I saw the young man who had said "Good lord!" having apparently reached a similar decision. Anyway, I followed him out at a slight distance, and was relieved to see that he went to the room next door. I went to the dressing room.'

'How did Sylvia receive you?' demanded the inspector.

'Very well. She looked overjoyed to see me in fact. She said that she had hoped that I'd be there.' Bertram stared at the floor. 'I can't tell you how lovely she looked. I thought I loved her. For a few minutes I did. I forgot all about Celia. Why, Sylvia almost made me agree to marry her.'

'Almost?'

'Yes. But then all of a sudden she changed and became spiteful and vindictive. She said the most horrible things about Celia. She said how hideous Celia looked in her silver dress and she couldn't think how I could possibly ever have considered marrying such a woman, money or no money. It brought me to my senses, I can tell you. My mind was firmly set. Sylvia could look very lovely when she tried, and be quite delightful and charming and all that. But underneath she wasn't a bit like that. I knew that if I married her, once she had in her grasp all she wanted from me, my life would become a misery.'

'How did she react when you told her?'

'I didn't, Inspector. I'm afraid I'm something of a coward. I was certain if I did tell her, she would make a scene. She would most probably have gone out of the room that very minute and told Celia all about us. I couldn't take the risk.'

'So you killed her?'

'No, Inspector, of course not. What do you take me for? When I left Sylvia she was alive and well, I assure you. I decided that the wisest thing to do was to tell her the truth later when no one else was present. For one thing I'd have more time to soften the blow.'

'Are you asking us to believe that you told Miss Beckett that you would break off your relationship with Lady Celia and marry her instead?'

'Yes, I am.'

'That sounds a highly implausible story to me,' said Inspector Deacon. 'Shall I tell you what I think happened? I think you did tell Miss Beckett in no uncertain terms that your relationship with her was over. And I think, knowing what sort of a woman she was, she would not accept it. She went further and threatened to tell Lady Celia about the two of you. You could not risk that happening. You knew that she would always pose a threat to you for as long as she lived. So you decided to take matters into your own hands and put a stop to her. The little gold scissors were conveniently to hand and you stabbed her in the neck. She fell forward and hit her head on the chair back. You slipped out of the room and fortune seemed to favour you. In your absence the curtain had been deliberately set alight. It produced confusion and panic amongst the audience with people going this way and that trying to get out of the shop. It was easy enough for you to join one of the lines or clusters of people unobserved. You looked about for Lady Celia. You were keen to ensure that you were amongst the first to leave the premises so that you would not be there when the body was discovered.

'No, Inspector, it wasn't a bit like that,' cried Bertram.

'Wasn't it?' said Inspector Deacon, sounding sceptical.

'No,' said Rose. 'You see Mr Thorpe didn't murder Sylvia. Lady Celia did.'

Chapter Twenty-nine

A few days later and once again the little square room at Madame Renard's flat was witness to a small gathering. Arguably the room was just as crowded as before, but it had lost its claustrophobic feel. On this occasion there was a sense of eager anticipation instead of one of fear and apprehension. The fact that Inspector Deacon and Sergeant Perkins were not separated from the others and were very clearly off-duty helped to lighten the atmosphere further. Rose dispensed coffee and cake and they were all tucking in with free abandonment.

Mary was sitting on the sofa. She was very much a part of the group this time. Gone was the haunted look, which had been replaced by an animated one. Happiness suited Mary well, so much so that Jacques, who was lounging on the floor idly by her feet, was wondering why he had never noticed before how very pretty she was in a quiet, unassuming way. He really found it most appealing. To anyone who would listen, Mary was eagerly informing them that Madame Renard had promoted her to chief shop assistant, a role which brought with it additional responsibilities. She personally would be appointing the new shop assistants who would be reporting to her rather than to Madame Renard, would you believe?

Rose joined Mary on the sofa, and the policemen pulled up the two wooden chairs.

'Well, now that we are all assembled and the refreshments have been distributed,' said Jacques through a mouthful of cake, 'I really think you should begin, Rose, and tell us how you worked it all out.'

'Yes, do,' said Mary eagerly. 'Start at the beginning and tell us exactly how you did it.'

'Well,' said Rose, pausing a moment to take a sip of her coffee, 'I suppose that it all started when we found out that Lavinia would not be attending the fashion event.'

'Yes, that rather put the fly in the ointment, didn't it? I say,' said Jacques, 'did you ever find out why Lavinia was unable to attend? Was she really ill?'

'Yes,' Rose said. 'She had chicken pox! Don't laugh, Jacques, it's not nice. According to Cedric, she was literally covered in spots and wouldn't let anyone see her. He was sworn to absolute secrecy, as were the servants. The last thing in the world she could do was model clothes.'

'Poor Lavinia,' said Mary. 'I do hope she hasn't been left with any scars.'

'One or two very small ones on her face. She is quite convinced that her looks are ruined.'

'That sounds like our Lady Lavinia,' said Jacques. 'But do go on, Rose. We want to know how you solved this case. How did you know that the murderer was Lady Celia?'

'Well, I didn't at first of course. But there were a few things that struck me as rather strange from the very start. To begin with I couldn't for the life of me understand why Lady Celia had decided to model the garments at the fashion show in place of Lavinia. She and Lavinia weren't great friends. I rather got the impression that they disliked one another. And Lady Celia wasn't a bit interested in clothes and her build was not suited for that of a mannequin. She must have known that the garments, which had been made to Lavinia's measurements, would never fit.'

'Yes, I thought that was a bit odd myself,' agreed Mary. 'From what little I saw of her, she struck me as very bored by the whole thing.'

'Another thing that struck me as rather surprising,' continued Rose, 'was that Sylvia knew that Lady Celia Goswell was one of the daughters of the Marquis of Perriford. Her picture had appeared so infrequently in the society pages that few people would have been familiar with her name and certainly not with her father's title.'

'Sylvia knew, didn't she, that Lady Celia was a rival for the Thorpe chap's affections?' said Jacques. 'I suppose Lady Celia had also found out about Sylvia?'

'Yes, she must have done. Unbeknown to Bertram Thorpe, of course,' said Rose. 'I think Lady Celia was curious to meet her rival. Lavinia's illness gave her the perfect opportunity to do so. I remember that she was very keen for me to point Sylvia out to her when it was first mooted that the girl model the outfits.'

'It must have upset her dreadfully when she saw how beautiful Sylvia looked in your silver gown, Jacques,' said Mary. 'No wonder she was so furious with Sylvia for making a face at her behind her back and why she insisted that she should not be allowed to wear the dress. It also explains, doesn't it, why she was so angry when Sylvia did wear the gown. She really did make the most frightful scene, demanding that the poor girl be sacked.'

'That's all very well,' said Sergeant Perkins, stretching out his legs in a comfortable fashion. 'But I still don't see how you worked out Mr Thorpe was her young man, Miss Simpson. Everything falls into place once you knew he was, as you've just shown us, but how did you get there in the beginning, that's what I'd like to know. You're not telling us that it's just because he called out her name, are you?'

'No, Sergeant. There were a couple more clues that Sylvia herself let slip. She knew that the silver gown made her look like a princess and she was absolutely determined to wear it at all costs, even if it meant losing her job. I couldn't understand why she would take such a risk and then I remembered what she had said to me. *I think it's just the sort of dress that would make a man fall in love with a woman, don't you… or propose marriage …* That is why she wanted to wear the dress. She was fairly certain that Bertram Thorpe would be attending the fashion event and she wanted him to choose her over Lady Celia. She felt fairly sure that he would, if he saw her in that dress.'

'I suppose it must have seemed to her a risk worth taking,' said Mary. She sounded rather doubtful. 'But he might not have turned up.'

'Yes, but he did, and he almost succumbed to Sylvia's charms,' said Rose.

'And then he remembered what Sylvia was really like when she wasn't wearing my gorgeous gown to mask her imperfections,' said Jacques. 'I'm sorry, Mary, you're quite right to look so appalled. I was being flippant, which was beastly of me. You know I was fond of Sylvia, warts and all.'

'You must explain to us, Rose, how you knew that it was Lady Celia who killed Sylvia and not Bertram Thorpe,' said Inspector Deacon, who had all the while been listening attentively. 'I've been trying to work it out myself. It seems to me that the facts are such that it could just as easily have been either one of them. It is perhaps fortunate for us that Lady Celia has made a confession.'

'I realised that it must be one of them but, as you say, it was difficult to determine which one. I am fairly certain now that Bertram Thorpe suspected Lady Celia's involvement in Sylvia's death, but had no wish to incriminate her. I think he felt he was in part to blame for what she'd done.' Rose paused a moment to take another sip of her coffee, which was rapidly going cold. 'It's Marcel Girard I have to thank for arriving at the truth. The information we gleaned from his interview and to a lesser extent from yours, Jacques, and also from Bertram Thorpe's, helped considerably.'

'What did you learn from us precisely, Rose?' asked Jacques.

'After you came out of the storeroom, following your conversation with Marcel about the silver gown, you fully intended to go to the dressing room and see Sylvia. You didn't because someone else was already in there with her. You said she sounded excited. According to Bertram Thorpe's own account, as far as Sylvia was aware he had agreed to give up Lady Celia and marry her. It therefore made sense to assume that Bertram Thorpe was her visitor. Now, when we come to Marcel's account, it is a different picture. I think we can safely assume that Mr Thorpe returned to the shop shortly after you did, Jacques. It was then that Lady Celia took the opportunity to visit Sylvia. She was still in the room with her when Marcel came out of the storeroom. I have two reasons for supposing this. Firstly, Marcel heard Sylvia give what he described as an awful and malicious laugh. It is just the sort of laugh Sylvia would give when telling Lady Celia that Mr Thorpe had decided to marry her.'

'Well, I can well imagine she might have liked to gloat about it in front of Lady Celia,' said Jacques. 'It's just the sort of thing Sylvia would do. But I wouldn't say it was very conclusive. Would it stand up in a court of law do you think, Inspector?'

'There's more,' said Rose quickly. 'When you visited Marcel in the storeroom to discuss the silver gown, you told him about the scene Lady Celia was creating in the shop. Marcel had taken a particular dislike to the woman and consequently resolved to stay in the storeroom. From what I can gather, he subsequently got rather bored and changed his mind. He decided to go to the dressing room and chat to you and Sylvia. On his way, he looked through the arch into the shop. He gave us a very detailed account of what he saw. He saw you, Jacques, trying to put out the fire and your mother shouting instructions to Mary. He did not see Sylvia whom he rightly deduced was still in the dressing room and –'

'Ah … I think I know what you're driving at,' cried Jacques. 'The one person he wanted to avoid at all costs was Lady Celia. It stands to reason then that the one person he would notice when he looked through the arch was Lady Celia, yet she is the only person he didn't mention seeing. For the very simple reason that she wasn't there. She was in the dressing room with Sylvia.'

'Bravo, Mr Renard,' said Sergeant Perkins. 'Perhaps you might consider a position in the police force.'

'I think not, Sergeant. It's the life of a fully-fledged designer for me. Whoever set fire to the curtain,' he paused to cock an inquisitive eyebrow at Rose, 'obviously very much regrets their actions. They have paid Mama very handsomely for the damage, so much so in fact that she has decided to undertake major alterations to the shop and this flat in order to create for me my very own design studio.'

'Yes, Madame Renard is very excited about it all.' enthused Mary. 'She has been talking about the House of Renard. She thinks that soon we will be able to move to larger premises and have a more fashionable address.'

'Yes, we'll give Thimbles a run for their money, see if we don't,' agreed Jacques. 'Mama was afraid that she would lose customers but actually the opposite has been true. She received so many enquiries about my silver gown that she made Elsie run up a copy and has displayed it in the shop window for all to see. You probably saw it when you came here, Sergeant? You wouldn't believe how many orders we have received for it. I was very cross with her at first. It seemed such an awful ghoulish sort of thing to do.'

'I admit I had some reservations about it,' said Mary. 'But really, I think Sylvia wouldn't have minded. She loved being the centre of attention, didn't she? You'll think me very silly, but I almost feel that her memory will live on in that dress.'

'Well, all I can say is that I am glad some good has come out of all this,' Sergeant Perkins said. The others concurred and there was a slight pause.

'Do you think Lady Celia planned to kill Sylvia, Rose?'

'No, Mary, I don't. I think she saw Bertram Thorpe leave the shop and go into the dressing room. She waited for him to return and then went to confront Sylvia, probably to tell her to leave him alone. Sylvia then laughed in her face and told her that it was she Mr Thorpe was going to marry. I believe Lady Celia picked up the scissors in a fit of rage. I don't think she really meant to stab Sylvia with them.'

'And it wasn't that that actually killed her,' said Sergeant Perkins. 'It was hitting her head on the chair back that did her in, wasn't it, sir?' He looked at the inspector for agreement. 'I don't reckon they'll hang her, do you sir?'

'No,' said the inspector. 'I believe there'll be a recommendation for mercy. Her father will no doubt employ the best barrister in the country to conduct her defence. He might even argue that it was an unfortunate accident that had little, if anything, to do with his client.'

'I'd like to see him try!' snorted the sergeant. 'Me, I think they'll send her to prison for a few years at least. According to Mr Thorpe, he'll be waiting for her when she comes out. He feels that guilty about it all, so he does. And, for what it's worth, I think he's right to. If he hadn't been carrying on with the two of them, this tragedy would never have happened.'

'Rose,' said Jacques, 'would you mind if I have a quiet word?'

'No, of course not. Why don't you carry through the crockery and you can dry while I wash up.' Rose looked about the room. Mary was busy chatting happily to the two policemen. It seemed to her that Mary was making quite an impression on the young sergeant. 'I don't think the others will miss us for a while.'

They made their way into the other room and pulled back the imitation linen curtain to the makeshift kitchen-cum-bathroom. Rose set to washing up the crockery, piece by piece, in the sink before handing each item to Jacques to dry with a tea towel.

'My mother took your advice. She told me the secret she's been keeping hidden all these years.'

'I'm so glad. It will be a weight off her mind your knowing.'

'She thought I would be terribly shocked to hear that she and my father were never married. Her name's really Aubert not Renard, but then of course you knew that. She said she and my father planned to elope but that my father was killed in a motor accident before they could marry. I'm not sure that I believe that bit of her story,' Jacques paused a moment in the act of drying a cup, 'but she must have loved him very much to give me his name, Jacques Renard, don't you think?

'Yes, I do.'

'All these years she has pretended to be a widow. I don't know how to tell you how grateful I feel to her for all she has done for me. It can't have been easy for her bringing me up by herself while building up her business. She did it all for me, you know.'

'Were you very shocked to learn the truth?'

'That's what's so funny. I think I've always known it, without knowing, if that makes any sense. You see, it had always seemed rather strange to me that we had no living family or relatives to speak of. My mother never really liked to talk about them. It was as if they belonged to a past, forgotten life.'

'In a way, I suppose they did.'

'It was rather careless of my mother to leave that letter lying out on her desk addressed to Madame Aubert, wasn't it?' said Jacques. 'Is that what made you guess the truth?'

'Yes,' said Rose. 'I couldn't understand why she had been so upset when I picked up some of her papers that had been scattered on the floor. I'd glanced at them idly when gathering them up, as one instinctively does without thinking, and she practically snatched them away from me. From what you said in your interview, she reacted in a similar way when she caught you going through her papers looking for your sketch. I racked my brains trying to remember what I'd seen and remembered that a piece of correspondence had been addressed to a Madame Aubert and I wondered whether she was in fact you mother. If she was, there was really only one logical explanation as to why she would pose as Madame Renard.'

'I see. You put two and two together and came to four, just as Sylvia must have done,' said Jacques. 'You're awfully clever, Rose, but I expect you already know that. No, don't try and protest, a woman really must accept a compliment when it's given.' He became serious. 'One thing has been worrying me terribly about all this. I know Sylvia had her faults, but I can't quite bring myself to believe that she sunk so low as to blackmail my mother.'

'I don't believe she did, not really. I think she merely hinted to your mother about what she had found out. It understandably put your mother in a panic. She was very careful how she treated Sylvia from then on, lest she should say anything. It meant that she was obliged to tolerate her many faults.'

'Ah, there you two are,' said Inspector Deacon, appearing from behind the curtain. 'Miss Jennings is asking for you, Monsieur Renard. Allow me to take on your drying up duties.'

'Righto, Inspector.'

Jacques darted eagerly out of the room.

'There's not much left to do, Inspector. Only this cup and saucer and we are finished.'

'Actually, I offered to do this because I wanted to have an excuse to talk to you.'

'Ah, how very useful washing up is in that respect,' said Rose smiling.

'It is indeed. Look here, Rose. I'm not much good at this sort of thing.'

Rose dropped the cup she had been washing. A cold sensation of panic came over her like a wave.

'I –'

'Please let me finish. I want to apologise for my attitude towards you during this investigation. I haven't been quite myself since being shot. It's put me on edge, you see, always fearing the worst. I was dreadfully afraid that you would place yourself in danger. I wanted to protect you. I couldn't bear the thought of anything happening to you.'

'It's all right. I understand. It was awfully kind of you to care so much about my safety. I daresay I can be quite annoying when I put my mind to it.' She smiled up at the inspector and felt the wave of panic subside. Much to her annoyance, she also felt a twinge of disappointment.

'Rose, there's something else. Something I want to tell you. You must know how –'

'I'm leaving Renard's,' said Rose very quickly. 'That's why I wanted to help solve this case so very much. I thought I owed it to Madame Renard. She's dreadfully upset that I'm going. I couldn't leave her with an unsolved murder on her hands as well.'

'Leaving?'

'Yes. Didn't you hear Mary say how she was in charge of appointing the new shop assistants? They're to replace me, and poor Sylvia, of course.'

'But why? I thought you liked it here.'

'I do, but –'

They heard someone walk into the room. The next moment a figure appeared beside the curtain.

'Hello, you two. That fine sergeant of yours said you were here, Inspector. It's good to see you again, Deacon. I heard about your shooting. A dreadful business. Glad to see you've fully recovered. Darling, have you told the inspector our news?'

'Cedric!' cried Rose, and promptly rushed into the arms of Lord Belvedere, who looked somewhat surprised but not at all displeased by the turn of events. 'I'm so glad you're here.'

'So am I,' said the young earl. 'My business at Sedgwick finished earlier than I had anticipated so I decided to motor down today instead of tomorrow. Hope that's convenient. Are you all packed? I'm staying at my club tonight and thought we could have a spot of dinner together and then go on to a night club after, if you'd like to, of course.'

'That would be delightful.'

'Oh, I say, Deacon, do beg my pardon, how terribly rude I'm being.'

'Not at all, my lord. You mentioned some news?'

'Yes, hasn't Rose told you? I thought she might have done. We haven't given it out yet. There will be an announcement in the newspaper tomorrow.'

'An announcement?'

'Yes. Rose and I are engaged, Inspector. She has very kindly agreed to marry me and become the next Countess of Belvedere.'

'I say, that is good news. May I offer my congratulations, my lord? And to you too of course, Miss Simpson.' Inspector Deacon made a half bow, which prevented Rose from seeing his face.

'Thank you. Now, I don't want to appear rude, Inspector, but I'm afraid we really must go. Rose, I hope you don't mind, but I've arranged for us to drop in on a couple of friends of mine who are dying to meet you before the big day.'

'Not at all,' replied Rose, wiping her wet hands on a towel.

'I say, you probably won't ever have to do that again, darling, wash up, I mean,' said Cedric laughing. 'You'll have a house full of servants to do that sort of thing for you.' Holding Rose by the hand, Cedric turned to look back at the inspector. 'Goodbye Deacon. I daresay our paths will cross again.'

'I look forward to it, Lord Belvedere,' said Inspector Deacon, catching Rose's eye. Try as she might, she found it impossible to read his expression.

Printed in Great Britain
by Amazon.co.uk, Ltd.,
Marston Gate.